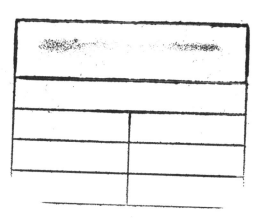

THE BOURNE ASCENDANCY

ROBERT LUDLUM'S™

THE BOURNE ASCENDANCY

Eric Van Lustbader

LARGE PRINT

Oxford

First published in Great Britain 2014
by
Orion Books
an imprint of The Orion Publishing Group Ltd.

Published in Large Print 2015 by ISIS Publishing Ltd.,
7 Centremead, Osney Mead, Oxford OX2 0ES
by arrangement with
The Orion Publishing Group Ltd.
an Hachette UK Company

CIP data is available for this title from the British Library

ISBN 978–1–4450–9982–8 (hb)
ISBN 978–1–4450–9983–5 (pb)

Printed and bound in Great Britain by
T. J. International Ltd., Padstow, Cornwall

For Victoria, as always . . .

CHAPTER
ONE

Seven ministers entered the famed Al-Bourah Hotel in Doha. Seven ministers from Jordan, Syria, Qatar, Iraq, Lebanon, the United Arab Emirates, and Yemen, grim-faced, all carrying briefcases locked to their wrists by chains, each needing their personal thumbprint to open. They held themselves like kings, these ministers, and in some cases they were as powerful as the kings of past ages. They were accompanied by their bodyguards — men grimmer still than their masters, as heavily muscled as they were armed, ready for any sudden noise or movement.

In the vast lobby, the entourage passed between two rows of gigantic marble pillars, then through the elaborate security screening process their respective countries had paid for, commanded by a dozen uniformed, battle-hardened mercenaries hired specially for this occasion.

The ministers and their bodyguards rode in a pair of elevators to the top floor, walked silently down a thickly carpeted hallway studded on either side with more mercenaries, and entered an enormous light-filled conference room.

They took their places around a polished rosewood table, thumbed open their hard-sided steel-and-titanium-reinforced briefcases, removed files red-stamped TOP SECRET. Their bodyguards uncapped iced bottles of water, sipped the water first, then poured it into glasses that had been hand-washed by trusted personnel. With military precision, the bodyguards stepped back to a spot just behind and to the right of their respective masters.

Besides the bottles of water, oversized cut-glass ashtrays had been set out in front of each chair. More than half the ministers shook out cigarettes and lit them. They inhaled deeply and gratefully.

Behind them, through bulletproof windows, Doha was already baking in the morning sun. Heat ignited ripples that rose up the glass-and-steel sides of the sleek modern buildings like smoke. Beyond the grand Corniche, the bay, for which it was said Doha had been named, sparkled like a latticework of diamonds in the raking sunlight.

The minister from Qatar, being the representative of the host nation, began to speak.

"We are here today to answer the call of a catastrophic problem," he said. He was a small man, distinguished-looking in his robes of state. "Over the past eighteen months, a series of deadly arms shipments have made their way into the African nations to the south — countries notable not only for their oil, but also for natural gas, diamonds, uranium, and rare earth elements."

2

The minister paused at this juncture to take a sip of water. As he did so, he took the opportunity to look around the room, regarding each face separately. "Thinking of the nations not represented here," he continued, "Egypt is in such continuing flux no coherent leader can as yet be recognized, let alone be counted upon to speak for the nation as a whole. As for Saudi and Iran, well, they are both the subjects of our discussion this morning. Nothing could be gained by inviting representatives from their countries." He cleared his throat. "And the less said about Israel the better."

"All Israelis are terrorists," the minister from Iraq said, distaste twisting his thick lips. "Their so-called country was founded by terror and now they subjugate the Palestinians in ever smaller quarters through terror tactics well known to us all."

The minister from Qatar, staring at the Iraqi, was silent for a moment. "Quite so," he said at last. Turning his gaze elsewhere, he went on: "To date, our best people have been unable to trace the source of the shipments. What we do know is that they contain ever more modern, and therefore deadly, armaments. The endpoints of these shipments are leaders of various local insurgent groups — terror cells bent on death alone." Here he lifted an iPad from the dossier. He tapped its screen, and projected onto the opposite wall was a list of the enemies of the states, enumerating their kills, destruction of property, enslavement of children and young adults, and the success rate of their various indoctrination programs.

"As you can see, the success rate is phenomenally high." He used a laser pointer to underscore his words. "Extreme poverty, disenfranchisement, a promise of martyrdom as well as money for their families bring recruits at such a pace that the high death rate of these recruits becomes meaningless." He switched off the screen. "Thus we see with our own eyes the truth of the Western criticism of radical Islam: It demeans life as it devalues it."

At this, the minister from the UAE rose. "This cycle of radicalism must stop," he said. Unlike the minister from Qatar, he was a tall man — majestic even — dark of eye and hair, with skin like ancient leather: cracked and worn, but still tough as nails. His fist pounded the table. "While the terrorists proliferate, wreaking havoc in their wake, it is we who reap the whirlwind they have created. We wish an end to the purposeful violence, a violence that rebounds onto us. It is our people who are dying in consequence."

He sat, having said his piece. The minister from Qatar nodded, as did most of the ministers ranged around the table. The minister from Syria, who had been watching the proceedings with a particularly keen eye, noted the others' reactions.

At a break in the meeting, he left the table and went down the hallway to the men's room. Ensuring it was empty, he wedged a piece of wood under the door to keep it from opening. Then he stared at himself in the mirror. He touched the bulbous prosthetic nose, removed the plastic inserts that puffed out his cheeks.

4

He rearranged his beard, first applying a bit more spirit gum to several key spots.

Still, Jason Bourne scarcely recognized himself.

That was, of course, all to the good. If he didn't recognize himself, no one else was going to either. For many years, Bourne had been living off the funds he had provided for himself, lodged in a Zurich bank vault. Now that those funds finally had been used up, he needed a new way to make a living.

For the past year he had been hiring himself out to the highest bidder, impersonating ministers and businessmen who were scheduled to attend high-level diplomatic and business meetings in hot spots around the globe. Rather than risk assassination, these ministers hired him to take their place. In the jargon of the trade, he had become a Blacksmith. And what a Blacksmith! In the space of twelve months he had amassed almost as much money as he had originally stashed in Switzerland.

He took out a mobile phone with software that scrambled all his calls, both incoming and outgoing, and pressed a speed dial button. The moment Sara Yadin answered, he recited chapter and verse the information on the terrorist groups in Africa that had been projected onto the conference room wall.

"More later," he said, cutting the connection.

He did not normally pass on the relevant product he gathered at these meetings to third parties. He did so this time because he loved Sara, an operative of Mossad. He did it also because of his ever-deepening friendship with Sara's father, Eli Yadin, Mossad's director. He wanted to keep them safe; this was an expedient way.

Smiling at his reflection, he reinserted the cheek prosthetics, adjusted them minutely, took one last look at himself, and, satisfied, returned to the conference room.

Apart from the mercenaries on patrol, the lobby of the Al-Bourah was a virtual ghost town. Not a guest came in or out, not a single limousine pulled into the semicircular driveway, not a soul could be seen passing by on the wide, curving Corniche. The security net was as taut as a drawn bow. It was all the phalanx of uniformed young men and women at the front desk and the concierge's station could do to hold back their yawns. Nothing to do, nowhere to go. They were forbidden even to exchange pleasantries, or the juicy celebrity gossip that usually fueled their workdays.

It was so quiet, in fact, that several of the mercenaries had taken to darting furtive looks at the various young women behind the concierge desk. Several minutes later, the most beautiful of these came around the end of the curved granite desk holding a tray in one hand. On the tray were a number of small cups of tea. The mercenaries' eyes fixed on her, first warily, then hungrily as she approached them, a provocative smile etched on her face.

She distributed the cups to the men, who sipped the tea gratefully. Only one declined her offer. She held out the teacup, but again he refused. By this time, his compatriots seemed to have developed rubber legs.

They staggered and lurched, then, in twos and threes, collapsed onto the polished marble floor. As the lone remaining mercenary in the lobby brought up his semiautomatic weapon, the concierge shot him through the temple at point-blank range.

That was the signal for the terrorists posing as hotel staff to spring into action. Racing across the lobby, they scooped up the mercenaries' weapons.

The four mercenaries stationed outside were frantically pushing their way through the revolving door. Two of the terrorists turned and fired their assault rifles in short, accurate bursts, killing the last of the ground-floor mercenaries, trapping them in a no-man's-land of shattered glass.

Now one of the terrorists spoke briefly on his mobile phone. Thirty seconds later three enormous American-made SUVs pulled up in front of the hotel, disgorging sixteen more men. The leading terrorists shot out what remained of the glass revolving door, and the cadre, at the center of which was its legendary leader, stepped over the corpses and entered the hotel.

Phase one had been accomplished without a hitch.

Upstairs in the conference room, the ministers had returned to their debate.

"There is every reason to believe," the Iraqi minister was saying, "that the illegal Jewish state is the entity behind these shipments. It would be just like the Mossad to fund terrorist cells bent on destabilizing countries from which they can never reap economic benefits."

A number of other ministers nodded their tacit agreement. The Qatari minister, rising to his feet again, turned to Bourne. "Minister Qabbani, we have not heard from you on this subject."

Bourne nodded. "Easy enough to hang Israel in effigy, but I am more interested in the actuality of the situation. It seems to me that there are entities with far more to gain from arming these cadres than Mossad."

"Such as?" the Iraqi minister said darkly.

"Such as Iran," Bourne said. "Such as Russia."

"Russia?" the Iraqi said, startled.

"China burns natural resources faster than any other nation. It has spent the last five years bribing and buying its way into the African countries with the richest sources of oil, natural gas, and uranium. Russia would dearly love to undermine China's incursions. What better way to do so than by financing cadres bent on destabilizing the governments of those nations?"

"In regard to Russia, our esteemed colleague makes an excellent point," said the minister from the UAE, even while the Iraqi snorted in derision. He turned his head. "You disagree, Minister Boulos?"

"Strenuously," Boulos said.

"Correct me if I'm wrong, Minister Boulos," Bourne said, "but isn't Russia a client of yours?"

The Iraqi bristled. "China has taken the largest stake in my country's oil industry."

"Which is why," Bourne said, "elements in the Kremlin have hired you to slip as many legislative spanners as possible in the works to deter China's advance."

The UAE minister's head turned on his neck like a falcon's. "Is this true, Boulos?"

"Of course it's not true!" But the louder the Iraqi minister's protestations, the less anyone was inclined to believe him.

Returning his attention to Bourne, the minister from the UAE said, "Have you suggestions for the way we might proceed from your thesis?"

From the elevators and the fire stairs the terrorists poured into the top-floor hallway. Three mercenaries already in the hallway who were in the terrorists' pay thrust knives into those nearest them, or else wound garrotes around their necks, pulling tight, holding on with a knee jammed firmly into the small of their victims' backs. The remainder were dispatched silently and efficiently by the newcomers, who, following hand signals from their leader, then headed toward the closed doors of the conference room.

"With the split within the FSB," Bourne said, "Russia's spying policies have become far more aggressive in both the defensive and offensive spheres. My contacts within the organization have confirmed that FSB-2, even more dangerous than FSB-1, has been responsible for —"

At that moment, the doors burst open and the atmosphere inside the room was shattered by the rapid fire of assault weapons wielded by four masked terrorists. Blood, brains, and shards of bones of the ministers from Qatar, the UAE, and Jordan sprayed through the air like an infernal fountain. The terrorists slammed the doors shut, locking in their victims.

Using the gore as cover, Bourne swung up his briefcase and hurled it at the terrorist closest to him. As the man was spun off his feet, Bourne grabbed one of the cut-glass ashtrays and smashed it directly into the face of the second terrorist. Blood fountained out of him as he was thrown backward against a wall.

His two compatriots were busy gunning down the ministers from Iraq, Lebanon, and Yemen, the last of whom had drawn a nasty-looking pistol from his briefcase. By this time, Bourne had claimed the weapon of the first fallen terrorist.

He aimed, squeezed off a short burst that flung the third terrorist off his feet, his chest a mass of blood and shredded tissue. The last remaining terrorist swung his assault rifle to bear on Bourne, but Bourne was already on the move, and a second burst from the weapon he wielded nearly cut the man in half.

Bourne stood. Through the red rain still falling, he checked the other ministers for vital signs. There were none.

Still armed, he turned from the carnage and opened the doors, to find the jihadist known as El Ghadan confronting him. El Ghadan, which meant "Tomorrow," was flanked by a dozen men armed with submachine guns, all aimed at Bourne.

El Ghadan stepped forward, took the automatic rifle from Bourne's hands, pulled off Bourne's beard and nose, and, smiling, said, "Hello, Mr. Bourne."

Part One

CHAPTER
TWO

El Ghadan gestured. "Please come with me."

Bourne said nothing, nor did he move.

El Ghadan said, "So the rumors about your stubbornness are true." His smile grew into a scar. "Search him."

A burly man stepped up and, his black eyes burning with hatred, patted Bourne down. He stepped back and nodded.

"Let's return to the scene of the crime."

A man grabbed each of Bourne's arms, turned him around, and frog-marched him back into the blood-spattered conference room.

"One, two, three, four murders," El Ghadan said as he took in the corpses of his men. He stepped in front of Bourne. He was not a tall man, but he was wide-shouldered. He had the narrow waist of a dancer, but that was where the resemblance ended. His coarse features, pockmarked cheeks, and enormous, powerful hands marked him as a laborer, a Bedouin born and bred in the terrible wastes of the desert.

"Martyrs, all." His lips were thick, his eyes narrowly focused, as if on the future rather than the present. Possibly that was how he got his name. "But that fact hardly absolves you of your crime."

15

Bourne had heard of El Ghadan, though they had never met. He had read his file at Treadstone, but though mostly accurate when it came to actual facts, files were notoriously incomplete — or, worse, inaccurate — when it came to the subject's personality. With fanatics like El Ghadan — and he was far and away the worst of the extremist bunch — understanding their personalities was the key to defeating them. Therefore, Bourne extended all his senses, focusing his attention strictly on El Ghadan.

"Aren't you concerned about the police?" he said.

"The police." El Ghadan laughed, the sound as harsh and dry as a desert wind. "I own the police here."

Bourne noted his response. Arrogance and contempt. When adversaries felt so in control of a situation that they considered you beneath them, you held a certain advantage. Bourne was building an invaluable knowledge base.

El Ghadan snapped his fingers and the two men holding Bourne sat him down on a chair between two of the fallen terrorists. He held out his hand, and his second in command slipped a tablet into it.

El Ghadan swiped the screen and turned it to face Bourne. On the screen was a live image of Soraya Moore, her daughter, and her husband — Aaron Lipkin-Renais, an inspector in the French Quai d'Orsay. The three were seated in a row, hands tied behind their backs. Soraya's daughter, not more than two years old, looked panicked; she started to cry.

Bourne felt his stomach contract painfully. His relationship with Soraya Moore was long, complicated,

16

and, at times, intimate. How had El Ghadan captured her and her family? His estimation of the terrorist rose exponentially.

Soraya was looking straight at the lens. Bourne had not seen her in over three years, but knew she had given up her co-directorship of Treadstone after marrying Lipkin-Renais. Not long afterward, she had moved to Paris permanently, starting the next phase of her life with him and her daughter, Sonya, who was born in the City of Lights. Nevertheless, her image was forever etched into his memory.

She had always been a beautiful woman — magnificent, even, being half Egyptian. It was strange, Bourne thought, how her extreme distress had made her even more beautiful — underscoring both the height and the winglike shape of her cheekbones, magnifying her large, uptilted coffee-colored eyes, which were brimming with a cold fury as well as terror for Lipkin-Renais and Sonya. He knew her well enough to understand that the safety of her family was paramount to her.

Unlike Soraya, Lipkin-Renais had his head turned, looking at something or someone just out of camera range.

In the stinking conference room, El Ghadan pointed a callused forefinger. "You know these people, yes?"

Bourne struggled now to keep his attention on the nuances of El Ghadan's voice.

"Well, you know the woman, for certain. Soraya. Soraya Moore. She is co-director of Treadstone — or rather, she was."

It was clear that he was boasting of his knowledge, a beating of his chest like a male mountain gorilla, but beneath that was a curious gloating Bourne needed to know more about.

"Odd that she chose the Frenchman over you, Bourne. But then perhaps not so odd. I daresay you'd make as poor a father as you would a husband."

The personal belittling was a sign of insecurity — even of fear, Bourne knew. What could El Ghadan be afraid of?

"Speaking of which, have you met Sonya? What a creature! Children of her tender age are completely innocent, don't you think, Bourne? And as beautiful as her mother, possibly more so. As she grows into womanhood, who knows?"

Here it comes, Bourne thought.

"*If* she grows into womanhood."

Bourne looked straight ahead, said nothing.

"Take him," El Ghadan ordered.

A hood was thrown over Bourne's head, and he was hustled along the death-strewn corridor, down in the elevator, past the carnage in the lobby, and out into one of the waiting SUVs. Someone stuck a needle in his arm. Dumped into the backseat, he struggled to stay conscious, but the drug was too powerful, and as the SUV took off, he passed out.

Returning to consciousness, Bourne experienced a short interim when all was calm, all was serene. Then, as if he had been struck by a bolt of lightning, the

18

recent past came roaring back, jolting him into complete awareness.

His first sense was that he was bound wrists and ankles to a ladder-back wooden chair. Looking around, he found himself inside a small room with bare concrete walls, no windows, one door, locked and guarded. The sole decoration was a thick afghan carpet hanging on the wall directly in front of him.

On his right side, El Ghadan sat in another ladder-back chair, a small octagonal table inlaid with Arabic script in mother-of-pearl between them. Bourne noted his posture: draped across the chair, one leg over the other. He might have given the full illusion of nonchalance had not his upper leg been swinging back and forth with a nervous energy. He lifted a hand and one of his men scuttled away, returning with a tray filled with two mugs of coffee, cream and sugar, and a plate of dates rolled in coconut.

El Ghadan gestured as the tray was set down. "Please, help yourself." He shook his head. "My apologies." He picked up one of the mugs. "Coffee? No." He sipped it himself. "Dates, then?" He held one out, popped it in his mouth.

He licked stray shreds of coconut off his fingertips. "I need something done," he said. "I need it done quickly."

"You have your own men, your own resources."

El Ghadan ignored him. "A week from now, in Singapore, your American president is set to broker an historic peace treaty between the Israelis and the Palestinians." He leaned forward even as he lowered his voice. "The treaty is hanging by a delicate thread. Without his help, without his guidance, it will never get done. I want you to see that the president never reaches the Golden Palace Hotel in Singapore, where the signing will take place."

"You're out of your mind," Bourne said.

"That is your response?" El Ghadan waited patiently, but when Bourne remained silent, he nodded. "So be it, then. A lesson in humility must be learned."

As if on cue, one of his men wheeled in a 24-volt car battery. Over his shoulder were two lengths of bare copper wire. He wore heavy-duty rubber gloves. He set the battery down beside Bourne, shrugged off the wire, and affixed one end to a battery terminal, leaving the other dangling off the corner.

Bourne watched with the kind of stoicism bred in the Treadstone program and put to the test a number of times in the field. The man wound the copper wire several times around Bourne's chest. When he was finished, he crouched down, nodded to his leader.

"Here's what's going to happen, Bourne," El Ghadan said. "Rashid is going to touch the unattached wire to the second terminal. When that happens twenty-four volts of electricity will run through your chest.

"Not enough to electrocute you, of course, but then, that is not my aim. No one learns a lesson from dying. No, the twenty-four volts will make the intercostal muscles around your lungs seize up. If Rashid here isn't careful, if the current stays on too long, you'll asphyxiate. But that will take time, and in the meanwhile the pain will be excruciating, like being on the verge of dying." He nodded. "Show him, Rashid."

El Ghadan's man touched the wire to the second terminal. Bourne was certain he had prepared himself, but the blinding agony that lanced through him made his body jerk. A great fist clamped down on his lungs and squeezed until his eyes began to water.

Rashid lifted the end of the wire off the terminal. Bourne's body collapsed, sweat ran down the sides of his neck, burned his eyes, flooded his underarms and groin. He knew he had to keep his wits about him, had to maintain at least a modicum of control. Otherwise . . .

Once again Rashid sent the current through Bourne. All the color leached out of the room, sounds were distorted. Bourne's head lolled, chin on sweat-streaked chest. His mind was in chaos, his thoughts fractured. He needed to remember something. What was it?

The current surged through him a third time, and all coherent thought fled him. The giant fist bore into him as if it were about to crush his rib cage, send the scimitar-shaped bones through his heart. The room turned red, then black.

"How are we feeling?" El Ghadan's voice floated ghostlike through the darkness. "Back among the living?"

All the lights in the room had been extinguished. Bourne took one shuddering breath after another, felt as if a freight train had run over his chest. Coarse fingers gripped his chin. A light shone in his eyes, blinding him. Someone pulled his lids apart.

"Pupils normal," another voice said. "A remarkable recovery."

"To be expected." This from El Ghadan. "We're ready for act two."

Someone pulled aside the carpet on the wall. Light flooded the room, coming through a one-way mirror. Bourne, struggling to focus, blinked furiously to clear his vision, then wished he hadn't bothered. He was observing the room he had seen on the tablet's screen. There were Soraya, Sonya, and Lipkin-Renais, bound, sitting in a line facing him.

El Ghadan was just visible, his face limned in profile on the other side of the octagonal table. "The little girl is terrified, Bourne."

"Sonya." Bourne's mouth was full of sand. His tongue felt swollen to twice its normal size. He tried to gather saliva. "Her name is Sonya."

El Ghadan shifted and his chair creaked. "In a moment Sonya is going to be so much more terrified."

Bourne jerked his head around. The terrorist's face was alight. "Don't do anything stupid," Bourne said.

"Stupidity doesn't enter into it." El Ghadan shrugged. "This is on your head, Bourne, not mine."

He made a sign. Bourne saw Lipkin-Renais's face go pale. A gunman stepped into view. Sonya screamed, her little body shaking as if with ague. Soraya's eyes opened wide in horror; she knew what was coming.

On either side of the glass, Soraya and Bourne shouted, "No!"

Sonya kept on screaming.

22

Bourne's voice was hoarse. "You don't need to do this."

El Ghadan settled back, as if about to watch his favorite movie. "Watch, Bourne. Your lesson in humility continues."

The pistol fired. Lipkin-Renais's blood, bone, and brains splattered over the cringing Soraya like pink hail.

El Ghadan rose, stood in front of Bourne, blocking his view, but the wails of shock, anguish, and grief remained in the room.

"Now," he said, "your conscience holds yet another sin."

He folded his hands in front of him, fingers laced, like a priest about to deliver a homily. "Here is what will happen if you do not comply. First Sonya will be shot in front of Soraya. Then Soraya will be taken to an interrogation cell where she will be systematically stripped of her will, of her personality — her very self. She will become a nonperson, nothing more than a slab of meat. Then I personally will flay the flesh from her one strip at a time, until her body is a quivering mass of bleeding sinew and fat."

He leaned forward, his hands still clasped, his voice low and conversational over Soraya's wails and Sonya's crying. "I have it on good authority that you are something of an expert in these matters, Bourne."

He stepped aside, once more revealing the horrific scene in the other room. Soraya was trying to take her hysterical daughter into her arms, but the restraints held her fast.

"Please," she shouted at the gunman. "I just want to hold Sonya." She stared up into his implacable eyes, the only part of his face visible through the scarf wrapped around his neck and head. "Please let me hold her!"

"Rejoice," the gunman said. "Your two-year-old hasn't been incinerated in a drone strike."

"How long do you think it will take her to die?" El Ghadan said. "Four days? A week? She looks a hardy soul, so I think longer, don't you, Bourne? And all the while the flies will land on her flesh, feeding."

"Enough," Bourne said.

El Ghadan cocked his head. "Are you certain, Bourne? I warn you, there can be no going back from this decision."

"Give me the details."

El Ghadan released a great sigh. "Gladly." He leaned across the table, his tone conversational, one friend to another. "Keep this truth close to your heart: You're mine now, Bourne. Mind, body, and soul."

CHAPTER
THREE

Camilla Stowe arrived at the West Wing while D.C. was still dark. She had never been much for sleeping, even as a child. Ever since President Magnus had asked her to join his inner circle as head of the Secret Service, she slept no more than an hour or two a night. That was fine by her. She always said, "I'll sleep when I'm dead."

A natural redhead, with green eyes shot through with brown flecks and skin looking like it had been dipped in milk, Camilla cut an enviable figure inside the Beltway. The effect of her pale face and petite, curvy body on the male population of D.C. politics on both sides of the aisle was startlingly lustful. Those who did not know her often mistook her delicate looks as a reflection of an inner fragility.

Her father was British, the immensely wealthy scion of an aristocratic family that for decades oversaw the expansion of the British Empire in Africa and India. He had insisted that she be schooled in England in a vain effort to keep her from returning to the States to join her mother in the military. Carla Stowe had been an ace marine fighter pilot in her day. By the time her daughter returned to her she was an ace flight instructor. Her classes were always full; everyone wanted a slice of her knowledge and war expertise.

Camilla had other ideas, joining Marine Intelligence as a lieutenant. She served in the Horn of Africa, Afghanistan, and Iraq, twice. She quickly made captain, before being aggressively recruited by the CIA. She left after eighteen months, unhappy with the Company's treatment of women. That was when she caught the attention of POTUS. He was looking for a new top cop to deal with the moral quagmire the Secret Service had become enmeshed in. He wanted someone to clean house, to reset the machine closest to him, which was responsible for his public and private safety. She was one of five candidates for the position, and the only female.

Magnus interviewed her for over ninety minutes, though he had made up his mind to hire her after ten. The truth was, he didn't want to let her go. At the end of her intake interview, he offered her the job, and she accepted. Later, he confided in Howard Anselm, his chief of staff, that Camilla had a core of steel that would bend but not break. "She's just what the West Wing needs," he said.

At the conclusion of her intake interview, POTUS promptly took Camilla to lunch, which meant a meal sent up from POTUS's private kitchen.

Magnus was a family man. Initially his telegenic wife ruffled conservative feathers by wearing sleeveless dresses, showing off her well-turned shoulders and upper arms, of which she was justly proud. But she carried herself with such spirited grace and was so unafraid to make fun of herself that even her worst critics eventually retreated into their bunkers, emitting only the occasional muted grumble. They had two children, an older girl and a younger boy, both of whom presented well for the cameras and were unafraid of either questions or crowds.

All this notwithstanding, it was noted by both Anselm and Marty Finnerman, the under secretary of defense for policy, both of whom had the most access to POTUS, that he was infatuated with Camilla. Whether POTUS and Camilla had had sex or were going to could not yet be divined, but putting their heads together, Anselm and Finnerman determined to keep an eagle eye on the two, the better to head off even the tiniest whiff of scandal.

That very early morning when Camilla arrived at the West Wing, the city had not begun to stir. Anselm's new assistant, Noreen, as young and beautiful as the previous one, informed her that he was already in his office. The door was open, the lights burning brightly, and the scent of freshly brewed coffee from his Nespresso machine wafted down the hallway, drawing Camilla toward it, away from the occupied Oval Office, as it was meant to do.

"Did you even go home, Howard?" Camilla said as she strode into his office.

"Frankly, I didn't see the point," he replied without looking up. His divorce was writhing through its final convolutions. "Too damn much to do for the Singapore peace summit."

He stopped writing, put down his pen, and flexed his fingers. He was a man who never used electronic means of communication. Not after the Snowden affair. Too insecure, despite the repeated reassurances of the cyber-guardians. It was handwritten drafts and typewritten finals for him and everyone on his staff. Back to the future. The really great thing about typewriters, he told anyone who would listen, was that each one had a signature as unique and distinct as a human fingerprint. If some memo went wayward, it was easy enough to trace it to the machine on which it had been typed. "The impreciseness of mechanics," he'd say, and Camilla, for one, believed him, switching over all Secret Service correspondence to mechanical means.

Now Anselm looked up. "Help yourself." As she went about fixing herself a triple espresso, he eyed her contemplatively. "And your plans?"

"You know my plans, Howard." She opened the half-fridge, poured a dollop of half-and-half into the white porcelain cup with the presidential seal emblazoned on either side. "I submitted them to you ten days ago. They've already been implemented. The guys regularly fucking those Colombian whores have been shit-canned. The rest of the crew is on lockdown, pending the final stage of my investigation." She added sugar, stirred, then lifted the cup to her lips and sipped. "Mmmm. That'll get a rush of blood to my head."

Then she turned to face him, a small, round man with short arms and legs and thin sandy hair brushed over his bald spot. He was round-shouldered, had the face of a bulldog, a nose like a mushroom or a failed prizefighter. Even in D.C.'s swampiest months, he wore thick wool suits, much-rumpled black suspenders, and heavy brogues that everyone suspected of containing lifts, indicative of his stern countenance and lack of a sense of humor. He appeared, in short, to be the perfect bureaucrat: half political engine, half desk.

"But you knew that, Howard. What's up?"

He gestured for her to sit. She was wearing a smart beige suit with matching pumps, an oyster-colored silk blouse, and a simple gold cuff. A Hermès scarf wound loosely around her neck like a pet serpent.

After she had settled herself and taken another dose of caffeine, he said, "I'd like you to clear your schedule for the next week, at least."

"My entire schedule? Why? What for?"

He had prepared himself for her.

"New information has come to light." Anselm took his time sipping his coffee, while his watery brown eyes behind round gold-rimmed spectacles scoured her face.

Instead of showing any sign of irritation, Camilla finished her coffee, rose, went back to the Nespresso, and made herself another double shot. When she was finished, she tasted it, then returned and sat down. Only then did she say, "Care to share?"

"There's been an incident in Doha," he said in a perfectly neutral voice, "involving ministers from seven Arab nations, who were holding a high-level summit there."

"I hadn't heard."

"For the moment, it's being kept from the newswires and Internet termites."

"That can't last."

"POTUS is determined to use what little head start he's been given."

Camilla regarded him over the rim of her cup. "What happened, exactly?"

"Six ministers dead, exactly. Along with over a dozen mercenary bodyguards and four jihadists."

"Christ. Do we know which — ?"

"The cadre was led by El Ghadan himself, by all accounts."

"He hasn't been seen in over a year."

"But his people, the Tomorrow Brigade, have been mighty active in Somalia, the Congo, Iraq, Syria, India, Pakistan, Indonesia — all over the fucking globe. He's a one-man wrecking ball."

"I've been keeping abreast of the reports. What would bring him into the open now?"

Anselm evinced a sphinxlike expression. "Excellent question."

Camilla waited, her double shot growing colder by the minute. When no answer was forthcoming she decided to press on. "And the seventh minister?"

Anselm's eyes behind his spectacles flicked down at his paperwork, then back up, all in the space of a heartbeat. "A man by the name of Qabbani. He's from Syria."

"What happened to him?"

"Vanished. As if he had never existed." Anselm looked at her darkly. "Except Minister Qabbani most

30

assuredly does exist. In fact, POTUS has just this hour spoken with him. Qabbani is safe and sound in Damascus, having never left."

"Then how the devil . . . ?"

"A Blacksmith."

Camilla shook her head. "I beg your pardon?"

"Blacksmith," Anselm repeated, enunciating the word carefully. "Someone who impersonates a dignitary, posing as them in world hot spots."

Camilla sat back and whistled. "There's a dangerous job."

"Dangerous for you when the Blacksmith you've hired is Jason Bourne."

Camilla was so startled some of her espresso slopped into the saucer. "What?"

"We believe Bourne is working with El Ghadan."

She shook her head. "Does that track?"

"There's simply no other explanation. How did the cadre gain access to a highly restricted area, so well guarded? Bourne is a master of infiltration. How did El Ghadan know that Bourne was impersonating Qabbani unless Bourne told him beforehand? All the ministers are dead except Bourne. You know El Ghadan as well as I do. He would never leave a witness alive. Ergo, he never had any intention of harming Bourne. Ergo, he and Bourne are working hand in glove."

"Even if everything you say is true —"

"It is. Jason Bourne does what he wants, when he wants. He's the most dangerous man in our neck of the woods, Camilla. A constant threat that gives POTUS gray hairs."

"Accepting all that, why in the world would El Ghadan team up with Bourne? From his dossier, we know that El Ghadan does not have a history of sharing power. Just the opposite, in fact."

Anselm leaned forward, the overhead lights sparking against his lenses, turning them briefly opaque. "All true, but here's what's just crossed the NSA's signals desk: El Ghadan is planning an attack so big, so important that even he needs help."

"But what would . . . ?" Camilla picked up on the sudden flurry of anxiety in the air. Then her hand flew to her mouth. "Oh my God, POTUS's summit in Singapore."

Anselm showed his teeth at last, tiny nubbins that glittered briefly as he drew back his thin lips. "This raid was a dry run. They got into the hotel, they overcame security, and then, the coup de grâce, they had someone on the inside." He lifted a forefinger like a college professor. "A little-known fact: Bourne is an absolute master of disguise. There's no one better."

Camilla stared at him, wide-eyed and mesmerized.

"Over the years," he continued, "this government has done everything in its power to bring Bourne to heel, to administer to him the justice he so richly deserves. How perfect, then, for him to engineer the assassination of the president of the United States, the man who issued his termination order."

His tiny-tot elbows stuck out as he leaned more heavily on his desk. "This is revenge, Camilla. Revenge, pure and simple." He took the cup and saucer out of her hand, set it aside. "We have to stop him. We have to end Bourne's reign of terror once and for all. This is the mandate POTUS has given us."

"Us?"

"The Company has been unsuccessful, so has the NSA. Even Treadstone, which has now been disbanded following the resignation of Soraya Moore and the severe wounding of Peter Marks. POTUS believes the time has come to think outside the box."

"Meaning?"

"If Bourne has a weakness, it's for people in distress."

"Do you have someone in mind, Howard?"

"Here's the brief." Anselm handed her a hefty folder.

"Good God, it's as thick as a brick."

"The Joint Chiefs put their heads together."

She opened the brief. "This plan must be something special if it got the alphabet soup to play nice with one another."

Anselm smiled. "It is special, Camilla. Very."

She began to read, then looked up, startled. "Wait a minute. This means —"

"It's you, Camilla. We've created a scenario expressly for you. We're sending you into the field as the center. Your brief is to terminate Jason Bourne with extreme prejudice."

CHAPTER
FOUR

Eli Yadin, director of Mossad, was tacking into the wind, sails straining, taking full advantage of the weather. His boat, a thirty-three-foot sloop he sailed himself, was perhaps a nautical mile off the coast of Tel Aviv. Sunlight winked in and out from behind puffy cumulus clouds. He looked up, grinned at his daughter Sara. He had taken her out on the boat as a celebration of her recovery from her near-death knifing. They had broken bread together, shared a bottle of rosé, had even gone for a brief swim.

Then his phone rang — not his mobile, but his sat phone. For a moment they stared at each other, recognizing the portent of disaster. He handed her the sail lines and went belowdecks to take the call.

It was his asset-in-place in Doha.

"Director, a Quai d'Orsay operative was just dropped off at the French embassy doorstep."

An icy ball of fear formed in the pit of Yadin's stomach. If it was him . . . "Dead or alive?"

"Half his head has been blown off."

"Not a professional assassination, then."

"Probably not."

34

Yadin looked out a window. Tel Aviv seemed very far away. Nevertheless, his world had found him. He dreaded asking the fateful question.

"His name?"

"Aaron Lipkin-Renais. I know the Frenchman was only an occasional, but still I thought his death important enough to —"

"You did the right thing." Yadin squeezed his eyes shut for a moment. Dammit, he thought. Dammit to hell. "Now tell me all of it."

"Sara!" Eli Yadin called. "Sara!"

The wind was in her hair, the sun in her eyes. She had never looked more beautiful, he thought, nor felt more precious to him.

"What is it?" She tied off the line, came toward him as he took the wheel.

Tears overflowed her eyes when he told her. "How?" she said. "How did it happen?"

"Aaron had been missing for two days, along with his family. His daughter had been ill; it was assumed he had taken the family away for a rest. Twelve hours later, he still hadn't responded to the emergency signals from his own office. His colleagues were canvassed. He'd said nothing to any of them. He, his wife, and daughter had vanished."

"Then he washes up dead outside the French embassy in Doha?" Sara shook her head. "It makes no sense." She sat on a teak taffrail. "What about his wife and daughter?"

"Nothing," Eli said. "Not a word, not a sign."

35

Sara looked away, didn't bother to pull her hair back from her face.

"I know you and Aaron were close." When she did not immediately respond, Eli went on. "Did your situation change after he was married?"

She looked at him sharply. "Why should it?"

Eli shrugged. "A man marries, he has a child. Priorities change."

"They didn't for you, Abba."

Now it was his turn to give her a sharp look. "Do you resent me for that?"

"How can I resent you, Abba? You're the bravest man I know."

"Sara."

"Now Aaron is dead, his wife and child are missing."

Eli made a course correction while he considered a moment. "We've got a most vexing mystery on our hands."

Sara squared her shoulders. Her feet were braced at shoulder width. She was clearly gathering herself. "Abba, I need to find out what happened. I want to go to Doha."

Without a word of protest, Eli turned the wheel over, headed the sloop back to Tel Aviv. He did not care for the idea of sending her to Qatar, but when she used that tone of voice he knew from bitter experience not to cross her.

"Sonya."

Silence.

"Sonya!"

36

The darkness exploded into light and Sonya, sobbing, ran into her arms. "Darling, I'm here." Soraya gathered her daughter up, cradling her, rocking her back and forth. "Sonya, I'm here. It's all right. It's all right," she crooned.

They had been allowed out of the room in order to use the bathroom. A jihadist had remained with them as Soraya washed them both down with the soap and washcloth provided, used the toilet, before they were escorted back to their cell.

Now she tried not to think about Aaron, about how his corpse, cut loose, had lain between her and her daughter, a terrible reminder — if any more were needed — of their captors' ultimate power. Now he was gone. God alone knew how they had desecrated his poor body. It was impossible not to think of Aaron. God in heaven, he was dead, his life winked out in the space of a heartbeat. The reality of it was almost too much to bear, and, strong of mind and body as she was, so well trained by Treadstone's most accomplished masters, she felt certain she would have broken down were it not for Sonya. She had to remain strong for her daughter. Her primary duty now was to keep Sonya calm, to reassure her that everything was going to be all right. Mourning for Aaron must wait until they were both far away from here — wherever *here* was — and safe. So, like the best agents, she placed her grief into the farthest corner of her mind, reverently sealing it off for the time being.

"Darling," she said in her steadiest voice, "I'm here. You're safe."

"Mommy!"

That little voice, as familiar to her as her own, now full of anguish and terror, almost broke her heart.

"I couldn't see you, Mommy."

"I was right here, sweetheart. Right here all the time."

"I couldn't see you!" the child repeated, as children do.

God, keep me strong, Soraya prayed. Let me protect my child and I will love you forever and ever. "If the lights go out again, here's what you do, muffin. Listen to my voice. Follow it in your mind and you'll find me."

"I won't be able to!"

"Yes you will, muffin. Remember Scheherazade? Remember the stories she told the old king, the stories I sing to you in Farsi as you go to sleep every night?"

"I remember them all, Mommy."

"Of course you do, muffin. Your memory is like a long, gorgeous river. Now think back to the song of Dinazade in the Cave of the Djinn. Do you remember how dark it was in the cave?"

"Very dark."

"So dark that Dinazade could not see a thing."

"And she had no lamp to light. And outside it was nighttime, a night with no moon or stars."

Soraya smiled to herself. Sonya was such a remarkable child. "Yes. But Dinazade had to find her way. What did she do?"

"She heard the wind blowing through the cave. She followed the sound of the wind."

"And what happened?"

"She found the many-roomed house of the djinn."

"How?"

"Their voices sounded like the wind when they spoke to her."

Soraya began to sing in Farsi: *"I will come for you when the moon is full to melon-bursting / When the trees shiver and bend to my will / When darkness lulls you to sleep / I will come / I will gather you in my arms and sail with you to shores unknown."* Her voice almost cracked. "Now, sweetheart, does my voice sound like the wind?"

"Yes, Mommy."

"Then follow it and in the darkness you will find me, and like the djinn did for Dinazade, I will keep you safe from harm." Soraya sang, almost in tears, *"For I am the sun and I am the moon / The stars, they do my bidding / None dare stand before me / For I am made of air and sea and sky / When you are with me / When I hold you / You are in the arms of God."*

"So you've agreed to it."

"Yes, sir, I have."

President Magnus frowned. "For Christ's sake, Camilla, don't call me 'sir' when we're alone."

Camilla's generous lips curled in a cat's smile. "As you wish, Bill."

The two of them were sitting on one of the two facing sofas in the Oval Office. In front of them glowed

39

the iconic seal of the president of the United States, woven into the majestic blue carpet, reminding all who entered just where they were.

"You've read the brief."

"I have."

"All the way through."

"I've memorized it. It's quite complex."

"It has to be. With the summit only a week away, surely you can see that."

"Why not postpone the summit? Or at least change the venue."

Magnus shook his head. "Too late. Besides, I'll be goddamned if I'll let a terrorist threat disrupt the culmination of the most important peace process of our lifetime."

"Of course. It's just that —"

"I know." POTUS sighed. "Why did you say yes, Camilla? Was Howard that persuasive?"

"You know me, Bill," she said. "I'm a patriot at heart. That's my training. I go where my country needs me most. I *will* protect you. As the head of Secret Service that's my job."

"And the rest of Secret Service?"

"Cleaned up, as you directed. Besides, Warren has been with me every step of the way. He'll do fine until I return."

POTUS seemed uninterested in Warren, her deputy. "What about your own needs?"

She pursed her lips, which, though she did not know it, made her look all the more alluring. "Now you're being disingenuous. It's not my needs you're referring to."

"*Our* needs."

She stared at him, breathing softly. By any measure he was an impressive man: tall, square-shouldered, oozing masculinity. Women loved him, men envied him. His skill as an orator was outstripped only by his ability to connect with individual people, be it a foreign leader, a legislator, or the common man or woman. He had won the last election in a landslide, and, remarkably, his approval ratings had stayed high into this, his second year in office, traditionally the most perilous, as the honeymoon effect wore off. Not for William Magnus. Not at all.

"I was amused this morning," Camilla said now, "the way Howard tried to waylay me."

"Let me guess," POTUS said. "With his Nespresso."

She laughed; they laughed together.

"Come over here," he said, patting the fabric next to him.

"I don't think that's a good idea."

His face clouded over, his wide-set gray eyes darkening. "Nothing's a good idea anymore," he grumbled.

"Now you sound like a little boy."

"I want what I want. We all do. It's a primal human trait."

"Primal animal trait, you mean."

He shrugged, ran a hand through his thick salt-and-pepper hair. "What's the difference?"

"In this case, none."

He shook his head, looked for something for his restless hands to do, found only her. "You know the brief's hidden agenda. It's an evil plot dreamed up by Howard and Marty to keep us apart."

"Maybe it's not so evil."

"You don't know what you're talking about."

The phone on his desk rang, but he made no move.

"Aren't you going to answer that?" Camilla asked, knowing he wasn't.

Magnus was looking at the American flag furled on its stand behind his desk. "I was just thinking . . ."

The ringing stopped; the silence in the Oval Office was absolute. Sound bafflers and frequency-modulating surveillance jammers made it so.

"I was just thinking," POTUS began again, "what it would be like to take you, wrapped in the flag."

"You see," Camilla said, "Howard and Marty do have your best interests at heart."

He turned to her, his expression now slightly hostile. He could be mercurial that way. She had learned this very quickly.

"Do you?" he said.

She considered a moment. "To be honest, I don't know whether it's in my best interests either."

"*It.*" His hostility was more evident. "You won't even use the word."

"There are many words for what we did."

As quickly as it had appeared, his hostility vanished. He grinned at her. "Don't you want to come over here and fuck me again?"

42

"You see, that's just what I mean, Bill. I have no intention of becoming the other woman, outed by God alone knows who, hounded for the rest of my life. Monica Lewinsky finally had to flee the country, for God's sake."

"You're not Monica Lewinsky."

"She and Clinton only did it once."

"Supposedly."

"You and I did it once, and luckily for us we didn't get caught."

"We're not going to be outed, Camilla."

"And you — you'd face impeachment in this very puritanical country." She shook her head. "No, once was enough."

He looked genuinely stung. "You can't mean that."

"Of course I don't mean it, Bill. But also I do. Very much so." She stirred. "Come on, we're both too smart for this."

"The heart wants what it wants."

"Cock, Bill. Cock."

He smiled, sadly, a little boy again. "Okay, okay. I take your point." His expression became suddenly serious as he half turned toward her. "But look here, Camilla, promise me you'll take care of yourself."

"Of course I will. I always do."

He nodded. "I know that, but . . . this is different. You're going up against Jason Bourne."

"He's been a thorn in the CIA's side for years, not to mention the NSA and you. But he's just a man — one man. And the Black Queen brief is correct: This is the only way to get to him. He won't come at you at your hotel — it's too heavily defended. He might be able to get in, but he'd never get out."

"So it will be at the Thoroughbred Club. The day before the summit begins, when I, along with the other heads of state, have been invited to sit in the presidential box to watch the races. An atmosphere of mutual enjoyment, a loosening of the neckties and all that."

She smiled. "And he won't ever see me coming. He'll be on the lookout for someone else — a DOD assassin, a man, you can be sure of that."

"Indeed I am." A frown overtook his face. "But, Cam, horsemanship —"

"Is essential to my cover. That's how I'm going to gain access to the working part of the Thoroughbred Club. I'll be in the area that Bourne is sure to infiltrate. That's his specialty, according to the brief. He'll blend in, become part of the rank and file. That's how I'm going to locate him."

Magnus's face twisted briefly. "Well, I know firsthand how good you are at the art of seduction."

"Who said anything about seduction?"

"First you charm him, then you kill him. The brief suggests an old and proven method. Honey's the best way to trap a dangerous assassin. It works. From Mata Hari all the way down to —"

"Bill, for Christ's sake!"

"That's a compliment, dammit!"

Shaking her head, she smiled, but it was a rueful smile. "Time to end it, once and for all." How many layers of meaning in that statement?

Magnus frowned, still clearly concerned. "The operation may not be as straightforward as the brief makes it out to be."

"What do you mean?"

"Briefs have a tendency to make everything seem cut-and-dried. Do x, and y happens. One move follows the next in logical progression. But the field doesn't always progress that way. The field is chaos; people who are logical by nature die out there, wondering how it could be that their life is ending because the mission went off the rails in an insane twist the brief never covered. In the field, other, hidden factors are always at play. Factors the authors of the brief know nothing about."

"I'll be careful, Bill. I told you."

"I want you to come home," he said, "with or without Bourne's head. But don't you dare tell Howard I said that."

"I make it a rule never to tell Howard squat."

"Good girl." He nodded. "And you're sure you're up to this?"

"Bill," she said, rising, "if I had a cock it would always be up."

She went to the door, turned to him, and smiled sadly. "You see how emotions fuck things up? We're fearing for each other's lives instead of concentrating on the situation at hand."

CHAPTER
FIVE

It was a terrible thing to wake up in Doha alone and in despair.

"If you look for them," El Ghadan had told Bourne before they slipped the hood over his head and took him away, "you will not find them."

It was a terrible thing to wake up in Doha alone and helpless.

"If you look for them," El Ghadan had said just before they had dumped him at the edge of the desert, "I will kill them myself, one slow inch at a time."

The heat was intense, the sun blinding, almost hallucinatory. And perhaps it actually was, because, squinting into the white glare, Bourne saw an Arabian oryx, its body white as milk, legs black as night, a splash of the same ebon hue pigmenting the center of its muzzle. The oryx stared at him with a rare intelligence, as if to say, You fool. Then it tossed its head, as if in contempt, its magnificent, impossibly long horns seeming to rake the sky.

Bourne blinked and it was gone. Picking himself up off the dusty verge, he commenced to walk in the direction of the city, until, hours later, a truck stopped beside him. Drenched in sweat, he climbed in beside the driver.

"What are you doing way out here in the middle of nowhere?" the driver said in Arabic, as he ground the gears out of neutral.

"Having a conversation with an oryx," Bourne replied, staring ahead at the city towers shimmering in the heat haze.

The Museum of Weaponry, in the Al Luqta quarter of Doha, was not open to the public. A letter was required from the Museums Authority before entrance could be gained. No such permission was needed, however, for Abdul Aziz, or Zizzy, as his intimates called him.

Abdul Aziz lived like a pasha. Not a modern-day pasha, whatever that might be, but a pasha from the opulent days of the Ottoman Empire. In fact, for him the Ottoman Empire was in many ways still alive, for his shipping empire extended as far as the Ottomans' had in its heyday. It was almost as lucrative, too, though in reality, what could compare to the wealth of the Ottomans? Apart, of course, from that of the Vatican.

Zizzy was an Arab who successfully negotiated the modern world while keeping the seven pillars of Islamic culture vibrantly alive. How he managed this almost superhuman metaphysical juggling act was a mystery to all, including his family. But everyone who knew him was grateful for his ability to defy gravity, as it were.

Jason Bourne was one of those. Bourne had encountered Zizzy some years earlier when both men were on assignment in the Sinai. Zizzy was inspecting a site he was considering buying. Bourne had penetrated the site in pursuit of a small cadre of terrorists who had blown an Egyptian church sky high, killing almost a hundred worshipping Copts, many of them women and children.

Zizzy had proved his astonishing marksmanship by shooting dead the last of the terrorists who had lain in wait for Bourne. Zizzy had used an L115A3 AWM sniper rifle, arguably the best in the business. One shot, one kill. That was the sniper's code — one, as it turned out, Zizzy adhered to religiously.

Zizzy was fiercely loyal, well connected, a man with an irreverent sense of humor who did not automatically view all westerners as inherent enemies of Islam. He possessed a deep and abiding hatred of extremism, of terrorists who, in his opinion, distorted the teachings of Islam to suit their own purposes. "Islam is a religion of peace," he was fond of saying with a ferocity that could keep a pack of jackals at bay.

But straddling past and present had its price. He was, in his own way, as much an outsider as Bourne. The two men had hit it off at once.

After the truck driver let him off, Bourne made his way back to Minister Qabbani's hotel room, took a long shower, first hot, then cold, shaved, and dressed. The pain hit him the instant he toweled himself off. The hot water had lulled him into believing the aftermath of his torture wouldn't be so bad. He was dead wrong. The pain flashed through him, constricting his chest, bringing back the session with the car battery.

Opening the room's safe, he pulled out a small rucksack. He stared at it a moment, thinking of his last, abortive identity, thinking of Soraya and Sonya, thinking of Aaron, his brains exploding from a head that resembled a dropped melon. With a supreme effort he blocked all the flashing images. Then he made the call.

Zizzy met Bourne at the entrance to the Museum of Weaponry, where they were let in by a wizened old man with a hunchback and a mad gleam in his eye. Being in constant contact with such a display of exquisite weapons dating back to the sixteenth century could do that to you, Bourne supposed.

Swords from all the great dynastic families of the Middle East were represented, including one belonging to King Faisal of Saudi. But by far Zizzy's favorite was the dagger once belonging to Lawrence of Arabia. To him it was the crown jewel of the collection, the weapon he returned to over and over.

"A great man, that Lawrence," Zizzy said as they stood in front of the case housing the dagger. "A man who understood Islam, a man who appreciated the seven pillars of Islam's wisdom. Of course, he was considered mad by the British. They said he'd gone native. Poor things. They never understood."

He pointed to the scabbarded dagger, curved as a houri's slipper. "It doesn't look like much, does it? If you saw it in a bazaar, you'd most likely pass it by. You wouldn't think that the future of Islam in the desert resided there. But it did. It does."

Having spoken his heart, Zizzy turned to Bourne, his expression somber, even worried. "My friend, what has happened?"

"Anything of mine is yours for the asking."

Bourne, sitting across from Zizzy in a café that was a small part of a shopping arcade Zizzy owned, nodded. "I appreciate that. As always."

In sharp contrast to the hypermodern boutiques surrounding it, the café was done up in authentic *Arabian Nights* style. Walking in was like stepping into a sultan's palace of three hundred years ago. The place was packed with westerners and locals alike, its reputation for excellent food known throughout Doha's hotels as well as its expat community. Its buzzy atmosphere was perfect for keeping important conversations private.

Unlike Bourne, who was in Western gear, Zizzy was in traditional dress — watery blue *thoube* over loose white cotton trousers. His head was covered in the traditional *ghutra,* in a black-and-white check, held in place by a doubled black coil, the *iqal.* To show his Bedouin roots, Zizzy's *iqal* had two tassels hanging from it, which Bedouins used to tic — or hobble — their camels at night to keep them from wandering off.

Sweet mint tea was poured and an array of small dishes were set out until the entire tabletop was covered. When they were alone again, Zizzy said, "Now, tell me what brings you to my great city."

"Work," Bourne said.

"Yes, work." Zizzy nodded. "Always work with you, my friend." He scooped up a bit of hummus with a triangle of pita, toasted a golden brown, chewed reflectively. "Eat, my friend. Eat! You cannot starve yourself! Nothing can be as bad as that."

Zizzy gave the aspect of a mythical creature — his goggle eyes and beaked nose dominated a sun- and wind-darkened face. He had a wide forehead, as prominent as the prow of a fast ship. When he smiled, which was often, his teeth gleamed like little cakes of sugar.

As he watched Bourne pick at his food, he said, "I worry about you, Jason. I worry that one day I will find your perfectly preserved corpse half buried in the side of a sand dune." He laughed. "But then I console myself with the sure and certain knowledge that you are far too tough for that to happen." Popping an enormous date into his mouth, he sat back and said, "Now, tell me what has befallen you."

Bourne told him what had transpired at the hotel, both before and after the massacre. As he finished, he put a mobile on the table. "El Ghadan gave this to me. Every day at midnight he will send me a short video of Soraya and Sonya, along with the day's newspaper."

"Proof of life."

Bourne nodded. "It also contains a GPS that cannot be turned off."

"So he can monitor your every move." Zizzy shook his head. "He's got you in an escape-proof box. This is a disaster, Jason. A complete and utter disaster." He spread his hands, the food and drink forgotten. "How can I help, my friend?"

"My first impulse was of course to go find them, despite El Ghadan's explicit warning," Bourne said. "But then I forced myself to take several steps back and look at the situation objectively."

"That's good," Zizzy said. "Because as of now you have seven days until the Singapore summit, seven days before El Ghadan goes to work on your friend and her daughter, seven days before he reshapes your world."

Bitterness squeezed Bourne's heart. It was a fact, hard but true, that everyone who had ever mattered to him had been either exposed to mortal danger or killed. Pulling his mind back to the problem at hand, he said, "Zizzy, I need to know as much as I can about him."

"Not an easy task, my friend. El Ghadan's past is as heavily guarded as his real identity." Zizzy pulled at his lower lip, as he was wont to do when he had sunk deep in thought. "Well, I do think there is someone who might be able to help." He checked his watch. "And, as luck would have it, this is just about the right time to catch him."

"He might be Jordanian or Omani — there are people who believe that — but I'm not one of them."

So said the tiny man — he was barely five feet tall — with a huge head, a nose like a hawk's beak, the ears of an Indian elephant, and a halo of white hair tangled as a thorny bush. This was Nebuchadnezzar, known as Nebby. He could have been seventy or a hundred and seventy, it was impossible to tell. His eyes were bright with a mischievous intelligence rare in men a quarter his age.

Bourne and Abdul Aziz were sitting on a circular rug in the center of Nebby's living room. He had a small apartment on the outskirts of the city, where, as he put it, he could study the desert. What there was to see in the expanse of sand and wind was anyone's guess. According to Zizzy, the old man dealt in information, traded item for item. He owed Zizzy several favors, so in this case no payment from Bourne was expected.

Tea had been served by a young woman with dark hair and a ready smile. All around them were shelves containing artifacts from Nebby's long and varied life: shells from Zanzibar, carvings from Namibia and Ethiopia, strange voodoo-like dolls from Uganda that looked like preserved babies, Moroccan tiles and pottery. A Maasai chieftain's polished wooden stick, strange deep-sea fish, dried and preserved. The array was dizzying, virtually endless. The air vibrated to the energies of these shards of his past.

Nebby sipped his tea as daintily as an English nanny, set his glass down, and continued. "No, I'm not one of them. I think El Ghadan is Persian, and this is why. Unlike other extremists who hate the Saudis as much as they do the Americans, his fury is directed solely at the United States and Israel. This, to my mind, marks him out as Persian."

The ensuing silence went on so long that Bourne felt obliged to say, "What else can you tell me?"

"This is not enough?" Nebby cocked his head like a bird eyeing a choice bit of food. "No, I suppose for a man in your position it is not." He raised a finger, as if testing the direction of the wind. "There is a story I've heard, though whether to credit it is strictly your choice. This story concerns El Ghadan's son. Now, what makes this story interesting is that it is widely known in some circles that, though married, the man is an inveterate womanizer. Doubtless, these escapades have led to issue, both male and female. However, the story says that El Ghadan has one legitimate son. The boy, who might be in his early twenties by now, ran away when he was perhaps sixteen, give or take a year. Ever since then, El Ghadan has been desperately searching for him. To no avail." A cackling laugh issued from Nebby's lips. "Can you imagine? A child disappears and the great and powerful El Ghadan cannot find him."

"What is known of this son?" Bourne said.

"Practically nothing," Nebby admitted, "though several things can be intuited. I believe he is hiding in plain sight, which is why his father's people cannot locate him. They're looking in the wrong places."

"What does that mean, exactly?"

Nebby finished his tea. "Well, if I were him I'd have joined a terrorist cell — under a different name, of course. One that's as close as possible to his father's cells."

"Such as?"

Nebby shrugged. "It is believed that from time to time El Ghadan partners with people who can be of particular use to him. Currently, that would be Ivan Borz."

"The arms dealer?"

Nebby nodded.

"Do you know where Borz is now?"

"Rumor has it Waziristan, working with one of El Ghadan's cadres."

"I'm hungry," Zizzy said. "What about you?"

Zizzy led him to an opulent restaurant whose owner Zizzy knew well. Even though at this hour the room was packed, Zizzy's friend ushered them to the best table in the house, had a kettle of rare silver-tip white tea brought to their table, and spoke to them effusively for several moments before departing with a smile and a deferential incline of his head.

"Sorry, Jason," Abdul Aziz said. "Difficult to know whether our little visit to Nebby was of any use."

"Any bit of insight into El Ghadan I can glean is important," Bourne said. "Especially the news that he has a wayward son he's desperate to find."

"Leverage, yes?" Zizzy said.

"If he exists," Bourne said. "If I could find him."

They paused to order.

"Of most concern now," Bourne said when they were alone again, "is how El Ghadan knew I was impersonating Minister Qabbani."

"Do you think Qabbani himself is a conduit for El Ghadan?"

"Possibly. Qabbani was instrumental in making the summit happen."

"Yet he didn't want to go himself."

"That in itself means nothing. I was watching his face the entire time. I wouldn't have taken the commission otherwise."

"If not Qabbani, who betrayed you?"

"That's what I have to find out. I need a back door into the Ministry of Interior."

Zizzy grinned. "You know, I've been wanting to revisit Damascus."

"The place is an out-and-out war zone, Zizzy."

Zizzy winked. "That's what I mean." He took out his mobile. "I'll have my pilot set out a flight plan and warm up the engines."

Shortly after their meal had been served, Bourne noted a young man enter the restaurant and scan the interior with professional acuity before settling himself into a corner table, after which he never looked in Bourne's direction.

"We have company," Bourne said, and Zizzy nodded, not even bothering to query the acute left turn in the conversation. "At your four o'clock, corner table."

"Alone?" Zizzy asked, without turning to take a look.

"In here, at least," Bourne said.

"El Ghadan making good on his threats." Zizzy said. "This is positive news; it means he's predictable, which is more than you can say for most terrorists. If he's predictable we can stay one step ahead of him."

Bourne shook his head. "With the mobile he gave me he has no need to put eyes on me."

Zizzy frowned. "Then who's our friend over there working for?"

"We'll find out before we leave," Bourne said, "but right now I want to know why you want to put yourself in danger in Damascus."

"You came to me, Jason, remember?"

"I'm asking for help, not for you."

"Nevertheless . . ." Zizzy shrugged. "What can I say? I'm missing the old days. Listen, it's my plane, Jason."

"Okay, we'll go to Damascus together," Bourne said softly but firmly. "You'll help me get into the ministry. Then you're done."

"Jason. I'll miss out on all the fun."

"I'm not going to endanger your life."

"Am I mistaken in believing that decision is mine to make?"

Bourne said nothing.

"Well, as for my own situation, if you've been made, then I've already been linked to you. Better for both of us if we get out of Doha as quickly as possible."

"I'm sorry about that."

Zizzy snorted. "What are friends for, except to take a bullet for you?" Then, seeing Bourne's expression, he laughed. "Come on. I have it on the highest authority I'm going to live to a ripe old age, dandling great-grandchildren on my arthritic knees."

CHAPTER
SIX

Camilla, her well-packed weekender in hand, presented herself at the Dairy, where she was photographed and fingerprinted by security personnel. The Dairy was only a mile or so away from the Farm, but its purpose was very different. Whereas the Farm trained new recruits, refreshed the skills of field agents, and periodically updated them on the newest surveillance hardware and weaponry, the Dairy prepared elite agents for specialized assignments.

Both the Farm and the Dairy were in rural Virginia, a short helicopter ride from Langley. In the Dairy's case, it was set at an actual dairy, complete with a herd of milk-producing cows and a highly trained staff dedicated to the bovines. Needless to say, the director of the Company handpicked every member of the Dairy's staff, whether in the service of the facility's human guests or animal residents.

The Dairy's setting, amid bucolic rolling hills, lush stands of hardwood trees, despoiled by few roads and even fewer vehicles, was idyllic, but only the cows had the leisure to appreciate it fully. The Company's guests were kept far too busy to catch more than a glimpse now and again.

The Black Queen brief had instructed Camilla to report to someone named Hunter Worth. This resident turned out to be a woman with the face of an angel and the demeanor of a marine drill instructor. In fact, as Camilla quickly discovered, Hunter had been a marine herself, piloting jets just as Camilla's mother had once done, until a shoulder injury had forced her to find another path.

"How did you injure your shoulder?" Camilla asked, that first day.

"I fell out of a tree."

"What? You're kidding."

"I wish."

"What happened?"

"I was stupid enough to accept a dare. It had rained overnight, the bark was slippery. Boom, end of story."

"Sorry."

"Don't be. I love the Dairy."

"Isn't this kind of a" — she gestured with her arm — "closed-off life?"

"Not with Hulu Plus, Netflix, and iTunes."

"You mean — ?"

"Yeah, *Breaking Bad, NCIS, The Big Bang Theory.*"

"Fan, fan, fan," Camilla said, laughing. "And music?"

"Lots and lots of it."

"Lana del Rey, Artic Monkeys, Lorde."

"Fan, fan, fan."

They laughed simultaneously.

Camilla shook her head. "But you don't miss flying?"

"You always miss flying," Hunter said, sobering. "Didn't your mother tell you that?"

In fact, she had.

"Anyway," Hunter continued, "this is the next best thing, and, after all, you can't fly forever. Better to get out while you're still on top. Better for me, anyway."

"You're that competitive."

"Aren't you?"

Camilla thought about that for some time. "I suppose I must be. I never thought about it much."

"You had to be," Hunter said, "to wind up here."

It was a compliment, Camilla knew, but whether it was directed at her, the Dairy, or Hunter herself was debatable.

"How are you around horses?" Hunter asked now. She had not taken Camilla inside, hadn't shown her to her room, offered her a drink. She had been standing at the rim of the landing pad as the heli transport from Langley had touched down and Camilla had emerged bent over, half sprinting past the circumference of the still turning rotors.

"I'm not frightened of them, if that's what you mean," Camilla said.

Hunter was dressed in jeans, boots, and a denim shirt with the sleeves rolled up her sunbaked, freckled forearms. She wore her dark hair close-cropped, her gray eyes were hooded, and her grip when she had greeted Camilla was as dry and hard as firewood. "That's precisely what I mean."

They were walking across what looked like a college quad, a low, square space covered in well-mown grass.

A gnarled crabapple tree rose from each corner. In the center was a mature rose bush. Camilla was still carrying her weekender.

Passing between two stone buildings, they emerged into a field of wildflowers, beyond which was a barn, a rack of high-end racing and mountain bikes, and two horse riding rings made of split logs, western-style. The rings were large. One of them was simply packed dirt, while the other had red-and-white jumping stanchions of various styles and heights placed at regulation intervals.

As they drew closer, Camilla noticed an enormous packed-dirt oval stretching away on the other side of the barn. She could smell the horses, hear the flies buzzing. Ignoring everything else, Hunter ushered her into the barn, where several workers stood, seemingly waiting for their arrival.

"Done any horseback riding?" Hunter asked.

"When I was a kid I used to bareback."

Hunter raised one eyebrow. "You talking about riding or sex?"

Camilla laughed. "Both."

"Riding at this level is no laughing matter." She gestured. "Stash your bag over there beside the door."

Hunter led her to the stalls. Each one held a horse. They went from stall to stall, Hunter making sure Camilla stood as close to each horse as possible. She watched the deportment of the horses as they reacted to Camilla.

Hunter said, "If you approach a horse from the front, it will shy away. If you approach from the rear, you'll get kicked. If the kick gets you square in the chest, you're dead." She reached up, patted the horse on its muzzle. "Their eyes are on the sides of their heads. Not like ours. You have to remember that. Let the horse see you, then scent you. If you startle him you'll never be able to control him."

"This is crazy," Camilla said suddenly. "I'll never be able to do this in under a week."

"But you must. As a jockey at the Singapore Thoroughbred Club you will have access to all the vulnerable areas. That will give you the chance you need to find Bourne before he can assassinate the president. Anyway, leave your horsemanship to me. I'll get you up to speed and out to Singapore as ordered." They had stopped at the second stall from the end. "Camilla, meet Starfall." The horse was reddish brown with a white diamond-shaped blaze on its forehead.

Hunter stroked the horse's muzzle. "The horse has seen you, has smelled you. Now replace my hand with yours." Hunter lifted her hand away and Camilla placed hers on the muzzle, soft as velvet.

"Starfall," Hunter said, "meet Camilla."

The horse bobbed his head and snorted through huge nostrils. Camilla laughed in delight.

As Bourne and Zizzy wended their way between the tables on their way out of the restaurant, Bourne took a quick detour to the observer's table. He was reading a paper. The front page was all about a French citizen who had been found on the doorstep of the French embassy in Doha, shot to death. According to the story, the victim's identity was being withheld pending the family's notification.

"How can I help you?" Bourne said.

The young man looked up over his paper, said, "Shalom, Mr. Bourne. My name is Levi Blum."

Mossad, Bourne thought.

"What are you doing here, Mr. Blum?"

"Levi, please. I bring greetings from Eli Yadin."

"You needn't talk in Hebrew," Bourne said.

Blum directed a significant glance Zizzy's way.

"Zizzy, meet Levi."

Zizzy grinned, said in Arabic, "I can wait outside."

"No." Bourne, switching to English, put a hand lightly on his arm. He turned to Blum. "Well?"

Blum folded the paper, placed it on the table. "I'm to bring you to a secure location in Doha." He stubbornly kept to Hebrew.

Bourne shook his head. "I don't have time."

"Someone needs to see you, Mr. Bourne. A friend."

"I told you —"

"It's urgent." When Bourne made no reply, Blum hesitated, then, with obvious reluctance, added, "It concerns . . ." And here he pointed to the front-page story.

Bourne looked at him, then nodded, and Blum rose, tossing some bills down on the tabletop.

Zizzy frowned. "What?"

Bourne turned to him. "I need to make a quick detour."

"Jason, you can't. Not with that accursed mobile tracking your every move."

Bourne handed over to Zizzy the rucksack he'd taken from the hotel safe. "The mobile is inside. Go to the plane and wait there for me, will you?"

"Of course, but —"

"Don't worry, my friend. I'll be perfectly safe with Levi."

"It's not that." Zizzy waggled a forefinger. "This clever bastard." He meant El Ghadan.

Bourne smiled grimly. "Go on, Zizzy. I won't be long."

CHAPTER
SEVEN

Sara Yadin waited for Bourne in the rear of a diamond cutter's shop. The diamond cutter, a friend of her father's, was another of Mossad's occasionals, a stringer, a local man called on from time to time to deliver a message outside official channels or to provide a safe house for its agents.

Sara had entered Doha under deep cover. She was Martine Heur: a French Canadian, a diamond merchant from Quebec, and a devout Roman Catholic. Her gold Star of David, which she normally wore around her neck, was hidden on her person so well that no one else was going to find it.

While she waited, she watched the diamond cutter work. He was not a young man. His back was hunched, his hair white, his intelligent face as lined as tree bark. But his hands were rock steady. It was as if they moved of their own accord, as the master took up his tools and applied his loving touch to the diamond braced in its special vise.

"Madam," the diamond cutter said, "your beauty outshines most of my gems."

Sara laughed. "But not all?"

He smiled as the chisel came down, cutting the diamond so precisely it looked afterward as if nothing had happened.

"I am not in the business of inflating egos." He put down his tools, unstrapped his prize. "I am, however, in the business of telling the truth." He swiveled on his stool and faced her, the newly cut diamond held in his open palm. "When one buys and sells diamonds one learns that the truth is the one commodity one cannot do without. How many merchants have I seen fold their tents and fade away because they are cheats and thieves? The business does not suffer these people easily." He shrugged. "Some even wind up dead."

He handed her the diamond to look at. "But you, being a diamond merchant, know all this, yes?"

They grinned at each other.

"Stop over here. I'll just be a moment," Bourne said, and stepped out of the car. They had driven perhaps twenty minutes before he had Blum pull into a parking spot.

Bourne went down the block, into a mobile phone store, where he bought a prepaid mobile, already set up. Back out on the street, walking farther along, away from Blum and the car, he turned his back and dialed a long-distance number from memory, waited patiently for it to be answered.

"Deron."

"Jason! I haven't heard from you since . . . well, it's been far too long." Deron's deep, Oxford-inflected voice hadn't changed a bit. "Are you in D.C.? You should come on over." Deron lived in the northeast quarter, that is to say, the black ghetto. Though he was wealthy enough to live in the poshest D.C. enclave, he had returned from art school in London to settle in the neighborhood where he grew up, using much of his money to help kids who had no hope, who would otherwise have turned to crime. He had made his first fortune by forging fine art. He had then hired himself out as an art expert to individuals and museums that had been sold his art as the real thing. Eternally restless, he had lately turned to manufacturing specialized weaponry for a select clientele, which included Bourne. He still painted, but now it was strictly for his own enjoyment. Bourne could recall with perfect clarity the astonishingly accurate copy of the *Mona Lisa* hanging over Deron's living room fireplace. It was not only style that Deron could reproduce, but the artist's inner fire.

"I'm not even on the continent," Bourne said, then proceeded to tell Deron about the mobile El Ghadan had saddled him with. "What I need," he said in conclusion, "is for you to find a way to fool the GPS. I want El Ghadan to think I'm somewhere I'm not."

"No problem at all," Deron said. "Recently, a bunch of students at the University of Texas built a unit that spoofed the GPS of an eighty-million-dollar super-yacht, sending it incrementally off course without the captain or any of the crew being the wiser."

"Do you know how they did it?"

Deron laughed. "Please. I figured it out six months before they did. Okay, I need some info from you. Give me the mobile's model number, the version of the operating system, along with the baseband, kernel version, and build number."

Bourne recited the info he had memorized, having surmised that Deron would need it.

"Okay," Deron said. "I'll get right on it."

"How long will it take?"

"It can't be done all at once. I have to send out a series of weak civil GPS signals. Eventually they'll overpower the original sat signal and I'll be in. Once that happens, I'll contact you and you can tell me where you want the mobile to tell your watchers you're at. All told, it won't take more than twelve hours."

"Thanks, Deron," Bourne said.

"You can thank me by taking me out to dinner when you get back here."

"It's a deal," Bourne said.

"One caveat, Jason. This GPS switch has a half-life, after which it's hackable and, if by an IT tech with up-to-date knowledge, can be defeated."

"How much time will I have?"

"That, unfortunately, is impossible to determine. Too many variables. And of course, it may never lose its mojo."

They said their goodbyes and he pocketed his new mobile. Then he went back to the car, where Blum was impatiently tapping the wheel.

"It's beautiful," Sara said, handing back the diamond.

"Beautiful?" the diamond cutter said in mock offense. "Why, it's magnificent! Ten carats, flawless white. Please!"

"How much?" she inquired.

"This treasure will set you back a million-four American dollars. Then there's the setting to consider." He lifted a forefinger. "But for you, maybe a special deal can be secured."

Sara laughed again. "What a charmer you are!"

He winked. "It's how I make a living."

At that moment, a knock at the back door precluded any more banter. Two longs, a short, three longs.

The diamond cutter rose. "It is past time I made sure my patrons are being treated well." He took her hand, kissed it briefly. "It's been a pleasure, madam. Come back and see me when you decide to get married."

"You think I'm getting married soon?"

"I think you have come here for more than business."

Sara's pulse pounded in her ears. "How can you possibly know that?"

He smiled. "My dear, if I can hear the beating heart of this diamond, surely I can hear yours."

Sara waited until he had vanished into the front of the shop before opening the back door. There was Levi with Bourne.

As the Mossad agent stepped in behind Bourne, she held out her hand. "My business is private."

"Protocol dictates I don't leave you alone with an outsider."

"He's not an outsider."

Blum frowned. "Do you know something I don't know, Rebeka?" This was the name by which Sara was known inside Mossad, where it was unknown that she was Eli Yadin's daughter, who to the outside world was dead.

She leveled her gaze at him. "Guard the alley, Levi."

Glumly he nodded as Bourne closed the door, stood with his back against it. She faced him, silent, waiting for him to speak. She had set up this rendezvous after hearing about the massacre at the Al-Bourah during her initial briefing with Blum.

When he remained mute, she said, "Aaron is dead."

"You knew him?"

She nodded. "He was a friend. But he was also what we call an occasional."

"You mean between your small talk about art and film and music he slipped you interesting tidbits of product."

"Now and again. The arrangement suited us both."

"Really? What did he get out of it?"

"You must know. Aaron was half Jewish. He despised the gathering French anti-Semitism. He always said that when he got married and his child was of age he'd move out of the country."

Bourne watched her carefully. She had revealed another facet of herself: recruiting people she knew. Did he think she had done this with him? She could sense this made him wary. Time to return the subject to more familiar territory.

"Levi briefed me the moment I arrived. How did you escape the massacre?"

Bourne told her.

"You and Soraya —"

"Worked together," he finished for her.

"And you were close."

"That was a long time ago," he said, "in another lifetime."

"Are they hurt?"

"Not so far as I could see." He had deliberately omitted telling of his torture at El Ghadan's hands. She already had enough on her plate.

She stood no more than a hand's breadth away from him. She could feel his breath on her cheek, that familiar masculine scent she so adored. She wanted to ask if El Ghadan had hurt him, but immediately she checked herself. They had had their two weeks' reunion following her stint in the hospital, and a more kind and gentle man she could not imagine. But now, a year later, they were both at work in the field. Moreover, in a red zone, teeming with the enemy. It would not do to be running on emotion. She also knew that if he sensed any sign of personal emotion he would take it as a flaw in her character and be repelled. That was a thought too terrible to contemplate.

"Okay, then." She nodded. "So we go from here."

"The second lesson to learn about horses," Hunter said as they walked Starfall out of the paddock toward the empty ring, "is just how stupid they are. Forget Trigger or whatever other ideas Hollywood has put into your head. Horses are herd animals. They need to be led. If they sense you're afraid or reluctant to take charge, chaos will ensue."

"Chaos?"

"They'll do whatever the hell they want. Stop, crop the grass, amble along, anything but what you want them to do. They're lazy beasts, at heart." Hunter had a voice as hard and raspy as the callused palm of her hand, as if she smoked three packs a day or had had some surgical procedure on her throat. "So the idea is *intent*." She smacked the small English saddle with the flat of her hand. "Before you mount the horse know what you want him to do, where you want him to go, and at what pace — walk, trot, canter, gallop." Her gray eyes shot Camilla a look. They looked as if she had been through innumerable battles — not weary as much as wise. "Got that?"

Camilla nodded.

"This horse likes you. I felt it from the moment you two met," Hunter said. "He's a gelding, powerful, fast — not a workhorse. See by his sleekness, his long, well-formed legs? He's a racer. Exactly the kind of horse you'll be riding in the field." She patted Starfall's flank fondly. "We'll start you off on him, then graduate you to a horse that won't be so fond of you. You'll need proficiency on all of 'em. Where you're headed you won't get to choose."

Camilla felt her heart thudding wildly in her chest. "You're going to teach me how to win? Really?"

Hunter looked at her in a way that made Camilla believe she could see right through her to the fear.

"First things first, darlin'. Now c'mon, mount this beast. And remember, from the left, always from the left."

The moment the door closed in his face, Levi Blum looked left and right down the alley. Finding he was alone, he drew out a small black box, placed it against the door. He fitted himself with a wireless earbud, switched on the Bluetooth connection, and began to fiddle with the dial on the front of the box. It took only moments to get the electronic ear focused on the two voices in the room beyond the door. He switched on the recording device hidden within the electronic ear.

"The problem is El Ghadan. How the hell does he know so much about you?" Rebeka's voice came through loud and clear.

"That's what I have to find out." Now Bourne's voice.

Rebeka: "You have less than seven days to carry out the mission. How can you — ?"

Bourne: "Let me worry about that."

Rebeka: "About the mission: You're not actually going to kill the president of the United States?"

Bourne: "What choice do I have? El Ghadan was all too clear about what he'll do to Soraya and Sonya if I don't."

Silence for several long beats. Blum, feeling pins and needles in his left leg, shifted from one foot to the other.

Rebeka: "You have another choice, you know."

Bourne: "I don't."

73

Rebeka: "You could find them and —"

Bourne: "El Ghadan has already taken care of that possibility."

Rebeka: "I know, but . . ."

Another silence.

Bourne: "I know what you're implying. Tell me this, if it was Aaron who was being held captive, what would you do?"

Rebeka: "I'd do what needs to be done. Mossad does not negotiate with terrorists."

Bourne: "And if in the process he died?"

Rebeka: "Then so be it."

Bourne: "There is a two-year-old child involved."

Rebeka: "I understand that."

Bourne: "You are as remorseless as the God of Abraham."

Rebeka: "That was how I was raised. That is how I need to be. My people are given no choice. Are you surprised?"

Bourne: "Not in the least."

A third silence. No, not quite a silence. Blum tried dialing in more closely, but all he seemed to hear was what might be the sliding of fabric against fabric, or possibly something else altogether. A hissing like the imagined conversation between two serpents.

Then, abruptly, Rebeka spoke: "That's it, then."

Her voice was louder, closer to the door, and Blum hurriedly detached the box, plucked the bud from his ear, jammed them both deep in the pocket of his trousers.

74

Not a moment too soon. The door swung open and Rebeka emerged, Bourne several paces behind her. Their business completed, they exchanged no words of farewell.

"This way," Rebeka said, leading Blum down the alley in the opposite direction Bourne took.

"Do we have an assignment?" he said, hurrying to keep up with her.

"Yeah," she said tersely. "Keep the fuck out of the way."

CHAPTER
EIGHT

"Everything go all right?" Zizzy said when Bourne climbed into the shimmering leather and chrome interior of the Gulf-stream G650.

Bourne seated himself across from Zizzy. "Nothing has gone right since I got here."

Noting his grim expression, Zizzy said, "Should I be alarmed at Mossad's presence in my city?"

"No one's planning an invasion or a coup," Bourne said shortly.

"Well, that's a relief." Zizzy grunted, picked up a phone, and called for the Gulfstream to get under way. "Strap yourself in."

Bourne sat back, closed his eyes. The jet engines' whine rose in pitch, the brakes came off, and the plane taxied, turned onto the head of the runway.

"You know, I'm getting worried about you," Zizzy said, after takeoff.

"Who's your contact at the ministry?" Bourne said, as if he hadn't heard.

Zizzy regarded Bourne for a moment, as if trying to find the fly in the ointment. "A pig, that's who," he said, apparently giving up. "Bugger looks like one and acts like one. He's as rich as Croesus, as degenerate as

Caligula. Drinks in secret, and don't get me started on his harem of young girls and boys."

Bourne opened his eyes. "I didn't know you were so indiscriminate about your friends, Zizzy."

Zizzy laughed. "Business often makes for uncomfortable bedfellows. And believe me when I tell you that Nazim Hafiz is very good for my business. He knows how to keep my deals running smoothly and without interruption, no matter how shitty things get in Damascus."

"What deals would those be, Zizzy?"

"You know perfectly well: platinum, palladium, my usual strategic metals. But I've more recently planted my flag in titanium — cars, planes — tough and lightweight. Titanium's the future, Jason."

Bourne swallowed, cleared his ears. "How does Hafiz feel about westerners?"

"Hates them like poison," Zizzy admitted. "But you are my friend. He'll make an exception."

"I'm not going to take the chance."

Zizzy flagged down an attendant, ordered sweet Moroccan tea for them both. "Please! Jason. He will have no choice."

"Of course he'll have a choice. People always have choices."

Zizzy looked at Bourne queerly. "I'll make sure he doesn't. It's all part of the game."

"This isn't a game."

Bourne said this with such force that Zizzy looked taken aback. "What's gotten into you, my friend?"

Bourne stared at Zizzy mutely.

"For the love of Allah, this is me who's asking."

Bourne looked away for a moment; when he turned back he looked stricken. "A year or so ago someone close to me died. I tried to save her, but couldn't. After that . . . I don't know, this shadow life seemed to lose its appeal. I was cajoled back with the prospect of revenge on the man who had her killed. But after that . . ." He shrugged. "I went into business for myself as a Blacksmith."

"Until this dire threat reared its head." The tea came, was poured into two narrow cups of colored glass woven with gold filigree. Zizzy handed one glass to Bourne, took up the other. He sipped meditatively. "You know, my friend, there is always going to be someone or some*thing* that will bring you back into what you call the shadow life. This is the way of it. You've lived so long in the margins you would not be comfortable in the light, living the rest of your days among civilians."

"These civilians," Bourne said, "have lives too."

Zizzy leaned forward. "They exist in another world altogether, a place that can no longer support you. No point in fooling yourself, my friend. Neither of us would find happiness there."

Bourne considered a moment; he seemed distinctly uncomfortable continuing the discussion. "I don't want to be introduced to Hafiz as a westerner."

Zizzy spread his hands. "What? You don't trust me to handle him?"

"Why take the chance," Bourne said, "when we don't have to?"

In another half hour Bourne was asleep. He dreamed of
Soraya and Sonya. They were in the water — a shallow
part of a vast sea. Soraya was holding Sonya to keep her
chest and head above the surface, but every once in a
while a wave would swamp them. Sonya sputtered, then
laughed, turning her head this way and that to see what
had hit them and where it had gone.

In the manner of dreams, Bourne was not in the
water with them — he was an observer. The sunlight
that illuminated them, indeed, that sparked the tops of
the waves, did not touch him. He was in shadow —
permanent shadow. And even from within the dream he
understood this much: Soraya, who had lived in the
shadows with him, had chosen to leave, she had chosen
to move into the sunlight. She had become a civilian.

The instant he realized the barrier that had come
between them, he saw an enormous shadow cutting
through the water. It was huge, this shadow, like a
drowned ship. But it wasn't a ship.

The thing was making directly toward mother and
child. Soraya and Sonya were in mortal danger. Bourne
tried to call out to Soraya, but either his voice box was
paralyzed or she couldn't hear him from the other side
of the barrier. Then he tried to get to her, but even
though he saw the scene before him with perfect clarity,
he could not reach them. He was the only one aware of
the danger. He tried to will himself into the water, to
move heaven and earth in a last-ditch attempt to save
them, but it was to no avail.

Then the shadow was upon them, Sonya's face twisted in the same terror and fear he had seen in her when her father was shot in the head, except it wasn't Sonya and she wasn't being held by Soraya. He was watching the demise of Sara and the little girl that was their dream child.

At that precise instant he jerked violently awake. Ignoring Zizzy's curious gaze, he rose, went unsteadily up the aisle to the toilet, where he splashed water on his sweat-streaked face.

For a long time, he stared at himself in the mirror. It occurred to him then that he'd been happier as Minister Qabbani, despite the brevity of his time in the disguise. Being someone else, someone other than Jason Bourne, seemed peculiarly appealing, and he had to wonder whether that was why he had told Zizzy he wanted to meet Hafiz in disguise.

After a time, he returned to his seat, where he was subjected to Zizzy's concerned scrutiny.

Zizzy handed him a glass of ice water, watched him gulp it down. "So she's gotten that deep under your skin," he observed.

Bourne put the glass down. "Who?"

"The woman you tried to save; the woman who was killed."

"Why are you so concerned?"

"We're heading into a war zone — do I have to remind you? My life is on the line as well as yours. If you're having nightmares that make you cry out in your sleep, I could easily become worried that your mind isn't focused correctly."

"It's nothing. Forget it."

"Carrying a dead person on your back isn't nothing, my friend. I should know."

Bourne remembered now. Zizzy's sister had fallen in love with a Danish engineer. Their older brother had gotten the engineer kicked out of Qatar, then he had killed their sister, for which he had been hailed as a true enforcer of Islam. Zizzy had been so incensed that he had broken off all ties with his family and to this day had not seen or spoken to any member. He had not gone to his father's funeral or, several years later, his mother's.

"On the day she discovered our brother had found out about her liaison, my sister came to me in private," Zizzy had once told Bourne. "'I love him,' she told me. 'I want to marry him. He has promised to take me away from this godforsaken country.' Tears leaked out of her eyes, rolled down her cheeks. 'I want my own life. Only you can understand this. Brother, I beg you to help us. I beg you to shield me from what I know is coming.' And what did I do? I went about my business, hid my head in the sand, telling myself that our brother could never do such a barbaric thing, that that was not the kind of family I had been born into. Then, before I knew it, it was over. She was dead and her lover was gone. 'Now it is as if nothing happened,' my brother said to me. 'I have erased the shame our sister brought upon this family.'"

Bourne asked now, "Have you been to your brother's grave?"

"Why would I want to do that?"

Zizzy's brother had died under mysterious circumstances two years after he had killed their sister. It was unclear to Bourne whether Zizzy had murdered him. He had never asked and Zizzy had certainly never volunteered the information.

"I dug the grave myself," Zizzy added, as if suddenly struck by the memory. "That was more than enough."

There was a silence between them, thickening like glue.

"I should never have questioned you about the woman," Zizzy said at length. It seemed clear he had realized Bourne's motivation for bringing up his brother. "That was wrong of me."

"Forget it," Bourne said.

Zizzy stared at Bourne for a moment. "I did it," he said so softly Bourne had to strain to hear him. "I killed him." He looked Bourne straight in the eye. "I had to. I hadn't protected my sister in life. I had to protect her in death."

"I understand, Zizzy."

Zizzy let out a long-held breath. It was like the scrape of the desert wind over an endless ocean of sand. "With what you did for that woman I knew you would."

He leaned forward, held out his hand. "Are we good?"

Bourne took it in his. "Good as gold."

Blum breathed a sigh of relief when he and Rebeka parted company. Something about her made him question himself, as if her presence caused him to peer into his own insidious nature. That was all nonsense, he told himself as he turned the corner and entered a crowded marketplace. His own guilt was imbuing her with supernatural powers.

It was natural, his handler had warned him, to feel guilt, even remorse, at what he was doing. The important thing was to keep those feelings in perspective, to remember the account that had been opened for him in a venerable Gibraltar bank. Each and every month an agreed-upon amount was deposited — money that when it reached a certain level would become what he thought of as his trajectory money: the means by which he could escape the constant pressures and terrors of his current double life. His handler had generously provided the scenario: Blum basking in the sun of some tropical South Pacific island, a fat joint in one hand, a lissome young thing in the other, with nothing on the horizon but to eat, drink, swim, sleep, get high, and fuck. "All this can be yours," his handler had said. But what had come to Blum was product useful to Mossad gleaned from his handler and, very slowly, a local network he had cobbled together, making sure of cutouts along the way so no one member knew of the other's existence. The problem had been sending the product home. Being watched so closely he had yet to find a way to do it.

Passing between a silk merchant and a coppersmith, he pulled out the electronic ear he had used at the diamond cutter's. The audio data was recorded onto the phone's 64GB micro SD card. This was the moment when his life split in two. Minor product was one thing; it kept his handler at bay. But this was major.

If he failed to deliver this product he would immediately come under suspicion, but if he did send it he would be betraying the people he worked for, the country that had raised and nurtured him. Perhaps this moment was inevitable: the moment when a vital piece of intel would fall into his hands. There were two paths to follow now, and he must step out onto one or the other.

The market spun on around him, people going about their daily lives, shopping, chatting, laughing, even. He felt cut off from them, as if he were living in another dimension. He could see and hear them, but he stood firmly outside them, apart — he was Other, and the sheer loneliness was overwhelming.

He had been fed this fantasy of nirvana from the moment of his recruitment, but was it how he really felt now that he had begun to betray his country? There was another way out, but it did not involve wild riches, sun-splashed beaches, and bikinied women flitting around him like butterflies. It was a darker road, filled with peril, and perhaps death.

He held the SD card in his hand for a moment before he dropped it on the ground, and stepped hard on it, grinding it to pieces. Then, filled with dread for his own safety, he walked on. Pausing at a stall, he bought a half pound of fresh-roasted pistachios, popping them one by one into his mouth as he strolled deeper into the market's maze.

A moment later, he abruptly stopped, turned away from the flood of people, and vomited into a dust-coated corner.

CHAPTER
NINE

Camilla was sore all over. She ached in places she hadn't thought about in years. She felt as if Starfall had stomped all over her. When she told Hunter this, her trainer said, "That's what hot baths and liniment massages are for. Get used to it. This is only the beginning."

Camilla might be complaining to Hunter, but she was pleased with her progress. By the end of the day, with a deep blue dusk settling over the Virginia mountains, she had been urging Starfall into an easy gallop around the ring. Uncertainty had given way to an incredible sense of elation. As Hunter had predicted, the feel of the muscular beast between her legs provided her with a surge of power. She wanted to charge into battle, to sweep aside the enemy, to keep going until she reached the foothills of the darkening mountains.

Of course, she did no such thing, and as if divining her thoughts and emotions, Hunter admonished her when she at last drew Starfall to a stop and dismounted beside her trainer.

"Don't allow your emotions to run away with you." She took the reins, walking Starfall out of the ring, back to the paddock. "It's easy, to do that, isn't it?"

"Yes."

"Never lose the sense of who you are and what the horse is. Though he may seem like more, Starfall is only a vehicle, that's all. If you lose your perspective you'll botch the end of it, the most important part. Sure as we're walking here you'll get hurt, possibly very badly. You need to keep your wits about you, remember everything I'll be teaching you. Then, when the moment comes, you'll be all right. You'll be perfectly safe, I promise."

Much to Camilla's surprise, after the promised hot shower and massage, she was instructed to meet Hunter back at the stables, where she was taught how to brush down Starfall and feed him. Then it was time for dinner, which was served — again, a surprise — in the barn. She and Hunter ate with the horses all around them.

Then it was time for sleep — or so Camilla thought. It wasn't long, however, before Hunter's purpose was made clear to her.

Night riding.

"There is a strict deadline," Hunter said. "It's crucial you spend as much time around horses as possible before you're inserted into the field." She led Camilla back to the stalls. "You'll be among professionals — all experts. Forget this for even a moment and you're finished. They will smell a plant six furlongs away. My job is to make you as genuine as a copper penny."

She grinned. "When you arrived this morning, you asked me whether we really had enough time to get you battle-ready." Her grin widened as she opened the door to Starfall's stall. "Darlin', believe me, when you leave here, you won't have a worry in the world."

Sara Yadin, who had reassumed her role as Rebeka, who once again thought of herself as Rebeka, slid behind the wheel of her rented car, but she did not fire the ignition. Instead, she stared sightlessly out the windshield and thought about the last moments of her meeting with Bourne.

She had been about to tell him that she was going after Soraya and Sonya when he had pulled her to him, given her a spine-tingling kiss, then had whispered in her ear, "Don't go after Soraya and Sonya, and don't go near El Ghadan."

When she had tried to pull away far enough to look him in the eye, he had held her fast. "He's going to expect that sort of frontal assault." Bourne's words filled her ear. "He's already prepared for it, believe me."

"Then what?" she whispered back. "I'm not going to stand idly by while —"

"No one's asking you to, least of all me. You're far too valuable an asset."

"What are you proposing?" she asked.

"Go sandcrabbing. You're in the perfect place to dig up dirt on El Ghadan."

"Every secret service on earth has been trying to do that for years, without success."

"But here you are in Qatar, in the center of the web."

"You think Qatar is his territory?"

"I've been working as a Blacksmith for a year. He had fifteen chances to trap me before this one. Why would *you* choose the summit in Doha?"

"He was running a difficult operation. It demanded complex logistics," she whispered. "The hotel had to be secured, the personnel suborned, the surrounding area swept clean. And the police —"

"Yes," Bourne had whispered in her ear. "The police is the place to start."

The police, Rebeka thought now. El Ghadan could not have pulled off such a complicated raid without involving elements within the Doha police.

Pushing her sunglasses up the bridge of her nose, she switched on the ignition, put the car in gear, and pulled out into traffic.

Bourne was right. It was time to go sandcrabbing.

Barring a White House crisis, Howard Anselm and Marty Finnerman made it a habit to meet for a late dinner three times a week. Both men, being creatures of strict routine, always ate at RNR Steak on 22nd Street NW. Partly this was because RNR Steak was one of the newest power spots inside the Beltway, but mainly it was because Finnerman and the chef, Richard Renaldo, were longtime friends. There was always a table for them, no matter how crowded the room. Often, when they were finished with their business, Renaldo would join them for an after-dinner drink, but in any event he always sent out special plates of food. The two men never bothered to consult the menu.

A sultry evening hung heavily over Washington, so it was a relief for Anselm and Finnerman to enter the cool, dim restaurant interior. They were greeted by the manager, who led them to their usual table. They sat in plush chairs, surrounded by dove-gray walls with butter-yellow accents. Here and there, large paintings of indeterminate age and dubious quality adorned the walls, interspersed with brass sconces radiating indirect lighting.

Finnerman, who always chose the wine, picked an Argentine rosé, and the men settled in for the rest of the evening.

Their discussion followed a particular form. As the chief architect of the administration's national security policy, Finnerman always began, while Anselm listened, inserting an appropriate or pointed comment when required. Tonight, however, it was Anselm who made the first comment.

He leaned forward, his forehead creased with worry. "Marty, I think we ought to find a way to postpone the peace summit."

Finnerman goggled. "Have you lost your mind? We can do no such thing. You know it as well as I do. The planning has been in the works for more than a year."

Anselm licked his lips as if they were chapped and dry. "I'm concerned we've pushed Camilla into the deep end."

"Of course we've pushed her into the deep end. That's the point of the brief. Where the fuck is this coming from all of a sudden?"

"I got a call from Hunter!"

Finnerman grunted. "Hunter!"

The wine came, the waiter uncorked it, went through what Anselm felt was the pretentious and boring ritual of smelling the bottom of the cork, pouring a bit into Finnerman's glass, watching indulgently while Finnerman swirled the wine around, smelled it, swirled some more, then tasted it. Anselm began to grind his teeth.

"I know what you think of her," Anselm said when they were alone again, "but she's the best horse trainer at the Dairy."

"Also our best butch since Janet Napolitano."

Anselm picked up his glass and took a nice swig of the wine, which was refreshing but a bit too mineral for his taste. "You know what they say about hard-core homophobes."

"I do," Finnerman said, "but don't let that stop you from telling me."

"Any boys in your closet, Marty?"

"Very funny," Finnerman said sourly.

Anselm set his glass down. "I'm not kidding. If there is one you'd best fess up now so we can deal with it before it stains POTUS."

"Stop it," Finnerman said tartly.

"I know, you don't allow homos in the Pentagon. What? You have a machine at the entrance that —"

"For Christ's sake, enough!"

"Then give a serious listen when I voice some concern about our plan."

The first course was laid out before them: gleaming stone crab claws set amid a profusion of micro-greens.

"Okay, okay." Finnerman reached for the nutcracker that had been delivered with the claws. "Christ almighty, Howard." He split apart a claw with uncommon violence.

Across from him, Anselm allowed himself a secret smile.

"My concern is for the aftermath."

"The aftermath?"

"Hunter told me that Camilla is exceeding all expectations."

"So?"

"What if she survives?" he said.

Finnerman dipped a chunk of pink-white flesh into a small bowl of drawn butter. "The way we set things up that's not possible."

"But what if she does?"

Finnerman sighed. "If you don't get to the point soon I'll be too old to understand it."

"We need to enlarge the dinger's brief," Anselm said, using the accepted marine slang for a crack marksman.

Finnerman bisected the piece of flesh in a mincing bite. "In what way?"

"He's to dispatch both of them — Bourne *and* Camilla."

Finnerman, chewing meditatively, stared hard at Anselm. "You're not joking."

"You know me better than that, Marty."

Slowly and deliberately, Finnerman set down his fork. He waved away the waiter who was coming to ask how they were enjoying their stone crab claws. "Well, fuck me."

"It has to be done," Anselm said, "when you consider the big picture."

Finnerman sat back. "The big picture is the threat assessment we got from our old friends at Gravenhurst. The entire structure of POTUS's initiative toward the peace summit in Singapore is built on their product."

"I'm talking POTUS and the girl."

"Oh, for shit's sake, Howard, the girl's a minor graft onto the larger scheme of things."

Anselm's eyes were glittering. "She's a constant temptation. And you know POTUS."

Finnerman's mood had turned distinctly gloomy. "I know as you see it your primary job is to keep POTUS from all temptation, but dammit, you've got to keep your eye on the bigger prize."

"And yet it's always the small things that put a spanner in the works, as our Brit cousins like to say. That was why I chose Camilla for this brief: Get her out of D.C., put her in a dangerous position, let her self-destruct." Anselm, warming to his thesis, completely ignored his food. "But after Hunter's call I got to thinking: What if Camilla doesn't self-destruct? Why, then we need someone on-site to make certain she never returns to D.C."

"The dinger."

Anselm nodded. "The dinger will leave her in the dust."

"And there's no other way?" Finnerman knew there was no other way, but he was the kind of person who needed reassurance.

92

"Not if we want to be sure to close the circle," Anselm said. "Not if we want to keep POTUS safe."

"You really are the limit, Howard."

"You know I'm right."

Anselm took up his fork and began to attack his crab claws. Soon enough, Finnerman joined him.

CHAPTER
TEN

There was a cloud, black and oily, hanging over Damascus as they descended onto an open runway. Zizzy's pilot had told them that they had twice been advised by the control tower to change runways. One of them had a smoking crater along one side.

Tracers filled the air, rattling the airport buildings, most of which had had the glass of their windows shattered. Soldiers with assault rifles were everywhere, and the smell of cordite and building rubble was muddled with the stench of human sweat and fear.

"Not to worry," the pilot said as he ushered them across the short expanse of tarmac to the arrivals terminal, "most of the city is still intact."

But temporary redoubts of sandbags were everywhere. Bullets whined like mosquitoes, then abruptly vanished.

"Call me when you want to go home," the pilot said, just short of the terminal. "Hopefully the plane will still be in one piece." He laughed, but they all knew it was only half a joke.

Inside, the air-conditioning was kaput. The electricity was barely working. A harried-looking immigration official took their passports, along with the wad of money Zizzy handed him. He spirited the baksheesh away and stamped their passports without bothering to look at them. Fear seemed to have exhausted him.

"Each day that dawns, the rebels become bolder," their taxi driver told them. "The city is totally divided." He was a thin man in his mid-fifties with a burned face and a Syrian's blue eyes. "I've seen everything here, but the last year has been hell on earth." He swerved to avoid a pair of burned-out cars. One had slammed into a tree whose foliage had burned away. A body still lay half out of the vehicle. The stench of roasted human flesh was nauseating.

"Take my advice," their driver said, "turn around and fly out of here while you still can."

The hotel Shahakbik was nice enough — or at least it had been until a shelling had damaged one wing. Still, the rest of the establishment seemed to be running more or less normally. It had a generator that was called upon four or five times a day when the electricity ceased to function.

Bourne and Zizzy were shown adjoining rooms, which overlooked an inner courtyard, lush with fig and lime trees, bougainvillea, and fragrant rose bushes. Intricate latticework balustrades curled around the circumference of the courtyard. Sunlight slanted down, then was obscured by foaming black smoke. Occasionally, the thump of artillery shells detonating could be heard. Prints shuddered against walls; a bit of plaster fell onto the rug.

Bourne lay down, clothes and all, and stared at the ceiling until at last his eyes closed and he passed into merciful sleep.

Soraya's head snapped up as a blaze of lights blinded her. In the absolute darkness, she had fallen into an exhausted doze, a shallow sleep in which her senses never let go of her daughter. Beside her, Sonya awoke with a squall of terror.

"Sonya!" Soraya did not want to shout, did not want to give her captors the satisfaction of hearing her give voice to her fear. But she was a mother now, and her child was her only concern. Her will to live rose and fell on Sonya's future.

Please God, she silently prayed, give Sonya a long, happy life, and do with me what you will. This was the prayer she had repeated over and over again ever since the darkness came down, ever since there was nothing else to think about.

"What do you want with us?" she said now. She could see nothing beyond the blinding light. "Why are you keeping us here?"

The only reply was the insectlike whirr of machinery. Then someone emerged from the absolute darkness into the dazzling light. He went not to her, but to Sonya.

"What are you doing?" she said in alarm. "Don't you dare hurt her!"

But a moment later, Sonya was plopped into her lap.

"Mommy! Mommy!" Sonya's hot, damp body pressed against her, the little arms thrown around her neck. Sonya's cheek, wet with tears, sliding against her face, brought Soraya's own tears welling up. She would die — offer herself — if only they would spare her daughter. Then she caught herself. She couldn't die; she needed to keep Sonya safe.

With Sonya squirming against her, she gathered all her strength, whispered in her daughter's ear, "This is a game, muffin, so we must both play along. Because, you see, if we play along we'll be fine. Everything will turn out all right. We'll be able to go home and everything will be as it was."

"But what about Daddy?" Sonya whispered back. "Daddy won't come back with us, will he?"

My daughter is too smart for her own good, Soraya thought. I must teach her how to harness that amazing intellect of hers. And just like that a new wave of terror and despair washed over her: What if I don't make it out of here? What if we don't make it out of here?

"Mommy, what is it? Why are you shaking?"

"I'm . . ." Soraya grew fierce, gathering herself for the sake of her child. "Mommy's just a bit cold."

"Here," Sonya said, "I'll hold you closer, Mommy. I'll warm you up."

Then Sonya's arms were being pulled away from her, Sonya screamed, and Soraya said, "Remember what I told you, muffin." And at once Sonya stilled herself. She allowed herself to be set on her mother's lap, facing the lights.

"Hold still," a harsh voice ordered, but Soraya did not know whether it was directed at Sonya or herself.

She became aware of the rustling of paper, and, squinting, she saw the ghostly silhouette of someone holding a newspaper in front of her face. Another silhouette, barely glimpsed. Someone else was taking a photo of first the front page of the newspaper, then of her with Sonya. Her mind struggled to clear itself from the fog of terror and lack of sensory input.

"Speak," the voice said.

Her head turned from her daughter and she looked into the camera. "Listen, we are being —"

"That's enough!"

Proof of life, she thought suddenly, and with that knowledge came the reason for their incarceration. Ransom seemed too far-fetched to even consider. Which left only one possibility: Her captors wanted someone to do something for them. But who? Who did she know who would be important enough for them to kidnap her and her family? And then she understood. Her husband's murder had been an object lesson, proof positive of her captors' seriousness, intent, and control.

Again, who would they want to coerce?

And then the answer bloomed in her mind, as bright as the lights illuminating her and her daughter for the camera.

Bourne.

Bourne didn't return to consciousness until the western sunlight, striking the windowpane, crept across his face like a stealthy insect. He had dreamed of darkness falling, of eyes in the dark, of feeling an overwhelming urge to get away as they closed in, but he couldn't — he was bound in wires. And then the light snapped on and he saw that he was in a spider's cocoon of high-tension wires. A buzzing began, like a swarm of bees, rising in both volume and pitch. Then the pain hit him, arching his back and taking away his ability to breathe . . .

He opened his eyes, anchored himself in the hotel room, in reality. As he sat up, he glanced at the mobile El Ghadan had given him. A message had come in while he was asleep.

At midnight, he had been dead to the world.

He watched the short video that had been sent him. He saw the newspaper's date, then, as the paper was whipped away, Soraya and Sonya. Soraya looked dazed, her face sweat- and tear-streaked, haggard and careworn. The baby was crying. Then, all of a sudden, the sound switched on. He heard a rough, commanding voice, Soraya's response, before she was cut off. Then the screen went black.

He sat for a moment, thoughts chasing themselves down a black hole. Then he gathered himself, forced himself to play the video again. This time, he looked at the edges, searching for some detail that might give him a clue as to where they were being held, but the camera was so tight on the newspaper and faces that there was virtually nothing to see.

Then he plugged in the pair of earbuds that had come with the burner phone. He listened from the instant the audio came on to the instant it was switched off with the video.

He threw the mobile onto the bed as if it had bitten him. As he rose, about to pad into the bathroom, the mobile buzzed. He scooped it up, knowing who would be on the other end.

"What are you doing in Damascus?" El Ghadan asked.

"Looking for the right bomb maker," Bourne said.

"Ah, that's how you're going to do it?"

Bourne turned to the window, stared out at the sun-bleached city. It was already afternoon; he had slept right through breakfast and lunchtime. Fighter jets screamed overhead. He could see their contrails writhing like sky serpents. "I don't work well with someone looking over my shoulder."

"Get used to it," El Ghadan said. "I'm tracking your every move."

Bourne tossed the mobile back onto the rumpled bed, shed his clothes, and stood in the shower for fifteen minutes. He tried to empty his mind, to think of nothing, but the image of Soraya and Sonya refused to be driven away. The image brought up anger, the anger made him want to return to Doha immediately, find out where they were being kept, and . . . and then what? That way lay only death for them. Hot water ran down him, inundating his face and head, pounding his shoulders and back. Patience, he told himself. Be patient. Because patience was the only thing that could save them now.

CHAPTER
ELEVEN

Thirty minutes later, Bourne showed up at Zizzy's room. "The proof of life came in at midnight," he said, brandishing the mobile.

"Right on time. They're both all right?"

Bourne nodded.

While Zizzy scared up Minister Hafiz, Bourne took his rucksack into the bathroom. Inside was an odd-looking vest. His entire complement of theatrical makeup and prosthetic devices were sewn into the lining. He removed his clothes so as not to mar them with the makeup he was about to apply.

He paused as a mortar shock wave caused the building to tremble. That was close, he thought. Zizzy popped his head in. "We're on. An hour from now. That give you enough time?"

Bourne nodded, and Zizzy's head vanished. A moment later, tinny music from the radio began to blare, drowning out the sporadic bursts of small-arms fire.

Twenty minutes later, he emerged from the bathroom, transformed. He was dressed in robes and patterned headscarf. He no longer had need of a fake beard, as his own had filled in enough.

"Who the hell are you?" Zizzy said, switching off the music. "You look like a Circassian warrior."

The ride across the city was like a fever dream. Streets of beautiful houses, mosques with slender minarets, shops selling silks and Damascus steel, then abruptly, blown-apart buildings, flattened vehicles. They passed a traffic sign so bullet-ridden it was impossible to read. A woman sat on a curb, head in her hands. Her wailing was like the scream of air-raid sirens. Smoke drifted, carrying the stench of oil and gasoline. They passed a wide boulevard filled with milling people. Bourne counted a dozen barbecued cars, blackened hulks, useless even as temporary shelters. Then they were back to neighborhoods untouched by violence and destruction. Normal life seemed to be going on here, as if in repudiation of the escalating crisis gripping the country.

Mercedes were rolling cheek by jowl with armored cars, even a tank. Traffic slowed to a crawl. Up ahead two military jeeps were parked, their heavily armed occupants checking IDs before vehicles were allowed through. To one side, a shell crater caused everyone to merge right, further slowing the proceedings.

A spray of screaming military jets winked silver across the sky.

When their time at the barrier came, invoking Minister Hafiz's name was enough to get them waved impatiently through. With the checkpoint behind them, the taxi driver returned to his voluble self. Zizzy had called him from the hotel. The wad of cash Zizzy had waved at him had almost made his mouth water.

"Assad's amnesty program has motivated pockets of rebels to drift back to his side now that it looks like foreign intervention is nothing but a fantasy. Meanwhile missiles, car bombs, who knows what else are killing our children all over the country, especially in Aleppo. Believe me, Damascus looks like the Garden of Eden compared to that hellpit." He shook his head ruefully. "Every day the situation becomes more chaotic, and chaos is the mother of evil. There is no letup. What could be worse? My country is now the largest jihadist staging area in the world."

He dropped them in front of the Ministry of Interior, of which the Ministry of Industry was a part, a blocky multistory building with a filigreed façade. It was ringed with soldiers sporting AK-47s and shoulder-fired rocket launchers. Several mortar emplacements were visible behind sandbag barriers. Off to one side, a line of gleaming Mercedes, BMWs, and motorcycles were parked, waiting for their minister masters.

Again, Zizzy invoked Hafiz's name. They showed their IDs. Bourne was now Yusuf Al Khatib, one of the many legends whose documents were hidden within his rucksack. One of the soldiers thumbed a walkie-talkie, spoke into it, then nodded at his compatriot, who stepped aside so they could enter the ministry.

The three-story entry was as chilly as a New England winter. All that was missing was snow. They took the elevator up to the third floor, accompanied by an armed guard who eyed them with paranoiac suspicion.

Minister Hafiz, a slender, elegant man, sat behind a Louis XIV desk that looked as if it had been looted from the Louvre. A couple of chairs in the same style and a very expensive Isfahan carpet were the only other items in evidence. They were all that was required to make an impression on the average visitor. Apart from a dusting of plaster on the floor, no tangible evidence of the battle raging in the city existed here.

Hafiz leapt up when he saw Zizzy, greeted him warmly. He wore a summer-weight Western suit that somehow did not quite fit him, as if he had pulled it out of someone else's closet this morning. Smoke-hazed sunlight slanting through the window highlighted his deep-set eyes and hawk nose. His slicked-back hair gleamed richly. Through the window a nearby mosque raised its carved minaret like a flag of victory. The call to prayer, one of five times daily, was being sung by a muezzin.

Bourne was introduced, but Hafiz did not wave them toward the chairs. Instead, he signed to them to follow him. They filed out of his office, past his secretary frowning over her computer terminal as she inputted the day's information. Hafiz led them down the main corridor and into the fire stairwell. He waited until the metal door snapped closed. They were surrounded by bare concrete. The temperature had shot up to oven level. None of them seemed to notice.

"It's getting sketchy out there," Zizzy said, hooking his thumb toward where a window might be if they had still been in the minister's office.

"Despite ruling for two decades, being Alawi has been no picnic," Hafiz grumbled. "The Iraq war ruined the country. It disgorged thousands of Iraqi Sunni seeking refuge here. And what happened? The inevitable, that's what. The Sunni majority became overwhelming. You think the rebels want democracy? Well, some of them, maybe. But there are a whole hell of a lot who are Iraqi Islamics, and others like the al-Qaeda-backed al-Nusra Front, Hezbollah, and El Ghadan's Tomorrow Brigade — jihadists using the current chaos to spread more chaos."

He jammed his hands into his trouser pockets, his shoulders rising, which made the suit jacket appear even more ill-fitting. "Do you know what will happen to us Alawis if the Sunnis ever gain power? We'll all be rounded up, set against a wall, and shot. That's no exaggeration."

He craned his neck, peering as far down the stairs as he could, as if he expected an enemy lurking in the shadows. Satisfied, he turned back to them. "The West hates Bashar, but do you know the current president's history? He went to England to study and work. He was happy there. He'd washed his hands of Syria altogether. Then his older brother — the heir to their father's rule — went and slammed his two-hundred-and-fifty-thousand-dollar convertible into a round-about, totaling it and himself. Bashar was recalled under enormous pressure."

Hafiz shrugged, his expression turning more mournful by the moment. "He was a reformer. For five years he gave the Syrian people a taste of freedom.

Then the war came and, along with it, the Sunni refugees. His father's old-line inner circle threatened him. They told him that if he didn't clamp down on the Sunnis they would kill him. So what choice did he have? Not only were the reforms rolled back but the Iraqi Sunnis were persecuted — tortured and, in many instances, killed. Now you see the result — over one hundred thousand Sunnis killed."

"Once the genie is out of the bottle . . ." Zizzy let the first part of the statement speak for itself.

"No kidding." Hafiz's look of disgust was unmistakable. "We're holding on with everything we have against both the rebels and the jihadists. I'm afraid it's a losing battle."

"That's the reason I came in person," Zizzy said. "I want to get you and your family out of here before it's too late."

"It's already too late," Hafiz said. "I appreciate the offer, Zizzy, but Damascus is my home. I cannot abandon it to the ravening hordes."

Zizzy allowed a moment of silence to underscore the gravity of the situation before he nodded. "I understand, Nazim." He gestured toward Bourne. "However, as long as we're here, I'm wondering if you could do me a favor."

Hafiz spread his hands. "Anything, Zizzy. You have only to ask."

"Actually, it's a favor for my friend, Yusuf."

Now Hafiz stared at Bourne with keen interest. "How can I be of assistance to you, Yusuf Al Khatib?"

"You know, I am sure, Minister Qabbani."

Hafiz nodded. "Naturally. Though we are in different departments, we manage to cross paths now and again. Budget meetings and so forth." His eyes narrowed. "There was a recent incident in Doha, I believe. The minister would have been killed had he not had the foresight to hire a Blacksmith."

"You know about that," Bourne said.

"But of course." The ghost of a smile played around Hafiz's wide mouth. "Qabbani fought tooth and nail to gain the funding to pay for the Blacksmith."

Interesting, thought Bourne. "Minister, why do you think he fought so hard?" A less seasoned agent might have added, "Could he have had foreknowledge of the incident?" But Bourne wanted to see if Hafiz would come to this conclusion on his own.

"To be honest, Qabbani wanted to weasel out of the summit," Hafiz said. "When that didn't work, he went the Blacksmith route. He argued he'd be safer here in Damascus than at the Doha summit. As it happened, he was correct."

"Lucky guess," Bourne said.

"I'm not so sure it was a guess."

"What do you mean?" Bourne said.

Hafiz returned to his recon of the lower staircase before answering. "It may be nothing, but there was some chatter —" He stopped abruptly. "You know, I'm not sure I should be repeating unattributed rumor."

"Humor me," Bourne said.

Hafiz appeared to consider this a moment. "Well, hall gossip had it that there was an ulterior motive behind the Doha summit."

"Was there anything more detailed?"

Hafiz heaved a sigh. "According to the rumor, the summit had an artificial air to it, that it was planned for a specific purpose."

"Which would be?"

Hafiz shrugged. "My best guess would be that someone here inside the ministry knew the massacre was going to happen. Ever since Qatar has been providing arms and materiel to the rebels here, it's been on our shit list."

Bourne shot Zizzy a quick glance before he said to Hafiz, "Could there be any hint of the foreknowledge in the ministry files?"

Hafiz frowned. "I doubt it."

"Personal emails? Appointments? Missing periods from a minister's calendar?"

"Who knows?" Hafiz said. "But it would be easy enough to check."

He led them out of the fire stairs, back into the refrigerated hallway. In his office, he crossed the Isfahan on his way to his desk.

"I have access to almost every level of electronic communication," he said. "And what I don't have ready access to, I can obtain, no prob —"

A tinkling of window glass, a spray of blood as Hafiz's body spun around and fell to the carpet.

CHAPTER
TWELVE

Sandcrabbing was not a particularly glamorous undertaking. In fact, it was shunned by many field operatives, or at least shunted off onto underlings. It was also never less than difficult, depending as much on raw intuition as on grubby digging. For Sara Yadin, the difficulty was compounded by the fact that she was a female in an Arab country. Had she been in Riyadh, for instance, where women were not even allowed to drive a car, instead of in Doha, a far less restrictive city, her job would have been impossible.

But Sara was unflaggingly intrepid. Even her few detractors, who thought that too often she flew too close to the sun, grudgingly admitted to that.

Start with what you know, her training had taught her, and move on from there.

The reason her father hadn't objected to her coming to Doha was that he knew she ran a number of reliable contacts and conduits here. The trouble was, having been recuperating in hospital for months, she hadn't been in touch with them for a while. The first one was out of the country, the second knew nothing, and the third was in hospital and unconscious, the victim of a stroke. She moved on to a man named Hassim, who owned Vongole, an upscale restaurant on a tony strip known as La Croisette.

Hassim wasn't at the restaurant, so she drove to his house, a walled villa of pale gold, beyond which could be seen the tops of date palms clattering in the hot wind. Through the open gate, she could see that the place was three-tiered, with flat tiled roofs and a shaded entry portico. Hassim's silver Rolls was in the driveway. She pulled up next to it, emerged into the blistering desert heat, and in the blessed shade beneath the portico rang the bell.

Hassim himself, rather than one of his servants, answered the door.

"Were you expecting me?" Sara said, half in jest.

"It happened I saw you drive up," he said as he ushered her inside. "It's a pleasure to see you, Rebeka, though your presence here seems a bit insecure."

"I know, but I don't have time for the usual dead-drop protocol."

He nodded. "Fair enough."

He led her through the octagonal entryway and into a large seating area. He was a small man, neat and fastidious. He and his family had made their fortune in oil, but, sensing the decline in fossil fuels, he had felt the need to diversify away from energy. Vongole was his third restaurant in Doha, the newest and the most successful, though as far as Sara knew they were all packed nightly.

"May I offer you a drink? Some chilled fruit juice, perhaps?"

110

"Thanks, Hassim." As pressed for time as she was, it would have been unforgivable to decline. "Whatever you have will be fine."

Crossing to a sideboard, he opened a small refrigerator, poured out passionfruit juice from a frosty glass pitcher. He brought the slim glasses over and they drank silently.

"So," Hassim said, "how can I help?"

Briefly, Sara recounted what she knew from Bourne about the massacre at the Al-Bourah Hotel, which was much more than had been reported in the local papers and TV stations.

"The inference I have made," she concluded, "is that the raid would not have been possible without police collusion."

"And you want a name."

"That's why I've come to you in all due haste."

Hassim nodded, but he didn't look confident. "That's not an easy question to answer."

"It's an eminently easy question to answer." She set down her empty glass and peered at him. "You get top police brass eating at Vongole virtually every night of the week. The emir's people as well, if I'm not mistaken. Surely you've heard something that can help me."

"I never said I didn't." But he had trouble meeting her eye.

"Hassim." She took a step toward him. "What's going on?"

"Something has changed," he said.

"Something? What, exactly?"

111

"Maybe from the emir on down, I don't know." His eyes flicked toward her as he licked his lips. "There's more money going to the Syrian rebels, for one thing."

"That's hardly news."

"Well, but the money isn't going to the rebels directly. It's going to a middleman who uses it to arm the rebels — or so the emir and his people believe."

She took a step toward him, could sense the fear coming off him like a rank perfume. "But the truth is —"

"Different," he said. He licked his lips again. "Listen, I —"

"Is it more money you want? I'll get it for you. A bonus."

"Money." He laughed nervously. "No. Not at all."

"Then what, Hassim? What can I give you in return for your complete cooperation in the matter?"

"Assurance," he said.

"You have it."

"Protection."

She nodded. "As well." What in the world has gotten him so spooked? she wondered.

"Along with a promise to extract me at a moment's notice."

"Okay. I can do that."

He nodded. "The money is going to this middleman. Tons of it."

"So you said, Hassim. Who is this middleman? An arms dealer? If so, I'm sure I know him."

"Oh, you know him, all right," Hassim said. "The middleman is El Ghadan."

112

Sara was rocked back on her feet. So it wasn't just the police who were colluding with El Ghadan, it was the Qatari government itself! No wonder Hassim had extracted those promises from her.

She pulled herself together long enough to ask, "Who's he dealing with in the police, Hassim?"

"The whole department, probably."

"You've come this far," she urged. "You might as well hit the finish line."

"Right, sure." Hassim looked disgusted, but whether it was due to the tale he had to tell or with himself was impossible to say. "But for this I need to make a call." He rose. "I'll be right back."

Sara watched him pad out of the room. She desperately wanted to follow him, try to overhear at least his side of the phone conversation, but she didn't dare take the chance. She was following a slender thread, and because it was the only thread she had, she was not prepared to put it in jeopardy by doing something rash.

Instead, she stood up, roamed about the room, examining a cut crystal ashtray here, a bronze statuette there. She picked up a shell, pink as the inside of an ear. To her surprise, it was made of a kind of resin. She turned it over, but there was only the mark of another seashell, tiny, stamped in gold.

She put it down as Hassim bustled back. "It wasn't easy, but I got it."

"Do I note a hesitation in your voice?"

Hassim cleared his throat. "I'm a restaurateur now, pure and simple. While you have been out of sight, I've been expanding my empire. That's what I'm concentrating on now."

"Are we done, then?"

He looked at her with a mixture of sadness and relief. "This is the last bit of product, Rebeka. I can't afford to keep sticking my neck out."

Something inside her hardened. "I understand your position, Hassim, but calling it a day isn't so easy."

"Nevertheless, that's what I'm doing." He regarded her steadily. "That's the price of this product. I tell you, I'm out. That's it."

"Take it or leave it, huh?"

He licked his lips, nodded.

Sara took a deep breath, let it out very slowly and evenly. "Let's have it, then."

"I have your word?"

"You do."

"His name is Khalifa Al Mohannadi," Hassim said. "He's a colonel in the National Tactical Command Center here in Doha."

"NTCC," Sara mused. "He's antiterrorist, then. You sure about this? Your source is reliable?"

"One hundred percent."

"A colonel in NTCC in bed with El Ghadan. That's a joke."

"If it is," Hassim said, "it's a sad one for my country."

Sara's look was unfocused, her mind far away, spinning like a top. "Qatar has always found a way to keep itself balanced amid constant Mideast turmoil," she said. "I'm wondering why it feels a need to secretly align itself with the most dangerous terrorist alive."

114

CHAPTER
THIRTEEN

Zizzy ran to Hafiz and, keeping out of the line of fire through the shattered window, knelt down beside him.

"Is he dead?" Bourne said, staring out the window.

"Still breathing."

"Stay with him." Bourne sprinted to the door.

"Where are you going?" Zizzy asked, but Bourne was already gone.

One motorcycle in the line parked outside the ministry had keys in the ignition. Mounting the cycle, Bourne fired it up, racing away before any of the guards had a chance to react. Heading toward the barrier at speed, he waved at the soldiers manning it. They lifted the barrier just enough for him to duck under it as he thundered down the street, heading for the mosque from which he judged the shot had been fired.

Arriving, he slowed, circled the building several times while studying it. To use a mosque as cover for a violent act was strictly forbidden, but he knew that wouldn't stop a rebel, for whom the exigencies of war overrode his moral code, or a jihadist, who had only death in his heart.

Similarly, he knew the sniper would not be in a hurry to leave his cover. In the first place, any haste would make him stand out among the worshippers, and might even incur their wrath. In the second place, he would doubtless be assured that no one had an inkling where the shot had come from, let alone set out to find him. It was Bourne's good luck to be in Hafiz's office when the minister was killed. The sniper's line of sight was readily available to his keen and practiced eye.

The day was waning, the sun already sunk beneath the smoldering skyline. Overhead, a pair of jet fighters returning from their strafing mission twinkled like stars, high up enough to catch the sun's last rays.

Bourne watched the first of the worshippers, prayer rugs tucked beneath their arms, slipping on their shoes as they exited the mosque. He waited, his eyes seeming to penetrate the burgeoning mass of men, searching for the one man of interest to him.

As the crowd thinned somewhat, he saw him. He was a tall man, with the build of a wrestler. His hair was dark, curled and oiled, and he buried his knuckles in his thick beard as, no doubt out of habit, he glanced around.

Bourne turned away, bent down, asked a passing boy the way to the Technical Computer Institute at Bostan Addour. The boy had no idea, but that hardly mattered. The sniper had not gotten a look at Bourne's face as he scanned the immediate environment.

As Bourne turned back, he noted that the sniper's prayer rug was larger than most, in order to conceal his rifle, Bourne surmised, even though he had doubtless broken it down, unscrewing the long barrel, placing it beside the stock. The man had the face of a wolf, his eyes wary, his manner calm and methodical. His skin was as rough as sandpaper, dark as stained mahogany, pocked as if from a scourge that had attacked the populace of his boyhood village.

Bourne tracked him as he ducked into a beat-up beetle-brown Skoda sedan that slid to a stop in front of the mosque. The driver was the only other person in the vehicle. Choosing a safe distance, Bourne followed the car as it slid through the evening traffic. Blue shadows lay in the street like exhausted dogs. The shelling had stopped, at least for the time being, and an eerie calm had descended over the city. To some, huddled in doorways or looking up to the sky, the quiet seemed more unsettling than the mortar bursts and the small-arms fire, and their terror made the air shimmer with bleak anticipation. At any moment, the shelling would begin again, but when? For civilians, the pause was an effective form of torture, fraying nerves to the breaking point.

The Skoda led Bourne down narrow streets lined with concrete-block houses with overhanging upper stories, their blank faces marred by spray-painted graffiti proclaiming the victories of the rebels or the self-righteousness of the jihadists. Beyond, the dusky hills were coming alive with thousands of lights, as if they were home to swarms of fireflies.

At length the Skoda turned down a darkened street, poorer than those that had come before. On the left, Bourne could see a difference in the buildings' façades.

The structures were larger and lacked windows, which led him to believe the street was lined with warehouses. At least half of them had sustained damage, a few were crumbling altogether. Many had been abandoned.

Which was the point, he saw, as the Skoda stopped in front of one such warehouse. The sniper hopped out, his prayer rug and its unholy contents left behind. The Skoda drove slowly off.

The sniper gave a series of rhythmic knocks on a worm-eaten wooden door, and it was opened immediately. He stepped inside and the door slammed shut behind him. Bourne slipped off the motorcycle, walked the hundred or so yards to the warehouse door. He repeated the rhythmic knocks. Again, the door was opened immediately. Bourne stepped inside, struck the man he saw in the side of the neck, then slammed his head against the wall.

The man collapsed. Bourne quickly went through his clothes, retrieved a dirk with a wicked-looking curved blade and an old Russian Stechkin automatic pistol. The tiny entry gave way to the vast interior, now reeking of rot and neglect and human sweat. Metal barrels lined the wall on his left, a crate or two on his right. Otherwise the warehouse was empty. The stench of vehicular exhaust came to him, not as stale as one might have expected.

Against the far wall, a steep flight of narrow wooden stairs led up to a second-floor office with a line of windows that overlooked the warehouse proper. Through one of the windows, Bourne could see the sniper. He was talking animatedly with two men, neither of whom Bourne could make out clearly.

Cleaving to the left wall, he made his way toward the office, using the stacked barrels as cover. He passed small puddles on the concrete floor, black, viscous as pitch: automotive oil. Clearly, heavy trucks of some sort were being run in and out of here on a regular basis.

Up ahead, the figures in the office were still in deep discussion. None had yet turned to look out the windows. Bourne was moving, half bent over, between the stacks of barrels, when the driver of the Skoda tried to slip a knife blade between two of his ribs. They were the correct ribs — the ones safeguarding his lungs.

At the last instant Bourne's senses had prickled, and he was turning as the tip of the blade flashed toward him. Grabbing the extended wrist, he jerked the arm toward him, turning back away from the attack, using the driver's own momentum to lead him around and down.

He slammed the edge of his hand into the driver's collarbone. The driver groaned, and Bourne knocked the knife out of his fist. He was cadaverously thin, all ropy muscle, without an ounce of fat on him.

Completely ignoring the pain of Bourne's blow, the man whipped his wrist free. Using his left shoulder, sharp as a pointed stick, as a cudgel, he jolted Bourne back into the barrels. Reaching up, he brought one of the teetering barrels down on Bourne's neck and shoulder, driving him to his knees. Time enough for him to draw a Tokarev pistol and point it at Bourne's forehead.

As his finger tightened on the trigger Bourne pressed the Stechkin into his abdomen at an upward angle and fired. The driver stumbled backward. He tried to re-aim his pistol but the bullet Bourne had fired point-blank had torn through his innards, lodging in his heart. His eyes rolled up as he fell backward onto the oily cement.

The noise of the shot ricocheted around the nearly bare space, catching the attention of the three men in the office. They stared out of the windows as Bourne covered the rest of the distance to the rear of the warehouse.

They were all in motion as he mounted the stairs two at a time. He couldn't see them now, but the reverse was also true. He reached the top without incident and hauled the rickety door open.

Then the blast blew the office apart.

CHAPTER
FOURTEEN

Khalifa Al Mohannadi, the NTCC colonel, was not much of an office man, Hassim had told Sara. In fact, he was the antithesis of a paper-pushing bureaucrat, even though paper-pushing was the very heart of his job description. Three sergeants, specifically hired for the purpose, worked more or less around the clock in eight-hour shifts to dispense with the mountains of paperwork that daily flooded his office. After a week of being bothered by a fly-swarm of calls asking for his approval on this matter or that, he equipped each of them with a rubber stamp of his own signature he had had manufactured to employ to his absence. Now his days and nights were free of bureaucratic annoyances, leaving him free to pursue his own interests.

These included gambling and golf. Given that gambling was illegal in Qatar, Hassim said that the colonel often flew to Dubai to indulge that particular passion. But since most of his time was spent in Doha, Khalifa could most reliably be found at the Doha Golf Club.

Naturally enough, the two courses were not open at night, but the clubhouse, Hassim informed Sara, was always ablaze with light and local luminaries, who dined there and afterward enjoyed a cigar or two on the expansive terrace that overlooked the championship course's eighteenth hole. In fact, evening was the best time to catch Khalifa, Hassim had said, as his parting bit of product. The colonel loved the clubhouse best when it was filled with Doha's elite, when his very passing through the rooms caused ripples of conversation, when the eyes of beautiful young women turned in his direction. The colonel was a bachelor, and wielded his single status like a fisherman's net to snare a new woman every week or, if the spirit moved him to keep one around long enough, every month.

Sara spied him the moment the solid Thai teak doors were opened for her and she entered a vast space — one of many — clad in polished gypsum and marble. A central fountain cooled the air, and beyond she could make out not one but two interior waterfalls cascading down walls of hand-hewn gypsum bricks.

The colonel cut a striking figure — slim and tall, with the well-turned legs of a fencer. His shoulders were square, his back ramrod straight. His curling black hair gleamed in the light, thick, luxuriant, with attractive speckles of gray here and there on the sides. Even while talking to a handsome young man, his deep-set coffee-colored eyes worked the room, skipping from one woman to the next, searching for what Sara intuited was a new conquest.

Then his gaze fell on her, and she almost staggered under the assault. Never before had she felt a man so completely undress her with his eyes. Her initial horror turned to anger as her sense of being violated came to the fore.

And yet, the field agent in her taking over, she walked directly toward him, returning his too frank gaze with a silent defiance that she suspected he would find intriguing.

Her instincts were, as usual, impeccable. She watched with the kind of fascination a mongoose has for a cobra as he broke off his conversation, excused himself, and strode confidently toward her. He wore a Valentino suit over a cream-colored silk shirt open too far down his chest. As for herself, she had gone shopping at a number of Doha's best boutiques before deciding on a simple yet elegant spaghetti-strap Vera Wang dress in deep blue shantung silk with, in deference to the religious culture, a short jacket over it to cover her upper arms and shoulders. A slit up the side showed just enough leg, in her considered judgment, to be provocative without looking slutty. For that reason, too, she had chosen pumps with a medium heel.

"Good evening," he said. "My name is Khalifa Al Mohannadi."

She took his hand. His grip was dry and strong, just like his voice.

"Martine Heur," Sara said in a perfect French Canadian accent.

"Welcome to the Doha Golf Club."

"Are you the owner?"

Khalifa chuckled. "But, no, madam, you have mistaken me."

"I was told the owner was tall, slim, and handsome."

"And instead you have found me." He looked pleased. "Shall I take you to the owner? I know him well."

"No," Sara said, eyeing him. "Not now."

He smiled winningly. His teeth were strong and white. "Would you care to take a drink with me?"

"I'd like that."

With a courtly nod, he led her through the room to a smaller one fitted out like an Arabian salon. Plush sofas, chairs, and loveseats were scattered about, each grouping with a low table and, it seemed, its own server. Sara chose a chair, and Khalifa sat across from her with the table as a barrier between them, as Sara wished. A server approached them.

"Have you eaten?" he asked. "The club has a full menu."

"Tea will do me, thank you." At this early stage, it would have been a mistake to get into a long evening with him. Leave 'em wanting more, her father had taught her.

The colonel ordered tea for both of them, then sat back, elbows on the chair arms, fingers steepled meditatively. They were the long fingers of a pianist or a strangler. The nails were neatly groomed, she saw, and gleaming. He had a small scar just below the outer corner of his left eye. It was white on his otherwise dusky face, almost livid.

"What, may I ask, brings you to Doha?" Khalifa said.

"Diamonds," Sara replied. "I buy and sell them."

"Where are you based?"

"Mainly Amsterdam."

"Amsterdam." He raised his head to stare at the ceiling. "Such a beautiful city."

"Do you know it well?"

He lowered his eyes to her. "Not well. No."

"Pity." She was aware that he was putting her through a light interrogation. She didn't know whether to be alarmed or flattered. Perhaps he did this with all his potential conquests, although, interestingly, he had failed to mention his military rank or that he was in the military at all. "You should return sometime."

The tea was presented on a chased silver tray; the service of pot, two cups and saucers, sugar bowl, creamer, and a small plate with an artful fan of lemon slices was exquisite. The server bent to pour, but Khalifa waved him away.

He poured the tea himself. "Cream or lemon?"

"Lemon, please."

As he handed her the tea, he said, "So, how is business?"

Carefully, she placed a frown on her face. "It would have been brisk," she said. "I had any number of appointments lined up. But then the terrorist attack drove all my clients underground, as it were. Now no one is interested in buying diamonds, or, it appears, much of anything else for that matter."

Khalifa nodded sagely. "True, it was a tragedy. But rest assured it was an isolated incident, never to be repeated."

125

Sara sighed. "I wish my clients felt as certain as you seem to. To a man, they're terrified."

"Unfortunately, there is risk now, all through the Arab world. I am devastated your business has suffered at the hands of terrorists."

"It isn't the first time."

The colonel raised one eyebrow. "Oh?"

"Yes. Three years ago." Sara took a sip of her tea, but it was too hot. She set the cup and saucer down on the tray, folded her hands demurely one atop the other. The pause was deliberate, to extend the anticipation, after she had whetted his appetite with the promise of a tale right up his alley.

"I have a source in Botswana," she continued now. "I have known him a long time. He's a friend as well as a business contact. He and I were almost killed by a cadre that had crossed over from South Africa."

"I commend you on your escape."

"My friend lost an arm."

He inclined his head slightly. "My condolences. I am truly sorry, Martine."

And there it was, Sara thought, the transition from interrogation suspect to attractive woman. Nothing like an old war story to bring two soldiers closer together.

"And now," he said, leaning forward and taking her hand, "you must have dinner with me."

Sara feigned looking at her watch. "But I —"

"No, no, I insist." He grinned, one comrade to another. "We will have the best dinner in the Middle East, guaranteed. And while we eat, I will tell you some stories I think you will find most interesting."

126

The blast split the office door apart, but it was an old door. It was made of hardwood, thick as a man's forearm. Even as it shattered, it shielded Bourne from the full brunt of the explosion. As he was thrust backward, he grabbed hold of the handrail to stop himself from tumbling head over heels down the stairs. Though the rent slabs of wood clattered down the stairs, amid tinkling glass shards glittering like a hail of ice, Bourne did not. He held on, slipping once on the treads, righting himself, his free arm thrown up to cover his face.

Then he launched himself up the remaining steps, hurtled into the gutted interior of the office. Smoke and flames obscured it for a moment, then he spied the door in the far wall. Leaping over a chair that had spilled on its side, legs crisped, back still burning, he reached the door, used fabric from his clothes to protect his hand from the heat as he turned the metal knob, wrenched open the door.

He sped down a metal spiral staircase as fast as he could, listening to the clang of shoes on the treads below. The light was dim. He was obliged to be guided by sound alone. Pausing for a moment, he listened to the heavy tread, heard three sounds, overlapping.

Three men: the sniper and the two others he had observed in the office before they blew it up. Slipping off his shoes, he continued down the spiral in utter silence. Down below, at the bottom of the well, a bare light bulb hanging from a length of flex burned fitfully.

127

The sounds on the stairs had ceased, but shadows flickered like the dying flames in the office above.

Bourne's gaze rose up from the bulb to where the flex went into the ceiling between two water pipes that ran horizontally parallel to each other. He was quite certain that the men would wait in the sub-basement to be sure he was dead or wounded badly enough not to follow them, because this was what he would do in their place. In that event, their attention would be focused on the narrow twist of the stairs.

Currently he was in darkness, but that would change the moment he descended far enough for the light bulb to pick up his legs. Putting his shoes back on, he calculated the distance to the water pipes, then leapt, grabbed them, swung toward the heads of the men, and let go.

He landed in the midst of them, bowling over one, slamming his forearm into the throat of another. Both were down. As the first man rose up, using the wall as leverage, Bourne kicked out, burying his shoe in the man's chest, cracking his sternum. The man went down again, and this time stayed down.

The second man grabbed him from behind, sought a choke hold on his windpipe. Bourne shoved him backward, his spine smacked the facing wall, and the air went out of him. Bourne grabbed the wrist curled around his throat and twisted it down and back, breaking the arm at the elbow.

The man cried out, scrabbled for the pistol tucked into his belt, but Bourne shoved his head down until the chin cracked against Bourne's rising knee. The man groaned, his eyes rolled up, and he collapsed.

A quick glance affirmed that neither of these men was the sniper. That left the third man. He heard a door slam, and took off, but the hard truth was his torture at the hands of El Ghadan's men had hurt him more than he had been willing to admit. His pain threshold was exceedingly high, but even he could not endure a near asphyxiation without consequence, and he felt it now as he ran down the darkened corridor and up two flights of rickety wooden stairs. Slower than he'd like, slower than he needed to be in order to catch up to the sniper. Pain gripped his chest as if the cruel electric hand El Ghadan had put to him was again squeezing the breath out of him. He stopped, nauseated and dizzy, slammed his fist against the concrete wall in rageful frustration.

Pushing through a metal door, he found himself in an unfamiliar back alley, deserted in both directions. From not far away came the cough of a car engine starting up, the screech of tires laying rubber, then nothing but the myriad background groans and sighs of the partially blacked-out city, as it experienced another exhausting lull in the continuing civil war.

As he went back inside, his own mobile buzzed. A text from Deron. *Inside. Awaiting instructions.* Some small bit of good news, anyway. Bourne texted back details as to where he wanted the tainted mobile's GPS to point to over the next week. It occurred to him then that he could return to Doha and start his inquiry into where the jihadists were holding Soraya and Sonya, but instinct told him that their lives were too precious to leave to chance. One false move on his part, one whispered word to the wrong person, and they would die horrible deaths. This was a path he refused to take. No, he decided, far better to remain on the course he had chosen: wend his way through the labyrinth into the dark heart of El Ghadan's network, in the hope of discovering leverage he could use against him to secure Soraya's and Sonya's release.

He returned to the two fallen terrorists. One was still alive. Crouching down, Bourne hauled him to a sitting position, slapped his face twice. The man's eyes opened. Bourne struck him again, and the eyes focused on him.

"The sniper," Bourne said in Syrian-accented Arabic. "Who is he and where did he go?"

The terrorist looked at him dully.

"There is no way to avoid telling me what I want to know."

The terrorist's expression did not change, nor did his lips move.

Bourne pulled out the dirk he had taken off the driver in the warehouse proper. The curved blade caught the wavering light of the light bulb above their heads.

"In two minutes," Bourne said, "you'll tell me everything."

Actually, it took four minutes, but all things considered, Bourne thought, that was acceptable.

CHAPTER
FIFTEEN

Khalifa Al Mohannadi took Sara to dinner at Red Pearl, an elegant restaurant nestled within a posh resort on its own island. The trip by launch took only five minutes, but as the boat glided between two piers decked out with electronic torches, Sara found herself in another world.

They headed into the very heart of the resort, along an artificial river lit up in shades of red and hot orange. Above them curved what could only be described as a shell lined with mother-of-pearl. A brace of uniformed female attendants who looked like runway models greeted them with wide smiles, helped them off the launch, and ushered them to a table beside a lagoon stocked with exotic fish, whose astonishing colors glimmered like gems in a sunken treasure chest.

"Well," Khalifa said, after they were seated, "what do you think?"

"There's nothing like this in Amsterdam," Sara replied, looking around.

"Or anywhere else," Khalifa said proudly. "Not even in Dubai."

Salads came, filled with exotic seafoods, then lobsters that Khalifa said were flown in from Zanzibar, "because they're the best in the world," and they were, too, at least in Sara's estimation.

She was practiced at small talk, polished at subtle flirting, and she did both through the first two courses, but she was troubled that after an hour and a half she knew Khalifa no better than she had at the golf club. He was as practiced as she was at engaging small talk that revealed nothing of himself.

He had promised her "stories," and, patient as a spider, she waited for him to begin. He was like a wild animal, untrusting of strangers, and she knew that any sudden move on her part would startle him into a silence from which she might not be able to coax him.

"What was the name of your contact in Kenya?" he said at length.

"Botswana," she said, knowing his mistake was deliberate, knowing too that he remembered she had not mentioned her contact's name.

"That's right, Botswana."

Between them rested the empty carcasses of spiny red lobsters, glistening tufts of pink-white flesh tucked here and there, the only meat left on shells otherwise picked clean.

"There are three kinds of people one encounters," he said, seemingly changing subjects. "People you can trust, people you can't trust, and people you kill."

"That's a cynical view of life." She almost added, Isn't that the view of a soldier? But she wasn't about to let on that she knew who he really was.

He shrugged. "One's view of life is shaped by one's experiences, isn't that so?"

"To a degree."

"No," he said, the flat of his hand cutting through the air. "It is so. Period."

The waiter came and cleared away their plates. He returned with the dessert menu and left them to decide.

Because Khalifa had presented her with an opening, she said, "Now you've made me curious. What sort of experiences are you referring to?"

"Why are you curious?"

She shrugged. "It isn't every day I meet a man who mentions killing, let alone so offhandedly."

He regarded her levelly. "Amsterdam is an oasis of calm in an otherwise war-torn world. Here in the Middle East, here in Doha, we do not have the luxury of being calm."

"Are you making fun of me?"

"Not at all. I'm trying to get at a truth."

So am I, Sara thought, but you're being obdurate. "So does this mean you have killed people?"

"If I have, it's been for a good reason."

"You've never told me what you do, Khalifa."

He smiled. "I'm a businessman."

"Everyone I meet is a businessman," she said. "What kind are you?"

"The successful kind," he said, and dropped his eyes to study the menu. "Something sweet to end the evening?"

Hunter refilled her mug. She took her coffee strong and black, no sugar. "There's a man I want you to meet when you get there."

Camilla regarded Hunter from across the table, her forkful of poached eggs halfway to her mouth. "Get where?"

Hunter took a mammoth bite out of a square of buttered toast onto which she had loaded a heaping tablespoonful of scrambled eggs. "Where you're being sent." She chewed and swallowed in a convulsive gesture. "Singapore."

Camilla resumed eating. Her inner thighs and lower back ached so much she already assumed she'd never be rid of the pain, though Hunter had assured her otherwise. Outside, it was still dark, but sunrise was not far away.

"Why?"

"Jimmie Ohrent will take care of you."

Camilla frowned. "I can take care of myself, thank you very much."

Hunter sipped her steaming coffee, her eyes slitted. She had the look of a carnivore, which at this moment meant she wanted more bacon. "As I understand it, you're Howard Anselm's creature."

"Where in the world did you get that idea?"

"From Howard."

Camilla was taken aback. "Howard Anselm is chief of staff, not director of the Company." She tossed her head. "Anyway, I work at Secret Service."

"And yet here you are at a Company facility." Hunter rose, crossed the room, got herself several more slices of bacon, came back, and sat down. She ate one strip in two bites, folding the meat over on itself. "I know who and what you work for."

Camilla felt herself bristle. "Do you?"

Seemingly unfazed, Hunter said, "Let me ask you a question. How well do you know Howard Anselm?"

Camilla shrugged. "Well enough, I suppose."

Hunter pursed her lips. "You poor thing."

"What the hell does that mean?"

Hunter wiped grease off her lips, stood up. "Let's get over to the stables."

Camilla sat for a moment, too shocked to move.

"Oh, come on," Hunter said. "Sulking doesn't become you."

On the way over, rain began to fall — just a drizzle, really, but a certain gloom hung over the Dairy that seemed to seep into Camilla's bones. She felt as if she had stepped into a hole she hadn't noticed before. The feeling of helplessness did not sit well with her.

At the stables, Hunter watched her saddle Starfall. "I've known Howard Anselm a long time. He uses me like he would use a sponge, to soak up the messes people make — him included."

Camilla tightened the cinch. "I don't see how that applies to me."

"Still in a pet, I see." She opened an adjoining stall, led out a horse named Dagger, and made ready to saddle him. "Of course it applies to you — and to POTUS."

Camilla froze. Her heart thundered in her breast. "What . . . what are you talking about?"

"This little caper Anselm cooked up with the connivance of Marty Finnerman."

"Howard told me it was the Joint Chiefs of Staff who —"

Hunter snorted. "Yeah, right."

Camilla hung on to Starfall as if without him her knees would buckle. "So what are you saying?"

"Camilla, darlin', your boss — the man who really runs you, pulling the strings from on high — has decided that you pose too great a danger to *his* boss. Which is why he's sending you to the other side of the world."

"That makes no sense. They're sending me to the place where Bill is going to be. Why not leave me here?"

"You're the head of the Secret Service. Your job is to be by POTUS's side. You will be in Singapore with him, but they've ensured you will be apart from him. The brief they've given you directs you to find and terminate Jason Bourne. You won't have time to engage with POTUS and it will lead you into potentially lethal danger." Hunter took a step closer to her. "Listen to me. If you find Bourne — and that's a big if — he most certainly will kill you."

Camilla opened her mouth, seemed to have lost her voice, then started over again. "How many people know?" Her voice was somewhere between a whisper and a croak.

"Besides you and POTUS? Just the three of us: Howard, Finnerman, and me."

Camilla rested her forehead against Starfall's great curving neck, taking what solace she could in the strength of its musculature. "Jesus."

136

"The point is," Hunter said, "the damage is contained."

"Why not just fire me?"

"And risk POTUS's reputation, not to mention his ire? For one thing, it's POTUS himself who must fire you. For another, you'd still be in D.C., still close at hand, and, out of the limelight, that much more available."

God, Camilla thought, she's right. "I've become a locked box, hidden away in some dark and deserted corner where no one will look."

Hunter looked at her with a kind of pity that frightened Camilla. No one had ever looked at her quite that way.

But then Starfall stamped his right foreleg, lifting his head and snorting, and she put her palm against his soft muzzle, and he settled. She looked into his huge, pure brown eye, saw herself reflected there. The reflection resolved itself in her mind's eye.

In that moment, she saw the conversation from a different angle, and a thought occurred to her, like a light bulb turned on in a comic book thought balloon.

She turned to Hunter. "You don't like Anselm much, do you?"

A slow smile spread across Hunter's face. "A dirtbag who treats me like a sponge and you like a clay pigeon? I hate his fucking guts."

Sara excused herself. Her bladder was full. Maybe it was from the juice she had drunk at Hassim's, but that seemed like ages ago. More likely, Khalifa was making

137

her nervous, which in turn made her more nervous. She hadn't been in the field for over a year. She felt rusty, a step behind where she needed to be. She squared her shoulders. There were remedies for that, and she knew how to employ all of them.

An attendant escorted her to the W.C., which she thought silly and way over the top until she discovered how convoluted the path was. On her own, she would have needed a map and a compass.

Unsurprisingly, the W.C. was as big as most medium-size cafés. It was altogether possible, she surmised, to get lost in here as well, not the least because all the walls were either mirrored or pure white marble polished to such a gloss that in a pinch they could have stood in for mirrors.

She peed in a stall, one among many, then went to the sink to wash her hands. Instead of a liquid in a dispenser, the soap, small and pink, came individually wrapped. She plucked one from a bowl, tore off the cellophane. She was about to put her hands under the faucet when she realized that the soap was in the shape of a shell. Pink as the inside of an ear, she thought. She turned the soap over, and there, imprinted on it, was a tiny gold shell, just like on the resin shell she had picked up in Hassim's living room.

The drizzle had turned to mist, blotting out what would have been the sunrise. There was light on the fields of the Dairy, but that light was as gray and wan as an old wedding dress. The fields were wet with dew, the

138

horses' hooves obscured by mist pouring over the hills like watered-down milk.

Hunter had led Camilla not to the ring, nor the oval racetrack, both of which were far behind them, but into the lowlands into the south reaches of the Dairy's vast acreage. The two rode side by side, their mounts at an easy canter. They were accompanied only by birdcalls and the chirp of crickets, muffled and mysterious in the mist.

"What you have to understand, first of all," Hunter said, "is that Howard Anselm is the most powerful man in D.C."

"Come on," Camilla said skeptically. "More powerful than POTUS?"

"What you have to understand, second of all, is that POTUS has a fatal flaw that must at all costs be kept from the public. He's a serial offender." Hunter turned her head, her eyes glittery in the misty morning half-light. "You weren't the first, Camilla, and you won't be the last. But because of your position, you're for sure the most dangerous."

"I would never do anything to hurt Bill's reputation."

"But there it is, you see. You called him 'Bill.' The president of the United States. No one calls Magnus 'Bill,' unless —"

"I get it," Camilla said with an uncomfortable upsurge in her heart rate. "But that's over now. Bill — POTUS and I had it out before I left."

"You told him it was over."

"I did."

"But here's the thing, Camilla, he's POTUS. It's over only when he says it's over."

Camilla looked out over the partially obscured hills. "That's a depressing thought."

"Maybe, then, it's a good thing you're on your way out of the country."

"Not if what you say about Anselm is the truth."

"Of course, but I'm going to protect you from him."

"Tell me more about Anselm."

Hunter eyed her critically. "Are you sure you want to know?"

"I wouldn't have asked otherwise."

They had entered the farthest reaches of the Dairy's south boundary. Beyond were hidden fortifications and security measures best left unseen. The two women wheeled their horses around, heading west. Neither was ready to return to the inner precincts yet.

"Howard has been around Washington all his life," Hunter said. "His father was a senator, his mother is a state supreme court justice. Both sides of his family are in the center of the Beltway power grid. Howard was snatched right out of Yale into Gravenhurst, D.C.'s most powerful conservative think tank. Its members include some of the most influential politicans, economists, industrialists, judges, and image makers in the country."

"Yes, I know. But its origins and aims are as mysterious as those of the Masons."

Hunter nodded. "That was where Anselm became aware of Magnus. He arranged a meeting. He saw something he liked. A lot. Howard guided Magnus's every brilliant political move. And he protected Magnus against the man's own worst instincts. Magnus is a great politician, no doubt there, but he's as perpetually randy as a satyr.

"At first Howard tried to curb him of his habit. But that only led to a disaster Howard just managed to contain. After that, he was forced to change tactics."

"Cleaning up after Magnus."

Hunter nodded. "No other choice."

"And that's where you come in."

"You know Anselm well enough to know he isn't going to get shit on his shoes. He hires other people to rake out the stables."

"And you were the logical choice?"

Hunter smiled archly. "I've made a few mistakes in my life — youthful indiscretions, you might say — while I was a marine pilot."

"He's blackmailing you?"

Hunter barked a laugh. "Blackmail is one of Howard's least egregious sins, believe me."

They had come to the edge of a dense stand of trees. Neither horse seemed inclined to enter the thick-limbed interior, where night still dwelt and shadows flung themselves in an eerie dance. The women did not feel compelled to press on either. By unspoken mutual consent, they headed back to the racing oval.

Camilla, bent over Starfall, dug her heels into his flanks, experienced a fleeting moment of joy at the immense power of him as they galloped home.

CHAPTER
SIXTEEN

Bourne called Zizzy. "Meet me at the Bab Sharqi entrance to the Medhat Pasha Souq."

He was tired and hungry beyond imagining; he could not remember when he had last eaten a proper meal. He longed to see Sara, but his mind, for once playing cruel tricks on him, was atremble with the crush of asphyxiation, the images of Soraya's vacant stare, the child's tears, Alain's head, made grotesque by the bullet's devastating impact.

The roiling clouds, their underbellies livid with the reflection of rocket bursts, swirled above emptied-out streets quivering with the concussions. Small-arms fire had started up again, a firefight somewhere in an adjacent neighborhood.

Bourne picked his way through the rubble-strewn streets and avenues, lanes and back alleys, some still smoldering, others picked clean by both man and dog, toward the great souq. He could see its lights rising, a benevolent glow amid the flaring iron-blue malevolence shredding the city.

Zizzy was waiting for him, a nighttime silhouette against the electric energy of the market. Without a word, they passed into the souq, wending their way between spice stalls, candy makers, leather crafters, and, of course, Damascus-steel purveyors. Near the center, they found a café, half filled with old men arguing the merits of the war. Some were loyalists, others not, but to a man they bemoaned the invasion of their beloved country by jihadists.

Bourne and Zizzy took seats near the rear, where they were afforded an excellent view of passersby as well as the people entering and exiting the café. A waiter was at their table at once. They ordered plates of meze, and mint tea, Moroccan-sweet.

Zizzy glanced at Bourne, but said nothing of his ragged state. "Pity Hafiz is in a coma. He might have provided the proof you needed that Qabbani leaked your information to El Ghadan."

"I doubt that," Bourne said after a time.

The food came, a flurry of small plates, and they dug in. They ate silently, with an economy of motion, as soldiers will do in the field.

"Qabbani had nothing to do with it," Bourne said at length. "But your old friend Hafiz did."

"What?"

"The shot came from the mosque's minaret," Bourne said.

Zizzy seemed not to care. "How d'you know Hafiz was guilty of betraying you?"

"He was working me over like a pro," Bourne said, still studying the street out in front of the café. "Leading me toward Qabbani, away from himself."

"What if Hafiz was telling the truth?"

"No one here tells the truth." He returned to his food. "Recall I was hired by Qabbani. Hafiz of course didn't know that. He had no way of knowing that I was aware of Qabbani's private motivations for attending the summit. Qabbani had to tell me, since I was impersonating him."

"I don't get that," Zizzy said. "Why would Qabbani confide anything in you?"

"Because in Doha I was going to be him. He had a side deal going with the minister from Yemen."

Zizzy's eyes narrowed. "What kind of a side deal?"

"Qabbani was an arms dealer. He was supplementing his government income."

"As if that wasn't enough!" Zizzy snorted.

"For people like Qabbani," Bourne said, "nothing was ever enough."

"But doesn't that put him squarely in your sights vis-à-vis El Ghadan?"

"Just the opposite," Bourne said. "Qabbani was using the summit as cover. The last thing he'd want is for it to be disrupted and for his business partner to be killed." He put down his knife and fork, pushed his plate away. "What's the long-range prognosis on Hafiz?"

Zizzy shrugged. "Doctors. Once they tell you something you realize how little they know."

"Go back to the hospital," Bourne said. "When Hafiz wakes up, I want you there to ask questions."

"*If* he wakes up," Zizzy said morosely.

Sara had plenty of time, wending her way back to her table where Khalifa waited, to work out what she must

144

do next. There was no question in her mind that Hassim owned Red Pearl. Was it coincidence that this was the restaurant Khalifa had chosen for their dinner? Long experience in the field had taught her that in the shadow world she inhabited there was no such thing as coincidence.

From this non-coincidence, she deduced that Hassim and Khalifa knew each other. Were they also business partners? What worried her most was that Hassim had lied to her. Perhaps he had nothing to do with El Ghadan. But why had he led her to Khalifa? And, most ominous of all, did that mean Hassim had blown her cover? Did Khalifa know he was dining with a Mossad agent? If so, her life was in imminent danger.

This was one of the reasons why a field agent's life was so hazardous: Contacts, loyal for so long, needed constant attention — flattery, money, whatever would ease their particular insecurity. Without that attention, their insecurity was in danger of growing to proportions they could not tolerate. Then they'd break, and when they did the opposition was always there to welcome them with open arms if they were still worth anything, terminate them if they weren't.

It seemed unlikely that anyone was going to kill Hassim, no matter what he had done in the past. He was far too influential, knew too many secrets not to be of use to someone. In this case, that someone looked to be Khalifa Al Mohannadi.

The colonel was waiting patiently, staring at a lithe young model type as she passed along the opposite side of the lagoon. Sara had deliberately chosen a route

where she could observe him unseen until the last
moment when she had to break out of the crowd and
head directly for his table. It was often instructive, she
had been taught, to observe a target or a prospective
contact in a moment of relaxation, the better to read his
frame of mind by his expression and the movement of
his eyes.

Khalifa was utterly at ease, and this told her much of
what she needed to know: He had none of the swagger
and arrogance that burst upon a man's face when he's
sure he's bagged a beautiful young woman. He had
none of the tension that comes into a man's body when
he is anticipating having sex with a new conquest. To
the contrary, Khalifa had the look of a man who was in
the right place at the right time. A premonition caught
in Sara's throat, almost making her choke. He knew
who she was, all right, and Hassim was the only one
who could have told him.

He was drinking black coffee so strong she could
smell it while she was still a table's length away.

"Pour me some, would you?" she said to the waiter,
who had sidled up beside her and was now hovering
with the unctuous attention of an undertaker.

"At once, madam."

The coffee was already poured by the time she sat
down.

"I was just musing," Khalifa said. "I have a
speedboat. I've been waiting for the full moon to take it
out at night." His head swung toward her, a smile
hooked onto his face like the visor of an Ottoman

146

helmet. "How pleasant, is my thought, to be on the water with you, Martine."

At once, a fist of ice formed in the pit of Sara's stomach, its fingers opening, spreading a certain queasiness through her.

Her eyes brushed over her watch. "It's getting late."

That masklike smile stayed firmly in place. "I would consider it a personal favor."

"I have several early meetings tomorrow."

"Come, come." With a flourish, he rose. "I haven't even told you my promised stories." He extended a hand across the table. "They're worth a late night. You will be greatly entertained, I promise."

Sara rose. "Don't you need to get the check?"

"All taken care of."

Did that mean the transaction had taken place while she was away from the table, or that he had no need of paying here?

The moment she slipped her hand in his, she felt the strength of him pulling her along. She came around the side of the table and they walked out, him never letting go of her hand.

Camilla was brushing down Starfall, crooning softly to him in a sure sign the two had bonded. Hunter moved along the stalls, out into an afternoon now sprinkled with sunlight pierced by racing clouds, the last of the gloomy morning swept away like so much dust.

"It's us against them." Hunter turned, looking back at Camilla. "You know that, don't you?"

Camilla, finished with her grooming, gave Starfall a nuzzle, then, wiping off her hands, she came toward Hunter over the packed earth and straw.

"Tell me," she said.

Hunter sighed. "Men. They're always trying to take advantage of us, to pull the wool over our eyes, make us look the fool."

"I've had my fair share of bad encounters, but —"

"It's to prove their superiority," Hunter said over her. "Especially now when we're beginning to flex our muscles, so to speak, all over the world." She took a deep breath of the piney air. "D'you think the rise in gang rapes in India and elsewhere is a coincidence?" She shook her head. "Men are frightened. Men were always frightened of women, but until now they always had ways — laws, even — to keep women in check, to keep them beneath them, subservient."

Camilla thought about this for a time. "Why do we frighten them so?"

Hunter grinned as she pushed the sleeves of her denim shirt up her forearms. "Because they can't understand us, and because they need us so much. Celibacy is not a natural state for man nor beast." Her grin widened. "You only need dig into the past of virtually any priest to determine the truth of that."

Camilla thought about Bill Magnus, and about Howard Anselm, both manipulative, devious creatures. She realized now how Magnus and Anselm were cut from the same cloth, how their loyalties were to one another, not to anyone else, most assuredly not to any female. Magnus, who was married with two beautiful

148

children, was a serial cheater. Did he love his wife? In that kind of heady atmosphere who could tell? She doubted that Bill himself knew. He was married to Anselm, till death do them part. That was the bitter truth of it.

"If you don't stop that little bitch crying," said the masked jihadist, "I will."

Soraya's heart rate shot higher. She could feel the pulsing of blood in her temples, in the side of her neck. "She's hungry," she said. "You've given her too little to eat."

A slap to her face rattled her teeth.

"Feed her yourself. Let her take the tit."

"She's two years old. I don't have any milk."

"Pity."

Soraya struggled to keep herself from falling into a rageful despair. Keep your wits about you, she admonished herself, no matter how they taunt you.

"If you want her to stop crying," she said, "you need to give her water and food."

She turned at the sound of the door opening. Another masked jihadist appeared in the soft light — thank God the room was in darkness only during the nighttime hours. He ordered the first jihadist out of the room, which the man did reluctantly. The second jihadist held a glass of water, which he tipped to her lips.

"Sonya first."

She watched with grateful eyes as the glass was held up for Sonya to drink from. Then it was refilled, and she drank greedily. Moments later, a shallow bowl of boiled chickpeas, along with a round of stale flatbread, was dropped into her lap.

"Thank you," Soraya said. She almost gagged on those two words, but they were important to say, especially now that he had done something for her. He had broken routine, even if it was in a minor way.

"How are you holding up?"

"How do you think?"

To her ears the voice held a different tone. Was that a softening, or just a figment of irrational hope? No, she said to herself, as she began to feed Sonya. Hope is never irrational. Hope is the most rational of emotions. Hope is what keeps us alive. Sometimes, as now, hope is all we have.

She looked up from feeding a ravenous Sonya and said, "Do you have children?"

"Allah has not blessed me."

"Yes, children *are* a blessing, and still you do this to us."

"We are under orders not to harm you or your daughter in any way." He took the empty plate from her. "When either of you need to use the facilities, just call out."

"What is your name?"

But the jihadist was already on the other side of the room. The door closed behind him. She winced when she heard the lock being thrown.

CHAPTER
SEVENTEEN

"Ever hear of a nightclub called the Golden Horn, Zizzy?"

"Not here in Damascus, anyway."

"I'm not surprised." Bourne looked out the window of the rattletrap taxi. "Its existence has been pushed way underground."

"Whether there's a war on or not," Zizzy said, "kids will be kids."

"And jihadists will be jihadists."

Zizzy's head turned so quickly the bones of his neck cracked.

"The Golden Horn is where we'll find the sniper who shot Hafiz." He tilted his head. "We're almost at the hospital. I'll drop you there and we'll rendezvous back at the hotel."

"When?"

The taxi had stopped. Bourne leaned across Zizzy, opened the door for him. "When I get back."

It was no wonder Zizzy had never heard of the Golden Horn. It was hidden away in a shattered neighborhood, in the basement of a bombed-out metalwork factory. No one was around to see Bourne clamber out of the taxi and pick his way across cracked concrete and tufts of weeds that, like jihadists, were too tenacious to die out.

Spotlights lit the night. The tramp of foot soldiers on the move soiled the silence of the all but abandoned neighborhood. Small-arms fire started up, at first short, sporadic bursts, then longer, sustained ones that made it clear the shooters had found their targets. A *boom!* and the ground shook, and a plume of black smoke rose lazily into the night sky, blotting out lights, turning the city darker.

Bourne had been told to enter the wreckage of the factory from the west. He could see why: All the other entrances were either blocked by brickfalls or had been obliterated entirely. A large truck lay on its side, like an extinct dinosaur. Firebombs had brought it down, tossed it into the air like so much confetti. The hulk was as bare as a skeleton picked clean by jackals. Tires, headlights, radio, steering column, engine were all gone. As he passed, a brace of yellow dogs that had made it their home reared their feral heads, bared their teeth at him, and barked hysterically.

The factory's interior was a maze of corridors, half-hallways, offices without ceilings, sometimes without walls as well. Rubble lay strewn everywhere, and not a soul in sight. Behind him, the sky lit up a lurid red, then came the *whump!* and subsequent percussion of another rocket landing.

He found the interior staircase. Apart from an initial fall of concrete and glass, kept in place as camouflage, it had been swept clean. He descended to a square

152

landing from which the stairs turned back on themselves. As soon as he started down again, he felt the *thump-thump-thump* of the music's electronic backbeat. Drums kicked in, then the wisp of a melody. A heavily amplified and reverbed voice started to scream what were likely meant to be lyrics. On the other hand, the singer might have been in his death throes.

The area below him was as luridly lit as the agonized sky above the city. A series of red bulbs illuminated a concrete landing only slightly larger than the one above and a metal door so dented it looked like it had taken a beating from a charging rhino.

Standing in front of the door were two shadows, smoking. Hooded eyes regarded him. As he headed for the door, Bourne heard the click of a hammer being cocked. One of the shadows pointed a revolver at him. It looked old enough to have come from the Russian Revolution.

"Business?" the armed shadow said. Either he was thirteen or he was a natural soprano.

"Meeting Furuque." Furuque was the name of the sniper, divulged to Bourne under extreme duress.

"Who?" said the armed shadow.

"Furuque isn't here," his companion said at precisely the same time.

"Shit!" one of them exclaimed.

"Get your story straight, boys," Bourne said. "I know he's here. I just spoke with him." He brushed past them and opened the door so quickly they had no time to answer, let alone stop him.

153

Instantly he was slammed by a wall of sound, amplified to an ear-splitting level. The place was packed with pogo-jumping teenagers. The unmistakable scent of pot mingled with the reek of sweat. Somewhere along the long slab of bar to his left liquor was being poured. In a country of strict rules, it was clear there were none here.

Bourne moved through the crowd. Again, patience was going to be his best friend. It was impossible to proceed quickly through a room jammed wall to wall with writhing people. He cut the space into quarters, then into eighths and sixteenths, looking for Furuque, methodically eliminating people in ones, twos, and threes.

Twenty sweat-stained minutes later, he was nowhere. He was on his way to the bar — the only section he hadn't checked out — when the door to the men's lavatory swung open. Two young men emerged, hand in hand, the afterglow of sex surrounding them like an air bubble. Beyond them, just before the door swung shut, Bourne saw Furuque. He was standing alongside the line of sinks, half turned away from the door, talking to two earnest-looking young men wearing knitted Muslim kufi hats. Bourne pushed the door open little by little until he could see the trio again.

He entered, went to the first sink, turned on the taps. As he washed his hands, he strained to listen to what Furuque was saying. The sniper was speaking very slowly and distinctly in order to be heard over the amplified ruckus.

154

Bourne heard only snatches: "disbelievers . . . fighting in the cause of taghut . . ." *Taghut* was the Islamic word for anything worshipped other than Allah — in other words, Satan. "It is the Quran that will remain unchanged, preserved for all time by its holy protectors, after all the other so-called divine books have turned to dust . . . The Jew, the American, the infidel has caused expulsion, destruction, and devastation . . . blood pouring out of Palestine must be avenged . . . calling you to Islam . . . complete submission to his laws . . . To right the injustices, we must pledge ourselves to death and more death until we are free of . . ."

Furuque was in the full throes of his jihadist manifesto, oblivious to anyone around him save the two young men. Bourne was about to grab him, when the world crashed in. The music screamed to an abrupt halt, replaced immediately by shouted orders and the tramp of military boots massing at the edge of the dance floor. In an instant, semiautomatic fire began just beyond the lavatory door. Cries of shock, shrieks of agony, the imprecations of an aborted counterattack were met only by a withering spray of bullets.

The sounds of mass hysteria could be heard beyond the closed door. Then the door was abruptly wrenched open by the stoned and sex-besotted teenagers racing out of the line of stalls as if their lives depended on it. And it did, but like lemmings they were racing directly into the jaws of death that awaited them on the bloody, corpse-strewn dance floor. The sobbing of the shocked

155

and wounded rose, the backbeat of a new form of music, mechanized and terrible.

The Syrian army had found them and, true to its nature, was determined to leave no one alive.

CHAPTER
EIGHTEEN

Khalifa's powerboat, a beautifully sleek thirty-three-foot pleasure craft with a water-level aft platform for diving, was waiting for them at the head of the artificial river that had brought them to Red Pearl.

As she was pulled aboard, Sara finally understood that the trajectory of her investigation in Doha had been preordained, that she had been led to this moment from the instant she stepped over Hassim's threshold.

And in fact, here was Hassim himself, because this powerboat belonged to him, not to Colonel Khalifa. He did not speak to her, could not even meet her gaze. He busied himself piloting the boat down the river and out into freer water.

It was no surprise to her that they were not headed back to Doha. Not yet, anyway. Certain matters had to be resolved, and she had no doubt the colonel was going to do his best to resolve them.

The Persian Gulf was vast, its dark waters here and there spotted with oil tankers lumbering to or from the straits that led out into the Gulf of Oman and thence to the Arabian Sea. This was the major route for bringing Middle Eastern oil to the West. Out here, there was no one to see them, no small craft to intercept them or question the powerboat being in these waters. And if there were, the two men aboard would only have to exert a fraction of their authority to exempt themselves from official scrutiny.

"Please sit," Khalifa ordered, leading her to a white vinyl cushion. Turning to Hassim, he said, "Slow it down now. We're in the deep water."

Sara knew what that meant. They were going to drown her.

To her surprise, Khalifa sat down beside her, as if the two of them had embarked on a nighttime pleasure cruise just as he'd falsely promised at Red Pearl.

"It's peaceful out here, no?" He lifted an arm in a sweeping gesture. "We're cut off from everyone and everything. No one need ever know what will transpire here tonight." He smiled at her. "Every word, every deed . . . Everything will be lost, hidden, drowned for all time. As far as the three of us are concerned, tonight will become a mystery, a page torn out of history and destroyed."

He turned his head, spoke again to Hassim. "That's enough now. Power down and drop anchor."

He rose, opened one of the storage lockers, dragged out a set of thick chains. Sara shuddered. She could already feel the cold links being wrapped around her like an industrial cocoon. With that weight, she would plummet a long way into the black depths of the gulf. No chance to escape; no way out. She crossed one leg over the other, bent down to grope for the gold Star of David attached to the thin gold necklace wound around

158

her left ankle. Just the touch of it comforted her, but it was cold comfort. She had nearly died once; she had no desire to repeat the process to its conclusion.

Having turned off the engine, Hassim unbolted the anchor and heaved it over the side. The boat rocked gently. Apart from the slap of the waves against the hull, all was silent. Not a single bird flew overhead; all the gulls were tucked in safely for the night.

More than I can say for myself, Sara thought. Lucky gulls!

The horizon was suddenly lit up with blinding electricity, but it was only heat lightning. No sound accompanied it, making it seem unreal, as if it belonged to another world. In the same vein, Sara could feel herself standing apart from her body as her mind retreated from what she knew was going to happen.

The end of all things, at least for her.

Hassim turned from his chores. "What now, Khalifa?"

The colonel smacked his hands together to rid them of the thin layer of muck from the chains, which were old, rusty, looking like they had been salvaged from a bombed-out garage.

"Now," he said, drawing a CZ-99 semiautomatic pistol, "we deal with people who cannot be trusted."

Colonel Khalifa pulled the trigger.

In the chaos, Bourne lunged for Furuque, but he was thwarted by the flood of young men attempting to flee the lavatory. All were in a panic — all except Furuque, who, slithering like a serpent, managed to reach the rear wall of the lavatory, break out the window with an elbow, and crawl through in a clatter of glass shards.

Semiautomatic fire was now a steady crackle on the other side of the door. Cries and shouts were intermittently audible, but these eventually fell away, then ceased altogether.

Bourne grabbed one of the two young men Furuque had been haranguing and, pulling him by the back of his shirt, dragged him against the lessening tide, toward the back wall. Boosting him through the window, he leaped up, quickly following him.

They found themselves in a narrow concrete canyon that had once been used to stack crates but was now thick with rubble. On the far wall was a metal ladder leading up to ground level. The kid headed for it, but Bourne pushed him back, flattened him against the wall of the club. Just in time, too, as a powerful handheld searchlight probed the canyon, picked up the shattered window, then the ladder, and, with a raised shout from just behind it, winked out. The sound of pounding boots slowly receded, replaced by the grinding of gears as various heavy vehicles pulled out.

When the night had returned to an uneasy silence, Bourne signaled to the young man. They picked their way across the blasted ground. He went up the ladder first, poking his head over the top, taking in the immediate environment. It was as deserted as it had been when he had arrived. No one would know what had taken place just below — unless one was unlucky enough to enter the underground club, strewn with the dead and dying. They were just kids. Now their short lives had been snuffed out.

Looking over his shoulder, he gestured for the recruit to follow him. He gained the surface, reached down, hauled the young man up the last several rungs.

They crouched in the scraggly tufts of grass for long moments. Bourne listened, watched a dog snuffle its way among the rubble, then lift its hind leg, urinate on a lump of concrete. It scented, turned its narrow head, its yellow eyes, in their direction. It growled, then padded on, forgetting all about them.

But someone else remembered, and he came at them now out of the shadows, striking Bourne a full body blow. They were both cast backward to the edge of the concrete canyon.

Bourne smelled him, felt him, saw him at last in the feeble light dribbling out of the lavatory window below them.

It was Furuque, the sniper.

The roar of the pistol was momentarily deafening.

Sara lurched to one side, but it was Hassim who received a bullet through the heart, not her.

"Good God!" she cried. "Why did you kill him?"

"A man who can be turned is a man who cannot be trusted." The colonel holstered his pistol. "A trader in secrets who cannot be trusted must be killed."

Sara remembered Khalifa's discourse at dinner on how he divided people into three categories. She couldn't say that he hadn't warned her. It was simply that she had been too out of touch to get it. Silently, she berated herself for her stupidity, vowed it would never happen again. Her operational edge was coming back, fast. But was it already too late?

He came and sat with her again, but this time she was acutely aware of the gun in his armpit. She watched Hassim's body roll back and forth, with each pass spreading more blood across the deck. Khalifa appeared indifferent to the mess.

"So," he said with a heavy sigh, "there is the matter of what to do with you."

Sara almost said, What do you mean? But that would have been stupid, and she had already made enough stupid mistakes this evening. "What did Hassim tell you?"

"That you're a Jew." Khalifa's broad shoulders lifted and fell. "That's the most important thing, isn't it?"

To these fanatics, she thought bitterly, it always was.

The colonel's gaze turned toward Hassim. "You know, this man would still be alive now if not for you."

"You shot him."

"Because you turned him into a spy."

"He did that himself."

"Did he?" The colonel fairly spat out the words. "Get up now and drag him aft."

Sara did as she was told. Khalifa pushed with his shoe while she hauled Hassim's corpse onto the aft platform.

"Now get back here."

There was no question of jumping ship; this far out she'd never survive. She did contemplate rushing Khalifa, but that was precisely what he wanted her to do; she could see the wicked desire in his eyes. She was damned if she was going to make this any easier for him.

"I never used coercion," she said now.

"Of course not. You people never do." He pursed his sensual blood-darkened lips as he shoved her back onto the bench. "Filthy Jews! You've taken everything from us, and then, as if that weren't enough of an affront, you brought the Americans to our doorstep to kill our men, women, and children. The Americans are like an infection, crawling into everything, corrupting it, debasing it." He hawked onto the deck, his spittle turning pink as it mingled with Hassim's blood. "I've hated you Jews all my life, but never as much as I do at this moment."

"Too bad for you."

The colonel grunted. "I'm not the one who is about to die, Jewess." He stood up abruptly, drew his gun. "Take off your clothes."

"I only get naked for gentlemen."

Khalifa dealt her a backhanded blow with the barrel of the gun. It was both casual and devastating, knocking her clear off the bench and onto her knees. The metal bit into her flesh cruelly, drawing blood. He unwound the short jacket from around her, flicked the straps off her shoulders.

"And take it slow, rotate your hips."

"Really, Colonel, I'm one hundred percent kosher." She righted herself, would not wipe the blood off her cheek. It dripped off her chin onto the dress. "I'm too pure for the likes of you."

Growling, he grabbed her elbow, his fingers digging painfully into bone as he hauled her to her feet. He brandished the gun. "No more talk. Just do it."

"Or what? You'll shoot me?" Her eyes appeared luminescent as she glowered at him. "That seems preferable to whatever you have planned."

"Not if I put a bullet into your knees, one after another. I'll shatter them, then go after your other joints. That is a long, slow, painful death, I can assure you."

Sara could imagine this wasn't the first time he had made that same threat — or carried it out. She did nothing for a moment, to give herself one last bit of dignity. She stood still as a statue, her shoulders and back bare.

"Now roll those hips," Khalifa said. "Swivel them like you mean it."

"Your own private porno film."

"Snuff film is more like it." He kissed the side of his pistol. "Your time pretending to be a lady is at an end. Get it going, filthy Jewess. You know how. You're nothing more than an animal anyway."

With a sigh, she moved and the dress fell away from her torso, pooled onto her hips. The freshening wind caused her nipples to stiffen. With a sick feeling in the pit of her stomach, she pushed the dress over her hips. It cascaded around her ankles.

Now Khalifa could not disguise his lust. "No underwear."

"In this heat what's the point?"

164

She had meant to distract him, even for a moment, but she needn't have bothered. Khalifa was no longer looking at her. She turned, following his gaze aft.

She gave a little scream as Hassim's body jerked and shuddered, as if it had been reanimated. Was he still alive? It couldn't be; he had taken a bullet through the heart. Then he jerked again, his body drawn farther aft, and she saw the triangular dorsal fin. Hassim lay on his side, his left arm in the water. The shark came up and snapped at the arm. The corpse was now half in the water, writhing as the enormous, prehistoric jaws ripped hunks of flesh from him. Blood spread in the water, attracting the shark's brethren. Hassim was slowly being turned into chum.

"Poor Hassim. Look what you've done to him." Khalifa's gaze returned to Sara. "Step out of the dress," he ordered. He grabbed her elbow again, half dragging her down onto the aft platform. The last of Hassim vanished into the churning water; there was still plenty of him to go around. He walked her to the edge.

"In you go."

Sara cast a fearful glance behind her. "No. You can't do this." Now she did prepare to strike out at him, but she had left it too late. "I'll dance —"

The flat of Khalifa's hand struck her between the breasts so hard it took her off her feet. She screamed as she crashed into the water. She came up spluttering, only to see the colonel crouched above her like a grinning god.

Grasping her hair, he forced her head back down beneath the water, where the great shadows writhed in the blood-clouded water and bits of flesh floated past her.

Then the side of a shark — a monstrous twelve-foot bull shark — struck her a powerful blow, sandpaper skin abrading her flesh, adding her own blood to the widening feeding frenzy. The shadows converged on the blood and sinew, the bones, muscle, and fat. They were coming for her.

Part Two

CHAPTER
NINETEEN

The shark came directly at Sara, its mouth already half open, bloody ribbons of what had once been Hassim's calf trailing from between its teeth. Sara grabbed one of Hassim's femurs, almost entirely stripped of flesh, and thrust it through the water, timing and point of impact more important than speed. The knob of the bone struck the shark square on its snout, hurting it as well as startling it. Whipping around, it turned tail, in search of a meal that wouldn't fight back.

Against her instinct, she let herself sink down into the bloody maelstrom, and, just as she had hoped, felt Khalifa let go of her hair. At once, she reached up, grabbed his forearm before he could withdraw it from the water, and hauled herself up.

Her head broke the surface. Khalifa, who had been in the process of leaning back, bent down again to shove her once more under the waves. As he did so, Sara launched herself upward. She still had hold of her Star of David. Its six gold points shed water, glittered in starlight, and she buried it, point first, into his right eye.

Throwing his head back, he roared in pain. Sara, clinging to his arm, rose up with him, her feet scrabbling on the slippery hull, then gaining purchase until she was on board. He came at her, maddened as a wounded bull. She knew at once his momentum would drive all the wind out of her. Still, she waited until the very last instant before sweeping her leg across his leading ankle. Thrown off balance, his momentum too great to break, he struck the gunwale, his upper body starting to go over.

He grabbed her, determined to use her as ballast to bring him back onto the deck, or, as a last resort, to pull her in with him. She jammed her thumb into his ruined eye, then jerked hard on the gold chain, extracting the star, along with the vitreous humor of his eye. He screamed again, groping more desperately for her.

Dancing away, she lowered her shoulder and, using the full weight of her body, rammed him at just above the height of the gunwale.

Over he went. She heard the splash, saw a fountain of seawater, then the dorsal fin, cutting through the water toward him. He tried to rise up, but his sodden clothes weighed him down, and he could get only his head and one shoulder out of the water.

"Help me!" he cried.

She stared down at him without pity. Her cheek and side burned like fire.

"Fuck you," she said. "Fuck you."

"Ahhhgh, no!"

His body convulsed as the leading shark took its first bite out of him. He shrieked, his body shaking violently as the shark whipped its head back and forth.

170

Then the others nosed in, claiming their own portions of the feast. For a short time, Colonel Khalifa was visible, one arm upraised, fist clenched against the agony as more chunks of flesh were torn off him. The water began to boil, he vomited blood, and was borne under, never to reappear.

Furuque was on top of Bourne, his weight pressing down on Bourne's rib cage. Bourne's mind rushed back to the hotel conference room in Doha, wires strapped around his chest, while the low-voltage current from the car battery constricted his breathing, on the way to asphyxiating him. He gasped, a blackness boiling at the periphery of his vision, where Soraya and Sonya sat, incarcerated, helpless, surely terrified.

Furuque was pounding him with a fury beyond the rational. It was the fanatic's release, his justification for all he said and did. He was motivated by rage — the particular rage of the oppressed, the person who believed everything had been taken from him, the person who had nothing, and therefore had nothing to lose but a life in the service of Allah.

This ideology made Furuque a particularly dangerous opponent, especially for an emotionally and physically depleted Bourne. El Ghadan had bested him. Worse, he had managed to burrow into Bourne's head, having successfully exploited his weakness.

All this went through Bourne's mind while Furuque, in his single-minded rage, was inflicting great damage with his balled fists. Bourne found his head and shoulders hanging over the concrete edge of the

171

canyon, the rubble-strewn floor yawning below him. Clearly, Furuque was determined to shove him over, to watch him break his back on the canyon's twists of metal and jagged lumps of concrete.

Furuque's furious countenance was just above him. Bits of food clung to his thick, curly beard like spiders to their web. The exhalations from his mouth were vile, as if the accumulated bile of dogma was eating through the lining of his stomach.

Bourne's hands, pinioned at his sides by Furuque's knees, were for the moment useless. He let his head drop over the open space, and Furuque, gloating, let his own head follow Bourne's down until they were almost nose to nose. Without warning, Bourne slammed his forehead into Furuque's nose, splitting the cartilage beneath the skin, driving it into his sinus passages.

As Furuque reared back in shock and pain, Bourne twisted his shoulders. Furuque's position was upended, and Bourne, taking immediate advantage, shoved him over. For an instant, the sniper, blood pouring from his ruined nose, teetered on the brink, as Bourne had moments before. Bourne shoved him again. But as Furuque was about to fall, he grabbed Bourne's shirt front and held on.

The two plummeted down. Furuque's shoulder blade caught the corner of a concrete block, shattering it. Bourne came down on top of him and rolled off, the small of his back slamming into the rubble. The breath shot out of him, and for a long moment he lay on his back, unable to move or even to breathe deeply.

After a short time he found the strength to roll over, gain hands and knees. In this position, he looked down at Furuque. The sniper lay with his eyes open, the pupils fixed, staring into another world. He was dead, and a brief exploration of his body turned up the reason. Bouncing off the concrete cube, Furuque had landed on a nest of twisted iron rebar, one length of which had pierced his side and kidney.

Bourne, gradually regaining himself, cursed under his breath. With Furuque dead, he had no way of discovering who the sniper worked for or why he had been assigned to assassinate Minister Hafiz.

He rose, still shaky, and slowly made his way toward the ladder leading out of the canyon. But with one hand on an iron rung, he heard a sound above his head, and, looking up, saw crouched above him the young man he had helped out of the lavatory. He was grinning at Bourne.

He held the Stechkin automatic pistol Bourne had taken off one of the terrorists in the warehouse, and was now pointing it directly at Bourne's head.

Sara sat on the bloody deck of Hassim's pleasure craft with the crazy thought that all the pleasure had been drained out of this one. She laughed out loud — a strained laugh that had about it the sharp edge of hysteria. It was one thing to stare death in the face, she thought, quite another to escape being eaten alive by a shiver of sharks. Drawing her knees up against her bare breasts, she wrapped her arms around her shins, rocking back and forth.

In her left hand she still held her beloved Star of David, sticky with Khalifa's eye matter, the consistency of custard. She dearly wanted to wash it clean, to see the six points glimmering again in the starshine, but she could not get herself to move. It was at this precise moment that she realized she was trembling uncontrollably.

Far away, she heard a deep boom rolling across the bosom of the Persian Gulf. She managed to turn her head, saw in the south that the stars had been obscured by clouds, blacker than the night. Embedded within, lances of lightning split the clouds with blue-white electricity. The atmosphere had thickened, the scent of rain was like a spice sprinkled over the waves, and a heavy sea was rising from the depths of the oncoming storm, freakish at this time of the year.

Sara knew she had to weigh anchor, make for shore at all due speed, otherwise the storm would catch her in deep water. This boat was a pleasure craft, not made to withstand six-foot waves. She risked shipping too much water, or even capsizing.

These thoughts galvanized her out of her temporary paralysis. Not bothering to waste time dressing, she went to the bow, hauled up the anchor, stowed it, then went to the wheel and fired the ignition.

The powerboat coughed to life. The huge engine rumbled, as if impatient to get going. Switching on the GPS, she identified the coastline, pressed the home button, and watched as the GPS plotted her course. Then she bore down on the throttle and the powerboat leapt forward in its own brand of mechanical joy.

Oddly, this display of pure energy lifted her, and she stroked the lacquered Macassar ebony trim of the wheelhouse with genuine affection.

Running before a storm had its own pleasures, as well as its dangers, which only accelerated her exhilaration. She had cheated death, she had overcome terrible odds, and here she was, driving a million-dollar boat, splay-legged, powerful, naked as a jaybird.

A strange thought occurred to her now. She had returned to the field, where she was always closest to death. And yet it was precisely here where she felt safest. She knew the territory, and the expertise she brought to bear on navigating every square inch of it was what, for her, made life worthwhile. Away from the field, she had been asleep; here she had come fully alive again.

Behind her, the wind had picked up. Though not yet at gale force, that too was coming, along with opaque sheets of black rain that already blocked her windward quarter. But up ahead, she could make out the beckoning string of lights, like a necklace of glowing pearls, which marked the safe harbor of Doha's coastline.

She would make it with moments to spare. Time to climb back into her dress, pull her jacket close around her. Time to clean her Star of David. Time to return to civilization.

CHAPTER
TWENTY

William Magnus, the president of the United States, was in a low mood. It was the kind of mood no one, even Howard Anselm, dared disturb for fear of being cut down at the knees.

POTUS stood in the Oval Office, staring out one of the windows. Night had fallen on the capital, the bright lights illuminating the reinforced concrete antiterrorist barriers. Looking at them depressed him further; they made him feel like a prisoner.

He stood immobile as a sentinel, as if he were one of the many that patrolled the White House grounds inside the high black-painted fences. Half draped in the same Stars and Stripes flag with which, days ago, he wished to wrap Camilla, he tried to sort out his thoughts after a long day of meetings, phone calls, arguments, and a parade of fifteen-minute appointments.

That he hadn't taken the opportunity to fuck her wrapped in the flag, even against her wishes, ate at him like a tapeworm. She had said no, but so what? Women always said no, it was part of their nature. It was also true in his considerable experience that with women no most often meant yes, at least when it came to sex.

176

They liked to appear demure, chaste even, but break through that porcelain exterior and they were as wanton as any man — sometimes even more.

Magnus stood with his hands clasped at the small of his back, head up, chin jutting forward. A pussy, he thought, is like the weather. When it's wet, it's time to go inside.

He chuckled, and for a moment his mood lightened. But then he thought of Camilla, her unwillingness to continue what they had started. And why? He'd never had such astonishing sex with any woman before. He knew she felt the same way, so why did she want to end it? The Monica explanation? He didn't buy it. He had plenty of safeguards in place to ensure that kind of debacle never happened to either of them. He was the most powerful man in the free world — possibly in the world, period. Women were drawn to power as men were drawn to beauty. What the fuck was Camilla's problem?

He sighed deeply. What, then, should he do? He knew, of course, but part of him did not want to stoop to such adolescent behavior. And yet he knew he would. No thought, no counteraction would stop him.

Sighing again, he broke away from his sightless vigil, went to his desk, and sat. From a locked lower drawer, he extracted a lightweight laptop. The instant it finished booting up, he clicked on the eye icon. A CCTV picture appeared, showing him Camilla's room at the Dairy.

And there she was, in all her naked glory. She was padding out of the bathroom in a cloud of, he imagined, fragrant steam, drying her hair with a fluffy white towel. Ah, to be that towel, he thought. His heart hurt. And it was at this moment that he sat back with an audible gasp.

It wasn't just that he wanted to fuck Camilla — he wanted to *be* with her. He loved her! He, the president of the United States, married with two children and a dog, all beloved by the American people.

He put his head in his hands, closed his eyes in agony. His heart beat like a trip-hammer, paining him. All at once, he lashed out with his right hand, sweeping the laptop with its incriminating, reprehensible, wicked video across the room. It struck the wall, as he had meant it to, shattering to pieces.

Immediately, the Oval Office was filled with Secret Service agents.

"Get out of here!" Magnus shouted. "Get out and stay out!"

When Howard Anselm was read in on the incident ten minutes later, he began to worry in earnest.

"*As-salam alaykum*," Bourne said. "My name is Yusuf Al Khatib."

The young man stared down at him. Then he grinned hugely. "Eisa. Thank you for saving my life."

Bourne climbed up the ladder. When he reached ground level, Eisa handed over the Stechkin grip first.

"You need a better weapon, Yusuf. That gun is ancient."

Bourne put the Stechkin away. "Let's get out of here before the Syrian army decides to take another look."

178

They crossed the junkyard field surrounding the factory. Apart from the hulks of bombed-out cars, the streets were empty. Another of Damascus's eerie silences had descended like storm clouds across the city. Sections were brightly lighted, like any other city across the globe, but here and there, entire neighborhoods were blacked out, either from a loss of electricity or from the citizens laying low, not wanting to draw attention to themselves. Then shelling began again in the outskirts of the city, lighting up the night.

Eisa kept his head down. "Why did Furuque attack you like that?"

"Blood feud," Bourne lied. "Uncles."

Eisa nodded. "My family, too, is split in half." His Arabic was odd — not stilted or poor so much as spoken with a curiously flat accent.

"Where are you from?"

"Pittsburgh," Eisa said. "That's in the United States."

A chill went through Bourne. "Was the other young man with you at the club also American?"

"Everyone at tonight's recruitment is American," Eisa said. "We're true believers. We've come to join the jihad."

Bourne took a moment to allow this news to sink in. "How many of you are there?"

"I don't know. I'll see tonight."

Bourne was shocked. He had of course heard of Americans being recruited to the jihadist cause, but not in wholesale numbers. This was a new and horrendous development. "Furuque was recruiting you."

179

"Indoctrinating, actually. I recruited myself. Well, not exactly. I made a friend through the Internet."

"Facebook?"

"No, that's too public. A fantasy chat room. We're both fanatics of this game. Anyway, we got to talking about other things. He's lonely, doesn't have any friends."

"Why not?"

"He says he's a runaway. His father's trying to find him, but he's been ducking him for years. He's been using a false name and everything."

"What's his name?"

"I shouldn't tell you. You might be one of his father's people. His father's very powerful, he says."

Bourne laughed. "You can be sure I'm not. I work for no one."

They had come to a cross street. A traffic light blinked intermittently, only half alive, like much of the city surrounding it.

Eisa studied Bourne. "I'm going to meet him."

"He's in al-Nusra Front?"

"No," Eisa said. "The Tomorrow Brigade."

El Ghadan's army. "Is that where Furuque was taking you? To join them?"

Eisa nodded again. "There's a staging area in the western quarter of the city. Nairabein Park, opposite the Zee Qar Battle Square. I was supposed to go with him tonight."

"Do you know how to get there?" Bourne asked.

Eisa shook his head. "I only arrived yesterday."

El Ghadan's mobile buzzed in Bourne's pocket, reminding him that it was now midnight and with it would come another proof-of-life message. At least, he thought, continuing to move away from the factory, El Ghadan no longer knows where I am.

"I'll take you," Bourne said, returning to Eisa. His heart rate was accelerated. Of course he would take Eisa. "These recruiting sessions are chaotic, more often than not. Tell me your friend's name. I'll help you find him."

"Aashir," the boy said. "His name's Aashir."

The rain inundated Hassim's boat. But Sara was near the dock; there would be no problem taking it in. Once again, she thanked her lucky stars she had been brought up on her father's boat. The care and feeding of motorboats was second nature to her.

Dockside, after the boat had been lashed to its slip, she sluiced the deck free of any remaining blood, dumped the chains overboard. Then she leaned over the gunwale, washed her Star of David thoroughly in the turbulent water. As she came back up, she noticed an object lying on the deck, only visible at this extreme angle. She turned, picked it up. It was Khalifa's mobile.

She stepped off the boat in a veritable downpour. Already wet, she was instantly soaked to the skin. From a slope-roofed building up ahead, the harbormaster emerged at a swift pace. He opened a large, windproof umbrella, hurried to her side, and ushered her into his office. He was a bald, pudgy man with the hunched back of a beetle and weather-reddened hands like lobster claws.

He bade her sit down, then grabbed two large towels from a stack possibly meant just for occasions like this one, and opened them for her until she was completely covered. Turning away, he brewed her some tea, but as soon as he brought it, he sat down opposite her and said, "Madam, what has happened?"

Sara knew she would be asked questions, perhaps many questions, but her greatest ally was the weather.

"The storm came in unexpectedly. For some reason, Hassim had forgotten to turn on the radar, maybe it needed to be fixed, I don't know." She took a slow sip of her tea, batted her eyes at the harbor-master, and said, "Thank you for this."

He waved away her words, his extreme concern still on his face. From a desk drawer, he brought out a large and much-dented first aid kit, from which he extracted alcohol, an iodine compound, and bandages. He brought out a hand mirror, set it so she could see her reflection, bade her to clean the cut on her cheek. He made no move to touch her, which for him would be an unforgivable breach of etiquette. So unlike Khalifa, who had had no qualms grabbing her, hurting her, trying to kill her.

She began to clean the wound, which had already started to swell. He had not seen, and she would not show him, the scrapes along her side from her encounter with the shark. The wound burned, but the seawater had cleaned it well enough, she felt.

"And Hassim?" the harbormaster said softly.

Sara sighed, summoned the memory of swimming with the sharks, and tears came to her eyes naturally. Natural was best, she had been taught.

"There, there, madam." The harbormaster was rocking back and forth as if in prayer. "Do take your time."

She nodded gratefully, sipped more tea, now that she had finished cleaning up her face. "There was another man on board. I was his guest, actually. We were having dinner at Red Pearl, it was getting late. Even so, he suggested we take a moonlight cruise. I . . . I didn't want to, really, but he was so insistent . . ." She hadn't wanted to mention Khalifa, but people had seen the two of them climb aboard Hassim's boat. She lowered her head. "You know how men can be . . ."

"Yes, madam." The harbormaster bobbed his head. "Indeed I do." He wiped his lips. "Madam, who was the other gentleman with you and Hassim?"

"His name was Khalifa," she said. "Khalifa Al Mohannadi."

The harbormaster sat up straight. "Colonel Al Mohannadi?"

Sara shook her head. "He never mentioned he was a colonel, or even that he was in the army."

"Hardly the army," the harbormaster said under his breath.

Sara cocked her head. "What?"

"Nothing, madam." He waved away her query. "Nothing. Please go on."

Sara told the story she had concocted on her way in: How the storm had come up so suddenly, and with

183

such fury that the men had been taken completely by surprise. How a wave had taken Hassim clear off the deck before either Khalifa or she could do anything. Still, Khalifa, hero that he was, tried, and was swept overboard for his effort.

"This is a sad story," the harbormaster said. "A tragedy." He rose, refilled her glass. "Is there anyone in Doha with you? Anyone I can call?"

She pulled out Khalifa's mobile. "I'll do it."

The harbormaster nodded. "As you wish." He pointed. "I have several chores that require my attention, but I'll be just through that door if you need me."

"Thank you," Sara said. "You've been extremely kind."

When she was alone, she called Levi Blum. He didn't answer, so she left an urgent voice mail for him to come fetch her at the marina.

Then, idly, she began to scroll through the list of Khalifa's recent calls and texts made and received, and she discovered one item that made the silken hair on her arms stir.

The mobile buzzed while Levi Blum was still in bed. He did not answer it. He was not in bed alone. Darlene was with him, or, more accurately, under him. He had hooked up with Darlene almost eight months ago. They had found each other in Nite Jewel, a sumptuous club used by expats and business transients alike as a hangout — a place to get together in every sense of the word.

184

When Blum had first spied her, she had been with another man — a swarthy Indian Blum loathed on sight. In the way of Indians, the man was as limp as a noodle, the kind of person of ambiguous gender for whom Blum felt only contempt. On the other hand, the Indian was bloated with wealth, a peculiarity, he learned later, that Darlene considered a magnetic character trait.

She was hardly alone. In his time in Doha, Blum had encountered this type of woman again and again. Sadly for him — since he was as yet far from rich — they were gorgeous, the kind of woman he dreamed of at night, alone in his bed.

No matter how charming or witty he made himself, without the requisite wealth he struck out again and again. It was depressing on so many levels that he considered using his local network to dig up dirt on Darlene's flabby Indian mark. But he was Mossad; he knew better than to use company assets for personal gain.

And yet he had to find a way to make his fortune — another way. He was at that moment ripe for being suborned. There were those who had become aware of him, who had been watching him as casually as a friend, but tracking him constantly. He remembered the precise moment he had cottoned on to them: a familiar face, smeared in reflection in a mall shop window. He had gone into the shop, looked around thoughtfully before picking out a shirt. By the time he paid for it, he was certain he had eyes on him.

After that, he no longer dreamed of Darlene or the other gorgeous women displayed like precious gems at Nite Jewel. He dreamed of his tailing eyes. There were five of them, on him in random shifts. This was smart tradecraft, as regular four- or six-hour shifts were too easy to spot.

So he bided his time until someone made contact, in the gentlest possible way, again, as if he were an old friend. The payment metaphorically laid on the table was far too generous for Blum to pass up. He realized that he had been given a one-in-a-thousand chance, the chance field personnel prized above all others. He was doubled, and now he would double back. A perilous game, to be sure, but it was the only one he would play.

His newfound wealth had attracted Darlene — a shallow triumph, it was true, but for an opposite-sex also-ran like Blum, a satisfying one nonetheless. Now that he had caught his prize, he wasn't about to curtail their time together for anyone or anything, but then the phone rang again, this time with a special ringtone he had devised to alert him to the identity of the caller.

Groaning, he broke his intimate contact with Darlene, rolled over, reached for the mobile on his bedside table. Crawling after him, Darlene slid her mouth all the way down his phallus. Then, in a way he had yet to understand, her tongue began to swipe him up and down. Then she started making those sounds deep in her throat that always egged him on, faster and faster . . .

He closed his eyes for a moment, the ecstasy sweeping away all thought and sense of obligation. Far

186

more quickly than he could have imagined, his pelvis lifted off the bed and he pulsed in her throat, again and again, while she emitted a long, drawn-out sigh.

Too soon, he flipped over the mobile, confirmed the identity of the caller. He had left no message, but then he never did. Checking the previous call, he heard Rebeka's voice asking him to pick her up at the marina immediately. His heart skipped a beat. Why the hell was she calling on Khalifa's mobile?

With heavy thighs and lips that felt bee-stung, he rolled out of bed, padded across the room into the bath. He turned on the shower taps, stepped in, and began to soap up. Moments later, Darlene joined him, rubbing herself along the length of his back and thighs.

But there were some things that trumped even his time with Darlene, and with an inward groan, he broke their connection, stepped out of the shower, and quickly dried himself.

"Where are you going at this time of night?" she said with a sexy pout. "To see another woman?"

CHAPTER
TWENTY-ONE

Bourne left Eisa at a late-night café. He called Zizzy to check in, told him to come as quickly as he could and to bring certain items with him.

"Hafiz is dead," Zizzy said mournfully when he arrived by taxi twenty minutes later. He handed the driver a fistful of money and told him to wait.

"So's his killer." Bourne redressed himself, shoved all the other items Zizzy had brought into the pockets of the wide trousers he wore underneath the robes, then turned to his friend. "Zizzy, I want you to check out of both our rooms, call your pilot, and fly back home to Doha."

"Without you?" Zizzy was aghast. "Are you crazy?"

"That's yet to be determined," Bourne said.

Zizzy regarded Bourne for some minutes before giving way. "And you?" he said with genuine concern. "Where are you going?"

"The less you know the better. Now get on with it."

"But really —"

"Do as I say," Bourne ordered. "You've done enough."

With Eisa in tow, Bourne drove through rain- and windswept streets.

Nairabein Park was not large. It was ringed by parked cars, and it was surrounded on three sides by apartment blocks. Nevertheless, it held several advantages, chief among them that it was deserted at this time of the very early morning. It was also located close to the western edge of Damascus, and was therefore out of the line of fire between the antagonist forces, at least for the time being.

In any event, according to what Furuque had told Eisa, it was the place of choice for the Tomorrow Brigade's recruiting efforts. The leaders had chosen well, as the park was unlovely even by the lowest of urban standards. There were trees, true enough, but they were broken up by concrete barriers topped with crescent iron bars. Lately, much of it had become a staging area for abandoned earthmoving equipment, idled by the civil war that had brought construction and real estate investment to a standstill.

The rain had subsided to a barely felt drizzle by the time Bourne parked the stolen motorcycle near Zee Qar Battle Square. He and Eisa crossed the virtually deserted road, heading toward where a group of young men were ranged around a makeshift podium on which stood three men, their bodies clothed in white, their heads and faces wrapped so only their eyes and mouths were visible. The man in the middle, clearly the cadre leader, was in mid-spiel. The men flanking him were armed with assault rifles, as were approximately a dozen terrorists patrolling the periphery of the park.

★ ★ ★

Bourne spoke to one of the jihadists who emerged from the shadows to accost them. He used Furuque's name, placed his hand on Eisa's shoulder, calling him Furuque's latest recruit, saved at the last moment from the raid on the underground club.

The terrorist nodded and they were through, approaching the fringes of the semicircle surrounding the leader, whose sonorous voice was raised and perfectly audible without the assistance of amplification.

"We must fully understand the role of the Muslim Brother in the West," he was saying as they edged through the crowd of upturned young faces. "The process of settlement, of being embedded, is a jihadist process. You *ikhwan*" — here he invoked the Arabic word for brothers, especially brothers in a militia — "must understand that your work is a kind of grand jihad in eliminating and destroying Western civilization from within and sabotaging its miserable structure by your hand and the hands of like believers so that it is eliminated and God's religion is made victorious over all others."

His eyes blazed and his face seemed to be alight with the inner fire of his fervor. He was a tall man with a face like a fist. Like all demagogues, he employed his voice like a weapon, at times blunt, at others surgical.

"Without this level of understanding," he continued, "we are not up to this challenge and have not prepared ourselves for jihad yet. It is a Muslim's destiny to perform jihad and work wherever he is and wherever he lands until the final hour comes and there is no escape from that destiny."

Bourne looked around at all the rapt faces, Eisa's included, and a terrible suspicion crept over him, one that was soon enough borne out by the leader's words.

"*Ikhwan*, our plan for you in North America is good, our plan for you in North America is solid. We have five phases to our plan. Phase One: a discreet and secret establishment of elite leadership. Phase Two: a gradual appearance on the public scene ... establishing a shadow government. Phase Three: escalation prior to conflict and confrontation with the rulers. Phase Four: training in the use of weapons domestically and overseas in anticipation of zero hour. Phase Five: open public confrontation with the government through exercising political pressure. Seizing power to establish an Islamic Nation."

The leader paused, his head turning slowly as if looking into the eyes of each and every recruit. "You are here now to begin Phase Four."

In the small hours of the morning Doha's Corniche was all but deserted. The scimitar sweep, the march of needle-sharp high-rises lit up like New Year's fireworks was breathtaking, making the cityscape look like a colossal carnival from another planet of the distant future. But as the government liked to say, "In Qatar the future is here."

Sara, feeling as if all she wanted was to sleep for the next twelve hours, walked along the water, watching a slow-moving fishing boat parallel her route, the crew

191

making ready the giant nets before swinging away, moving out into deeper water. Watching it sail off, Sara shuddered, remembering her literal brush with the shark. Her side burned horribly.

Having reached the Corniche, she had directed Blum to park, then, without a word to him, had got out and begun to walk. At some point she heard him trotting after her to make up the distance between them. She had Khalifa's mobile in one hand.

When he reached her side, he said, "You look like you've been to war. Will you tell me now what the hell happened?"

That was when she pressed the redial key on Khalifa's mobile. A moment later, Blum's mobile buzzed. Automatically he brought it out, took the call without looking at the screen.

"Hello?"

Sara, turning to him, held up the colonel's mobile for him to see. "Khalifa's dead, Levi. That's what happened to me tonight."

Blum looked from one mobile screen to the other. "*Ben zona*." Son of a bitch.

"Just so. What did you tell him about me?"

"Nothing. I swear. He knew about you already."

Hassim, she thought dully. And then, "You and Hassim."

Out in the gulf, the fishing boat was now no more than a smudge against the horizon along which oil tankers crawled like a line of ants, bearing their burdens.

192

"Part of the job," he said, nervously licking his lips. "Let me explain."

"What job? Levi, what fucking job!"

Her voice, powerful rather than raised, caused him to wince. *"Kusemec!"* God-fucking-dammit!

"If you're going to explain, do it now."

"Not while you're ready to bite my head off."

Grabbing hold of his arm, she swung him around to face her. "That's not the only thing I'll bite off. Give it the fuck up."

She watched his face, pale and drawn, grow as big as a moon. Then it started to shimmer like the moon's reflection on the water. Streaks of blinding light crossed her vision field, as if she were moving at the speed of light.

Then a pool of darkness opened up in front of her, into which she pitched. She fell, and kept on falling.

"No," Hunter said, leading Camilla away from Starfall's stall. "Tonight you'll be riding Dixon."

The stable was ablaze with light, as if awaiting their arrival. They stopped in front of a stall near the end. A black stallion lifted his head, eyes blazing. His nostrils dilated as he scented her. He bared his teeth.

"Lovely," Camilla said.

A sly smile informed Hunter's face. "Lead him out and saddle him."

The instant Camilla unlatched the door, Dixon stepped back, tossed his head, and snorted in a most unfriendly manner.

"Has anyone ridden him?" she asked.

Hunter laughed. "I have. You want me to saddle him for you?"

Camilla held up her hand. "To what end?"

"Atta girl!" Hunter stepped back, leaned against the far side of the stall area.

Camilla entered, reached up to grab the horse's bridle, and almost got her fingers bitten off.

"Fuck me!"

Hunter, unconcerned, crossed her arms over her breasts. "You know how to approach him, Cam. Take it from there."

Camilla nodded, moved to the side of the stall so Dixon had a better view of her. She smiled at him, started to talk to him softly the way she talked to Starfall. The great eye observed her with what seemed to be a fiendish intensity. Then the horse moved, pinning her against the side of the stall.

"Hunter!" Camilla called softly, her heart pulsing wildly in her throat. She craned her neck, only to find that Hunter had disappeared. She was on her own.

Slowing her breathing, she returned to talking low to Dixon — a kind of singsong that one might croon to a colicky baby. "There, there, big boy, you and I are going to be friends, I know that, I can feel it, there's something between us. Yes, you can feel it too, can't you?" And with that, she reached up very slowly, running the flat of her hand along his jawline, gentling him. "There, you see, it's just me, me and you, we're gonna ride today, aren't we, we're gonna have fun, just the two of us, you'd like that, wouldn't you, big boy, I bet you would."

194

That huge eye continued its enigmatic contemplation of her as she continued her melodious litany, and, as if by magic, Dixon stepped back. She did not move, but the breath came easily to her now, and she slid her hand down his face to his muzzle. He snorted and his head bent to her.

Then, grabbing two handfuls of his mane, she vaulted up onto his back and, without saddling him, rode him out of the stables, into the star-filled night, where Hunter, already astride her mount, was waiting.

The recruitment meeting was at an end, the armed jihadists taking the young Americans under their wing, guiding them to a pair of large military trucks with tarp tops and wooden benches beneath. Bourne, still with Eisa at his side, moved ever closer to the vehicle into which the recruits were climbing. Herded like cattle, Bourne thought.

When the first truck was filled, the jihadists began to stock the second. At length, Eisa was helped into the back of the vehicle. Bourne was about to follow, when one of the jihadists took his arm and stayed him.

"This way," he said, leading Bourne around to the side of the truck, to where the leader stood, flanked by two bodyguards.

"*La ilaha illa Allah*," the leader said. There is no God but Allah. "One of my men came to me. He told me you are a friend of Furuque's."

"Furuque is dead," Bourne said. "Eisa was one of the two recruits he was talking with when the club we were in was raided by the army."

"And how did the club come to be raided?" the leader asked.

"That I could not tell you."

"Then tell me your name, please."

Bourne did.

"Yusuf Al Khatib, I have never heard of you. I have never heard Furuque speak of you." He wiped at his beard just beneath his ruby lower lip. "Further, I am unaware that Furuque had any friends."

"First of all," Bourne said, "now that you know mine, may I know your name?"

The leader stared at him for a long moment. "Abu Faraj Khalid."

"I never said I was a friend of Furuque's, Abu Faraj Khalid. You did. Snipers like Furuque do not have friends, that's a truism. Snipers are loners."

"Hmm. And how would you know that, Yusuf Al Khatib?"

"I, too, am a sniper," Bourne said. "Furuque and I knew each other in that way." He smiled. "It is like a fraternity. A closed fraternity."

Faraj stroked his beard, his black eyes never leaving Bourne's face. "Well, that is an interesting story, my friend. If it is true."

"Why would it not be true?"

"Yes indeed, why?" Faraj snapped his fingers and one of his bodyguards held out his weapon for Bourne to take.

"That's an AK-47," Bourne said. "What do you expect me to do with it, mow down that line of trees?"

"You have your own weapon?" Faraj said. "Where is it then, sniper?"

"Back at the club. I was fortunate to escape with Eisa. A recruit is more important than a rifle."

"*Mashalla.*" What Allah wishes.

"*Allahu Akbar,*" Bourne replied. God is great.

"Tell me, Yusuf, what weapon were you obliged to leave behind?"

"An L115A3 AWM."

Faraj cocked his head. "American, is it?"

"British." Bourne knew very well the leader knew it was British.

A slow smile curved Faraj's wide mouth into the shape of a dirk's blade. He snapped his fingers again, and a moment later, out of the lifting gloom of night, a weapon was handed to him. He held it for a moment, then lofted it to Bourne.

Bourne caught the AWM properly, pulled back the bolt, checked that the .300 Winchester Magnum was in the chamber, that it was a live round, then switched down the bolt.

Faraj turned. He pointed to a distant streetlamp, its fizzing bulb dimmed and about to go. Bourne judged it to be about five hundred yards away, well within the limit of the AWM's effective range. But there was still a bit of fog, moving in slow undulations across the park. The light waxed, then waned, vanishing for moments into the mist, before reappearing like a sad moon, past its prime.

Bracing himself against the side of the truck, he took aim through the scope. Ignoring the fog, he

197

concentrated on the light, waited while the mist thickened and then pulled apart like gossamer strands. Waited, then slowly squeezed the trigger. The report sounded just before the light blew out.

Faraj turned back to him. On his face was a wide smile.

"This is excellent," he said. "Most excellent!"

He took the rifle from Bourne, tossed it to one of his men. "You are a man whose skills we can use. Is that of interest to you?"

"I would not have shepherded Eisa through the city had it been otherwise," Bourne said.

"The lamb! Yes, the lamb!" Then Abu Faraj Khalid threw his arms wide and embraced Bourne.

"*As-salam alaykum wa rahmatu, akhoya, Allahi wa barakatuhu,*" he cried. Peace be upon you, my brother, and Allah's mercy and blessings.

CHAPTER
TWENTY-TWO

When Sara woke, she felt warmth on her face, a light, then a window onto the coming dawn bloomed in her vision.

Someone said, "Go get him. She's awake."

A moment later, Levi Blum's face appeared, hovering over her.

"What . . ." Her mouth felt full of cotton. She tried to swab her lips with her tongue.

"Here." Blum lifted her head so she could get a straw into her mouth.

She sucked on ice water, a little at a time. When she'd had enough, she nodded, and he took the glass away.

She tried again. "What happened? Where am I?"

"I brought you to our doctor." The Mossad employed a permanent doctor in all their fields of operation. "You passed out right in the middle of a sentence. I had no idea what was going on so I did what I thought best. Rebeka, your side is a mess. What happened?"

She told him about the nightmare ride on Hassim's boat, Khalifa shooting Hassim, then turning on her and what transpired after. "The shark scraped me up."

"That's one thing," he said, "but the doc found a deep wound underneath, not quite fully healed."

Sara closed her eyes. She'd been too preoccupied to realize that the shark had turned into her on the same side she had been knifed in Mexico City last year.

"There was more bleeding than I guess you realized," Blum was saying now.

Then something occurred to her, and she struggled to sit up. "The mobile," she said. "Where is Khalifa's mobile?"

"Here." Blum handed it to her, then propped her up with a number of pillows. "It was on the side table. Did you think I'd appropriate it?"

"Frankly, Levi, I did."

He nodded. "I don't blame you." He sat with his hands in his lap, fingers intertwined, like a schoolboy called to accounts.

"You were working with Khalifa. He almost killed me. This is the end of your career in Mossad, Levi. Believe me when I tell you this."

"Ah, Rebeka, I know it looks bad, but before making a judgment you'll regret, I beg you to listen to what I have to tell you."

"What could you possibly have to say to me that would mitigate what you've done?"

"Yes." His head bobbed up and down. "In your place I'd say the same. But then, too, I might take a step back and listen."

Sara let go a long sigh. Then she nodded. "You have three minutes."

"But —"

"Make the most of them, Levi."

"Right." He swallowed. "It's true that Colonel Khalifa came to me, but it's also true that he'd already had me under surveillance."

"What?"

"That's right. I was blown the moment I landed in Doha. Don't ask me how or who. I don't know. But when he made his pitch I knew I only had two choices: Do as he said or abandon ship. For me, the second option was out of the question; screwing up this assignment I'd be drummed out of Mossad instantly. Anyway, I thought, if I'm to double, why not double again?"

"You mean you meant to gather product on him to deliver back to Mossad."

"Right."

"Yet you didn't."

"Rebeka, I have material, I just didn't dare send it. He had me under the microscope from the get-go. I couldn't chance it."

"Then you should have pulled yourself out."

"And miss this opportunity? Besides, he would've had me locked down the moment I showed my face at the airport."

Her eyes turned steely. "How much, Levi?"

"What?" When he was startled he reminded her of a bird about to take wing.

"How much product did you give Khalifa?"

"The bare minimum to keep myself running."

"And the quality?"

"Bits and pieces. Here and there. You know."

"You blow any of our agents?"

"Absolutely not." He shrugged his coat-hanger shoulders. "Anyway, he wanted something very different."

"Like what?"

"Like details of our operations in western Pakistan."

"Western Pak. Really?"

Blum nodded. It was getting on her nerves.

"He said nothing was going to be disturbed," he protested. "That it was strictly a monitoring he wanted."

"And you believed him?"

"Call Tel Aviv. See if we're still intact."

"I will, believe me."

His head continued to bob up and down, like an Adam's apple on a thirsty drunk. "Anyway, I know we are. Intact, I mean. Fully."

"I need a list, Levi. ASAP."

"Way ahead of you on that, Rebeka. I used the doctor's laptop to access my encrypted files and had the relevant ones printed out for you."

He handed her an envelope. She knew almost nothing about Mossad's ops in western Pakistan. In any event, the contents of the envelope didn't seem all that thick. She took a quick look, her eyes skimming the list of product Blum had passed on to Khalifa. As he said, all tracking movements, all in and around the borders of Waziristan. She shoved the sheets back.

"All right," she said, still weighing the envelope like an assayer toting up the value of an ore find. "Let's give it a go."

He nodded. "Sure, I saw a chance to make some heavy money, but I also figured if I gained Khalifa's trust I might be able to discover how he'd fingered me so quickly."

Her stomach clenched. "Someone inside Mossad is dirty."

"Well, that's what I thought too. It's the logical conclusion, right? But then something totally unexpected happened." He glanced at his watch. "Rebeka, my three minutes are up."

She gave him a sour smile. "Go on, Levi. Don't be an idiot. But you damn well better have gold-nugget product for me."

"Wait. I've opened up an entire vein of gold."

"Don't oversell, Levi. Just sell."

He relaxed somewhat as his confidence built back up. "So here's what happened. Khalifa had arranged a regular weekly rendezvous for us. It moved around, as good security dictates. In this case, a round robin of five restaurants, always at an hour in the middle of the afternoon when, because they were very expensive and not at malls, they were closed to the public.

"Anyway, one afternoon I arrived early — early enough to see Khalifa huddled with another man. With this man were four gorillas — not Doha police, not Qatari army, or intelligence. They weren't connected with Qatar at all."

"What were they?"

"Military, or rather ex-military. They're Chechen."

"Chechen?" Sara's head reared back against the pillows. "Are you certain?"

"Absolutely. I took photos with my mobile."

He brought it out, scrolled through, then handed her the phone. Sara saw Khalifa in a dimly lit space — the rendezvous restaurant — huddled over a table with a man whose profile was partly obscured by shadows. Another photo showed the other four men. Clearly they were not Arabs.

"In this light and distance how on earth did you get such good shots?"

He ventured a grin, obviously pleased with her reaction. "Camera on my mobile is fantastic. Forty-one megapixels. Aces in dim light. And all without a flash."

Sara nodded absently. She returned to the photo of the men. They could only be bodyguards. As she scanned each face a sense of disquiet built within her, as if her momentum was propelling her along thinner and thinner ice.

"Keep going," Blum urged, and she did. "I spent some time digging."

Now she arrived at other photos of the same men. These were file shots, identified by Interpol, marked as extremely dangerous. The next photo in the group was a grainy close-up of the man meeting with Khalifa. The last one identified him.

"Ivan Borz," she said in a breath.

"The one and only."

Sara felt as if she had fallen through the ice. "My God."

"Ivan Borz, the biggest arms dealer this side of Viktor Bout. In fact, now that Bout is behind bars, Borz is the man when it comes to global arms shipments."

204

"But Borz is into much more," Sara said.

Blum nodded. "The so-called Wolf isn't also known as the Poppy Man for nothing. He controls the world's illegal trade in opium and heroin." He took his mobile back from her. "But, frankly, I don't think it was Khalifa's ambition to get into either of these areas. He was in bed with Borz for an entirely different reason."

Sara stared at Blum for a moment, wondering at how easy it was to misjudge people. "Go on," she said.

"Borz is tied very closely to El Ghadan. In fact, Borz is El Ghadan's spymaster."

"That's how El Ghadan was able to gain access to the Al-Bourah Hotel here in Doha — through Khalifa."

"Yes. And I was well on my way to monitoring Borz through Khalifa."

"Did you find out anything?"

"Something very, very big is on the immediate horizon. That's why Borz ordered the eyes on me. He doesn't want intervention, doesn't want anything disturbed. Let sleeping dogs lie, you know? He just wants to make sure we're not on to his new op, whatever it is." Blum did not look happy. "But now that Khalifa's dead, how in hell will we find out what it is?"

Faraj had Bourne sit up front with him in the cab of the second truck. The vehicles pulled out into a sunrise turning the sky the color of a battlefield streaked with blood. They rumbled through the streets, passing more burned-out cars. Cyclists veered away from them, and pedestrians stopped what they were doing, averted their faces, as if the devil himself were abroad in their city.

205

Almost immediately, shelling began in another neighborhood, and Bourne could only imagine the assault was a diversion to keep the army occupied while Faraj and his contingent made their way to their destination.

"Without us," Faraj said over the roar of the engine, the grinding of gears, "your country is without hope."

Bourne, posing as a Syrian, had told the leader he had been born in Latakia, a city far to the west, on the Mediterranean coast.

"My father and brother are dead," Bourne said. "Together. In one instant, gone. My mother never recovered. She went mad with grief."

Faraj nodded, scrubbed at his beard. "It is a common enough tragedy, yes? And, you know, tragedies by their very definition should be anything but common."

"Not these days," Bourne said. "Not here."

"Tell me about your home, tell me about Latakia."

"It's a port city, very busy these days." He had chosen Latakia because much of Zizzy's business with Hafiz had passed through that container port. "It's also under attack from ISIS."

Faraj gave Bourne a sideways glance. "That Iraqi al-Qaeda group is by far the most dangerous to your country, and to us as well. ISIS tried to merge with al-Nusra but we took the initiative and spiked the nascent alliance. Do you know why? Its slogan is 'From Diyala to Beirut.' ISIS wants to spread to the length and breadth of the Ottoman Empire, and in the process stamp out all other jihadists who are not as extreme as it is. That would include us. Al-Nusra, us, we're all kind compared to ISIS."

Bourne decided to make Faraj's thesis personal. "My father and brother were killed fighting ISIS in the north. First the Turks, then the Israelis, then the Americans, and finally Iraqi fanatics. ISIS has been murdering, kidnapping, and torturing people in Raqqa and Aleppo. They needed to do something."

"They died as martyrs. We all aspire to such deaths." Faraj sat back, combing his beard absently as he mused. "We face a grim future, my friend. The economies of the world have left us behind, with no hope of catching up, let alone keeping pace. We are remnants, soldiers of a bygone age, fighting the good fight for Islam and Allah. We seek to turn back the world clock, but it is a proven fact in Saudi, in Tunisia, in Morocco, and especially here and in Egypt that the modern world is inimical to sharia law."

Bourne was both startled and fascinated to find a jihadist leader who was so clear-eyed about his situation. "Then what are we to do?"

"Fight on," Faraj said, "and just possibly we will win. It took the deaths of thirty percent of the young boys in the American South for the North to win their Civil War. Those boys had much to live for. Ours do not. Their poverty, their future is so bleak they have little or nothing to lose. Joining our cause is their way to glory."

He turned his fierce, feral gaze on Bourne. "And we have so many, my friend, so very many, all willing to die for our cause. The Americans can never kill enough of us. This war will have a very different outcome."

Some time ago, they had passed beyond the western boundary of the city, and now Bourne understood there was another reason for setting the recruitment in Nairabein Park. They swung off the highway, away from the seemingly endless line of rumbling trucks on their way into the city.

They headed south, then southwest, into the countryside.

"Tell me," Faraj said, "are you prepared to leave Damascus? Are you prepared to leave your homeland?"

"In your service, Abu Faraj Khalid, of course."

The leader nodded. "Good."

The journey continued. Bourne took out his prepaid mobile, dialed into the Mossad server. There was a message for him. It was encrypted. He retrieved the message, then spent the next ten minutes decrypting it in his head. It was from Sara, and it contained high-level product vital to him. Deleting the message, he cleared the phone's history, then turned it off and put it away.

He looked up to find Faraj regarding him levelly. "A love letter?"

Bourne laughed. "If I had a woman I would only cause her grief."

Faraj nodded, as if in understanding, one warrior to another.

Five minutes later, they stopped before a gate in a high cyclone fence. More jihadists appeared, hailed by Faraj. One of them unlocked the gate and the group followed the trucks into the compound, locking the gate behind them.

They went around to their left and Bourne saw that what he had at first taken for a training facility was in fact an airfield. A Boeing C-17 military transport sat at one end of the runway, its rear door gaping open, waiting for its cargo to march on board.

The trucks pulled up behind the plane. The troops on the ground helped the recruits down, guiding them into the belly of the C-17. Faraj climbed down, Bourne following, and they stood, waiting for the transport to fill up. Faraj spent a few moments in consultation with the pilot and navigator. The early morning air force sorties were causing a last-minute change in course until they cleared Syrian airspace.

"Where are we headed?" Bourne asked, as he and Faraj followed the cockpit crew toward the C-17.

"Home," the leader said without breaking stride.

But Bourne, following the jihadists up the stairway into the cockpit, had seen their destination on the revised flight plan, and he knew Faraj had told him his first lie. Western Pakistan, more specifically, Waziristan, wasn't home for these people. It was sanctuary.

CHAPTER
TWENTY-THREE

"The eyes were pulled the moment news of Khalifa's death reached his people."

"Are you certain of that?" Sara said.

Blum nodded. "I was clean when I brought you here."

She regarded him critically. "Have you been here before since you arrived in Doha?"

He shook his head. "This is the first time."

"Nevertheless, they might have pulled the old ones for new ones," she told him. "It won't hurt to take another look."

"We're the watchers," Blum said. "But who's watching the watchers, eh?"

She and Blum had been installed in the doctor's private quarters, which he shared with his wife. She was a plump woman with a sunny disposition. She happily fed them, then went out to buy fresh clothes for them as if they were her own children. "Our two sons are off in England at college," she had shyly confided to Sara. "And I always wanted a daughter."

Blum returned with news that the immediate vicinity was immaculate, which contented Sara, at least for the moment. As it turned out, he had done more than compile product on Khalifa. There was material on his six lieutenants for Sara to pore over.

"This is A-prime product, Levi," she said, glancing up from the text he had given her.

He was like a puppy, eager to play. "Juicy, huh?"

For though the product had little in the way of military secrets, it was chock-full of the private peccadilloes of four of the six men, more than enough for her immediate needs.

"How did you find out all of this?" she asked, suitably impressed. "They had eyes on you the entire time."

"But not on the local network I assembled. I have five operatives, all fiercely loyal, fueled by their hatred of the government's sub rosa policies." He had stopped fidgeting. "That gave me breathing room."

"To pursue your personal fortune," Sara said tartly.

"To a dual purpose. I led them on some merry chases," he said, with the tone of a sixty-year-old agent nostalgically recalling his fieldwork. "Plus which, there were times I was working when they were certain I was debauching myself."

"At Nite Jewel."

He nodded. "As you can imagine, the eyes aren't comfortable there."

"Good to know." She glanced through the product. "This one," she said, pointing to Lieutenant Mahmoud Tamer. "Call him. Set up a meet late tonight at Nite Jewel."

Blum looked doubtful. "I was Khalifa's personal asset. Tamer doesn't know me. Why would he come?"

"He'll come," Sara said with absolute confidence. "Tell him you know who murdered his boss."

She jolted awake into the glare of artificial light, but now, after days of captivity, Soraya was finally able to summon her wits. They had been days of fear and uncertainty. Now and then, her initial terror yielded to the banality of the evil that held her and Sonya captive. These were only men, after all — dangerous men, to be sure, but without superhuman powers.

Soraya had been through the full Treadstone course of training, which included ways both physical and mental to combat abduction, incarceration, and enhanced interrogation. No course, however, could prepare you for having your two-year-old child kidnapped along with you.

Which was why she needed to have all her faculties about her, to think things through clearly. God knew, she had enough quiet alone time in between meals, when Sonya was sleeping.

Where was she? Still in Doha; they had not been transported out of the killing room. So, step one: in Doha.

Step two: How many men were guarding them? She had encountered three already. Though their faces were always masked, everyone had a distinct natural scent, including the guard who was marginally more civil to her than the others. But beyond those three she had no idea how many more El Ghadan had installed outside the room.

Step three: Were they in a warehouse, a fortress, a safe house? The only people who knew the answer were the jihadists themselves.

She was sitting on a wooden chair with a ladder back. She rose, made a circumnavigation of the room, which, apart from the door, was entirely featureless. For a moment, she stood in front of the door. Then, as if with a will of its own, her hand reached out, turned the doorknob.

At that moment, the lights were extinguished, and Sonya cried out.

"Mommy!"

"I'm here, muffin." Soraya backed away from the door. "Remember what I told you. My voice is the voice of the wind. All you need to do is follow it."

When she was far enough away from the door, the light blinked back on. Sonya ran to her, and Soraya scooped her up in her arms. Sonya was trembling. Soraya carried her to the chair and sat down with her in her lap and as she soothed her child tried to order her thoughts.

The lights winking out at the precise moment she grasped the doorknob was no coincidence. They were being observed, possibly from behind the mirror on the opposite wall. But could there be other means of observation she did not yet know about? She looked up at the four corners of the room, where the walls met the ceiling. At first she could discern nothing. But then she saw what appeared to be a small crack in the plaster, high up. She saw the end of a fiber optic cable, a tiny eye observing her with cruel indifference.

Then the door opened. A jihadist entered with their breakfast.

Somewhere outside her prison, another morning had dawned.

Late in the day, when the sun was nothing more than a line of burnt sky on the western horizon, Dixon threw her. They were galloping full out across a rolling field. A thick stand of oaks flashed close by on their left. On their right, the field dipped down into a swale filled with wildflowers.

A fox, sleek, ruddy, and muscular, dashed from out of the oaks directly across their path. Startled, Dixon pulled up short. Camilla lost her grip on the reins, tumbled head over heels over Dixon's lowered head. Tucked in, she landed on one shoulder and rolled. All the breath was knocked out of her, but she was otherwise unhurt.

She lay for a moment, staring up into the piebald sky, slightly dazed. What came to her mind was an afternoon much like this one, when she had been a girl of about eight. She had been running full tilt across a field, neck and neck with Beatriz, her older sister. All she saw ahead of her was the finish line: the yellow-green foliage of the weeping willow at the end of the field, a demarcation where the ground fell off precipitously onto the banks of a deep, still lake, filled with frogs and water skimmers with the angular legs of an architectural drawing.

Camilla was winning — six steps ahead of her sister, seven — when she tripped, trying to avoid a startled

214

rabbit. She fell hard into the thick grass, where, as now, she lay, dazed and gasping for breath. Her knees were scraped up and bloody, burning as if an iron had been pressed into them. Still, she did not cry.

At length, she rolled over onto her stomach, lifted herself onto her elbows, and looked for Beatriz, whom she expected to see crouched over her, a worried look on her face. Instead, she saw her sister at the finish line, dancing up and down, her arms raised in victory. "I won! I won! I won!" Beatriz's excited voice cut like a buzzsaw through the birdsong and the insects' hum. Camilla was about to shout at her to come back, tell her she was hurt, but then she clamped her mouth shut grimly. Beatriz wasn't coming back for her; no one was. And with that her tears slipped their bonds, rolled down her cheeks in hot rivulets.

Now, as she heard hoofbeats coming slowly toward her, she wanted to tell Hunter to stay away, that she didn't need her help, certainly didn't want her pity. She needed nothing and no one; she was an adult now, could take care of herself, thank you very much. Read as a child, remembered in adulthood, the words of Queen Elizabeth I, Tudor, resounded again in her mind: *I have found treason in trust.*

Long moments passed. As she continued to stare upward, repeating her shining idol's words, Dixon's great head came into view. He stared down at her, snorted, shook his head. His huge eye observed her with a clear and certain intelligence, Hunter's theory to the contrary be damned.

"It's all right, Dixon, really, it is."

She rose on one knee. The horse lowered his head toward her.

Reaching up, Camilla's hand found his muzzle, stroked it. "It's okay, Dixon. I know you didn't mean to stop short, I know you didn't mean to throw me. And I'm fine, see?" She rose slowly, put her arm over the horse's back, leaned against him, her cheek against his. He whinnied, bobbed his head up and down, as if in agreement.

"We're good," she whispered. "I promise we're good."

And then, hugging him all the tighter, she had herself a little cry for the loss of herself in the vast arena dominated by men. What could her life have been if she had chosen another path? But what path? she asked herself. Be a wealth manager, like her father had wanted? Be a deeply unhappy fighter pilot instructor, her best days behind her, like her mother? Or be a surgeon like Beatriz, bone weary, twice divorced? She shuddered. Those were lives for other women, not her.

Trust, she thought. In an animal, once given, trust is never corrupted or overthrown. It abides.

"Are you hurt?" Hunter called. She had wisely stopped her mount a distance away. "Shall I call an ambulance?"

Camilla shook her head, her face buried in the horse. "I'm fine." Her voice was clear and strong. "We're both fine."

Their room was still cloaked in darkness when she heard the door creak open. By smell alone, Soraya knew who had come in. She also knew what kind of food he was carrying.

Willing herself to breathe deeply and slowly, she waited for him to cross the room. The light came on and she blinked, her eyes narrowed against the glare. Sonya slept on, curled in her lap. Instinctively she wrapped an arm around her daughter.

"I know it's you," she said. It was the man she had spoken to yesterday. She peered up into his eyes, which were all that was visible of his face. "Won't you tell me your name? Then we can talk more freely."

"Move the child," he ordered.

"She's still sleeping," Soraya said. "Leave her in peace."

After a small hesitation he centered the tray of food on her upturned palm. "Call me Islam," he said then.

Soraya began to eat. "You're always here, it seems," she said between bites. "You must hate it almost as much as we do."

"Of course . . . Well, what do you expect being cooped up in this place for days on end? I'm not used to it."

"Who is?"

He bent toward her. He reeked of cheap cigarettes and stale sweat. These people didn't know the meaning of showers, she thought. It had been at least two days since she or Sonya had cleaned themselves. The thought depressed her, so she banished it. She needed to keep herself positive at all costs, not only for herself but for Sonya as well. It was the only way to survive.

"What is that face you're making?" he said. And then, more forcefully, "You are offended by my smell, infidel, is that it?"

Soraya paused with a bit of food halfway to her mouth. Abrupt changes in a captor's demeanor were also a part of the hostage process. She knew she would have to inure herself to it. But his sharp, menacing tone had awakened Sonya. There was fear in her eyes as she looked from the jihadist to her mother.

"Mommy?"

"It's all right, muffin," she said in as calm a voice as she could muster. "Everything's fine."

"Fine? No, it's not fine. I think you can't stand the sight of me," Islam shouted. He ripped the tray from her hands.

"Islam, I don't know what you're talking about. Truly."

He bent toward her again, his nose almost touching hers. "Did it ever occur to you that you're the one who smells, that I can't stand the stink coming off you, that I gag repeatedly while I'm in here with you?"

Soraya knew she had made a mistake by letting her feelings show, even for an instant. She gestured. "The tray, please. At least let me feed Sonya."

Islam leaned over the little girl, but when he spoke it was to Soraya. "From now on, you'll smile when you see me, won't you?"

"Of course," Soraya said, but her attention was on her daughter. "Of course I will."

But it was too late. Sonya was crying inconsolably.

218

CHAPTER
TWENTY-FOUR

"First order of business," Eli Yadin said, "is to get you out of Doha now. I'm assembling a Kidon extraction team even as we speak."

"Director, I don't think that's a good idea," Sara said.

She had instructed Blum to fetch them a pair of prepaid mobile phones. It was the only way she could be certain their conversations would not be overheard by Khalifa's NTCC people. He might be dead, but she was certain his orders regarding Blum remained in effect. Her first call was to her father, through a scrambled circuit. The moment she had finished briefing him, he hung up on her.

It was an hour before he called back. During that time, she composed an encrypted text containing Blum's golden product: the connection between El Ghadan, Khalifa Al Mohannadi, and Ivan Borz. This she sent to a private mailbox on an encrypted server, to which Bourne had access twenty-four/seven.

"I don't care what you think, I'm pulling you," Eli said hotly when he called back. He had not bothered with the niceties of a salutation. "I never should have let you go in the first place, Rebeka." On a live op he would no more think of calling her Sara than she would refer to him as Father.

"I'm glad I came here, otherwise we never would have unearthed the connection between El Ghadan and Ivan Borz, through Khalifa."

"The immediate problem is that Khalifa is dead, a colonel in the Qatari National Tactical Command Center, no less. From what you've told me, there are witnesses who saw you and Khalifa get on the boat together. The harbormaster can identify you. Khalifa's people will come after you with everything they've got." There came the sound of shuffling papers. "The Kidon team is operational. In three hours you will be picked up. In the meantime, stay inside and don't show yourself at the windows."

Eli cleared his throat, as if he were about to choke on his own rage. "Now I want to talk to that prick Blum."

Sara opened her mouth in order to continue her defense, then thought better of it. When her father was in a red mood there was no talking rationally to him. Perhaps it had not been such a good idea to allow his daughter to become an agent of his, she thought morosely, as she shoved the mobile at Blum.

"Here," she barked.

Blum took the phone gingerly, as if it were a bomb about to explode. He looked like he wanted to chuck it out the window, anything but get ripped to shreds by Director Yadin.

"Listen, you little shit, I ought to have Rebeka shoot you on the spot, but since our people have confirmed

220

your product — at least the bones of it — I am of a mind to keep using you."

"Thank you, Director."

"Don't thank me, Blum. You're still on probation. We've pulled our people out of Waziristan, burned the residence. We have to start all over because of you."

"Rebeka told you I couldn't risk contacting you."

"There were ways, Blum, if you thought about it, but you were too lazy. I always felt that about you, that's why you were posted to deadhead Doha."

"Supposedly deadhead."

"Don't editorialize."

"Yes, sir."

"The question is whether you're simply lazy or whether you're nuts."

"I might be both, Director," Blum said with no little sheepishness. "But I also put my life on the line redoubling on Khalifa. He was one tricky bastard."

"Even so," Yadin said, "the jury's still out on you, Blum. Just do as I tell you. I informed Rebeka that I was going to extract her, but that was just to scare the pants off her."

"If that's even possible," Blum said, glancing her way.

"Well, you're right there. She's fearless. But that's sometimes to her detriment, which is why I'm assigning you to protect her."

"What?"

"You looked out for yourself pretty well in a difficult situation, Blum. You're to help her any way you can. You're to guard her with your life. If she dies on your watch, Blum, no matter the circumstances, I will stake you out in the desert, no joke. Are we clear?"

"I understand, Director."

"I hope to God you do. Now, put her back on the line."

The moment Blum handed her the mobile, she said, "I believe the recent events have given us an extraordinary opportunity here in Doha."

"How d'you mean?" Yadin said tersely.

Then she told him, step by step, detail by detail, with the particular brilliance no other field agent could hope to duplicate.

Five hours later, the doctor's printer chattered to life again.

Lifting off, the C-17 swung over the city in a northeasterly direction. Bourne, peering out the Perspex window, watched the long lines of people, carts, and rattletrap vehicles heading out of Damascus, out of Syria, out of the war, for refugee camps in other countries, including, ironically enough, Iraq. He heard Faraj give the pilot a sharp order, and the plane banked slowly, for the moment heading due east.

Then Faraj clambered out of his seat, crouched beside Bourne. "Listen, Yusuf, my friend, I just got word of something and I want you to see it. I want you to see what is really happening in your poor country."

On Faraj's orders, the pilot took the C-17 lower still, until houses rose up before them. People looked like no more than ants scurrying over the ground, away from a fierce rocket barrage. Oddly, the impacts sounded soft, almost muffled. What kind of ordnance, Bourne wondered, was in the payloads?

It wasn't long before he got his answer. Swirling clouds of dust arose from the strikes, rolling along the streets and byways of the suburb of Ghouta, where men, women, and children ran screaming, stumbled and fell, clawing at their faces, gasping for breath, convulsing as the dust clouds converged, swirled over them, undulating like some many-headed serpent.

The serpent devoured the men, the women running with their arms thrown around the narrow, bony shoulders of their sons and daughters. A pregnant woman fell behind, then fell permanently, crying out, clutching her belly. People stumbled over her, in their desperation to escape trampling those who had already succumbed. But there was no escape; the invisible serpent, borne by the winds, traveled faster than they could.

As the plane swung around to the north again, away from the horrific effects of the barrage, Faraj said, "This is your army at work, Yusuf, the so-called defenders of Syria. Not content with bombing their populace, they are employing sarin gas, a weapon of mass destruction."

Bourne checked himself from grabbing a parachute and jumping out of the C-17, but what could he do against the army's attack? So he sat and watched, helpless and in turmoil, as the plane banked away, leaving the grim massacre behind.

"This is what we have to deal with, Yusuf," Faraj said. "Every day another atrocity. And not just here —

Yemen, Iraq, Iran, the list goes on and on." His hand gripped Bourne's shoulder. "Which is why we will do what we can, in every way we can, to bring Allah's will to Muslims everywhere."

"You said we were headed home," Bourne said.

"Home. My friend, people like us, we have no home. We are ejected from one place to another. We are pariahs, forced out of the places of our birth, always on the run, squeezed into the margins of society."

"But you have a plan."

A dark glint came to Faraj's eyes. "A plan, yes. Years in the making, now about to come to fruition. I won't lie to you, Yusuf, it is a daring plan, a plan only people kicked to the curb, people with nothing to lose, could imagine, let alone execute.

"But we have, my friend, and we will. We will execute this plan. Our time has arrived. The Great Satan has sung his siren song."

It was almost two thousand miles due east from Damascus to Waziristan. The C-17, not the fastest plane, rumbled along through a cloud-filled sky. Bourne was still brooding over what he had been witness to. He had seen many atrocities in his time — and no doubt more that he could not remember — but this one stood out as the most heinous. Chemical warfare had been internationally outlawed for a long time. Like poisoning wells, it was an offense that could not be excused, an offense that demanded the most severe punishment. His utter helplessness ate at him. He was a man who, having lost his own self in the fog

224

of a forgotten past, saved himself by saving others. There was nothing he could do, and yet he was moved to do something. He looked over at Faraj and thought that there must be a way to find a chink in El Ghadan's armor through him.

He rose, crossed to where Faraj sat, crouched beside him as, before, Faraj had hunkered down beside him, providing commentary to the sarin gas attack. "Matters are not as simple as they used to be," he said over the roar and jangling vibration of the engines.

"I disagree," Faraj stated flatly. "There is us and there is the Great Satan."

Bourne countered. "All this hatred of the Great Satan disguises the complexity of the problem."

Faraj turned to him, his thick eyebrows raised. "Which is?"

"Islam itself," Bourne said. "We are like a soldier, fractured in a battle eons ago, whose parts are now warring with one another. Sunni against Shia, Alawi against Sunni. And then there are the Saudi, their sticky fingers in everyone's pies, whom we all hate and fear. The Iranians, Afghans, the Pashtun warlords of western Pakistan, hounded into the mountains, the Punjabis, who bow to no one. The list goes on and on. The bloodshed isn't simply the Great Satan's doing, Faraj. We also have to take responsibility."

Faraj grunted. "You are a man with strange ideas, Yusuf."

"Strange ideas are what's needed now. I have not come to this conclusion lightly or over a short period of time."

225

"You talk like a leader, not a loner, a sniper."

"I suppose you could say that being alone is what has given me the time to formulate my strange ideas."

"And do you seek to impose these ideas on others?"

"How would I do that, Faraj? I have no power over others, nor do I seek it."

"Then how do you propose to implement your ideas?"

Bourne smiled. "By exposing them to those in power. People who do hold sway over others. People like you, Faraj." He almost added, "El Ghadan," but it was too soon for that. The last thing he needed was for this necessarily paranoid man to become suspicious.

"What exactly are you getting at?" Faraj said now.

"Let me go at this from a different direction," Bourne said, after some time, though in truth he had already thought this idea through. "Why are you hiding out in Waziristan?"

"You know why. To keep the Great Satan's eyes off us while we are in the final stage of our plan."

"With half a dozen American drones per day raining missiles down on the area?" Bourne shook his head. "I don't think so."

Faraj's eyes blazed in fury, and Bourne knew he was playing this game very close to the edge. Unfortunately, it was the only play he had.

"Tell me then," Faraj said, "if you're so smart."

"You are besieged on all sides by the other powerful jihadist cadres — ISIS, as you yourself told me. Al-Qaeda, the al-Nusra Front, the Muslim Brother-hood, KOMPAK, Ansar al-Sharia, the Islamic Front in

Syria, Hamas, Hezbollah, shall I go on? No, I thought not. This is the problem you must face, Faraj. All these other cadres say they want the same thing as you do, but do they? They won't use your methods or your rhetoric, and they surely don't want you to gain in power and influence."

Faraj nodded sagely. "All this is true, Yusuf."

"Do you like hiding out in Waziristan?"

"Have you been to Waziristan?"

Bourne grinned. "That's what I thought. I have ideas."

"I'll bet you do." Faraj scratched fiercely at his beard. "But I'm not the one to talk with."

"No? But you are the leader."

"Of what you have seen, of what you will see when we land," Faraj said. "El Ghadan is the supreme leader of the Tomorrow Brigade."

"Will he be in Waziristan?"

Faraj continued to gaze at Bourne. Then he turned away.

"Are you certain?" Howard Anselm said.

"Here is the raw product," Marty Finnerman said, "straight from DOD's listening posts in Jerusalem and the Golan Heights."

And there it was, Anselm thought, staring down at the intel in stark black and white.

"The Israeli Knesset has agreed to continue the settlement building in occupied territories. And the number of Hamas-related bombings in Tel Aviv has escalated to an unconscionable level. Fifty-five killed so far in just the past week."

Finnerman and Anselm were in one of the SITCOM rooms in the Pentagon. The lights were low. All the eight screens ranged around them were active, showing lists of personnel, troop movements, animated maps of Iraq, Afghanistan, Egypt, and Syria, along with surveillance tape — via both drones and CCTV on the ground — as well as dizzying raw footage from mobile phones at the front lines in these countries.

Finnerman stood, bent over Anselm. "Events are coming about as our Gravenhurst colleagues predicted," he said. "We don't want peace. Gravenhurst's members and alumni, of which we are a part, are the political-industrial axis that makes this country run. Frankly, the concept of compromise isn't in our lexicon. Despite POTUS having come this far with the peace talks, they are going to end in failure."

"Which is why we came up with the contingency plan that depends on the summit's failure."

Finnerman nodded. "Look, we both know the Gravenhurst threat assessment is correct: Syria is the doorway to Iran, and whether we like it or not, Iran is the next stage in the war on terror. We neutralize Syria, we deprive Iran of one of its prime client nations in the spread of jihadism. We are taking this drastic step to ensure the security of the world — the security of our own country, which, according to Gravenhurst, has never been at higher risk, not even just before 9/11."

Extreme distaste had transformed Finnerman's face. "We're all but out of Iraq and we'll soon be leaving

Afghanistan. We have six hundred and fifty billion dollars' worth of high-tech weaponry at our disposal. It's high time we used it against a target that truly must be crushed."

Anselm shook his head. "You know what POTUS is going to say. The people have had their fill of war. More than."

"Then it's the administration's job to tell them how wrong they are, how their livelihoods, the very lives of their children and grandchildren depend on our intervention in Syria."

"The Russians have made it a very tough sell."

"We expose the Russian president for the opportunist he is. How difficult will that be? Nobody likes the fucker anyway. We'll have the help of both CNN and Fox, not to mention the *Washington Post,* as well as the outsized number of conservative and religious bloggers I have in my pocket. That doesn't even begin to include the senators and congressmen invested in our military complex." Finnerman grinned. "You're in your element, Howard. Rectitude, sir! Rectitude is the order of the day."

"Perhaps, but there's still POTUS to convince," Anselm said. "We knew that from day one."

Finnerman smiled his foxy smile. "On that front, fate has stepped in to help us. Look here." He directed Anselm's attention to the center screen, where a frozen frame of a surveillance tape had been put up.

"This just came through, transferred from one of our forward-position video monitoring posts in the Middle East."

Both men stared at the frame, which held the images of two men.

"The picture is so damn grainy," Anselm said. "Who the hell is it?"

Finnerman used the remote he was holding as a pointer. "The one on the left is Abu Faraj Khalid, Syrian cadre commander of the Tomorrow Brigade."

"El Ghadan's people."

"Right." Finnerman nodded. Ever since the tape had come in he had been working himself up into a righteous rage. "And the man next to him —"

"Looks like a fellow Syrian," Anselm said.

"Indeed." Finnerman fiddled with the remote, and the frame slid over so that the right half of the screen showed a close-up of Faraj's companion. "Then we ran our facial recognition software on him." He pressed another button on the remote and a dozen white triangles covered key portions of the face. They began to flicker so quickly the human eye picked up only a blur.

"Stop it, Marty. I'm getting a headache."

"Patience." The triangles came out of the blur and froze. "Ah, there we are." The photo of the two men disappeared, the face of the man in question slid to the left, and up came a photo of Jason Bourne, side by side with the blowup. The same dozen white triangles appeared on Bourne's face and began to pulse on and off in time to the ones on the so-called Syrian's face. "It's Bourne, sir. He's in disguise — a very good one. But the FR program sees through disguises to the real contours of the face."

"Bourne." Anselm seemed mesmerized.

"In the company of one of the most notorious terrorist leaders."

A slow smile spread across Anselm's face. "It's all true, then."

"Indeed," Finnerman said. "We now have the irrefutable proof to bring POTUS on board: Bourne is working with El Ghadan."

CHAPTER
TWENTY-FIVE

Sara dried her hair with a bathtowel.

"I like your hair dead black," Blum said. "It suits you."

Sara's eyes flashed. "Don't get any ideas."

"Not to worry." He laughed. "I don't go for girls with short hair."

Sara snorted as she turned to contemplate her reflection in the mirror. The doctor's wife had expertly cut off her hair while Blum raided the local pharmacy for hair dye and makeup, using the list she had given him.

Sara did look different, it was true. Though not as completely transformed as Jason could look, she knew she would pass for Qatari as soon as she donned the traditional clothes. The headscarf would help as well. She had also shortened her gait; pace of walking was something that could give even the best-disguised field agent away. The doctor's wife proved the most help, perfecting her makeup, fixing the robes and headscarf she had bought for Sara just so.

At last Sara and Blum were ready to venture outside.

It seemed like an age since she had felt fresh air on her face. The moon was out, shimmering along the sweeping curve of the Corniche. They strolled for a bit, as if they were lovers enjoying the sight of the high-rises lighting up the spangled night. A speedboat passed them on their right, leaving a phosphorescent wake, and Sara shivered as the memory of her mortal struggle aboard Hassim's craft pierced her to the marrow.

Nite Jewel was the kind of place that sent a limo for its regulars. Blum called, and after a half hour more of walking had brought them near to the time he had set for the meet with Lieutenant Tamer, the car pulled up beside them.

Nite Jewel was a stone's throw from the Corniche. Down a side street filled with darkened boutiques, its façade glowed and glimmered, a testament to its name. Depending from the canopy protecting the doorway was a grid of LED cylinders that bled one color to the other in an endless rainbow, bathing the patrons entering in a red, orange, yellow, green, blue, violet, purple glow.

The limo slid to a stop at the curb and Blum emerged first, followed by Sara in her traditional Qatari outfit. The doorman, recognizing Blum immediately, nodded deferentially and held open the heavy door coated with silver leaf.

Inside, it was darker than the city night outside. Gradually, as her eyes grew accustomed to the gloom, Sara realized they were walking down a passageway lit only by tiny, starlike LED bulbs randomly set into the black-painted ceiling. The walls, she saw as they neared the end of the passageway, were a patterned midnight-blue wallpaper.

Then they emerged into the club itself, and she blinked in disbelief. Whoever had designed Nite Jewel had fallen in love with certain Hollywood films of the thirties. The sumptuous room was composed of a three-tiered horseshoe of tables. At the open end of the horse-shoe was a stage occupied now by a jazz quintet.

Each table was intimately set with a fringed lamp that shed pink light and an old-fashioned telephone with which patrons, should they desire it, might call people at other tables. As they were shown to their table, Sara could see that though there was a sprinkling of twos and threes at the tables, the vast majority were occupied by individuals, more women than men, so far as she could see.

Blum had booked a table in the center, on the third and highest tier. Mahmoud Tamer was already in residence, nursing a glass of what looked to be club soda with ice. He was a glowering, intense-looking individual with pocked cheeks and the sloped shoulders of a tree dweller. He didn't look stupid, though, and in any event, Sara was too well trained to underestimate anyone from a first impression.

Tamer rose when Blum, still ahead of her, approached the table. He was in uniform, and a uniform could give even the ugliest man stature and gravitas. Just ask Mussolini.

Tamer slowly looked Blum over from head to toe, as if taking inventory prior to a cattle auction.

"Lieutenant," Blum said, affably cordial.

"Blum," Tamer replied. "I should have you arrested."

"On what charge?"

"On any charge I care to name."

"Would that be prudent, or even wise?" Blum said.

"I'm not in a particularly prudent frame of mind tonight."

"Your leader is missing." Blum nodded. "I understand."

Tamer plucked at his lower lip as if ridding it of a bit of tobacco. "I don't think you do, but have a seat anyway."

Blum, wanting to maintain control of the interview for the moment, remained standing. "There is a time for intimidation," he said, "and a time for negotiation."

"Tactical Command doesn't negotiate. I want the woman, Martine Heur, the Canadian diamond merchant seen getting onto Hassim's boat with Colonel Khalifa. According to the harbormaster, she was the lone survivor."

"Martine Heur is no longer in Qatar, that much I can tell you."

"It's hardly enough," Tamer sneered. "It's hardly anything at all."

"On the contrary," Blum said evenly, "it's more than you knew five minutes ago."

Tamer stared at him as if dressing down a recruit. When that silent intimidation didn't work, he shrugged. "So why are we here, to stand and stare at one another? You are wasting my time."

"And your time is so valuable." Blum indicated with his head. "Let's sit, then."

Tamer sighed to show his exasperation. Nevertheless, he sat back down, and Blum slid into the seat opposite him. Tamer looked up, surprised to see a female standing so close to them. Sara had positioned herself perfectly, using Blum as a shield so that until this moment the lieutenant hadn't seen her.

"What's this, then?" Tamer said.

Before he could make a move, Sara sat down beside him. He cringed away, as if she had leprosy.

"I won't sit here with a female," he said with clear distaste.

"You will," Blum said.

The lieutenant snorted. "Who are you to give me orders?"

He made to get to his feet, but Sara, extracting a scalpel she had taken from the doctor's surgery, plunged it though Tamer's trousers, just missing his thigh. It went all the way through the cloth, the tip burying itself in the seat. Tamer let out a low howl of approximately the same pitch as the sax solo up on the stage. No one appeared to notice either sound.

"That's more like it," Blum said.

Tamer, pinned like a butterfly on display, ignored him, glared at Sara.

He was about to open his mouth when the telephone on their table rang. Blum looked at Sara, who picked up the old-fashioned black Bakelite receiver.

"By all that is holy," a voice said in her ear, "you have just signed your own death warrant."

CHAPTER
TWENTY-SIX

When Camilla came down to breakfast it was, as usual, barely light. She looked for Hunter, but found instead a man with brush-cut hair, a mile-long stare, and the demeanor of a carnival barker.

"Morning," he said, in a thick burr. "Vincent Terrier."

"What? As in the dog?"

"I'm your new nanny."

Camilla didn't like him, liked his attitude even less. "I don't need a nanny."

He shrugged. "Difficult times."

She scanned the typed menu disinterestedly. "Where's Hunter?"

"Gone." He showed her some teeth. That, she thought, did not bode well for her.

He ordered oatmeal, which, according to his type, he called porridge, "with milk, no sugar." Camilla shuddered internally. She ordered her usual — two poached eggs, wheat toast — though in truth what appetite she had come in with had evaporated.

"You're mine now," Terrier said, for no particular reason she could see apart from further pissing her off.

She resented his tone as much as the phrase, which made her sound like an acquisition, like a car or a wristwatch. The food was placed before them, and he dug in as if he hadn't eaten in days.

"Am I being monitored?" she asked.

"Should you be?" he said between shovelfuls of porridge.

This man was from Anselm. Hunter had promised to protect her from Anselm; now Hunter was gone. Poof! Just like that. Suddenly she'd had enough of Terrier and his master, and, as she had once read in a Le Carré novel, people who have had enough want more. "I demand to know what happened to Hunter."

Terrier continued eating his disgusting, gluey mess without either answering or looking up.

She leaned forward. "Did you hear me?"

"Your eggs are getting cold."

She grabbed her plate, tilted it so that the eggs slid off into his bowl of half-eaten oatmeal. He paused with his spoon halfway to his mouth, staring down at the mess. Then he set the spoon very carefully back into one of the yolks, which had now spread over the top of the oatmeal.

"This is the Dairy," he said, just as carefully. "We don't ask questions like that."

"I am Camilla Stowe," she said with even more intensity. "I ask questions whenever I want, wherever I want."

He sat back, his eyes at last rising to meet hers. "So this is how it's going to be."

She didn't bother to speak; the answer was obvious.

238

"I want my old handler back."

"I'm afraid that is im —"

She rose and left the dining hall. Outside, in the clean, new-day air, she thought she'd feel better, but all she really felt was Hunter's loss more keenly.

Soraya loved her child more than life itself, but she had discovered, to her chagrin, that she was not a natural mother. Every single thing that an infant, and now a toddler, required of her was a struggle. Her life had been forever changed, it was not wholly hers anymore, and for someone who had spent years in the clandestine services, this change was not an easy thing to come to grips with, let alone master. Most days she was left with a feeling of guilt, which, if she wasn't careful, could become crushing, never more so than now. The fact that she hadn't been able to protect either Sonya or Aaron from the life she had led ate at her, as if it were a living thing in her belly.

"Mommy," Sonya piped up in her little voice, "tell me more about the djinns."

It was not until after Sonya was born that Soraya discovered she was a natural-born storyteller. Now she used those stories to weave a spell of calm and optimism around the two of them, protecting them from Islam and his cohorts, although she had increasingly come to feel that Islam could become useful to her. She had no illusions about jihadists; she'd had too much experience with them. But establishing a relationship with one — and getting him to tell her his name — was a great leap forward. She felt as if she could at least keep her head above water, and possibly at some point reach the shallow end of the pool into which she and Sonya had been dragged.

For the moment, she returned to the private inner world she was spinning for the two of them. Sonya had fallen in love with the djinn, obliging Soraya to make up endless stories about him. Curiously, this brought her closer both to her daughter and to motherhood.

"Once upon a time, there lived a lonely djinn. He was lonely because he lived in the center of the Gobi Desert, in a place his fellow djinns had long abandoned."

Sonya was between her knees, leaning her little body in. "Why did he stay, Mommy?"

"Because, my darling muffin, the djinn's father was buried beneath the very dune where he had lived his whole life. And although his fellow djinns had long since moved on, he could not."

"He didn't want to leave his daddy."

"That's right, muffin."

"I wouldn't want to leave my daddy either."

Tears leaked out of Soraya's eyes.

"Mommy?"

"Yes, precious."

"The djinn can do anything, can't he?"

"That's right."

"I wish the djinn was here, Mommy." Sonya's voice suddenly seemed smaller than ever. "Then he could bring Daddy back."

"Join me," the voice on the telephone said in Sara's ear. "Come alone."

240

Carefully, she lowered the receiver into its cradle and, staring at Lieutenant Tamer, said to Blum, "Someone has been observing us. I'm going over to his table now."

Blum shifted in his seat, but had the presence of mind not to crane his neck to look around the room. "Do you think that's wise?"

"I don't have a choice." Sara noted the slight smirk on Tamer's face. "You won't be smiling when I get back, I promise you."

"*If* you get back," he said.

Blum leaned forward, spoke urgently to her. "Who has been observing us?"

"I'll let you know shortly." She freed the scalpel. Then she leaned over and, with her lips almost against Tamer's ear, whispered, "The next time I use this on you you'll howl and keep on howling."

Then she scooted out, walked slowly and deliberately along the top tier to the table in the far corner, where the lamp had been turned off, as the voice on the telephone had instructed her.

A man sat alone, partly obscured. Without a word, she sat down opposite him. Even though he was in shadow, she recognized him instantly.

"Nite Jewel does not seem like your kind of place, El Ghadan," she said.

"You know my name," he said, "but I don't know yours."

"We'll keep it that way," Sara said, "at least for the moment."

"You speak Qatari Arabic perfectly, but you are not a native." His eyes narrowed. "You are not American either."

Sara smiled. "I very much doubt this is why you called me over."

El Ghadan clasped his hands on the table in front of him. "Why did I call you over, then?"

"It's clear your lapdog went running to his master as soon as he received the call from my friend."

"It was the prudent thing to do."

"Indeed." Sara strived to ignore his burning eyes. These fanatics are all alike, she thought. Nevertheless she was careful not to underestimate him, knowing not only his history but how cleverly he had trapped Bourne with Soraya and her family. This was a man who recognized the usefulness of psychology, and used it every chance he got. "And now here we are."

Silence reigned for a time. The quintet was on a break. A low murmuring filled the room. Now and again women, dressed like glamorous birds, rose from their perches, wending their way around tables to slide into places next to the single men who had offered telephoned invitations. The atmosphere was lush and sensual, a stark contrast to the fierce psychic war going on at the far corner table on the third tier.

"There is a mystery I'd like cleared up," El Ghadan said at length.

"Which one? There are so many."

Though his face remained impassive, a terrible animosity built inside him, caused him to clasp his hands so tightly the knuckles turned white. "Khalifa is

242

missing. Presumed dead. I take care of my people. I want to know what happened."

I'm in, Sara thought. "Believe it or not, I want to help you."

"And can you?"

"You've got a leaky boat, El Ghadan."

He blinked, the only sign that she had genuinely surprised him. "You are saying what?"

"You mentioned that Khalifa was one of your people."

"Yes."

"An important cog in your jihadist wheel."

El Ghadan tossed his head, abruptly impatient. "Yes, so . . . ?"

"You are a man of integrity, El Ghadan. I see this clearly. By this I mean that your beliefs are absolute, your aims motivated by ideology."

He shook his head, clearly baffled. "Having antagonized me, are you trying flattery now?"

Sara smiled benignly, leaning slightly forward. "Not at all. I cannot imagine what advantage that would bring me. No, I am in the process of warning you."

El Ghadan sat back stiffly. "Warning me?"

"Khalifa's motives were not the same as yours. He coveted money, nothing loftier. Which meant that he was for sale to the highest bidder."

El Ghadan's eyes narrowed. "And?"

"He was set to sell you out to the Israelis."

"That's an insane accusation," El Ghadan scoffed. "I knew Khalifa well."

"Not well enough."

She chose this moment to lay on the table between them the product Blum and his local network had so meticulously amassed on Mahmoud Tamer. She pushed it across for El Ghadan to read. It detailed the comings and goings of Tamer between Doha and Beirut, where he continued to drop thousands of dollars a month at Casino du Liban, gambling and bedding high-end call girls.

"I don't have to tell you," Sara said, "that a lieutenant's salary isn't going to pay for all that high living."

El Ghadan looked up, shaking his head. "What has this to do with Khalifa?"

"Tamer is one of his lieutenants. I have similar product on the others. It's the trickle-down theory, El Ghadan. His lieutenants were scraping the crumbs from his table. They were all dirty. It was the way Khalifa had of keeping them loyal."

He shook his head. "I don't believe it."

"You don't want to believe it." She passed to him the product Mossad, at her father's request, had manufactured. It was a spreadsheet of dates and times when large amounts of money were wired to a specific account in the Cayman Islands that, according to the material, Khalifa himself had opened. The damning part was the page on which the wiring instructions had been deciphered. They emanated from a shadow bank account in one of the half dozen Tel Aviv banks linked to Mossad. The Cayman account existed, the account records had been backdated. Apart from Khalifa's involvement, everything was real and correct. In the unlikely event that El Ghadan should dispatch one of his men to Grand Cayman, armed with a photo of Khalifa Al Mohannadi, the bank manager would tell him that yes, that was indeed the man who opened the account on such-and-such a date, and here was his signature. Mossad left as little as possible to chance.

In a sudden burst of disgust, El Ghadan pushed the product back across the table. "And Khalifa's end?"

"Came at the hands of Hassim, the boat's owner." This was of course another lie, but it was a necessary one. The day she started telling the truth to jihadists, Sara thought, was the day she needed to get out of this business. "Hassim discovered just how dirty Khalifa and his men were. They fought across the deck of the boat. A storm was approaching; it was a dangerous moment to be doing anything but running before it. Immersed too deeply in their mutual animosity, they ignored the storm, to their detriment. Locked together, each searching for an advantage, they went over the side."

El Ghadan took a moment to digest her story. Then he said, "And how do you know this?"

"The woman who was on board with them, the woman who survived —"

"The so-called Martine Heur."

"She is my friend. My childhood friend. We're closer than sisters. No sibling baggage, you see."

El Ghadan's eyes narrowed. "Surely that is not her real name."

"It is or it isn't. What's the difference?"

El Ghadan's eyes burned. "You know the difference."

"She is protected from you, believe me," Sara said flatly. "Besides, Martine did you a great service. And so have I." She glanced over her shoulder to where Tamer sat with Blum. "You need to clean house here in Doha."

Without another word, she rose. About to leave, she was halted by the sound of his voice. The quintet had started up again, Lerner and Loewe this time, and she was obliged to retrace her steps in order to hear what he was saying.

"How can I get in touch with you?" he asked.

"Why would you want to?" she said.

"I could use your eye on the Israelis. What do you say?"

CHAPTER
TWENTY-SEVEN

Waziristan was a place of no one's dreams. Caught between Afghanistan and Pakistan, seen from above it looked like it had been expelled by both countries. It bordered the state of Peshawar, was cracked by mountains, many of them impenetrable. It was inhabited by Pashtun tribes, who now shared their spiky, unlovely territory with elements of the Taliban, al-Qaeda, and possibly other hard-core jihadists. The Waziri, a rough, warlike people, kept these disparate cadres separated, like Siamese fighting fish, lest they wage a continuous war, one against the other, and in the process turn the country to ruin.

The C-17 circled the pressed dirt airstrip once, then pulled itself down in stomach-churning fashion before the nose could smack into the wall of granite that rose steeply at the far end. The plane hit hard, the tires smoking, the brakes shrieking like the ghosts of the Waziri dead.

Even in this great valley, they were high up. The air was clear, clean, and thin. The sky was very blue, almost dark overhead. Clouds clung to the mountaintops to the east, churning and gloomy. Occasionally, lightning flickered in their depths and deep rumbles of thunder like beaten drums rolled ominously through the valley.

Faraj's men were unloading the C-17 through its massive rear door. The American would-be jihadists marched down, stiff-legged from their uncomfortable journey seated on wooden benches. Most trotted off to relieve themselves, as the C-17 had no facilities on board. To one side of the strip was a line of buildings, looking more like temporary shelters, camouflaged in order to be invisible from above.

From these buildings men emerged. Bourne immediately caught their difference from the men with whom he had been traveling. Chechens, he thought. And he thought of Sara's encrypted text, which confirmed Nebby's intel: the invisible line connecting Khalifa, El Ghadan, and Ivan Borz, the Chechen arms dealer who had ably stepped into Viktor Bout's enormous shoes.

"This is the edge of nowhere," Faraj said, breaking into Bourne's musings, "the margin of society. The mountains of western Pakistan are crawling with people who have been forced out of the cities to the east for religious and ethnic reasons. They are treated like pariahs, and so they become pariahs."

It seemed to Bourne, listening to this thesis, that Faraj and perhaps many of his jihadist brethren were invested in being pariahs, a unique status that allowed them to preach to all and sundry just how awful their lives were, how little they had to lose because they owned nothing, and never would. So why not join the pariahs, why not embrace the status, why not allow it to empower you? This was the real message Faraj and his ilk were preaching. All the talk of Allah and the Great Satan was so much trapping. The Great Satan was what gave them pariah status in the first place. It seemed to Bourne that being a pariah gave Faraj a reason for being; that without it he would be nothing.

"But you have your plan," Bourne said. "Or should I say El Ghadan's plan. It's not really yours, is it? And if it works out, if I follow you correctly, neither you nor El Ghadan will be pariahs for much longer. I definitely want to be on the winning side."

Faraj watched his men form the new recruits up into ranks. "Once again, Yusuf, I don't know what to make of you. Are you a sniper, a philosopher, a would-be lieutenant?"

"Perhaps I'm all of these."

"And if you're not? If you're none of these?"

Bourne grinned. "You have already seen my skills as a sniper."

"And you have demonstrated your language skills. Furuque had no such aptitude."

"Furuque was limited. He was a pawn on a chessboard."

"But you're not."

"You have to make that determination, Abu Faraj Khalid, not I."

Faraj eyed him for some moments, as if struggling to reach a decision. "Come," he said at length, and without another word strode off toward the line of buildings.

"Stay out here," Faraj ordered before he ducked inside. Bourne watched the procedures the new recruits were being subjected to. Right now they were being armed with AK-47s. Several moment's later, Faraj emerged, beckoned to Bourne.

Bourne entered the middle building of five. It was long and low, like an Indian lodge in the American Southwest. But inside, it had more of the aspect of a Roman army tent. A man sat on a camp chair before a desk made of what appeared to be aluminum. Across the desktop were strewn various topographical and city maps, building blueprints, charts of all kinds, including city plats of sewer systems. These were marked up with a charcoal pencil — notes, connecting lines, queries. Battle plans, Bourne thought. And then he recognized the city against which Borz had set himself: It was Singapore.

Two huge, glowering Chechens flanked Borz's battle desk, as if they were bookends. Their narrowed eyes were wholly concentrated on Bourne; it was as if Faraj — known to them, and trusted — did not exist.

The seated man looked up as they entered. He unhooked his reading glasses, set them atop his work. He was a burly individual, with a bull chest and virtually no neck. His arms were short, as were his legs, evident when he rose and came around to the front of the desk, more to block sight of his workspace than for any form of courtesy.

This was Ivan Borz. Bourne recognized him from the photos accompanying news stories about him and his burgeoning alleged empire.

While Faraj made the introductions, Bourne studied Borz more closely. He had a wide nose that appeared to have been broken at least once. His ears were small, set high up on his head. His forearms were as matted with curling black hair as his skull was bald. His eyes, gray as the clouds that ringed the mountaintops outside, were extraordinary. Set deeply in his face, they were ringed with dark circles, pouched beneath. They maintained the absolute stillness emblematic of psychopaths and natural-born killers. It was as if all emotion had been leached from them.

He snapped his fingers. "Passport."

Bourne handed over his Yusuf Al Khatib passport.

As Borz leafed through it, Faraj said, "He's a first-rate sniper."

"Did I ask for your opinion?" Borz snapped. He sounded as if he had been gargling with glass, his voice deep and thick, and somehow strangled.

Faraj said nothing in return, keeping a silence that told Bourne more about Faraj's standing with Borz than any response could have done.

"Leave us," Borz said without looking up.

With a glance at Bourne, Faraj turned on his heel.

"You know what to do, Faraj," Borz said, just before the other left, followed, surprisingly, by the Chechen muscle.

Borz regarded Bourne as he took a pack of cigarettes off the crowded desktop, shook one out, lit it, and drew smoke into his lungs slowly and thoughtfully. He slapped the passport against the palm of his hand.

"Yusuf, do I know you?"

"We have never met," Bourne said.

"No? Are you sure we haven't run into each other somewhere?" Then without warning, Borz switched to Russian. "Is Yusuf Al Khatib your real name?"

Bourne looked blankly at the Chechen, shook his head, just as he would have if he did not in fact speak Russian. "Can you please use Arabic? You speak it very well."

"Is Yusuf Al Khatib your real name?" Borz repeated in Arabic.

"It is."

The Chechen took a sharp right turn, moving to an altogether different subject. "How well do you know Faraj?"

"Hardly at all," Bourne said, unperturbed. He would have been surprised if he hadn't been subjected to an interrogation. "We spoke briefly in Damascus, then more at length on the flight here."

"What is your impression of him?"

"As I told you, I haven't known him long."

"Precisely." Borz crossed his arms over his chest. "You have no dog in this hunt, as the Americans say. I'm going by instinct here, but you don't strike me as an ideologue. You don't follow blindly. Am I correct?"

"As it happens, you are." Borz had inadvertently given Bourne a gift of great value. It was clear that Borz was not an ideologue either. He was a clear-eyed pragmatist, following the scent of money wherever it might lead him. Kindred spirits — or, in this case, the illusion of them — were of vital importance out here at

252

the edge of the world, beyond the sway of even the most powerful exemplars of law and order.

"Then answer me this: How is it you hooked yourself onto Faraj?"

"Happenstance," Bourne said. "I got caught in a Syrian army raid, along with one of Faraj's people and two of his would-be recruits. I managed to escape with one of the recruits. He didn't know his way around Damascus, so I took him to Faraj's recruitment gathering. Faraj became interested in my skill as a sniper and asked me to come along."

"No," Borz said in precisely the same tone of voice. "I think you're a spy."

This was a well-traveled interrogator's trick: sharp turns in subject, only to return time and again to the core matter of interest. It was a proven method of separating truth from lies.

"I should take offense. Is this your famous intuition again?" Bourne said neutrally. "Who would I be spying for?"

"The Israelis are prime suspects. Until a few days ago, Mossad had a presence here; now it's gone. You could be the replacement."

"I could be," Bourne said, "but I'm not."

"Well, it's certain you're not American."

Bourne wondered how Borz could know that.

"So you blindly followed Faraj out of Damascus, is that it?"

Again, the sharp turn of subject.

Bourne smiled. "Not blindly at all. At that moment my continued presence in Damascus was too great a risk. I weighed the probabilities and used Faraj as my way out."

"In other words, you were opportunistic."

Bourne nodded. "By necessity, yes."

"Pragmatic as well. No one can understand this state of affairs better than me." His cigarette was almost burned through, but Borz ignored the lengthening ash at its end. "You weighed the probabilities." He chuckled. It sounded like he had swallowed his cigarette butt. "Let's sit and talk about probabilities."

At that moment, Bourne's keen hearing picked up a dreadful song. It was neither the muffled shouts of Borz's men, which had ceased some moments earlier, nor the keening of the wind swooping off the mountains.

"Down!" Bourne shouted as he leaped on Borz, driving both of them under the metal table. A heartbeat later, the world exploded all around them. The earth trembled, clods of flying debris punctured the building. Then the building itself disintegrated, and a wall of fire rose, roaring in their ears.

Camilla headed west. About a mile out, the diamond shadows vanished as clouds tumbled in, as if being pursued by the devil himself. The wind freshened, rustling the trees, and she felt the rain coming.

She altered course toward a thick stand of birches north of her. For a breathless moment, the tips flamed gold and silver in the last shard of sunlight before the clouds irised closed.

254

Approaching the trees, Camilla saw a figure on horseback off to her left, atop a small hammock shaded by a giant oak. The figure was entirely in shadow. For a moment, Camilla wondered if it was Terrier, or someone else dispatched by Howard Anselm, perhaps at Bill's behest. What if she had been deemed unreliable? What if she was never going to make it to Singapore? What if they meant to kill her right here on their own property? Suddenly, she felt alone and vulnerable. If she were thrown — or if she were shot — no one would know. She would disappear as surely as if her body was dropped into the ocean. She shivered at the gruesome thought.

Then, as she entered the tree line, the figure urged its horse forward, down off the hammock, heading directly toward her. She had a heart-stopping moment before she recognized Dagger, and then she knew.

Turning Dixon, she headed back out into the rain. The figure drew up beside her.

"What are you doing here?" Camilla said. "I was told you were gone."

"In the future," Hunter said, "after you leave here, you'll be told many things. Most of them will be lies. You need to be able to recognize them."

Camilla stared at her for a moment. "You mean that shit Terrier was a test."

Hunter grinned her huge, tomboyish grin. "That's precisely what I mean."

By mutual consent, they directed their mounts into the stand of birches, dismounted where the trees clustered most thickly, protecting themselves from the downpour.

All around them, the tiny forest swayed and glittered, but there was a coziness to it that sent Camilla straight back to her childhood, a house in the woods — just a hut, really — she had made, into which she retreated when her sister and father became too much for her.

"I said I would protect you," Hunter said, "and I meant it."

"I know."

They stood very close. The smell of the horses mingled with that of the wet leather of their saddles. There was also an undertone of something more intimate: Hunter's scent of clean, sun-washed skin.

"We made a pact," Hunter said.

Camilla nodded. "Yes, we did."

Hunter stepped forward, cupped the nape of Camilla's neck with her palm, kissed her. Lips soft as petals, half opened, tasting of apricots. They trembled slightly. Then both women pulled back.

Hunter's eyes searched hers. "Sorry."

"Don't be." Camilla didn't know what she was feeling. "It was a natural thing to do, I suppose."

Hunter laughed, deep in her throat. "There are so many reasons why I like you."

"I'm not gay," Camilla said.

"This isn't about being gay or being straight."

"Isn't it?"

"Not for me." Hunter said this tenderly, with no trace of snarkiness.

Camilla tried to kiss her back, a short, sharp, indecisive movement like a bird hopping out from the cover of a tree into broad daylight, but Hunter held her back, hands on her upper arms.

"Cam, do you trust me?"

Camilla nodded. "I do."

"Then you're a fool." Hunter's eyes searched hers. "I've lied to you."

"About what?"

"I was never a jet pilot. I said that because I'd been given your file and knew your mother was a marine pilot. It was a shortcut, a way to quickly bond with you."

Camilla said nothing; her heart beat fast, filling with a terrible despair. She thought again of her sister dancing at the finish line while she lay hurt in the grass. And now she thought of her father, with his elitist attitudes, his lip curled in the perpetual sneer only she could see. How he had looked down on her and her mother all her life, before finally turning his back and walking away with an heiress, a countess with residences in Rome and the south of France, the full package so far as he was concerned.

"I was a bad, bad girl," Hunter was saying now. "Anselm likes bad girls, because he can control them. I learned to ride horses in Mongolia. I was sent there by a private security firm hired by the Pentagon, after I had washed out of the Marines for standing up to a sergeant who tried to rape me."

Camilla shook her head. "That doesn't sound anything like bad."

257

"Wait," Hunter promised. "What was I doing in Mongolia? I was part of a small cadre sent to the Bayan Olgii area in the extreme west. We were supposed to be listening in on Muslim extremist groups infesting East Kazakhstan. Which we did. But I soon discovered that the real reason we had been sent there was to intercept a known drug pipeline between Russia and China, run by a Chechen by the name of Ivan Borz. Borz was just getting his feet wet in arms dealing, but he had made his fortune in drugs.

"Stupid as I was, I thought our mission was the intervention and destruction of the pipeline. Come to find out that, no, what our bosses wanted us to do was to take a piece of the pipeline. We were to contact Borz and convince him that from that moment on he needed us to protect the integrity of his pipeline."

"And?"

"He paid. It was easier, I suppose, than killing us and attracting more attention to what had been a perfect route."

"So your bosses extorted him."

"That's not all they did."

The rain was momentarily heavier, and Hunter retreated farther into the densest part of the stand of trees, where the horses could not follow. Camilla followed, suddenly eager to hear more.

"After the Mongolia success, they sent me to Iraq. That was my reward." There was real malice in Hunter's eyes, frightening in its intensity. "I wasn't there to protect any of the army brass. I wasn't there to provide threat assessment, though that was my official

258

brief. I was there with three of my Mongolia cadre for another intercept mission. Only this time it was against our own government. The money being flown into Iraq, Cam, you wouldn't believe it. A skid of money, shrink-wrapped, straight from the U.S. Mint. Millions, uncountable millions. We stole this skid — the whole thing — and found ways to expatriate it back to our bosses in D.C."

"How did you come to the attention of Howard Anselm? He found out about the mission and used it against you, yes?"

Hunter's laugh was harsh, as unpleasant as the malice still in her eyes. "If only. No, Anselm was a partner in the private security firm I worked for. He was the one providing them with the inside product that made them all fortunes."

Camilla backed up against a tree. She felt as if someone had punched her in the stomach. Sickened, she turned away for a moment.

"These people," Hunter said, "are monsters. They were born and bred to capitalism and the free market system, which to them means grab whatever you can and a good fuck you to everyone else."

Camilla could feel her close, pressed against her side, her lips whispering into her ear.

"The worst part is, these people pretend to be the moralists, the great patriots keeping our country safe, ensuring the security of not only the country but the world. What a joke! But it's a cruel joke, an abomination, the corruption of the power they have been given by the free market system."

Firmly but gently, she turned Camilla to face her. "I want you to help me, Cam. I want you to help me work against these monsters. I want you to help me bring them down."

"Me?"

"Yes," Hunter said, the intensity in her voice infectious. "You're in a unique position to make a statement — a statement that all the world will see and understand."

CHAPTER
TWENTY-EIGHT

Chaos in the aftermath of the twin explosions, and a ringing, deafening silence.

All around Bourne a fiery rubble, a heat so intense that his lips and the backs of his hands were already blistered. Beside him, Ivan Borz lay unconscious, not dead or dying. A whirling missile of corrugated steel, part of the blown-apart wall, had cracked the desk in two. But Bourne's instincts hadn't failed him: The desk had provided the best — the only — cover. It had protected them, but now the metal was heating to an unbearable level, and he knew he had to get them out of there as quickly as he could. No one was coming into what was left of the building. A bad sign: No immediate help could be counted on.

Dragging Borz out from under what was left of the desk, Bourne knelt to pick him up in a fireman's lift. As he did so, his gaze fell upon a fragment of one of the Singapore blueprints Borz was working on when Faraj had brought him in. He swept it up, folded it, put it in the pocket of his soot-smeared trousers. Then he settled Borz across his shoulder, stood, and searched through the flames for the quickest route out.

The quickest turned out to be among the most difficult. It was filled with flames and burning hot metal fragments. Nevertheless, it was the way to go. There was no telling when a secondary explosion, triggered by ammo or other war materiel in the adjoining buildings, might go off. He knew they would not be able to survive that.

His shoes started to smolder as he crossed the red-hot shards of metal. The intense heat blistered the soles of his feet. He kept going, around a fall of razor-sharp glass shards, twisted metal, frizzled wires, and small fires burning brightly like feral eyes in the dark. The crack and pop of stressed metal was all around them. On his shoulder, Borz began to stir.

Bourne, leaping a fall of soft glass, almost lost his balance. He staggered, repositioned the Chechen on his shoulder, and pressed on. He could see plumes of black smoke rising into the sky now; they were almost there. Then as he rushed through a last wall of flames his robe caught fire.

Laying Borz down, he threw himself onto the ground, rolling in the blackened dirt, smothering the flames. He returned to the Chechen, whose eyes were fluttering open. Borz's bodyguards came at a run, knelt on either side of their fallen leader.

"He's just shaken up," Bourne said. "He'll be fine."

"Go get the medic," one of the men shouted, and the other hurried off.

Standing, Bourne took in the devastation. The C-17 was a twisted wreck, shorn in two. The landing strip was blown apart. Clods of earth lay everywhere, as if a

262

gigantic hand had scooped out the packed dirt, tossing it every which way. The tail section of the C-17 lay in the smoking crater more or less in the center of the strip. But it was in the area surrounding the strip that the true nature of the disaster was revealed. Overhung by titanic billows of black smoke, swirled now with the winds off the mountains, the scene was one of blood and ash. The cries of the wounded rose and fell with the oily smoke.

Borz's Chechens, along with the remnants of Faraj's people, were recovering bodies, laying them out side by side. Bourne rose, moved toward the workforce. He counted a hundred bodies, some without limbs or with great holes carved out of their torsos. Moving closer, he recognized Eisa, his face black, his eyes frozen in amazement.

Bourne's gaze moved from face to face, counting as he did. His heart sank. So far as he could determine, every one of the American recruits was dead. And now the Chechens were brandishing mobile phones, taking photos of the overall scene before crouching to snap photos of the individual faces. Though their expressions were grim, they hardly seemed traumatized.

One of Faraj's men Bourne hadn't seen before was crouched over Eisa's corpse. When he felt Bourne beside him he looked up. He was very young. There were tears on his cheeks

"*Allahu Akbar*," he intoned. Allah is great. "Are you hurt?"

"*Alhamdulillah wa shukru lillah*," Bourne returned. Praise and thanks to Allah. "No." He crouched down beside him. "I met Eisa in Damascus. Did you know him?"

"We never met, and yet we were friends." He glanced at Bourne. "I am Aashir Al Kindi." He was a tall, dark young man of no more than twenty. His questing eyes were deep-set on either side of his hawk's nose. The corners of his lips were perpetually curved up, giving him a friendly, gently mocking air.

"Yusuf Al Khatib," Bourne said.

"You're the sniper Faraj picked up at the last moment in Damascus, yes? There's been a lot of chatter about you." He had returned his gaze to Eisa.

"Good chatter, I trust."

"I hear you can take off a lark's beak at a thousand yards."

"News travels fast." Part of Bourne's mind was still on the dead Americans, especially Eisa. "Perhaps we can bury our friend together."

Aashir was silent a moment, then he nodded. Together they took the body to the side. Aashir scrounged up a couple of shovels and they began to work.

"There is no cloth to wrap him in," Aashir said. "No one to say the prayers."

"I've buried many comrades," Bourne said. "I know the prayers."

Aashir paused in his digging. "Thank you, Yusuf."

They returned to their work.

"Was Faraj hurt?" Bourne asked after a time.

"Left shoulder," Aashir said. "It's nothing compared to what happened to —" But he stopped, unable to go on.

264

They finished their work and Bourne said the prayers. Then they covered Eisa.

Returning to where Borz still lay, Bourne saw the medic was almost finished tending to him. He was running a series of simple eye tests to determine if Borz had sustained a concussion. But when Borz saw Bourne, he waved the medic away. His bodyguards helped him to sit up, and Bourne crouched down in front of him.

"Thank you," he said in Russian, then, remembering, in Arabic. "I wouldn't have made it out without you."

"Your desk saved both our lives." Bourne gestured with his head. "All the recruits are dead, the C-17 is destroyed. What happened?"

"American drone strike," Borz said, wincing as he gestured for his men to raise him to his feet. "You buried one of the Americans."

"He was a friend of Aashir's."

"Still, you took him out of the line. You shouldn't have done that." Then he shrugged. "Let's get inside."

They proceeded in a halting manner to the last building of the five, which had come through the attack unscathed. It looked like a combination of schoolroom and barracks, with wooden desks and chairs in the front half, steel-framed bunk beds in the rear.

The bodyguards drew out two chairs and Borz lowered himself into one. Bourne took the other. Borz was given water and a couple of pills by the harried-looking medic, who after administering a superficial check of Bourne's faculties and reflexes scuttled back outside to do what he could for the wounded. Borz drank the water, threw the pills onto the floor, grinding them to dust beneath the heel of his combat boot.

When he spoke again his voice was steadier, more assured. "What happened is what was supposed to happen."

Bourne shook his head. "I don't understand."

"Precise coordinates were leaked to the Americans, as well as a precise date and time. A drone strike, Yusuf, with me as the target. The one thing I didn't count on was them sending in two drones. The bastards wanted to make sure they got me. They might have, too, if it hadn't been for you."

At once, Bourne understood why Borz had dismissed the possibility of Bourne being an American spy: They never would have sent one of their own into ground zero of a drone strike.

"You wanted this destruction?"

Borz smiled. "You're a clever man, Yusuf. Provide your own answer."

And then Bourne recalled the Chechens frantically taking photos of the dead recruits. They were going to disseminate those photos, proof that an American drone had killed a hundred young American boys. The fallout would be massive. The drone program, already under attack in the United States, would be dead, and the president's stature would take a major hit.

"Dupe the Americans into killing their own young men. The plan was brilliant," Bourne said, sickened by the utter barbarity of it. Eisa and those other kids never had a chance. They had been recruited as cannon fodder, as exhibit A in a PR stunt of Machiavellian cunning. Credit where credit is due, Bourne thought. He was up against two brilliant tacticians.

"It was," Borz acknowledged, "and from every angle. Listen, as far as the Americans were concerned, they traveled a long distance because they believed absolutely in our cause. 'To serve is to die,' as the Iranians say. That's what we promised them. They drank the sweet nectar of martyrdom."

"You know Iranians?"

"Does anyone know them?" Borz shrugged. "I do business with them from time to time. But only sporadically. They're — how to put it? — unreliable. They always have their own inscrutable agenda."

He turned away. Clearly, he had more important things on his mind. "Unfortunately, we had to sacrifice the plane," he said. "It was a necessity, but it will also present some difficulties for us. Namely, we're going to have to leave here on foot, and to do that in complete safety we're going to have to gain the permission of Khan Abdali, the local tribal leader."

"That's a problem?" Bourne said.

Borz laughed his weird laugh. "Problem would be an understatement. Abdali is a son of a bitch, one fucking nasty piece of work. He could easily turn us down out of spite. The predominant language here in the valley is a form of Pashto. I was hoping Faraj would bring someone who spoke Abdali's godforsaken dialect, but —"

"Not to worry," Bourne said. "As it happens, I speak Wazirwola."

"Rampant consumerism," Hunter said, rapid-fire. "That is capitalism's end. That is where America is now."

The rain had lessened to a drizzle. Above them, the sky was scrubbed clean, the last of the clouds shredded like gauze. They rode side by side, like companions in a Hollywood western. Six-shooters holstered on their hips were all that were missing.

"You have only to listen to the country's economists, who to a man shout at the tops of their lungs that since the Great Recession the only path to renewed prosperity is for the American consumer to consume more and more. Always more."

The sun, a red disk throwing off light but not heat, seemed to throb in the sky like a giant heart. A bluebird screamed a warning, headed for the safety of the trees, while high up a hawk circled lower. As if by mutual consent, the women slowed their mounts to a walk.

"Democracy is gone, corrupted beyond recognition." Hunter glanced at Camilla. "In your heart you know it even if you won't admit it. Since 9/11, we have been living in what amounts to a police state masquerading — not very successfully, I might add — as a pseudo-democracy. The Patriot Act is nothing more than a fascistic document that tramples all over citizens' rights. I mean, what does America export except Coca-Cola and 3-D movies? Militarism. Imperialism, colonization in the name of planting the flag of America's consumerism everywhere. The corruption and betrayal of the people spreads and

268

spreads. It's got to be stopped. There is no other choice for right-minded people like you and me."

Hunter, reaching out, put a hand on Camilla's forearm. At once, the horses halted, snorting.

"You were betrayed by both POTUS and Anselm," Hunter said more softly. "You're not alone." Her eyes searched Camilla's. "The choice is this: After being kicked in the head, you can either lie down and take it, or you can stand up and fight back."

Camilla's brows knit together. "I dunno, Hunter. Against such powerful men —"

"There is a way." Hunter's voice, though still low, became more urgent. "For decades now America has been entangled in unwinnable wars that have drained its finances and divided its increasingly radicalized political parties. Iraq is a hotbed of al-Qaeda activity. The government has turned Islamic. The war in Afghanistan has had the unintended effect of strengthening the Taliban's hand and making the country, along with Iran and Syria, one of the biggest exporters of jihadists. In addition, most of Benghazi has become another al-Qaeda stronghold. France and Britain are either ineffective or have withdrawn from the world stage, leaving America without effective allies. Why does the country continue on this path? What it refers to as policing the world is in reality imposing its corrupt values on other countries. Everyone sees it, except the Americans themselves.

"What passes for culture these days? Wall-to-wall Kardashians, a naked Miley Cyrus making faces at us, Jay-Z ranting at us while he rakes in millions. Adults are reading books meant for preteens. Hollywood no longer makes movies, just franchises. As for television, it's been reduced to trafficking in human humiliation in order to survive. And everyone rushing through the streets, furiously multitasking during the day, popping pills to sleep at night. America is in the late stages of decline. The game is up. The delusion is about to evaporate." Her grip on Camilla tightened. "You can do nothing, remain a victim of these powerful men, or you can make a difference. The choice, Cam, is yours."

"Islam can't be your real name," Soraya said.

He shrugged. "What does it matter? We are all the same."

She lifted her head. "That's what you're taught? That you're all interchangeable."

"No one individual is more or less important than the next."

"Does that include El Ghadan?" she said. "No. El Ghadan is your leader. He is as different from you as night from day."

He was so close that Soraya actually felt his smile through the scarf wrapped around his face.

"Are you trying to undermine his authority? Please. In the future keep your opinions to yourself."

While he had been talking, Soraya was studying him intensely.

"Now, come," he said. "Sonya is finished. You must eat."

His use of her daughter's name sent chills down Soraya's spine. This, too, was part of their system,

270

engendering a false intimacy. She was all too familiar with Stockholm syndrome, which had been incorporated into Treadstone's infamous anti-interrogation program, so harsh it finally had been shut down by the powers that be. She knew how to combat their system.

"Leave me alone, Islam."

He grunted, leaned over her. "What is the matter with you?"

"Please," she said. "Please leave me alone." She despised the weak, begging tone, but it was necessary. "I'm ill."

"Ill? What do you mean?"

"I want to sleep."

"You just woke up."

"Yes, yes, I'm ill. I have no appetite."

Crouching down, he stared hard into her eyes. "You're very pale."

She looked back at him, mute and unmoving.

"All right," he said. "I'll return in a couple of hours. If you're still feeling ill or are worse I will call in a physician." He continued to watch her, abruptly uncertain, it seemed. "You must miss your husband."

"Please." Soraya closed her eyes to keep back the tears.

"This is war, Soraya. He was the enemy, even if you and your daughter are not."

Soraya's eyes flew open. "Then let us go."

His smile seemed to have no emotion behind it, and again she was chilled by how alien his extremist views had made this young man. In another life he could have had a good job, gone back to his family every evening for a hot meal, and, once in a while, a clandestine bout of sex with a like-minded young woman. Instead, here he was, on the brink of death, his fondest wish to die a martyr. How horrible the world has become, she thought, to allow the creation of this man and thousands just like him, an army of unfeeling golems, marching to their certain deaths without a care or a flicker of emotion.

She shuddered.

"What is it?" Islam said. "Do you feel more ill already?"

I am ill, Soraya thought, because I have been a part of this work — a willing participant — and what toll has that extracted from me? Already, her few years with Aaron seemed like a dream, a life that belonged to someone else she had once glimpsed on the street. It was her former life at Treadstone that loomed large in her memory — vivid in every detail as if she had lived it all yesterday. There was nothing about those years she had forgotten or would forget. Each decision, brief, mission, every hour of her fieldwork was etched into her brain, never to be excised until the day she died. With a sinking heart, she understood that despite her best efforts, their incarceration had begun to get to her, to play tricks with her mind. If only Sonya wasn't with her. If only the sky was green, as in her stories about the djinn.

"Soraya?"

"It's nothing, Islam."

She could tell, even through his headscarf, that he didn't believe her. And that was good: She was drawing him closer to her.

CHAPTER
TWENTY-NINE

The stars had aligned for Sara. She had dealt harshly with Levi Blum's controller, and, through Blum's unorthodox but effective methodology, had inveigled her way into El Ghadan's inner circle.

And yet her enthusiasm was curbed by her field sense, now returned to her in full force, that something was not right. Feeling like the princess atop her stack of comfy mattresses still discomfited by the presence of the pea, she walked along the windswept Corniche alone and in a kind of permanent agony for Aaron, Soraya, and their daughter. The thought of Aaron's death and the others' continuing incarceration gnawed at her.

Having come this far, she felt as if she were in a trap, able neither to go on, because of Bourne's warning not to attempt to free Soraya and Sonya, nor to retreat, because of how near she was to her target.

With vivid clarity, she remembered her father's repeated admonition that sailing too close to the wind, though exhilarating, could capsize your boat. That was the situation in which she now found herself. With El Ghadan she was sailing very close to the wind indeed.

274

One false move and she could find herself without a craft, and drowning.

She was still in her Qatari robes and headscarf, not daring to be seen in public without them now. She had contacted her father via their ultra-secure line, giving him the new lay of the land. In response, he had sent her two pieces of product to pass on to El Ghadan. She was contemplating which one to lead with when a black American SUV slowed beside her.

The instant it drew to a halt, the shotgun door opened and a slim young man stepped out. He wore a Western suit and looked good in it. He didn't look like a jihadist, but Sara supposed that was the point.

Smiling, he opened the rear door, said, "Weapons?"

"In Doha?" Sara held her arms out from her body. "You tell me."

"Get in," he said with the kind of contemptuousness she had become inured to in Arab men.

She came off the Corniche, ducked, and climbed into the backseat. The interior of the SUV seemed as large as a studio apartment. Across the burnished leather seat from her sat El Ghadan, looking for all the world like a sultan of the Ottoman Empire.

"Good evening, Ellie Thorson," he said, using the name she had given him before departing Nite Jewel. "Are you well?"

She laughed. "You're not one for small talk, are you?"

El Ghadan made a face. "What gave me away?"

"Your lack of sincerity."

"I'll have to work on that."

275

"Don't bother."

The SUV pulled away from the curb, began its slow circuit of the city's crescent harborfront. Sara could tell the driver had no particular destination in mind. Not yet, anyway.

El Ghadan, head turned away from her, stared out the window. "You don't seem to exist, Ellie." His head swung around, his eyes fully on her. "Can you explain this?"

"I don't think I have to," Sara said.

"I don't like dealing with people whose identities are unknown to me."

"I don't like dealing with jihadists," Sara said evenly, "and yet here we are. Strange bedfellows."

"What?"

"Never mind."

"What is your real name?"

"I imagine El Ghadan is not the name you were born with."

"You must tell me."

"My anonymity guarantees my effectiveness."

She sat very still. He seemed to be weighing her words carefully.

"I have product for you, El Ghadan. Either we do business or we don't." She shrugged. "You're the one who needs an eye on the Israelis."

"I had one," El Ghadan said. "Or rather, Khalifa did. He was running the man who brought you to Nite Jewel."

"Blum." She nodded. "He wanted me to vet Khalifa's lieutenant."

276

El Ghadan grunted. "It seemed to me he also wanted you there for protection."

Sara allowed the ghost of a smile to cross her lips. "Perhaps that as well."

"That does not speak well of him, as either a Semite or a man."

Sara chose not to respond.

El Ghadan sighed. "I may as well tell you that my current thinking is to take you in and sweat you."

"Sure," she said. "What do you need me for? Did you clean house here? Yes? No? Go back to using Blum. Khalifa did that and where is he now?"

El Ghadan's eyes narrowed. "Are you saying Blum set up Khalifa's death?"

"I'm saying you'll never know. Does that make continuing with Blum a decent bet?"

"As it happens, Khalifa's house was rotten to the core."

"You're welcome."

He shook his head. "You're too smart to be a woman."

With no little effort, Sara kept her ghost of a smile, but her expression seemed frozen in place, as if she had looked upon Medusa. "For all the women of the world I take offense."

"You cannot fathom how offensive it is to have you in my vehicle." El Ghadan showed her his teeth. "Now I will see the product you have for me."

"I suppose it's offensive as well for you to have a woman as your eyes."

He looked away, staring out at the city through the smoked glass window. "You have a price, I imagine."

Sara named it, knowing it was very high. But then cheap product was of interest to no one.

El Ghadan snapped his fingers, and the man riding shotgun up front handed over an ostrich-leather case. Rolling the lock tumblers beneath his finger, El Ghadan opened the case, counted out the money, put it on the seat between them. Then he looked expectantly at Sara.

She handed over the part of the product her father had sent — an ultra-secret file the Scrivener Directorate at Mossad had cooked up. El Ghadan read it through twice before folding the sheet and putting it away. She waited for a comment. Outside, the Corniche flickered past, neon lights skimming the waves like flying fish. She longed to be out in the sea-soaked air, away from this monstrous creature who frightened her more than she cared to admit.

He gave her a portion of the bills on the car seat, put the rest back in the case. "The other half after your product is checked for accuracy."

"It's good as gold."

He appeared unmoved. "This is what we shall do. My choice is Blum or you, is that right?"

"Frankly," she said crisply, boldly, "I don't see that you have a choice at all." She was all in now, every chip she had on the table, riding on this one hand, winner take all.

"You see, if your product is good, then I believe you," El Ghadan said. "In that event, I must think the worst of Blum, and he will be shot dead, just like Khalifa's lieutenants."

Bourne was given a new robe, which more or less fit him. He declined a new pair of trousers, not wanting to transfer what he had in his pockets. In the meantime, Ivan Borz spoke to the wounded Faraj, left him in charge of the devastated field. He directed Bourne to a jeep undamaged in the twin blasts. Aashir, the group leader who had spoken to Bourne directly after the drone attack, was already behind the wheel. With Bourne and Borz in the back, Aashir drove them west for just over an hour. He drove with seriousness and complete command; it was clear he knew their destination and how to get there. Very possibly, Bourne thought, he had been there before with Borz.

The mountains, blue and purple, bearded crests barely visible behind clouds, reared up in front of them like wild horses. The air was as sharp as a knife edge.

"We are in Mahsud territory," Borz said. "All the tribes hate one another. No one can move freely in Waziristan without a chief malik's assurance of safe passage." He spat over the side. "It's like living in fucking Nazi Germany." Turning to Bourne, he said, "D'you know much about the tribes hereabouts, Yusuf? Speaking the lingo, you must."

"The Waziri fear dishonor over death," Bourne said. "They'll lie, cheat, steal, and flee in order not to be bested by any enemy. The most common mistake outsiders make about them is that they're cowards, when the opposite is true."

"So how would you handle them?"

"If you don't become one of them," Bourne said, "you have no standing with them."

Borz shot him a quick look. "How the fuck do you do that?"

"Good Lord," POTUS exclaimed. "This has disaster written all over it!"

His hand trembled as he read the SITREP Marty Finnerman had brought over from the Pentagon, along with Vincent Terrier, the fieldman whose network had tracked Faraj's C-17 to the remote valley of the Mahsud in Waziristan.

Morning light slanted in through the Oval Office windows. The reinforced concrete antiterrorist blocks, still in shadow, loomed larger than ever, marking the perimeter of the public sector of which the White House was the center.

"A hundred casualties — all of them young American boys." POTUS looked up at Anselm, Finnerman, and Terrier as if they were a trio of giant owls that had roosted on the corners of his desk. "How the fuck can this be justified, Marty? For the love of God, my drone program has just blown up in my face."

"Not so," Anselm said, knowing that the faster they fed POTUS their spin the quicker they could deflect him from his path to PR ruin. "First, we remind the public of the full list of terrorist leaders the drones have dispatched. We emphasize how much more secure the United States is now that these extremists are dead."

280

Finnerman took up the baton. "Next, we point out as simply and clearly as possible that these Americans were not only defectors, they were traitors to their country."

"We play up the fact that they were recruited here at home," Anselm went on. "We parade the recruiter, fill the press with photos of him, background on how insidious his network was until we rolled it up."

"Is this true?" POTUS looked from Finnerman to Anselm. "Do we have him? Have we rolled up his network?"

"We will have done," Finnerman said in the tone, both authoritative and soothing, POTUS responded to best, "when we go public with the story. Terrier here will make sure of that, won't you, Vinnie."

Terrier nodded. "You can count on it, sir."

Anselm gestured. "There, you see? The point is to get out in front of this, turn a potentially damaging story into one that underscores your administration's continuing dedication to national security."

POTUS wiped sweat from his upper lip. "But these young men —"

"Are traitors," Finnerman said. "And in times of war traitors are summarily executed."

"The point we'll make," Anselm said, leaning forward to better bring their plan home to POTUS, "is that these Americans were recruited at home, voluntarily and illegally, I might add, and traveled to Syria to be trained by Abu Faraj Khalid, one of the most notorious terrorist leaders."

"Who Terrier's network assiduously tracked from Damascus to Waziristan," Finnerman continued, "where we unleashed two drones to destroy him and interdict his plan to return these brainwashed American men as parts of local terrorist cells."

"By the time our media blitz is over," Anselm said, "you'll be hailed by conservatives and liberals alike as a hero. I'll wager even the Tea Party will be pleased."

"And then," Finnerman said when they were alone in the privacy of Anselm's office, "we can get on with our real business."

Anselm nodded. "Making POTUS look good when the peace summit falls apart next week."

"When Jason Bourne is shot dead in Singapore during his attempt to assassinate POTUS, we will release the photo of him with Faraj. That's all we'll need to convince POTUS and Congress that we need to go to war in order to protect him, the United States, and the free world."

CHAPTER
THIRTY

Khan Abdali was a cadaver of a man — tall and impossibly thin, with bony shoulders and long, ropy arms. His skin was as dark as stained teak, thick-looking, grained and lined as leather. It was impossible to tell his age; he could have been anywhere from fifty to seventy. He was dressed in white robes and loose trousers over which he wore a blue vest embroidered with tribal emblems. His gold-colored turban was as large as his head. But it was his eyes, dark, deeply inset in his face, hard as marbles, that caused him to fill up any room he entered or occupied.

The chief malik met them at the outskirts of the village. He was flanked by six of his heavily armed men, bearded, turbaned, all with black vests over white robes, all with assault rifles The village behind them was nothing more than a loosely grouped selection of concrete boxes, some whitewashed, some not, surrounded by pockmarked concrete walls. There were lines of dust-caked trucks, looking the worse for wear, having been driven hundreds of miles over the rocky terrain. Children climbed in the backs of the trucks, and above them, on a dusty promontory, two solitary sentinels, AR-15s at the ready, peered mistrustfully down from behind semicircular stone emplacements.

Bourne spoke the traditional greeting, right hand over his heart. Khan Abdali, clearly surprised, came forward and returned the greeting.

"You know our land?" he said.

"I spent three years here," Bourne said.

"And why did you leave?"

"Over a woman."

"Oho!" Khan Abdali threw his head back and laughed. "And did you take her?"

"From a malik of the Tori Khels."

"Bah! I spit on all Tori Khels!" And Khan Abdali did just that, hawking and spitting a huge glob onto the earth to one side. "And did this accursed malik come after you?"

"I let him," Bourne said.

Khan Abdali's shaggy eyebrows raised. "Did you now?"

"Yes. I confronted him. I told him I was a djinn. I told him I had put a spell on his woman and that if he did not leave us both alone I would put a spell on him and he would die a long, slow, agonizing death."

Now Khan Abdali was fairly shaking with laughter. Indeed, tears were streaming from his eyes and he could scarcely catch his breath. Gasping, he was finally able to say, "My dear Yusuf, you are a man of rare courage and imagination. I am grateful to welcome you into our village, despite the fact you are in the company of this impossibly rude Chechen."

284

Tea, preserved olives, and a sweetish flatbread were served in Khan Abdali's own house, the living quarters strewn with afghan rugs and Turkish brass oil lamps, any one of which could have held Bourne's fictional djinn. The walls were covered with black-and-white blowups of what appeared to be the chief malik's men and children. There were no photos of the village's women, which came as no surprise to Bourne, whose knowledge of the Waziri was such that he knew they valued their women above their religion. These people were not fanatics; they therefore did not understand the fanatics who had infested their mountains and valleys and did not much like them. It was only because the tribes were too busy with their internecine warfare that they did not unite to drive the fanatics out. Besides, Waziristan was vastly underpopulated. A couple of hundred fanatics made little difference to them, unless they became a nuisance. Or asked for favors.

"Your children are magnificent, Khan Abdali," Bourne said, being deliberately overeffusive. "My hearty congratulations."

The chief malik smiled, showing two gold teeth and more than one space between them. "Children and grandchildren, Yusuf, my brother."

"Truly Allah has blessed you."

"May his beneficent light be ever upon us."

The three men sat on one of the rugs, cross-legged, eating and drinking. Aashir lounged against one wall, burning eyes taking everything in, no matter how minuscule, while Bourne continued to chat with the chief malik, gaining information about the current state of tribal warfare in this part of Waziristan. He could tell that Borz was growing impatient, especially because he could not understand the conversation. When Borz began to fidget, Bourne felt compelled to admonish him to remain calm.

"Your friend has a harsh face," Khan Abdali said. "It complements his impatient manner."

"These Chechen," Bourne said. "Impatience is in their blood."

Khan Abdali, refilling Bourne's cup from a copper kettle, nodded sagely. "Such is the tragedy of men, always rushing headlong to their doom." He tipped his head discreetly. "And the young Arab?"

"His name is Aashir Al Kindi, and he has been kind to me," Bourne said. "That is all I know about him."

"I have seen him here before. He has better manners than the Chechen."

"I have no doubt," Bourne said.

"Perhaps you will teach him to speak our language."

"If we both find the time, I certainly will."

The chief malik nodded, apparently satisfied. "What is it the Chechen wants from me, Yusuf, my brother?"

"He requires safe passage for himself and his men."

"Direction?"

"Due west, into Afghanistan."

Khan Abdali heaved a great sigh. "I have no love for the Afghans, especially the Taliban who, due to the meddling of the Americans, have tightened their stranglehold on the country. I cannot abide their abhorrent views. They have warped religion into a

286

cudgel with which to beat senseless those around them."

"My friend considers the Taliban his enemy," Bourne said, "of that I can assure you."

Khan Abdali cocked his head as he gazed at Borz. "Will he kill Taliban when he reaches Afghanistan with our help?"

Bourne turned to Borz. "It seems he wants you to go to war with the Taliban."

"What?"

"That's his price for safe passage into Afghanistan. He wants Taliban heads."

Borz snorted.

"Watch yourself," Bourne cautioned.

"I am on a deadline. I cannot spare the time, Yusuf."

"I urge you to make the time, Borz. He won't budge, otherwise."

Borz considered a moment. "Tell him okay."

Bourne eyed him. "I won't do that if you're ordering me to lie to him."

"How the fuck is he going to know what we do once we're out of his accursed country?"

"Waziristan has sheltered you, kept you safe, even tolerated you bringing the American drones in. You will give your word and we will take Taliban heads."

Borz gave Bourne a murderous glare. "You said these people lie. So what is the problem?"

Bourne wanted to slam his hand into Borz's face. He set that impulse aside for another day. "I said they might lie in order not to be bested. These are honorable people, Borz. They're not extremists. They have tolerated you, but that could change at any moment. Frankly, Khan Abdali doesn't much care for you. If not for me you would have been sent packing."

Expelling a long held breath, Borz nodded. "All right, and damn him to the lowest level of hell."

Bourne turned back to the chief malik. "Khan Abdali, my brother, my friend is in many ways uncivilized. Nevertheless, he means well and is honorable. He gives you his word that after crossing over into Afghanistan, he will take many Taliban heads."

The chief malik stroked his beard thoughtfully. "I agree, Yusuf, my brother, the Chechen is uncivilized. On the other hand, he has you as a friend. I will agree to the safe passage, but I will have two of my best hunting maliks guide you. They will make the crossing with you. They will help you take Taliban heads."

And make sure Borz keeps to his word, Bourne thought, with a smile and the requisite effusive show of thanks to Khan Abdali.

Before departing, Khan Abdali took Bourne aside. "Yusuf, my brother," he said softly but intensely, "I fear treachery on every side of you." His breath was redolent of dates and preserved olives. "I wish you a long life." He took hold of Bourne's right hand, turned it palm upward. "To that end, I give you this." He placed something small but heavy in Bourne's palm, closed Bourne's fingers around it in order to hide it. "It is a *chīlai* — a bracelet. It is both a talisman and a weapon. Inside is a *mangèr*."

288

"A serpent?"

Khan Abdali smiled a curious smile. "This snake is only as long as your fingernail. But, Yusuf, my brother, it is coated with a fastacting poison. The *mangèr* will keep you safe in times of extreme darkness, yes?"

"Thank you, Khan Abdali." Bourne slipped the bracelet over his left wrist. "You are most generous — and most wise."

The chief malik nodded. "Safe travels, my brother."

The dust cloud the jeep threw up upon its rattling departure soon obscured the village and all its inhabitants.

Vincent Terrier sat in a windowside booth in Jake's World, a chromium-clad diner in rural Virginia with fifties-era aqua trim and picture windows overlooking the ashy parking lot and the interstate. From the parking lot, it looked like a vintage jukebox lying on its side. The outdoor lights were on as twilight was shouldered aside by the coming night.

Terrier dug into a slice of indifferent apple pie, sipped impoverished coffee, and thought of *Nighthawks*, Edward Hopper's iconic painting of the Depression-era patrons of a New York City diner. The painting perfectly captured the existential emptiness of Terrier's life, a life begun in the filthy tenements of Detroit, where his father had been an autoworker before being laid off, his emptied plant a symbol of Middle America's creeping death. And what of young Terrier himself: product of a negligent public school education, a state college where he was high all the time, and then

. . . work? Not on your life. Not a decent job to be had for a hundred miles around, though he washed dishes for a time and was a gravedigger for a cemetery sadist for barely six months. Otherwise, his needle was stuck on empty.

With no prospects and no future, Terrier had joined the armed forces, where he served three tours of duty in the Horn of Africa, Iraq, and, latterly, Afghanistan. It was in the Afghan mountain strongholds of the enemy that he received his Saul of Tarsus moment. The people he discovered in the caves high up in the mountains were women and children, some no more than a year old, ragged and perpetually starving. Their eyes were the eyes of old men who had seen too much of a life without either prospects or future.

As Terrier harked back to his own bankrupt beginnings, he at last understood how easy it was for the extremists to recruit these children before they even became men. The clever bastards gave the kids both prospects and a future, the only future available to them: They were fed, clothed, housed, armed, and all the while the poison of indoctrination was being pumped into them. For these kids it was a matter of survival, nothing more or less. Hate gave them a reason for being alive; the prospect of martyrdom, a promise that their deaths would be meaningful to both themselves and their families.

Terrier returned from Afghanistan a changed man, but not in the manner of many of his fellow soldiers. He applied to the DOD, and was immediately snatched up both because of his experience and his innate intelligence. He trained for six months at the Farm, then another three months at the Dairy, before being dispatched as a fieldman, returned to the hot spots of the Middle East with which he was so familiar. He spoke the lingo, he knew the minds of the people. He was the perfect weapon.

To the delight of his handlers and their masters, he unfailingly accomplished the objectives of his briefs. At some point, he came to the attention of Marty Finnerman, who, with his keen eye for talent, appropriated Terrier as his own dog in the hunt, running him on brief after brief, collecting invaluable product on the movements and the ever-morphing tactics of the elusive enemy.

Which was how Terrier had come to be brought by his handler into the West Wing to brief POTUS.

The lights in the diner shone off Terrier's empty plate, with its last bits of lard-soaked crust. Outside, a monstrous midnight-blue '72 Chrysler Imperial, in cherry condition, turned into the parking lot. Terrier raised a hand, called over the waitress, and ordered two coffees.

The searchlight headlamps of the Imperial were switched off. The wide grille reflected the diner's neon glow. He watched the figure exit the car, trot up the concrete steps, and enter the building.

Hunter looked around, spotted Terrier, and slid into the other side of his booth just as the coffee was brought to the table. She wore stained jeans, cowboy boots, and a denim shirt under a suede jacket, which she did not bother to take off.

"All that's missing is fringe on your jacket," he said with a wry tone.

"And fuck you too," Hunter said with a small laugh.

"Couldn't you come in a less conspicuous vehicle?" he said. "Like a Honda or a Chevy, maybe?"

Hunter sipped her coffee. "You love my Imperial."

And it was true, he did. It was a symbol of what America had been at its height and now was no more. It gave him a warm feeling in the pit of his stomach, a reaffirmation of the correctness of the path they had chosen.

"How are things at the Dairy?" he said.

"My, aren't you coy this evening." Hunter eyed him critically. "Your performance went down a storm. Camilla believed it completely."

"And have you taken advantage?"

"What d'you think?"

"So." He put his hands on the table. "What is your assessment?"

"She's going to be fine. She has precisely the right background, as you know, since you whispered her name in Finnerman's ear. That fucking father of hers embodies everything that's wrong with the consumerist imperium America has become."

"Kudos to her for seeing the truth," Terrier said. He drank off half his coffee, which was already cool. "Tell me she'll be ready by the time she's shipped off to Singapore."

"Stop worrying."

Hunter pushed her cup away; Terrier could scarcely blame her.

"Camilla is a very accomplished young woman; her ability to learn and absorb is astonishing."

Now it was Terrier's turn to eye her critically. "So that's how it is."

"I'm not sleeping with her."

"Yet." He gave a nonjudgmental laugh. "You still have a couple of days to rectify that."

Hunter grinned, then said, "What's doing in the world beyond the Dairy?"

He passed her a manila envelope. "For our mutual friend."

"Really?"

"It will seal the deal."

"Beautiful." Hunter slipped the folder onto the seat beside her. "Okay, then."

Terrier hunched forward. "The big boys are planning one massive spin on the drone strike debacle. Pulling out all the stops — the Americans were recruited on homeland soil, came to Syria of their own accord, indoctrinated by Faraj."

"In other words, traitors."

"Right. They posed a grave and imminent danger to America, blah, blah, blah."

"It might work."

He nodded. "Better than even chance." He shrugged. "But then again maybe not. There'll be plenty of outrage from overseas, not to mention the antidrone lobby."

"Which we encourage in every way possible."

Terrier leaned forward, lowered his voice. "But here's the kicker. Finnerman wants me to roll up a local network as the extremists who did the local recruiting."

"That's a joke," Hunter said.

Terrier nodded. "But only to us."

"Have you picked a likely target?"

He smiled. "What d'you think?"

One of the racing bikes in the rack outside the barn went missing while Hunter was fetching her Imperial. Camilla was on a narrow pathway above the road that Hunter took to Jake's World diner. The night was clear, and she had no difficulty in following the Imperial's wide red trail. She knew that if Hunter was going more than five miles, she'd lose her, but intuition told her that wherever she was going was close enough to the Dairy.

The ways in and out of the Dairy were heavily manned, of course, and there was no way Camilla could pass through without showing her credentials, which was out of the question. She was going AWOL, at least for a short time, and she knew she needed to leave no trace of her leaving or returning.

On one of her horseback rides, she had spotted what she believed was a hole in the net that surrounded the Dairy like a castle moat. She might have thought about riding Dixon, but she had been afraid of the sound of his hooves. Plus, his absence from his stall at this time of night would inevitably be recorded. The bike was silent, as well as compact. She had made the right choice — the hole in the Dairy's net proved impossible

294

for a horse, even without its rider. A large buck had tried to leap over the net, but its underbelly had caught on the razor wire atop it, and it had bled to death. Its weight had brought the net down without causing a break in the electronic circuit — a definite design flaw. Camilla walked the bike over the deer's back. Once, on the downslope, she had to reach out, grab hold of the tines of an antler to steady herself. She felt the innate power of the animal even in death, and briefly mourned its demise, which seemed as arbitrary and unnecessary as a soldier's on the battlefield. Still holding on, she blessed the deer for providing the bridge to her exit.

It was inevitable that the Imperial would get ahead of her, but that too was no problem, for she saw it heading directly for the bright jukebox lights of the diner.

Hunkered down inside her leather jacket and pedaling for all she was worth, she arrived five or six minutes after Hunter pulled up and went inside. Wheeling around to the rear, she surprised a trio of fat raccoons, who leered toothily at her from their spot beside two green Dumpsters. She shone her flashlight into their eyes, forcing them to lumber grumpily into the shadows.

Dismounting, she leaned the bike against the rear stairs, then trotted up and through the door, striding through the kitchen as if she belonged there. The staff was too busy to notice her, and in any event, she had reached the corridor where the toilets were located before any of them had a chance to turn from their duties.

She spotted Hunter right away, sitting on one side of the booth, talking earnestly, but she had to maneuver a bit to catch a glimpse of the person she was huddled with.

When she did, a chill slithered down her spine, as if someone had slipped a snake inside her shirt. Hunter was in conversation with Vincent Terrier, the man she had claimed to loathe, and by the look of high animation on her face Camilla could tell that their discussion was of a highly clandestine nature.

She took another step to the side, could lip-read some of what they were saying. Fuck me, they're in this ideological shit together. Terrier was the beater, driving me closer to Hunter, she thought, wiping away the beads of cold sweat that had formed at her hairline.

CHAPTER
THIRTY-ONE

Stars fell on the Mahsud's valley in Waziristan in such profusion that the sky seemed white in places. Deep in a night blanketed with an eerie silence devoid of either insect buzz or bird call, Bourne stood gazing at the wreckage of the C-17. The bracing air still reeked of burned insulation, burst-apart concrete, melted plastic, and the unmistakable horrific barbecue stench of charred human flesh.

"I can't sleep either."

Bourne turned to see Aashir slouching toward him, hands in pockets, head slightly tucked into his narrow shoulders. He stared mournfully at the ruined runway. "I never expected this."

"What did you expect?" Bourne said.

Aashir shrugged. "I didn't think about it. I was too busy planning my getaway."

"From what?"

Aashir didn't immediately answer, and when he did, it was obliquely. "I had a friend. A girl. That's not supposed to happen — or, anyway, it's not allowed. We met anyway. We thought we were being discreet, but, you know, there are so many wagging tongues, so many eagle eyes watching out for single men and women together. Spies, you know, with nothing else to do except enforce sharia law, tell their tales, and bring the hammer of justice down." He laughed bitterly. "Hammer of sexism is more like it."

Now Bourne was listening closely. This story interested him. It marked Aashir as someone other than an extremist. What he was doing embedded in Faraj's jihadist cadre was still a mystery.

"You won't tell anyone I said that, Yusuf."

"Of course not. As I've pointed out to Borz, I'm a pragmatist, not a zealot."

"Unlike Faraj and El Ghadan, whose infatuation with fanaticism is absolute." Aashir's voice, following his expression, had turned mournful, like a sax playing a minor-key melody. "They will kill and, eventually, be killed for it."

"And what is it you want for yourself, Aashir?"

"Freedom, I suppose." He shrugged again. "But, really, I don't know what that means."

"To be free."

"Yes."

Bourne wondered if anyone knew. Everyone was tied to their lives. Did that make them prisoners, or free men?

They walked side by side, staring straight ahead. It was a fact of life that it was easier to talk to a stranger about personal matters than it was to someone you knew.

"What are you doing here?" Bourne asked.

Aashir shrugged. "Can you think of a better place to hide?"

"You can't hide here forever," Bourne pointed out. "Besides, you know we're moving out as soon as all the wounded are in stable condition."

"Afghanistan is as good as here, I suppose." Aashir gestured vaguely. "Where else should I go, Yusuf? To the West? To join the people who dropped napalm, white phosphorus, bunker busters, air-to-ground missiles, and the largest array of state-of-the-art engines and vehicles of death ever assembled upon millions of innocent Vietnamese, Cambodians, Iraqis, Pakistanis, Afghans, not to mention Libyans and Yemenis?" He shook his head. "No. There is nowhere for me to go, except here with Faraj."

"As you yourself pointed out, Aashir, this is temporary shelter at best. Faraj and El Ghadan are bent on the destruction of not only their enemies but themselves. Where will that lead you? Injured, or dead, like those being buried out on the side of the runway? You don't want that. Go home. Home is where you belong. You have unfinished business there."

Aashir shook his head as they continued to walk out toward the mountains, away from the killing field, where the stench of death was being superseded by quicklime. "You don't understand."

"Tell me, then."

Instead, Aashir changed the subject. "I've heard you're an ace marksman. Is that true?"

"It is."

"Why do you do that?"

Bourne considered a moment. "There is a certain satisfaction in mastering a skill — any skill."

299

"Would you teach me?"

Bourne nodded. "If you wish."

Aashir cocked his head, regarded Bourne from the corners of his eyes. "What are you doing here, Yusuf?"

"I'm a misfit," Bourne said truthfully. "For as long as I can remember, I've felt like an outsider. I'm not like other people; I have different interests."

"Like staring into the war from the other end of a long gun."

"Yes, but that came later."

This was another of Bourne's innate skills, to listen to the questions, silences, and hesitations of another person, and from them intuit their secret histories.

Aashir, with his full attention on Bourne, said, "So tell me, what came first?"

"A feeling of being set adrift on an endless sea."

"Out of sight of land — and my parents." Aashir seemed to be musing to himself.

"Are they so terrible?" Bourne asked.

"My mother cried when I tried to talk to her, and my father — well, there's no talking to my father. His disappointment in me was like a third person in the room."

"Did you tell him?"

Aashir gave a sad little snicker. "My father is deaf to what he doesn't want to hear."

Bourne had met too many of those kinds of men. In fact his shadow world was rife with them. "Where are you running away from?" he asked.

"It doesn't matter."

The conversation was drawing them inexorably closer, as often happens when strangers meet in extreme circumstances, bond, and become friends.

"Your accent is Yemeni," Bourne said.

Aashir nodded. "You have a good ear, Yusuf. And you are Syrian, I hear. What part are you from?"

Bourne sensed it was time to draw the young man even closer. "I don't know."

Aashir laughed. "How could you not know?"

"I was shot." Bourne showed him the scar. "I fell into the water, was picked up by fishermen, who saved my life. They brought me to a doctor, who fixed my body, but my mind was another matter. I have amnesia. I can't remember anything before the time of the shooting."

Aashir stared at him, making eye contact for the first time since they started their walk, since they had begun to speak of things that mattered to both of them. "You don't remember your mother or father, if you had a family?"

"That's right."

"And your name?"

"I chose it." Bourne gestured. "I would give anything to know what you know — where you were born and raised, who your parents are, brothers, sisters, aunts, uncles, cousins. A place to call home. You shouldn't run away from all that; it's too precious." He stepped in closer. "But listen, you mustn't tell anyone. I gave Faraj a fiction about my background."

Aashir shook his head. "There's no need to worry. I don't tell Faraj anything. He's like my father. What would he understand, anyway?"

They continued to walk; Aashir scuffed at the ground with the toe of his boot. He appeared to be about to say something, then quickly, almost furtively, changed his mind. He looked up at the star-kissed mountains and said, "So what am I doing here, Yusuf?"

"That's a good question, Aashir, but now that we know each other a bit it's not so difficult to answer," Bourne said. "You're doing what every intelligent person your age does. You're finding out who you really are."

Aashir laughed then, and it was a laugh Bourne did not understand.

Sara was being followed. A man in front, a pair in back. For good measure, there was also a car. The owls were to be expected, and she was therefore reassured. The number of men El Ghadan had assigned to her was also reassuring, since it provided further proof that his base was in fact in Doha, as she had suspected. That meant Soraya and Sonya were still in Doha. Somehow, this comforted her, feeling closer to them. But she was still under strict orders from Jason to keep her distance. He had something planned, she knew that much. And frustrating though it might be, she had reconciled herself to not knowing what it was. Better for her, better for everyone, especially now that she had made contact with El Ghadan. It was imperative that he have no suspicion whatsoever that she had any connection to his hostages.

She turned down a street, passed under an ornate gate, entering the bustling Souq Waqif. Here the buildings were all traditional two-story structures of honey-colored stone or whitewashed limestone. Colorful awnings over the shop entrances fluttered in the breeze. Wares were set out — from spices to beaten brass to rugs, and small souvenirs for tourists, some made locally, other cheaper ones manufactured in China to Qatari specifications. Red, blue, yellow, and green parrots squawked on their wooden perches, pecking idly at their leashes or calling to passersby, seeking company or at least a few seeds to munch on.

The car was useless in the souq, which was one of the reasons Sara had come here. The other was Blum. She had successfully discredited him in El Ghadan's eyes, in the process turning his attention to her and away from Levi. This was the plan — at least the first part of it. That it was working perfectly made her uneasy. Often, she had learned, it was when things appeared to be rolling along smoothly that the mission was closest to having the wheels come off.

She trusted El Ghadan about as far as she could lift him, but he was her handler now. That had been the plan she had formulated on the fly as soon as she had recognized him as the man calling her in Nite Jewel. The second part of the plan involved returning Blum to the shadows, where he could again work in secret without being observed.

Of course, at some point in the near future she would have to kill him in order to satisfy El Ghadan. She knew without the jihad leader having to tell her that he would insist she do it; he was furious at having to use a woman as his eyes on Mossad.

Killing Blum posed no problem for her, but it might for Levi. That kind of internal joke was necessary now for her to keep her spirits up as she groped her way through the thorny labyrinth of being a double agent. She was used to leading a double life — if you actually ever got used to such a thing — but handling a triple life was a complication of an entirely different magnitude. If your mind wasn't meticulously and absolutely compartmentalized your artful play-acting could easily fray at the seams, exposing the truth beneath.

All the while she had been musing, she had been strolling at a leisurely pace through the vast market. The idea was to forget about her owls while at the same time keeping strict track of them. They needed to be lulled into a state of boredom more or less like that of the parrots.

She bought a silk scarf, a very old small bronze incense-holder, and an earthenware bowl. After her shopping spree, she sat at a café and spent forty minutes sipping an espresso that could have stripped the verdigris off her incense-holder.

While she sat, face tilted up into a stripe of sunlight falling onto the café terrace, she spotted Blum not once, but twice. He was moving along the second-floor balconies of several buildings across the dusty street. She could tell by the tension in his frame that he was aware of her owls. He never once looked in her direction. He was heading toward their planned rendezvous point.

304

With a deep sigh, she finished her espresso, dropped a few coins on the table, and, gathering up her parcels, rose and left the café. Her owls came with her. The three men, still one in front, two behind. Very unimaginative. By now they were like boarders who had overstayed their welcome — familiar but annoying, especially at this moment.

Keeping to her unhurried pace, she popped into another shop, checking out robes, then an adjacent one that displayed silver jewelry so well crafted she bought a bracelet, wide and gaudy, which she immediately slipped onto her left wrist. She paid too much but she didn't care; there was no time to haggle.

Exiting the shop, she made sure her owls caught a full view of her changed profile: parcels on one arm, the silver bracelet on the other. She turned down the main thoroughfare, which was thick with both locals and tourists. The constant crush made it difficult for the men behind her to keep her in sight; the one in front of her lost her completely. Picking up her pace, she brushed her way through the throng. Timing was everything.

At the very heart of the most congested section of the souq, she ducked into a shadowed doorway, where she stashed her packages in a cobwebbed corner, then skipped lightly up the narrow stone staircase to the second floor.

Behind her, on the thoroughfare, her three owls, front and back, converged on a woman laden with packages, the silver bracelet Sara had purchased on her left wrist. In the crush, Sara had transferred it to join two others. The woman turned, bewildered, but not half as much as Sara's owls.

Above them, Sara crossed one balcony onto another, where Blum was seated at one of the souq's most venerable cafés.

Taking command of the table next to his, she settled herself on a chair away from the balustrade and a view of the souq below. She took another espresso, but asked for a plate of almond cookies to help defray the damage to her stomach lining.

"How goes it?" Blum said

"I'm plotting your imminent demise."

He winced. "Will it hurt?"

"Think of a spiny lobster placed in a pot of water. The heat is slowly turned up. The lobster goes quietly to sleep, dreaming of whatever it is lobsters dream about."

They spoke in undertones, in voices that could not be heard over the murmur of the café patrons and the singsong calls of the merchants below.

Leaning over, she said at a more normal volume, "Pardon me, but I seem to be out of sugar."

He passed her the container stuffed with sugar packets. She plucked three out of the middle, then handed it back. "Thank you."

He saw a tiny hotel tube of toothpaste where the packets had been.

"The first squeeze," she said, back to the undertone.

"And that's it?"

She nodded. "That's it. Now for your update."

"Everything's in place."

Her eyes narrowed. "You're sure."

"Sure I'm sure."

"And there were no owls on you."

"None whatsoever." Blum glanced over the railing at the milling throng. As he did so, he took possession of the toothpaste tube. In the souq, the owls had split up, on the hunt for their missing target. A smile curved his lips like a bow. "I don't know what you said to El Ghadan, but I'm no longer a person of interest."

"Okay," she said, "then let's do this."

He nodded, paid for his coffee, and left via a side entrance that would let him out onto another street. Sara stayed put, slowly munching her almond cookies, and contemplating the death of Levi Blum.

CHAPTER
THIRTY-TWO

"Dinazade was lost in a sea of stars," Soraya said. Sonya was sitting on her lap, her drowsy head on her breast. "She had been lost for a very long time."

"Like us, Mama?"

"Yes, muffin, just like us." Soraya swallowed the lump in her throat.

"How did she get lost in the stars?"

"She was sent there by a wicked wizard who was jealous of Dinazade's beauty. He wanted her beauty for himself. When Dinazade refused, he sent her into a prison he said she could never escape."

"Did she escape, Mama?"

"Patience, darling. You'll have to wait for the end of the story to find out."

"Mama, I have to use the bathroom."

Soraya picked her head up, called for Islam. She had formulated a plan, and it entailed a trip to the bathroom.

Several moments passed, then the door was unlocked and Islam came in, his dark eyes on her.

"Are you feeling more ill, Soraya?"

"I am," she said. "Also, Sonya has to urinate."

He helped her to her feet. The days of constant sitting had affected her legs as well as her balance. She had tried to exercise, to walk, but Islam had stopped her, as if knowing her purpose. This was the one thing that terrified her; if she couldn't run with Sonya in her arms, how could she hope to escape?

Soraya took her daughter's hand, and with Islam close beside her, she crossed the room, went out the door into a featureless corridor. The toilet was the first door on the right. As usual, Islam came in with them. But there was a Western-style stall, into which she took Sonya, closing the door behind them.

"Shall I call the doctor, Soraya?" Islam said from his position beside the sink and mirror. "How ill do you feel?"

Soraya made retching sounds, then said, "It's just something I ate. A doctor isn't necessary, but I could use your help."

She heard him outside the door, and, signing to Sonya to turn around and press her face into a far corner of the stall, she opened the latch. The moment Islam entered, she hit him hard on the point of his chin. His head snapped back, slammed against the door. Dazed, he fell to his knees.

Soraya grabbed her daughter, stepped over Islam, and was about to cross the bathroom to the hallway when Sonya squirmed out of her arms and ran back to where Islam knelt, head bobbing.

"Sonya, what are you doing?" Soraya called in alarm. "Come back here!"

"Islam is hurt, Mama. We have to help him!"

Islam's head came up, his arm snaked around the girl, and Soraya thought in despair, the innocence of children.

She froze, tasting the freedom of the hallway just beyond the door. But that taste turned out to be a mirage. Islam rose and, taking Sonya's hand in his, led her out of the bathroom. He did not even look at Soraya, knowing that wherever Sonya went, Soraya would docilely follow.

Out in the hallway, two armed jihadists were waiting for them.

"You see how foolish you were," Islam said, when they were back in the prison room.

Soraya, terrified because he still had hold of Sonya, sat back on her chair, her hands clasped in her lap like a disobedient schoolgirl. Islam stood in front of her, holding Sonya close against his leg.

"Mama?"

Sonya's lip was quivering, and Soraya knew she was on the verge of tears. Her heart broke all over again. "Hush, muffin. Let Islam speak."

Islam said, "Because I genuinely care about your welfare, and to show you I am not the animal you think I am, I will give you a choice. Promise you will not try to escape again."

She looked at him defiantly. "And if I do not?"

"Then you will force me to take Sonya to another room. You will not see her again until this is all over."

Lunging, Soraya took Sonya, held her to her breast. Islam made no move to stop her.

"Mama," Sonya whispered in her ear, "are we lost in the stars?"

Soraya, tears trembling at the corners of her eyes, looked up at her captor. "I promise." She could not say it fast enough.

"Here's where you learn to fall."

Hunter, astride Dagger, twisted in her saddle to meet Camilla's gaze. It was a misty, windless morning, the eerie stillness seeming to be a harbinger of things to come. The boundaries of the Dairy were obscured and therefore an immense distance away. They were on the oval racetrack at last, with its low whitewashed fences and lanes for seven horses. Here was the final stage of Camilla's training.

"It's not necessary for you to win," Hunter said. "In fact, winning is peripheral to your brief. Finding Bourne and killing him is your order of business. But you'll be among professional jockeys. You need to be one of them, as good as they are — better, if I have anything to say about it."

During a long and sleepless night, Camilla had tried to work out the web of lies in which she was enmeshed. Right now she was being pulled in different directions. Finnerman and Howard had sent her on a mission to stop Bourne, but if Hunter was telling the truth then on another, hidden level, they wanted her gone, killed in the line of duty. One thing was clear, however. Hunter wanted something entirely different from her. She had made up her mind to be the model pupil, to do whatever she was asked while she was at the Dairy. But

311

after she was sent overseas, it was every woman for herself and devil take the hindmost. She had had her fill of being everyone's pawn, from POTUS on down to Hunter. It was time to make her own decisions, and what better place to start than in the field where her own eyes and ears would lead her onto the right path. Her dedication and hard work, rising within the military and subsequently the public sector, all in aid of finding herself a free woman at the top of the food chain — it had all been nothing but a mirage. She saw at last the real truth: No matter how high she rose, men were always pulling the strings, making her dance to their personal tunes.

No more. This she vowed, as a fragile dawn shuffled over the fields and downs of the Dairy.

"I'm not going to fall," Camilla said.

"Of course you're not. But I've been delegated not only to train you but to keep you safe up on your mount."

Camilla nodded slowly, unsurely.

"Okay, this is how you fall," Hunter said, taking off at a gallop.

She was bent low over her mount, her butt slightly off the saddle, perfectly assuming the position of a professional racing jockey. As she came around the first turn, she went head over heels, landing on the packed dirt on her right shoulder. She rolled away from the horse, got her legs under her, and stood up, none the worse for wear.

She whistled, and Dagger turned, trotted back to where she stood against the rail. Camilla urged Dixon forward until she was close enough to smell the lemon of Hunter's shampoo, mingled with the scents of the horses.

"Now it's your turn." Hunter leapt up onto Dagger's back. "Your toes will be in the stirrups. First imperative: Tip them out just before you pitch yourself off the horse. Second imperative: You must wait until your horse is into a turn. He'll be heading to your left, so you'll pitch yourself over his neck to the *right*. That way you'll be completely out of his way; he can't possibly kick you or, worse, trample you to death. Third imperative: Relax your body. This is no doubt the easiest thing to do, since you have already had extensive training in hand-to-hand combat. Fourth imperative: Land on your right shoulder. You'll simply tumble. Just let your momentum take you. You'll be fine. Guaranteed." She nodded. "Okay? Let's try it."

Camilla dug her heels into Dixon's flanks, but the big stallion hardly needed urging. He was off in a flash, taking the second half of the turn and heading into the straightaway. Hunter kept Dagger several strides behind her in order to see the scenario clearly, as well as to be able to come to Camilla's aid should something go wrong.

Halfway down the straightaway, Camilla set her mind on the precise moment she would take her fall. It would be just before the apex of the turn, so that Dixon would be pulling away from her at the maximum angle as she hit the ground.

The turn came up, she hit her mark, but her left toe got caught in the stirrup for just a split second. That was enough, however, to throw her off. Instead of falling, she was obliged to grab on to the saddle. There being no horn, her hand slipped off and she dropped. She grabbed the stirrup, but her feet were now dragging in the dirt. Her body began to twist as Dixon passed the apex of the turn, heading left into the homestretch straightaway.

Camilla tried to fold her legs up, but Dixon's speed was too great. Then she felt a strong arm reaching around her waist and heard Hunter's voice shouting, "Let go! Let go!"

Her terrified mind wanted to hold on for all she was worth, but she let go anyway, felt herself scooped off the ground, swung up and around until she was sitting uncomfortably behind Hunter, astride Dagger. Up ahead, Dixon had slowed, and now, seeing where she was, he turned back at a smart trot until she leaned over and took hold of his bridle.

As Camilla dismounted, Hunter said, "Not exactly how I drew it up. Next time, make sure your boots tips are square in the stirrups. Now mount up. Let's go again. I'm not going to be the one responsible for you getting your brains kicked in. A horse can do that, you know. One kick. Wham!"

The curve of the Corniche, now as familiar as home, stretched out in front of Sara. She felt the cool weight concentrated at the small of her back. The snub-nosed .38 El Ghadan had given her was loaded with hollow-point bullets filled with mercury. You had to be close to your target, but you didn't have to be accurate.

314

The weapon and its ammo were tailor-made for Blum's death.

It was after midnight. Clammy tendrils of fog, rising out of the water like a living creature, were driven onshore by an east wind. Up ahead, Camilla could see Blum silhouetted against the neon skyscrapers. Behind her, at a discreet distance, came the black SUV carrying El Ghadan, his driver, and two bodyguards.

This was a terminal rendezvous, without a fallback or any of the usual safeguards strewn as carefully as a minefield.

She smiled when she came up to him, but her smile was deliberately cold. They were being watched, possibly even recorded. This was play-acting of the highest level; it had to convince even the most hardened cynic.

"You really fucked up this time," she said. "There was no good reason to order Khalifa's death."

"I hated that fucker," Blum retorted, swinging into a rancorous mood from the get-go. "He made my life a living hell."

"He could have supplied you with invaluable product. You were impatient; you allowed your personal feelings to get in the way of business. You're supposed to be a trained fieldman, Blum."

He assumed an aggressive posture. "How could you know?"

"How d'you think? Martine told me."

"She had no business doing that."

"Because of your foolish action, Martine is blown; she almost lost her life. Now I'm involved."

As he took a step toward her, his stance moved from aggressive to belligerent.

"Careful!" she warned.

"Why don't you just get the hell out of my face? It's you who's gumming up the works, not me."

"I can't, Blum. You blew up your brief." Her fingers folded around the grip of the .38. "And now, you see, I have my own brief to complete."

She brought the .38 out, squeezed the trigger. The force of the bullet caught him by surprise. Blood bloomed on the right side of his chest as he was thrown backward so hard he stumbled and then, arms pinwheeling frantically, fell into the water.

El Ghadan stepped out of the SUV even before it had fully stopped. He took the .38 out of her hand, checked the ammo to make sure she hadn't replaced the live rounds with blanks, then gestured to his men.

They ran down the stone steps to the jetty, used gaffs to bring Blum's body to the surface. They hauled him up onto the jetty, while above them El Ghadan and Sara peered down.

"So?" El Ghadan called down.

One of his men squatted down, pressed two fingers against Blum's carotid artery. "He's dead," he said, glancing up.

"Roll him in with full pockets."

El Ghadan watched as his men stuffed Blum's trousers' pockets with rocks and bits of concrete. Then they rose and kicked him back into the water.

He sank before Sara had time to say a prayer.

316

CHAPTER
THIRTY-THREE

"Dinazade was lost in the sea of stars," Soraya sang to her daughter, and then abruptly stopped.

"Islam," she said, though her heart was thumping like mad in her chest. By now, she was used to the rhythms of her captivity; his visit was out of bounds. She pumped up her voice. "How good to see you."

The jihadist grabbed the back of a wooden chair, dragged it over in front of her a good six feet away, and sat down.

"How are you feeling, Soraya?"

"I'm fine." She was aware that her voice was overbright, and she struggled not to bite her lip in self-recrimination.

Islam seemed to smile. It was curious, she thought, how she could tell his expression even beneath the concealing headscarf.

"I know you wouldn't tell me the truth even if your life depended on it." He looked down at his hands with their cupped fingers, then back up again at her. "If you want anything —"

"You know what I want."

"Anything I am able to provide."

Sonya was squirming in her lap, but she remained silent, as she most often did when the two adults were speaking. Soraya knew their tones of voice disturbed her, but there was little she could do. "That's why you came in here."

"Yes."

He stared at her intently. She could tell that his smile had dried up.

"I don't think so."

"No? What do you think, then?"

"It's you who wants something from me, Islam. What could that be?" When he did not respond, she began a kind of singsong intoning: "'Call me Ishmael. Some years ago — never mind how long precisely — having nothing in my purse, and nothing particular to interest me on shore, I thought I would sail about a little and see the watery part of the world.'"

"I hate the sea," Islam interrupted. "I don't want to hear about the sea."

"This is a story about Ishmael, a young man close in name to you, and his captain, a man named Ahab."

"I said —"

"This Captain Ahab was obsessed, like El Ghadan. Ahab's obsession is Moby-Dick, the great white whale that took Ahab's leg and his first ship."

"Not interested."

"But surely you'll be interested in how it ends. Ahab finally finds his white whale — although many people, myself included, believe it's Moby-Dick who finds Ahab, in his new ship. The whale destroys the ship, Ahab, and all who are in it — except for Ishmael. He, alone, was the sane one on a ship manned by the insane. He, alone, is left to tell the tale."

Islam seemed unmoved by her impromptu parable of his own situation. "This is a Western story — one that does not belong to me. I want to hear that song you were singing."

"Not a song," Soraya said, "a story, a myth."

"What language were you singing it in?"

"Farsi. It's a story about Dinazade, lost among the stars."

So this is the reason for his unscheduled visit, Soraya mused. He heard me start to sing to Sonya. This is another step forward for us, she thought. I am drawing him closer and closer.

"Can you sing it in Arabic? I don't know Farsi."

"As you wish." She nodded, and when she recommenced singing her voice changed, as if by magic, the subtle shadings of Arabic different from those of Farsi. She had of course taught Sonya both languages. "Dinazade was lost for a very long time, although in the sea of stars time did not exist. There was never a day or a night. The sun did not rise, nor did it set. The sun was as lost as was Dinazade, lost on another world, in another sky, far, far smaller than the one that held all these stars.

"Dinazade's prison was beautiful, but it was a prison for all that, a prison without either walls or bars. The sea of stars was infinite. In all her wanderings, Dinazade had never come across another soul. Her prison was inhabited by no one else.

"Or so she thought."

Soraya settled Sonya more comfortably in her lap. She did not look directly at Islam, but in the corner of her eye she noted his rapt attention.

She continued: "At some point — it was impossible to say when, since in this prison time did not exist — Dinazade became aware of a stirring beneath her. At first it was just a ripple, so faint she at first thought she had imagined it. But then a second ripple passed over her, stronger this time, like the exhalation of a djinn.

"Gradually, she became aware of something rising up from the infinite space below her. It blotted out the stars as it rose toward her. More and more stars winked out, until she could make out something glinting like metal in the starlight from above. It was not metal. It was the scale of a fish — a fish so vast her eyes could not take in more than an infinitesimal fraction of it.

"On it came, growing vaster until it seemed to Dinazade that the fish was larger than the infinite space through which it swam. The fish's name was Bahamut, and he claimed that all of the world's seven seas could fit into one of his nostrils, like a single grain of sand in the desert.

"On Bahamut's back was a white bull, and on this bull was a ruby mountain, and at the peak of this mountain was a seraph. Do you know what a seraph is, muffin? A seraph is an angel."

"I like angels, Mama."

Soraya smiled, making sure it encompassed Islam as well as her daughter. "We all do, darling."

She took a breath, let it out slowly and completely. "Dinazade spoke to the seraph, begging the seraph to free her from the prison into which she had been so wickedly cast. And do you know what the seraph said to Dinazade, muffin?"

"What, Mama?"

"The seraph said, 'I see you are lost.' The seraph hovered over Dinazade, its expression unfathomable. 'Only you can free yourself, Dinazade.' Then the seraph came closer, the beating of its wings like the murmur of a bee when it lands on a flower. Dinazade stared into the seraph's eyes and saw only herself.

"The seraph whispered in a voice that made it clear it was revealing a secret, 'When you find yourself you will be free.'"

The instant Blum hit the water, after being knocked in by the force of the blank hitting him, he bit down on the tiny ruby pebble that had been embedded at the top of the tube of toothpaste Rebeka had given him in the souq. Fear was a palpable thing, a beast writhing in the pit of his stomach. He did not want to die. Of course he didn't. It was a natural reaction.

Intellectually, he knew that he was not going to die, but already his bodily functions were shutting down, his heart rate slowing, his blood pressure sinking. He thought of all the prep work Rebeka had done. He imagined how she must have walked down the Corniche, out of sight of the black SUV following a half mile behind, how she had extracted one bullet from the .38 El Ghadan had given her, thrown it into the restless, star-strewn sea. In its place, she had chambered a bullet from the several blanks of differing calibers she had made from the Mossad doctor's stores. Replacing the .38 at the small of her back, she had walked on toward her terminal rendezvous with him.

All going to waste now.

The world closed in on him as death rose up from the black depths, enfolding him. He longed to cry out, but he would not open his mouth for fear of drowning. He wanted to cry out: I'm lost! Please find me, someone!

It was death that found him.

The Kidon divers were waiting for him. Their orders were explicit, precise, irrevocable. Everything depended on clockwork timing. When Blum hit the water for the second and final time, they kicked out with their fins, closed in on him, and, like a pair of seraphs, enfolded him in their arms, emptying his pockets of rocks and concrete chunks, swimming toward safety and, for Blum, a return to life.

Camilla, pitching herself off her horse at the apex of the turn, falling perfectly, her relaxed body rolling over on her right shoulder, felt no elation at her success. Becoming aware of Hunter's applause, hearing her shouting, "Brava! Brava!" she felt no satisfaction.

Rather, she was plunged into a sense of loss so deep it seemed to cut her like a knife. She was alone. Alone and lost in a desert populated only by mirages. People who professed to help her, to be her friends, were nothing of the sort. They were merely kings, queens, bishops, and knights on a vast and unknowable

322

chessboard where she was the pawn being shuttled between them in order for one or another of them to gain advantage.

For Camilla this was a familiar sensation. She and her sister had been passed back and forth between her warring parents like burning coals too hot to hold for long. She could vividly recall wandering through the many rooms of the countess's villa, or attending dinners meticulously laid out by a platoon of servants, her teeth grinding at the phenomenal excesses of the super-rich that her father happily basked in as though bathed in Caribbean sunshine.

As she sat with her back against an upright post on the Dairy's racetrack, it occurred to her that she had no one to blame but herself. She had put herself into the emotional position she knew best, the one she had endured as a child. And with this knowledge came the revelation of just how utterly and irrevocably lost she was.

Hunter dismounted, led Dixon back to where Camilla sat. Dixon lowered his head, snorted as she rubbed her palm against his velvet muzzle. She pushed herself up as he urged her on with his head.

Hunter, all smiles, held out her hand for Camilla to shake. "That was perfect," she said, her enthusiasm seeming genuine. "Now we can concentrate on winning."

Was everything Hunter had said to her a lie, even her avowal of protection? It must be, she thought. It must be. She's just like my sister, my father. Another betrayal. POTUS, Howard Anselm, Marty Finnerman,

Terrier, and Hunter. How was it, Camilla wondered, that these people could be so completely duplicitous? How had they successfully walled off parts of themselves, becoming who they were required to be as the situation dictated? In the military, and later in the Secret Service, she had trained to be a protector, not an actor, not a liar, not someone who seemed to revel in preying on people's emotions.

As she gripped Hunter's forceful hand, she had a vision of herself as a tasty fish that had been thrown into a sea filled with ravenous sharks.

CHAPTER
THIRTY-FOUR

There were two reasons why the cadre didn't head out of the valley in the morning. The first was that the wounded required a bit more time to recuperate. The second was that intel relayed to Borz through a method Bourne was yet to detect had put a spy drone in the vicinity, possibly sent to check on the aftermath of yesterday's strike. In any event, Borz deemed it safer to travel by night, at least until they crossed the mountainous border into Afghanistan.

As he had promised Bourne, Khan Abdali had sent two of his best warriors. They were impossibly lean, tall and majestic as Maasai. In addition to the requisite automatic weapons and bandoliers of ammo, they carried at their waists broad swords that looked like scimitars. Bourne knew that the various Waziri tribes often settled their disputes with these swords, as had their fathers and grandfathers before them.

They were sun-fried and taciturn, always keeping to themselves. From time to time they drank water, but refused food; they carried their own: hard, unleavened bread, like the Jews, and chunks of cheese, white as chalk, harder than the bread. They made everyone, save

Bourne, uneasy, especially Faraj, who viewed them as spies.

"I don't like being watched," he said to Bourne at one point. "These people are nothing but trouble."

"No one likes to be cooped up inside all day," Bourne said, "especially these boys."

Because of the suspected American drone and its cameras, no one was allowed outside, in order to give the impression that everyone in the camp had been killed or had fled. Even the jeeps had been pulled into sheds.

Faraj didn't care what the Waziri felt. "Keep a close eye on them," he ordered as he stalked away.

At Aashir's insistence, Bourne spent most of the day teaching him to shoot the L115A3 AWM. They crept out into the blinding sunlight, Bourne showing him how to keep himself hidden in the valley's sparse vegetation.

"A sniper's dead meat if he's spotted," Bourne said in a hushed tone. "You'll be killed before you start."

They crouched among a cluster of boulders Bourne had selected. Bourne kept one eye on the skyline access points to the valley. He no longer needed his theatrical makeup. The sun had darkened his skin, his beard was now full. He was Yusuf Al Khatib.

After he was certain they were in the clear, he displayed the AWM for his pupil. "Pay close attention," he told Aashir. "You're learning on the best weapon of its kind."

Bourne shot a buzzard, showing Aashir how it was done. Then he handed over the AWM. Aashir missed

326

with his first two shots. Bourne counseled patience. Once, he took the AWM from Aashir and pushed him down among the rocks. Moments later, a shadow, as from a gigantic bird, passed over them, but there was no sound — none at all. Only a deadly silence. The shadow passed over again, more slowly this time. The utter stillness was almost unbearable.

Bourne forced them to stay hunkered down and unmoving for a full twenty minutes after the shadow had passed for the last time. Afterward, there were no more buzzards to shoot at. Bourne picked out rocks of different sizes and set them up anywhere from five hundred to a thousand yards away for Aashir to practice on.

Later, back inside one of the metal huts as Bourne was putting the rifle away, Faraj sauntered up to him. His left arm was tied tightly to his chest. Tiny dots of blood had seeped through the bandages.

"You should not have gone outside," Faraj said without preamble.

"I took Aashir shooting."

"Were you going to shoot down the drone?" Faraj's voice was withering. "You broke protocol. What if you had been seen and photographed? You would have jeopardized the entire cadre."

"Snipers are invisible. That's what makes them so deadly," Bourne said pointedly.

Faraj ignored him. "You should not have taken him."

"He wanted to go."

Faraj stared hard at Bourne. "Believe me when I tell you, that boy doesn't know what he wants."

"It was a good day for him, Faraj. Let it go."

Faraj's eyes narrowed. "You seem to have much in common with him."

Bourne glanced at him briefly. He knew Faraj was jealous of his relationship with Borz. "I don't know about that. He seems a bit lost. I'm teaching him to shoot, that's all."

"He is lost," Faraj observed, "but learning how to handle the long gun isn't going to help his basic problem."

Bourne wiped his hands on a rag, set it aside. "What is his basic problem?"

"I guess you're not as close with him as I thought," Faraj said, before walking away.

An electric atmosphere accompanied dinner. The knowledge that the cadre was going to move out at midnight had gripped everyone. It was a good night to begin their trek: Both moon and stars were hidden behind thick layers of clouds, dark, ominous, and heavy as metal. During dinner the wind off the mountains began to shriek like a creature in torment. Khan Abdali's men ignored it, as did most of Borz's Chechens, but Faraj and his cadre appeared ill at ease.

Aashir slipped onto Bourne's bench, set his metal plate down, and began to eat, as if the two had done this night after night for years.

"How's my skill — really?" he said.

"Anyone can learn to shoot accurately," Bourne said, "but it takes certain instincts to become a sniper."

"And I don't have them."

328

"I didn't say that, and I didn't mean it. We won't know until there are live targets to shoot at — moving targets."

"I shot down the buzzards."

"Buzzards aren't men." Bourne pushed aside his plate; he had no appetite anyway. "You have to learn your target, then anticipate movement — up, down, left, right, fast or slow. But without true fieldwork we'll know nothing."

"Then we're going to the right place." Aashir's fork clattered onto his plate. He seemed to have as little appetite for this food as Bourne.

"Afghanistan is never the right place," Bourne said. "It's the wrong place for everything — except death."

He rose, and Aashir with him. They went outside. The wind had ceased its eerie howling, but the still air was icy, laden with moisture.

"The rain will slow our progress," the young man pointed out.

"It won't slow the Waziri," Bourne pointed out. "We can't let it slow us."

Aashir opened his mouth, then closed it again, turning away, and again Bourne had the impression he was about to say something — something extremely difficult for him to get out. Whatever it was seemed lodged in his voice box, sticking there like a needle. He would get to it, Bourne knew, in his own time, at his own pace.

"Do you have a wife, Yusuf? Children?"

"I have no one," Bourne said. "I have myself."

They began to walk. They picked their way past the remnants of the C-17, then the mass grave of the American recruits — the cannon fodder for El Ghadan's plan. The trembling anticipation of the pullout was joined by the melancholy of death.

Aashir jammed his hands into his trouser pockets. "I've been trying to feel what it's like to not remember your family, your childhood, your growing up."

"Don't," Bourne said. "Consider yourself lucky."

"You don't understand."

"No one ever understands another person."

Aashir peered at him sideways. "Do you really believe that?"

The night was very dark; the encampment was in a mandatory blackout, no one allowed even to smoke outdoors. The two men could hardly see each other, but they felt each other's presence, larger than life.

Aashir went on without waiting for a reply. Perhaps he already knew the answer. "I have three sisters — *had* three sisters, I should say. They're dead now. Missiles, drones, I don't know. I'm the only male — the only son — and I'm such a disappointment."

"To your father," Bourne said, "or to yourself?"

"Does it matter? To my father I am a nonperson."

There was such a well of sorrow in Aashir's voice, Bourne was compelled to reply. "I should think it matters to your mother. I would think it would matter even more to you."

"My mother understands nothing except cooking and cleaning and raising her children. That's the scope

330

of her life, the same as her mother before her. Now she has no children to raise. She is completely lost."

"You could go back."

"I am not a child!" Aashir said hotly.

"But you seem to be the only one who understands her, who can help heal her pain."

"And who will heal my pain?"

It was a cry from the heart rather than a self-pitying moan. Bourne had no answer for him; he had no answer for himself.

Vincent Terrier was with Marty Finnerman at the late morning meeting with Howard Anselm at Finnerman's office in the Pentagon.

"We got the high-res photos back," Finnerman said as soon as Anselm had seated himself on a cane-backed metal chair. The Pentagon did not go in much for creature comforts.

With a nod of his head, Finnerman deferred to Terrier, who immediately spilled a dozen 11-by-14 blowups onto Finnerman's desk. As Anselm looked through them, Terrier provided the commentary.

"The drone made three passes over Faraj's encampment. We got his C-17."

Anselm tapped his forefinger on one blowup after another. "Blew it in two, I see."

Terrier bobbed his head the way a praised dog might. "That's right. Faraj's command building was also completely destroyed. Hopefully with Faraj in it."

"Mmm," Anselm said. "No activity."

"Abandoned," Finnerman agreed emphatically. "Everyone else dead."

Anselm glanced up. "Including the Americans."

"The American traitors," Terrier corrected him.

Anselm wagged a finger. "Wipe that smile off your face, Vincent."

"Vinnie's right, Howard," Finnerman interjected. "The drone strike was a complete success."

"I don't see any bodies," Anselm pointed out.

"Burned to a crisp," Terrier said. "Inside Faraj's command and control facility."

"What's this slight mound here? It looks like newly turned earth. There were survivors who took the damning photos, who buried the dead? I'd like eyes on the ground." Anselm sat back. "Marty, why don't you contact our friends at Mossad. You've told me they have a cadre not far from the valley."

"Had." Terrier seemed to make a habit of interrupting. "For some reason unknown to us, they've pulled out of Waziristan completely."

Anselm frowned. "I don't like that. What do they know that you guys don't?"

Finnerman made a show of laughing, but from the look in his eyes it was clear he wasn't pleased with the question. A moment later, Anselm understood why.

"I spoke to Eli Yadin this morning," Finnerman said. "I asked him that same question. I wanted to know why we were being kept in the dark." He put his hands flat on his desk as he leaned forward. "You know what he said? He told me there was nothing to interest them in Waziristan. At the moment, everything was quiet."

"In other words," Anselm said, "he lied to you."

Finnerman looked like he had just smelled three-day-old fish. "It wouldn't be the first time, and it won't be the last."

"But this is a crucial moment for us." Terrier, eager as his namesake.

"Not a time for the director of Mossad to be dissembling to a purported ally," Anselm added.

Terrier's head came up. "Purported?"

Finnerman shook his head. "Not now, Howard."

Anselm spread his hands. "Why not now?" His gaze moved to Terrier. "The Israeli Knesset has secretly okayed the expansion of settlements across the Green Line, the 1967 border, the latest of which is in the Jordan Valley, which the hard-liners are adamant to keep under its military control, arguing it's Israel's eastern security border. The prime minister has assured POTUS he won't sign the bill into law, but meanwhile the expansion has begun, one more reason this so-called peace summit is a sham. The Orthodox segment of the population has for some time joined with the hard-line conservative pols, keeping a hammerlock on Knesset policy."

Anselm leaned back, stared up at the ceiling. "You know, in a perfect world —"

"Humans don't — and frankly, can't — live in a perfect world," Finnerman cut in. "You know better than most how *imperfect* our world is."

"And getting more imperfect by the day," Terrier muttered.

"What?" Finnerman said.

Terrier shook his head. "Nothing."

"If we're finished debating intangibles." Anselm picked at a bit of imaginary lint on his trousers leg. "POTUS's thesis has never been that well thought out; the Israeli prime minister said as much."

Terrier looked from one to the other. "So now — what? How is this peace summit still happening?"

"It's happening," Anselm said, "because it has to happen."

Terrier opened his mouth then closed it with a snap. "You mean . . ."

"Yes," Anselm said, "it's one enormous PR stunt. To keep the status quo alive, to save face for everyone."

"And to keep the 'peace process' industries from imploding," Finnerman said, "depriving thousands of people of their livelihoods and companies of profits."

Including yourselves, Terrier thought bitterly, because you're shareholders in any number of those Gravenhurst-directed companies making money off of this phony peace process. How I despise you all.

"The bottom line," Anselm concluded, "is that this summit will benefit everyone involved. And when nothing substantial comes of it, the spin will be, 'POTUS tried, he got farther than any other president in a decade. Kudos to the hero.'"

Finnerman laughed. "And then everyone can go back to hating one another."

CHAPTER
THIRTY-FIVE

The Arab and chechen cadre moved out precisely at midnight. Black clouds roiled over their heads, fitful gusts of wind brought with them further hints of rain. The impending heavy weather actually bolstered their spirits, as the chances of their being spotted had been eliminated.

They could move freely, follow the two Waziri warriors with a complete freedom rarely afforded them. They were led toward the mountains, where a curious pale mist was creeping, as if to greet them or help shepherd them into eastern Afghanistan.

The time gave Bourne cause to think again of Soraya and Sonya. His mobile was of no use here, so he had no way of knowing whether El Ghadan had sent another proof-of-life video, no way to know whether Soraya and her daughter were indeed still alive. Despite El Ghadan's assurances, he knew the timetable was working against all of them. The longer Soraya and Sonya remained in captivity the greater their chance of being killed, no matter what Bourne did.

That he had a plan, that there was still a glimmer of hope, was cold comfort to him. That he carried with him a corner of a plan from Singapore, the place he needed to be, was like a light in the darkness. But there was still a ways to go; how Borz, Faraj, and their men were going to get from Afghanistan to Singapore was anyone's guess. And that was assuming they survived the Taliban.

For the moment, Bourne needed to put all his doubts aside. He was determined to keep his friend and her daughter from harm. He knew he would move heaven and earth to save them.

As they exited the valley, they also left level ground behind them. The way became rockier as the terrain rose steeply into the foothills, which all too soon morphed into a narrow, winding path, flanked on either side by stony ledges and imposing outcroppings.

Three hours after they left the valley, the path vanished altogether, and they found themselves at the complete mercy of Khan Abdali's men. This disturbed Faraj, but it seemed to faze Borz not at all. He followed the two elongated skeletons with absolute confidence, an attitude that, from Bourne's observations, appeared to annoy, then anger Faraj, who had been forced to cede control to the Chechen ever since the C-17 landed in Waziristan.

Now they were obliged to climb rather than march, grasping outcroppings, levering themselves along like lizards on a wall. The Waziri moved along the rock face as if wraiths, seeming to expend no effort as they mounted higher and higher, heading directly into the clouds.

The chilling rain came an hour later, drenching them at once. The Waziri appeared not to notice, and the

Chechens took their cue from them. Faraj and his grim-faced men soldiered on without either complaint or comment. They were inured to hardship — it was the only way of life they knew. To a man, they were fixated on their mission, their target, and the angels in the Promised Land that awaited their deaths.

"Now I will tell you something, Yusuf, that Faraj would not understand. In fact, it would offend him," Borz said to Bourne with the rain streaming down his face. "I love America. Yes, yes, it's true. You know why I say this, Yusuf? Because America has developed the greatest war machine the world has ever seen. American businessmen have turned the ideology of war into a multibillion-dollar business." He smiled. "Why do I love this? Well, that war machine is not wholly American. It has help from people like me." His eyes twinkled through the rain. "Rest assured, Yusuf, when America goes to war I make money. Lots and lots of money."

He would have gone on, but one of the Waziri warriors came up to Bourne, spoke to him in their strange dialect. Bourne nodded.

"What's he saying?" Borz asked.

"Around the next bend is Afghanistan," Bourne said. "The moment we cross over, we'll be in enemy territory. He wants you to order your men to be on guard."

The warning was duly passed from man to man, and weapons were brought to the ready. They continued on, around the curve in the rocks, clinging, slipping here and there, the rain ceaseless, the sky bearing down on them like a press.

And so into Afghanistan.

The terrain looked no different than it had for the last several hours, but then why should it? Western Waziristan flowed into eastern Afghanistan like a river to the sea.

Within a half hour, the Waziri had found a seam in the rock face. The path through it was narrow, with high walls looming on either side like giant sentinels. The rain struck the sheer rock and bounced off so that it came at the men both vertically and almost horizontally. The wealth of water had turned the path to runnels, racing streams through which the cadre waded.

Now the path pitched down at such a precipitous angle that they found themselves half sliding into what, in the almost hallucinatory light of the coming dawn, appeared to be a knifelike valley riddled on one side with caves that would afford them shelter from the incessant rain.

Though soaked, the men were forbidden to build fires, even in the depths of the caves. Though tired and hungry, they were restless, craving an enemy to attack and destroy. Finally, however, they hunkered down and ate in huge, voracious mouthfuls, like baby birds. The Waziri and Chechens sat with their backs against the wall, watching as the Arabs — Bourne among them — knelt facing Mecca and chanted their prayers in hushed voices.

"As I see these people praying," Borz said to Bourne when the session had concluded, "I'm reminded not of the billions of Muslims — including Chechens — but of the officials in Washington, D.C., making decisions that affect the entire world. We are thrown back to the days when Rome ruled the world through its corrupt popes, when thousands of men were thrown into battle in God's name."

He looked hard at Bourne. "Imagine what this world would be like if there were no religion." He laughed. "You and I, Yusuf, would be out of work. Whatever, then, would we do?"

Day had broken, sunlight was slowly prying its way through the thinning clouds. The rain was hardly more than a benign drizzle.

"Fetch the Waziri," Borz said. "I need details about the next stage of our trek."

Bourne was approaching them, at the mouth of one of the caves, when the shooting began. Automatic weapons fire shattered the dawn from multiple directions, and all around him Chechens and Arabs were spun around, fountaining blood and brains.

Part Three

CHAPTER
THIRTY-SIX

"Noreen? Are you fucking kidding me?"

Camilla stared at the sheaf of photos Hunter had shaken out of a manila folder.

"Noreen?"

"Of course Noreen." Hunter clucked like a mother hen. "Why d'you think Anselm goes through assistants like crap through a goose?"

"I haven't been at the White House long enough to . . ." Camilla's voice trailed off as she stared at a photo of Bill kissing Noreen — William Magnus, POTUS — while she was wrapped up in the American flag. "Was this taken in the Oval Office?" Her voice was sharp, pitched an octave higher than normal, with, to her chagrin, an edge of hysteria.

"I don't know. I wasn't told."

Hunter, a pro through and through, kept her tone at the midway point between cynicism and pity. She didn't say, I told you so, but she had every right to, Camilla knew.

The two women were in the barn, brushing down their respective steeds, following another perfect session on the racing oval. It was the dinner hour; they were alone. Hunter's timing had once again proved flawless.

"The soft white underbelly of Anselm's job."

"He pimps for POTUS."

"Crude," Hunter said, "but accurate."

Do I detect a whiff of triumph in her voice? Camilla wondered. She saw that these photos were meant as a coup de grâce, the hard evidence to push her all the way over to Hunter's — and Terrier's — side. If her background wasn't enough to get her to accept their philosophy, then by God, good old-fashioned jealousy would do the trick. And of course, from jealousy would come the need for revenge — at least in their minds.

Was there nothing to which these people would not stoop? Camilla asked herself, but she already knew the answer. No, there was absolutely nothing. These people — and she included POTUS and Anselm in the mix — were amoral. Time and again she had found herself wondering how people of high position like Anthony Weiner and Eliot Spitzer, not to mention the Secret Service agents she had canned because of their flagrant dalliances with South American whores, could do what they did, over and over. Did they not consider that they would be caught? No, they did not. She saw that now. Because, like POTUS, they believed themselves beyond judgment, above the law.

She experienced a sudden hallucinatory moment. She saw herself as she had been — as head of the Secret Service, as Bill's lover, as a victim. At the same time, she was aware of what she had become — a false pawn, a realist, but also a cynic. And then she looked at Hunter and saw two of her as well: the trainer, the protector, but also the false friend, the latest person to want to carry Camilla in her pocket like a coin.

Now, Camilla thought, when she thinks I'm most angry and therefore most vulnerable, she's going to make her pitch. Now I'll find out the task she and Terrier have in mind for me.

Still, she needed to prove her thesis to herself, she needed Hunter to drive the last nail into her own coffin, because for Camilla betrayal was far more serious than it was for the people surrounding her; it was not to be embarked upon lightly, with no thought to its consequences.

"What will happen to those photos?" she asked.

"Nothing," Hunter said in the most offhanded way. "These are the only copies. I'll burn them. The digital images will be erased. No trace of them will remain."

And there it was, Camilla thought. The last nail. The photos had been taken exclusively to induce her to act. And while she was about it, who was to say they were real? They might just as easily have been Photoshopped. She had no experience with fake photos, so there was no way to tell. And yet now that she considered it, there was a way for *her* to tell. The fact that Noreen was wrapped in the flag, just as POTUS had wished Camilla to be, was all the proof she needed. The photo was real, no question.

"Let's take a walk," Hunter said, ending Camilla's train of thought.

They had finished grooming their horses, fed them, replenished their water. Hunter picked up a kerosene lantern and what appeared to be a wicker picnic hamper, and they set out, heading due east, past the racing oval, over a low ridge and down into a swale. In the distance, the meadow where the cows grazed and lazed during the day stretched away, a deep emerald sea, dotted here and there with the desert islet of a tree or two.

Camilla thought about her reaction to the photos. She felt no anger, and certainly no regret. What she did feel, however, was shame. Shame that she had been a part of this sad parade of young women mesmerized by Bill's charisma, POTUS's power. She felt as dirty as a used washcloth. More than anything the photos made her itch to scrub herself down under a very hot shower.

The eastern half of the swale fell away gently, then, without warning, more steeply. This was a section of the Dairy Camilla had not explored. As if someone had rung a bell, the sun slipped behind the western hills and twilight was ushered in. Their elongated shadows turned blue, then vanished altogether. They picked their way downward.

The stream, when they came upon it, was as slow-moving as the cows that had been up on the pasture all day. With a seductive ripple, it curved indolently away from them. Hunter settled them on a wide grassy knoll. She opened the basket, which was indeed filled with food, along with plates, glasses, utensils, and a bottle of wine with a twist-off cap.

"I'm not hungry yet. How about you?" Hunter said without caring about Camilla's reply.

346

"What are you doing?" Camilla said as she watched Hunter shrug off her denim jacket, start to unbutton her shirt.

"Going for a swim." She shucked off her jeans. "I'm hot and sweaty, aren't you?"

She wore no underwear. Her body was lean, muscular as a teenage boy's. She had narrow hips, a narrower waist. A constellation of pale freckles arced across her chest, just above her small, hard breasts. Her thighs were powerful in the way of all athletes.

Hunter half slid off the knoll, then turned back. "What's the matter? Are you frightened of a little nudity?"

The splash of her compact body was small and sharp, like her words.

Camilla pondered a moment. This was 180 degrees from what she had expected. Still, she didn't think she had a choice. Stay on the bank and she would leave the Dairy without Hunter's aegis. Bad for her status no matter what she decided to do in Singapore.

She piled her clothes next to Hunter's. In doing so, she had to move Hunter's jeans. Feeling something in the back pocket, she slipped it out, unfolded it, and tipped it toward the orange-yellow corona of the sunset.

It was a photo of herself, a copy of the one taken when she had arrived at the Dairy. It was much creased, molded to the shape of Hunter's buttock, but otherwise well preserved. Carefully and thoughtfully, Camilla slid it back into the pocket of Hunter's jeans.

She started when Hunter yelled, "Are you coming, or what?"

Sliding down the edge of the knoll, she dropped the two feet or so into the stream. The cold water bit hard, forcing a gasp out of her. She surfaced, pushed her hair back off her face. Her skin was raised in goose bumps and her nipples were hard. She saw Hunter near her, and she felt heat rise up into her throat and cheeks.

"I thought you'd chickened out."

Cupping her hands in the water, Hunter splashed her, laughing as Camilla splashed her in return. They bounced around like girls at summer camp, and Camilla's hardheartedness began to slip away before she realized what was happening. She had been drawn closer to Hunter again, despite everything she now knew about her. Even more alarming, at the height of their innocent play, she felt the urgent rise of erotic need.

What is happening to me? she asked herself, just before Hunter took hold of her and kissed her hard on the lips. It was a different kiss than the one they had exchanged in the copse of trees, longer, both more erotic and more impassioned, so that Camilla found herself helpless to resist it. Maybe she didn't want to. She liked the taste of Hunter's lips and tongue — cinnamon and nutmeg (wasn't nutmeg a hallucinogen?). She liked even better the press of her naked body — its perfect balance of softness and firmness, which spoke of both dependability and determination.

She was being seduced. She knew it, and didn't care. At this precise moment, as Hunter bent to gently take her nipple between her even, white teeth, she wanted the other woman as much as she had wanted anything.

They toppled into the shallows, mud-spattered, entwined, and laughing. Camilla cupped the back of Hunter's neck as she drew her head up, kissed her with open lips and a questing tongue. Along with the lust she felt rising in her the anger she had been unconsciously tamping down. The two rose and fell in concert — light and dark, yin and yang.

Alpha and omega.

A reptile, sensing danger, absorbs sounds via the ground to detect the number and movements of its enemies. Bourne, lying on the floor of the cave near its mouth, listened for the vibrations of the Taliban. He pressed his ear to the earth, trying to shut out the explosive cracks of automatic fire.

The Taliban were in the deepest recesses of the cave, where, he surmised, a passage must lead up and out into the open air. This no doubt was where they had crept in. But how did they know the cadre had sheltered here? Had the cadre been under surveillance from the moment they had been led through the mountain pass into Afghanistan?

Faraj had another idea. He ran past where Bourne lay, heading directly toward Khan Abdali's men, crouched and firing back at the Taliban. He screamed and they turned just in time to receive facefuls of bullets from his AR-15.

Borz leaped up. "You fucking Arab idiot, what have you done?"

Faraj turned to him. "I did what you should've done the moment we set out."

"Really?" Borz stepped forward and shot him twice through the heart.

Faraj fell where he stood, his head in the lap of one of the Waziri, a fitting place for him to find his mythical angels.

Bourne, watching this interplay with fierce interest, shouted to Borz, "You've got to kill Faraj's men before they shoot your people."

Borz, it seemed, agreed wholeheartedly. He turned his attention from what was left of the Taliban and began to take down the remnants of Faraj's men as if they were pigeons in a shooting gallery.

Grabbing Aashir, Bourne pulled him around behind him, then pitched in, keeping his attention on the three remaining Taliban. "I have your back," he shouted to Borz. He advanced on the Taliban, the last request of Khan Abdali to take their heads echoing in his mind.

Then Aashir was beside him, gunning down an attacking Taliban, who had been coming at Borz from his left side. Bourne shot the second man, but the third took cover deeper inside the cave, beyond the firefight between Faraj's people and the Chechens. Both sides were fearless, but the jihadists, without their leader and in hostile territory, were vulnerable. One by one, the Chechens picked them off while sustaining a minimum of casualties. Still, many of them had been killed in the Taliban's initial surprise fusillade.

350

Aashir ran through the melee after the last remaining Taliban soldier. Bourne shouted at him to come back, but Aashir called, "Let me do this, Yusuf. I'll get him."

The young man wanted to bloody himself in the age-old ritual of becoming a man. As a result, he could get himself killed. Bourne took off after him, brushing past Chechens, bringing down a jihadist on his left, then another on his right. The Chechens laughed, tried to pat him on the shoulder or back as he and Aashir flew by. They were clearly impressed by the young man's courage and fortitude against the Taliban. After all, he had saved their leader.

He reached the stygian inner recesses of the cave without encountering either Aashir or the Taliban soldier. He had only a penlight Borz had given him. The pea-sized beam was worse than useless: Illuminating next to nothing, it yet served to pinpoint his precise location as accurately as a laser. He didn't turn it on.

Fingertips on rocks, feeling his way forward, he noticed the black turned to charcoal, then, in spots, to light gray. The cave roof was dotted with fissures through which light seeped down. This unearthly illumination allowed him to proceed forward with a good measure of confidence. Shortly, the sounds of soft footfalls against the pumice-like floor of the cave reached him.

The floor sloped down, even as the way tapered until it had narrowed to a width of perhaps two young boys standing side by side. Bourne paused for a moment, listening intently, but now that the firefight behind him had come to its bloody end, a ringing silence reigned, punctured now and again by echoes of questioning voices.

Not much farther on, Bourne identified Aashir's voice. Who was he with? Bourne had heard no gunshots, no moans of pain.

Despite the presence of light, he picked his way even more cautiously. Several times, hearing a pebble or small rock bounce along the floor, he froze, his entire mind tuned to the sounds. Always he continued on, into the silence, deeper and deeper into the living rock.

"Yusuf."

He stopped, waited.

"Yusuf, are you there?"

"Yes," Bourne said, and moved.

"Yusuf, please, I'm injured."

"What happened?" Bourne said, moving again.

"It's my leg. But I got him. The Taliban is dead."

He was sure now; it wasn't Aashir's voice. Was Aashir dead? Bourne looked around, found a ledge onto which he laid his penlight. "Tell me where you are, Aashir, and I'll come get you." He turned on the penlight, quickly moved aside.

A burst of automatic fire splintered the ledge, disintegrating the light. But Bourne was already on the move, sprinting forward. A bit of white material caught the light, then a sleeve. He leaped, driving his left shoulder into the Taliban soldier. They both tumbled backward onto the floor. Having dropped his assault rifle, the Taliban reached up, gripped Bourne's throat with his two hands, and gave a mighty squeeze.

Bourne drove his fist into the Taliban's abdomen, then against the point of his sternum, cracking it. Still, the Taliban only tightened his grip. Bourne could not breathe. Stars danced at the corners of his vision. His third strike shattered the sternum completely, driving bone into the Taliban's right lung, which immediately emptied of air and filled with blood.

Bourne pulled the hands away from his throat, bent the arms back. There was no resistance now. The Taliban was dying, drowning in his own blood. Bourne got to his feet. He wished he could take the head of this man back to Khan Abdali, to compensate him for the deaths of his warriors.

Taking up the fallen AR-15, he went in search of Aashir. As he went, he called the boy's name, but there was no answer. Every minute that passed was a tick in the direction of Aashir being interrogated.

Bourne found him bound, gagged with a wad of filthy cloth. There was a nasty bump on the back of his head, matting down his hair with sticky blood, but he was otherwise unharmed.

"I'm sorry," Aashir said when Bourne had pulled out the gag. "He caught me by surprise."

"We'll have to work on that." Bourne severed the knots that bound the boy's wrists.

"Thank you, Yusuf," Aashir said as he scrambled to his feet. "No one has ever treated me . . ."

His words petered out, and Bourne nodded wordlessly.

Aashir ducked his head deferentially. "Now I suppose we'd best get back to the others."

"I don't think so." Up ahead, Bourne could see a larger fissure of light, dazzling as a lightning bolt amid dark clouds. "I think we need to see how the Taliban got into the cave, where they came from, and if there are more of them."

When Aashir looked at him questioningly, Bourne added. "Maybe that will tell us how they knew we were here. Are you up for it?"

"Lead the way," Aashir said, shouldering his AWM.

CHAPTER
THIRTY-SEVEN

They dined in the night air by the light of the kerosene lantern, ravenous as beasts. Camilla scarcely tasted the food, but between them they drained the bottle of wine. Camilla had felt lightheaded as they levered themselves out of the river, rinsed off what remained of the mud, and sat trembling a little as the western sky slowly lost its color.

When Hunter dried her off with her own shirt, Camilla was certain the other shoe was about to drop. She was mildly surprised when it didn't, more surprised when Hunter didn't bring up anything more serious than early-period Rolling Stones versus middle-period Rolling Stones. They dressed, ate their meal, guzzled their wine as if they both had things they wanted to forget, chatted some more about the state of pop music, their favorite films, even while they cleaned up.

Camilla carried the lantern, Hunter the basket. They turned back to the barn, accompanied by the swaying light. Under any other circumstances the walk would have been romantic, but Camilla was on edge. Her mind was filled with so many conflicting emotions she found it difficult to sort one from another. She was still waiting for Hunter to drop the bomb. What did they expect from her? What did they want her to do? There were less than two days left at the Dairy before she needed to be in Singapore. The suspense was just about killing her.

And yet nothing happened. They reached the barn. The horses were asleep. Camilla did not know the time, but it seemed late to her. The moon was up by the time they made the short trek to the main house. On the way, they passed the bank of bicycles, and Camilla was reminded of her frantic trip to Jake's World, following Hunter.

Inside the main house, they said good night and parted as if nothing of an intimate nature had occurred. Camilla's confusion was in full bloom. She could not quite grasp what had happened, let alone what was happening now.

She went to her room, performed her nightly ablutions, and got into bed. She was in the middle of John Le Carré's *Absolute Friends*, and was engrossed not only in the characters but in the uncanny manner in which the underlying theme of the novel might have fit with the situation she now faced.

The lights were out in the room — only the bedside lamp illuminated a small oval encompassing the book and her hands, which held it open. She read five or six pages before her eyelids grew heavy and she found herself reading the same paragraph over and over.

She had just closed the book when she heard a soft knock on her door. She said nothing, but the door opened anyway and Hunter stepped silently in.

"Am I disturbing you?" It was almost a whisper.

Camilla honestly did not know what to say. Why was Hunter here at this hour? Did she want to crawl into Camilla's bed, hold her as she had held her in the aftermath of their lovemaking while the stream flowed endlessly around their small island?

Misunderstanding her silence, Hunter said, "I need to speak with you." The light from the hallway threw her into shadow. Nevertheless, her eyes glittered like an animal in the African bush.

Camilla patted the blanket. "Come sit beside me."

Hunter glided across the room. She was wrapped in a thin robe, but her feet were bare, pink and nearly perfect, save for one toe on her left foot shorter than the others.

"I don't want you to go," Hunter said the moment she reached Camilla's bedside.

Camilla was startled. "What?"

"To Singapore." Hunter sat close to Camilla. Her body seemed to radiate heat. "Don't go."

"I have to," Camilla said. "I was given a brief. I know my duty —"

"Jesus, who cares about duty?" Hunter took her hand. "Listen, these people have no loyalty to you. Why should you have any to them?"

"That's the way I was made."

"But if you go to Singapore you won't come back."

"You don't know that, Hunter. I may be able to get to Bourne before he gets to Bill. I have to believe that. There's always the chance —"

357

"No, you don't understand." Hunter's voice had turned urgent. "You were never meant to leave Singapore alive. The Black Queen brief — the one you were given — was designed to fail. You and Bourne are going to be shot dead in Singapore. Finnerman has already sent a top-notch dinger —"

"A what?"

"A long-gun assassin." Hunter's tone had turned impatient. "Christ, don't they teach you anything in the Secret Service?"

"We call them snipers."

"By whatever name they're sending in a professional in field wet work. Your presence at the Thoroughbred Club is merely a feint." Hunter leaned in. "Don't be pissed, Cam."

"I'm not pissed," Camilla lied. "I just don't believe a word of what you're saying."

"When have I lied to you?"

"How could I possibly answer that?"

Hunter looked genuinely sorrowful. "Turn on your mobile."

"Why? There's no cell service inside the Dairy. Deliberately."

"Indulge me. Please."

Camilla sighed, plucked her mobile from the top drawer of the night table. She fired it up. Sure enough, the no-service icon popped up on the top row of the screen. And yet a moment later the new email message icon appeared.

"How the hell . . . ?" Camilla looked up at Hunter.

"Open it," Hunter said in a voice both soft and tender. "Trust me."

Trust me. Those words ricocheted like a pinball off the fresh wounds of betrayal in Camilla's mind. Nevertheless, she opened the email. It had no subject line, no message either. However, two attachments had somehow already been downloaded. With no little trepidation, she opened the first one, discovered to her horror a PDF of an Eyes Only DOD file. The stamp across the covering page made it clear it came from Martin Finnerman's office.

Heart pounding painfully in her throat, Camilla went on to the next page. There was the watermark that could not be duplicated, authenticating the file. It was a brief — a dinger brief. The dinger in question was Benjamin Landis, code name Kettle. Where did they come up with these work names? she asked herself, because she was too frightened to immediately read Kettle's brief. But she couldn't help looking at him. A head shot was included. He looked like any middle management drone. A nobody. Nevertheless, an unnatural chill invaded her body.

As of their own accord, her fingers turned the electronic page, and she saw laid out for her the entire brief. It was concise, succinct, and to the point. In fact, it consisted of only one sentence: *You are hereby directed to terminate Jason Bourne before his final preparations for the assassination of POTUS have been completed.*

"Now the second," Hunter said, as if it were a command.

The second attachment was an MP3 — an audio file, which began to play the moment she opened it. She heard Finnerman and Howard Anselm talking about adding to Kettle's brief. They had decided to have Kettle terminate her in a way that would look like she had been killed in the line of duty.

Camilla dropped her mobile as if it were white-hot. She put her hand to her mouth; she felt sick in the pit of her stomach. Pushing Hunter aside, she leaped out of bed, ran to the bathroom, barely made it before what was left of their riverside picnic spewed out as she knelt in front of the toilet.

CHAPTER
THIRTY-EIGHT

"The product is solid." El Ghadan handed over the second half of the money.

"I've got a second bit of intel," Sara said.

"Well, aren't you the wonder."

She held out a small manila envelope. "This will cost you double."

"Is it worth double?" But he was looking at the envelope, not her.

"It's a map of Israeli missile deployments at the Syrian border."

"Done." He took the envelope, opened it, and scanned the intel before looking back up at her. "Now, how would you like to make even more?"

"How much more?"

"Leave this pittance in the dust."

"That depends." She looked at him steadily. "What do I have to do?"

He laughed. "Take a ride."

They were strolling along Doha's Corniche. She had quickly come to realize that this crescent was among his favorite places to talk. Out in the open and on the move, closely observed by his own team, he had nothing to fear from electronic ears. Besides, he was dressed in a summer-weight Dior suit, a Lanvin tie, and a Charvet shirt. Cuff links of gold knots gleamed at his cuffs. He was a walking advertisement for Western consumerism. Sara, as he had requested, was in Western clothes as well: a blue-green leaf-patterned dress with a wide belt, sensible flats that looked like ballet slippers.

The late morning was typically hot, the sunlight fierce, almost blinding. It winked off the windows and facets of the high-rises up ahead. At this hour, they were virtually alone on the Corniche, both tourists and locals preferring the shade and air-conditioning of the city's cafés or malls.

"Where might this ride take me?" Sara asked.

Instead of answering her directly, he said, "You know, Ellie, I must admit to not liking Doha. It has embraced Western culture too fervidly."

"And yet you spend time here."

He shrugged. "Qatar is convenient. Also, the government is, shall we say, sympathetic to my cause."

"Which is either ideological or mercenary," Sara said. "I can't make out which."

He laughed. "I am rarely given such an astute compliment, especially from a woman."

"I must have something between my legs other than a cunt."

He stopped abruptly and turned to her. "Why must you be so crude?"

"It's the only way to get your attention, to get you to understand that I will not be spoken to in that condescending manner."

362

"Every other woman —"

"Every woman needs to speak up for herself," Sara said flatly.

He watched her with his dark, predatory eyes. "Do you speak out of ideology or sanctimony?"

Sara's eyes blazed. She no longer cared whether the ice under her feet was becoming too thin to support her. "If you think me disingenuous why are you wasting both our time?"

There was a long silence. She heard the waves slapping against the concrete bulkheads, gulls crying overhead. She thought of Hassim and Khalifa, whose bones by now surely had been picked clean by the sea life. She thought of how close she had come to death, and mentally embraced her gold Star of David, symbol of everything she loved — her family, her friends, her country, Jason.

"Do you know where Street Fifty-Two is?" El Ghadan asked.

"That's in the Industrial Area, yes?"

He nodded. "First thing tomorrow."

"And what am I supposed to do at Street Fifty-Two?"

"Be my emissary," El Ghadan said.

She shook her head. "I don't understand."

His smile was cool and calculating, as befitting someone with the upper hand. "All will be made clear to you after you arrive."

The fissure opened up before them, like a doorway into Aladdin's world. They pressed themselves against the sheer rock walls and started their steep ascent. They did not have far to go. Bourne broke out of the cave first and stopped dead, waiting for his eyes to adjust to the sunlight. He allowed Aashir to come up beside him so he too could acclimate himself.

Bourne quartered the terrain. It wasn't long before he whispered, "Look off to our right. The high tor."

Aashir followed his direction.

"It's an owl's nest," Bourne said. "A watchtower."

It had a perfect view along the valley that led to Waziristan.

"That's how they spotted us."

"Two owls," Bourne said. "Perfect targets for the long gun."

Aashir unslung his AWM. Bourne put a hand on his forearm.

"Please," Aashir said.

"Two targets, Aashir. Not one."

"I know I can do this."

Bourne nodded, but unslung his own AWM.

Aashir moved a bit to his left, set the barrel of the AWM on an outcropping. He settled his right eye against the rubber cup of the rifle's scope.

"Take the one farther away first," Bourne said in his ear.

Aashir adjusted the AWM accordingly. "Ready," he said, and squeezed the trigger.

The report echoed over the mountains. A thousand yards away, the owl farthest from them threw up his hands and toppled over. Immediately, the second owl turned in their direction and began to fire with an assault rifle. Aashir moved the barrel of the AWM incrementally, squeezed off a second shot. He missed, and in missing, panicked. His third shot was wild.

Bourne brought his AWM up, but before he could get off a shot, the second owl launched something from the end of his rifle. It arced toward them.

"Down!" Bourne grabbed Aashir by the back of his robe, letting go of his hold on the rock. They plunged back through the fissure into the cave. Just in time, as the grenade struck the outcropping above and detonated, showering them in a cascade of rock shards.

Aashir, half blinded and coughing, staggered back against the vertical rock. Bourne was already moving upward, returning through the fissure, knowing the Taliban would be coming to make sure the grenade had done its work. His real fear was that the man had radioed his compatriots for reinforcements. Bourne's only hope was that his first order of business would be to take care of the men who had killed his comrade.

Bourne was halfway up when the rock face on his left sheared away, leaving him dangling by one hand. He reached out across the fissure, taking hold of an outcropping exposed by the rockfall. He tested it with part of his weight, and then continued his ascent. A moment later the handhold gave way and he was left dangling again.

As he struggled to regain his balance, a shadow fell over the top of the fissure. He looked up to see the Taliban soldier squatting at the top. He grinned as he aimed his AK-47 at Bourne. Then a single report careened crazily up the fissure, doubled and redoubled as it rose.

The Taliban's smile turned into a rictus, black lips drawn back from yellow teeth, eyes opened impossibly wide, giving him the appearance of a rabid animal. Then blood spurted from his chest, his eyes rolled up, and he vanished just as if he had been only a shadow.

Bourne glanced down, saw Aashir with the butt of the AWM jammed against his right shoulder, the long barrel raised, as if in a salute.

He extended a hand to Bourne. "I told you I'd get both," he said.

CHAPTER
THIRTY-NINE

Sonya was playing with the toys Islam had brought her gradually over the days: a rubber Arabian horse, a simple jigsaw puzzle in the shape of a dog, and a computer tablet on which she could learn prayer words from the Dua Surah Quran when either he or Soraya sounded them out for her.

Perhaps surprisingly, her favorite was the tablet, for then she could engage with Islam, whom she had come to like enormously. The feeling appeared mutual. When he brought their meals, he never failed to play with her, laugh with her, pray with her. Soraya would have liked to say that she hated this interaction, that she felt it a violation. After all, Islam could have been the one who had murdered her husband. That time was still jumbled in her mind, the terror, shock, and anguish obscuring all detail no matter how hard she tried to recreate the event. Of course, part of her did not want to envision it again; anyone in his right mind would understand. And yet, as a trained agent, she was bound and determined to remember it all — every last horrific second.

But on the other hand, Sonya was bringing him closer to them. The repeated evocation of positive emotion was her greatest ally. It ate away at the chains

367

of domination and subjugation that had bound her from the moment she and her family had been abducted. Just as important, it kept Sonya active, engaged, and happy. The child was far too young to dwell on the implications of their continuing incarceration.

Soraya heard Islam's voice intoning the prayer word Sonya had selected on the tablet. She heard her daughter's high-pitched voice repeating the word perfectly. And now that she thought about it, there was never a time when Islam had to repeat the word or correct her. That was how Sonya's mind worked. She had inherited all the best traits of her mother and her father. What frightened Soraya was that when she had grown up she would not remember Aaron, would not recall how gentle and wise he was, how much he loved her. Soraya knew that it was up to her to provide the memories — her and Aaron's many friends in Paris.

If they ever got back to Paris. But of course they would. Each hour of every day Islam's compassion for her and love for Sonya strengthened. Soraya knew that the time was drawing near when she could count on him as an ally in her plan to escape.

"You're all packed, Mr. President. Your bags are aboard Air Force One."

POTUS, seated at his desk in the Oval Office, lifted his head from his one hundredth or so reading of his itinerary in Singapore, both before the summit and during it. Who knew there was so much to see in the tiny city-state?

"Howard," he said, seeing his chief of staff standing in the doorway, "why so formal?"

"I have a surprise for you, Mr. President."

Anselm stood aside and William Magnus's two children entered the room. Teddy, his eight-year-old son, in his exuberance, actually burst in, running across the presidential seal on the carpet to throw himself into his father's arms. Charlie, his sixteen-year-old daughter, was more sedate in her entry, stepping carefully, as if the soles of her chunky shoes would mar the carpet.

"*Hullo*, Dad," Charlie muttered. She wore leather pants and a cropped sweater that clung to her no longer childish curves and left bare an inch of flesh at her waist.

"Well," said a beaming POTUS, in his most presidential tone, "what brings you two rascals to your father's inner sanctum?"

"*God*, Dad." Charlie fairly shuddered.

"I brought them, Bill."

And in walked Maggie, his wife of twenty-odd years — he could never remember the exact number. She was impeccably dressed, as always, today in a gray Chanel suit and shiny black Louboutin pumps. Her hair was as cropped as Charlie's sweater.

She strode across the room as if she owned the West Wing, bent from the waist, and pecked him respectfully on the cheek. "They're always badgering me to see you at work."

"*I've* never badgered you," Charlie said in her supercilious way.

Maggie raised one eyebrow. "About anything?"

"About coming *here*, anyway." Charlie had the mannerism, annoying to the rest of the family, of emphasizing at least one word in each sentence she uttered, as if she were a character in a comic book.

"Unfortunately," Anselm interceded, "the president has a full schedule today."

"When *doesn't* he?" Charlie muttered to no one in particular.

"Come on, crew." Maggie spread her arms. "Onward."

"You promised us sundaes," Teddy protested as he slid off his father's lap and went to the protective wing of his mother.

"And so you shall have," Maggie said, kissing him on the top of his head. "Come along, Charlene." She was already moving toward the door.

"In a *minute*, Mother." Charlie had come around her father's desk to stare out the window behind him. "What is it you *see* out there?"

The president swiveled around in his chair. "Are you asking me or telling me?"

Charlie turned to him. Her smile was as artificial as coffee creamer. "Who can see *in*?"

"What? No one." Magnus shifted uneasily in his chair. When had she become a woman? he asked himself. When had she put her precious childhood behind her? "What are you looking at?"

"I'm *wondering* if your *pants* are stained."

POTUS blinked. "I beg your pardon?" Could he have heard his daughter right? What on earth could she mean?

"I'll make this *simpler* for you, Dad." She leaned forward from the waist as his wife had done, but it wasn't to kiss him respectfully on the cheek. "Are. Your. Pants. Stained."

Magnus blinked. "Why should they be stained, Charlie?"

"A *human* stain, Dad."

The degree of contempt in her voice confused and astonished him. He stared up at her, still not quite getting it. His brain was slowed by shock, as if it were encased in a block of ice.

"But of *course* —" She threw Anselm such a poisonous look that he immediately scuttled out into the hallway. She turned back to Magnus. "Of course, you have *people* to take *care* of that for you."

Now Magnus was alarmed, but he still didn't know why. "Dammit, Charlie, start making sense."

Drawing closer, she whispered in his ear, "I *know*, Dad."

Magnus blinked. "Know what?"

"Your affair. And now I wonder if you ever *fucked* Camilla in *here*, where you *work* at making the world a *better* place." Seeing his stricken expression, she laughed softly, unpleasantly. "Don't worry. Even *Mom* doesn't know, though who's to say whether she *suspects*?"

And then she was gone, slapped out before Howard could intervene, or Magnus himself, reeling as much from her coarseness as from her accusation, could fabricate a chastising denial.

Instead of taking Aashir's hand and descending, Bourne went up into the sunlight, disappearing from sight. Shaking his head, Aashir slung his rifle over his shoulder and clambered up after him. There he found Bourne crouched over the second Taliban.

"He's dead," Bourne said.

"I made sure of that." The pride in Aashir's voice was evident.

"That was a mistake." Bourne looked up at him. "You should have wounded him. Now we'll never know whether he contacted a larger group, or whether we already dealt with them. He had important information to give us."

"I didn't think . . ." Aashir hung his head. "I was trying to make up for missing him the first time."

"This is a lesson you can only learn in the field," Bourne said. "Remember I told you that?"

Aashir nodded. Then he saw Bourne go completely still. "What is it?" he whispered.

"Third man," Bourne said. "At your ten o'clock."

"He's been lying low."

"Yes."

"That's the way of these people." Aashir slowly unslung the AWM. "Let me make up for —"

Bourne's hand clamped to his arm stopped him.

"Wait," Bourne said. "Wait."

Before Aashir could say a word, Bourne was off, scuttling to their right, over the rocks, moving in a deliberately noisy fashion. He was making himself a target, Aashir realized. Grasping the AWM, he slithered down, working his way slowly to the left in order to come around behind the third Taliban, whose focus must now be wholly on Bourne.

A shot rang out, and with it, movement up ahead and to Aashir's right. He saw the enemy then: a flash of black beard and gray turban. He fought down his instinct to shoot to kill, and, observing Bourne's warning, waited, patient as a spider. Waited until the Taliban showed enough of himself. Then he aimed the AWM, squeezed off a shot that caught the soldier in his right shoulder. The Taliban went down, tried to re-aim his rifle at the figure racing toward him. Aashir shot him in nearly the same spot. He went down and stayed down.

Aashir and Bourne reached the fallen Taliban at virtually the same time. The soldier was bleeding profusely. Bourne kicked away his weapon, went quickly and efficiently through his robes, relieving him of a handgun and a knife.

"Now," Bourne said, squatting beside him, "we talk."

The Taliban turned his head away, which brought Aashir into his line of vision.

"Where is your cadre?" Bourne said. "How many men?" He jammed the butt of the AWM into the wounded shoulder. The Taliban's teeth ground together, but he said nothing.

Bourne stood up, signed to Aashir, and went out of the Taliban's hearing. "We don't have time for a prolonged interrogation. I want you to turn away."

Aashir glanced over his shoulder at the wounded soldier. "I want to watch."

"Believe me, you don't."

Bourne returned to where the Taliban lay. The soldier looked up at him with bloodshot eyes, no expression on his face. Then Bourne bent down and, after a minute or so, Aashir did look away. Was it the wind making his eyes tear? When he wiped them clear and turned back, the Taliban was talking.

"My cadre went into the cave." The soldier licked his lips. "We're an advance scouting party. That's all there is."

Curious now, Aashir came and crouched beside the Taliban.

Bourne ignored Aashir. "Within how many miles?" he said.

"Fifty," the Taliban said. "Seventy. It's impossible to say." Even as he spoke, he took up a rock and, with a cry, drove it into the side of Aashir's head.

Aashir fell back, bleeding. Stepping over him, Bourne slammed the heel of his boot into the Taliban's throat, crushing it. The soldier gasped, gagging for air. Then his eyes lost their focus and his chest gave one last heave, then was still.

Aashir's eyelids were fluttering as he moved in and out of consciousness. Stooping, Bourne gathered him, slung him over his shoulder, and began the process of descending the fissure into the cave, returning to what was left of Borz's Chechen cadre.

CHAPTER
FORTY

"Why would you send me as your emissary?" Sara said. "Do you trust me that much?"

"My dear Ellie," El Ghadan said, "I don't trust you at all."

They were seated in a golden restaurant — walls, floor, and ceiling, all gold, all glittering as the early afternoon sunlight turned the floor molten, reflected upward, setting fire to the entire room. Apart from Sara, El Ghadan, and three of his men, no other patrons were in the restaurant, though it was the luncheon hour. Platoons of waiters with nothing else to do served them the food El Ghadan had ordered. Menus had not been provided.

"Not at this point in time, anyway." El Ghadan stirred honey into his tea. "I have devised a test for you, Ellie. This test can be given nowhere else but on Street Fifty-Two." He took up his cup and, with a peculiarly delicate gesture, sipped his tea. "Tell me, have you been to the Industrial Area?"

"I have."

"What were you doing there?"

"I was asked to find out if Arabian Switchgears was being used by al-Qaeda to transship weapons into Somalia."

He watched her as the food came, a kingly array of dishes set before them. He said nothing until the wait staff had retreated to their station at the rear of the restaurant. Outside, the sun had turned the water to thousands of tiny prisms.

"Eat, eat," he said, ladling mounds of food onto her plate like a mother who had taken a starving child in off the street. "This is the best food in Qatar."

"Better than what your followers get, holed up in the mountains."

"And what did you find at Arabian Switchgears?"

She met his steady gaze with her own. "You know what I found."

"That was a Mossad-engineered incursion."

"Allegedly," she said.

His lips curled in a dark smile. "So you work for Mossad."

Watch it, girl, she told herself. You're sailing too close to the wind. Now make this work. "I know people in the FSB, Al-Mukhabarat al-Ammah, CIB, MI6, BAIS, the Chinese Ministry of State Security, Mossad. Shall I go on?" She relaxed her face, laughing softly. "How do you suppose I obtained the product you wanted?"

He nodded thoughtfully. "Still more to you than meets the eye, Ellie."

She needed to change both the topic and the atmosphere. Her gesture took in the entire table. "Such luxury for a man who purports to hate Doha and its decadent Western ways."

El Ghadan put down his fork and sat back. "I keep wondering why you continue to goad me."

"Let's be honest, you and I hate each other — and yet we're mysteriously drawn to each other."

"I don't hate you," El Ghadan said.

"I'm being honest, why can't you?"

He took up his fork and began to eat.

"Yes, I see," Sara said. "It's impossible for you to be honest."

For a moment, his gaze turned toward the golden heavens. "Honesty. Let me see, you say we are drawn together. But to me the reason is not so very mysterious. We live in the margins, you and I, nevertheless we refuse to be marginalized. Systems of government, religions, ideologies rule the world, but they are all flawed. And into these flaws flows corruption, seeking to take hold. We are all human, after all; therefore, all corrupt."

"I could not disagree more."

"You disagree, Ellie?"

When he smiled — really smiled — as now, he became quite charming. From Sara's point of view, frighteningly so.

He spread his hands. "But corruption is the human condition. Every student of history knows this. C'mon, Ellie, you're digging in your heels for the wrong reason."

"And what would that be?"

"To spite me. To oppose me. To show you can fight me." That disarming smile again. "I already know this."

She brought food to her mouth, chewed, and swallowed. The best food in Doha, and it tasted like ashes in her mouth. Being with him was like being too near a black hole — all your energy was focused on not getting sucked in. She felt mentally and emotionally spent. She missed Jason more than she could say, and this too frightened her.

And yet from these depths inspiration sometimes came; she found it in herself to rally. "Tell me, what do you stand for? Sooner or later, we all have to make a stand, we who live in the margins. You're no exception." She looked at him shrewdly, beginning to warm to her subject. "You included religions as flawed, therefore corrupt. So you're not a fundamentalist. What then?" And then she decided to play her ace. "I'm thinking now that you're very much like your partner, Ivan Borz."

Outwardly, El Ghadan's expression did not change, but Sara, trained in divining details in subjects whose demeanor ranged from recalcitrant to hostile, felt the changes beneath his skin. He grew tense, his heart rate increased as, she supposed, his blood pressure rose. Direct hit!

"Borz is a businessman, plain and simple," she went on. "Nothing complicated about his purpose. He wants to make money; he wants power. That's you all over, isn't it?"

El Ghadan returned to his food, but he was attacking it now. "You have no idea what I want."

"Are you afraid to tell me?"

Now he appeared piqued. "Listen to me, Ellie." He leaned forward, his hands flat on the table, fingers spread. "While it's true that you and I live in the margins, there we part company. Do you know why?

Because you have everything and we have nothing. We have been thought pariahs for so long that this is precisely what we have become. So in a sense you have made us what we are."

His eyes, always wary, always calculating, seemed to burn in his skull. Something had changed in him. Naked emotion had laid his face bare, stripped it of artifice and bombast. "We have had nothing for so long that those who have everything become the target of our hatred and our violence. The fact that you want to push your values on us only enrages us more."

He appeared now to catch himself, to rein in his sudden outburst of anger, to retreat behind his implacable façade. "And as for me being here in Doha — I'm not here because I want to be in that SUV out there or eating this rich food. Wearing these Western clothes is a necessity, a disguise. It's my job to be here now."

He reached into the breast pocket of his suit jacket, pulled out a slim wallet. "Look at this thing. It's made of crocodile skin and cost five hundred dollars. Imagine! This is a coveted item in Western culture." He shook his head. "Who can fathom such an atrocity!"

The extremity of his rage had distanced him from her, had made of him a thunderous figure, at perfect odds with his civilized clothes. He looked as if he wanted to rip them off right then and there.

Instead he said, in a low, ominous rumble, "My purpose is to destroy the people who carry their lives in this." He shook the wallet. "Who live in expensive high-rises, wear expensive clothes, eat expensive food

— the people who have everything, while the dispossessed of the world watch with sunken cheeks and hollow eyes."

Sara's appetite flooded back. Her heart lifted. So she had done it. She had succeeded in getting him to reveal himself, at last, when all others had failed even to get near him.

"Now you are going to give me the 'This isn't killing, this is war' speech, right?"

His features darkened, like the sky anticipating a storm front. "No woman has ever talked to me the way you do."

"You frighten everyone, El Ghadan, especially women." She shrugged. "But then your stock-in-trade is intimidation — like Ivan Borz, like the worst criminal."

"Still you goad me." His eyes narrowed. "Why? What is it you really want, Ellie?"

She would not tell him that he had already given her what she wanted. "I want what all women want, El Ghadan: respect."

He wiped his lips with a napkin, took up an olive, glistening with oil, between his fingers. He was back on secure ground, back to having information she wanted. "When you get to Street Fifty-Two and accomplish what is required of you," he said, savoring the olive in the same way he savored his words, "you shall have it."

"You see how it is now," Hunter said as she wiped the sweat off the back of Camilla's neck. They were sitting on the bed in Camilla's room, the rumpled covers like sea foam caught in a single instant. "This is the world we're both living in. This is reality."

"No," Camilla said, her voice tiny and throttled by emotion. "This is deceit. This is hypocrisy. This is betrayal at the deepest level."

"Poor Cam."

Hunter stroked her back, but she twisted away. "Get off me. I don't want to have anything to do with you."

Hunter heaved a sigh Camilla thought a bit too theatrical. She rose and padded to the bedroom door. With her hand on the knob, she said, "You say that now, Cam. But, actually, I'm the only one who can save you from this shitstorm."

She walked out, timing her exit as perfectly as a veteran actor. And what, Camilla thought now, was the world she was caught in but a stage and all the players actors? Master performers. And what was she? An emotional wreck, an expendable walk-on. In terms of war, cannon fodder.

Putting her head in her hands, she bent over and wept, not only for this current act of betrayal, but for her broken childhood, the disciplinarian mother, the philandering father, the diffident and aloof sister. The Secret Service had been a way to wall herself off from all of them, a way to take a new path, a way to make a new life for herself.

Now here she was, on the vast, lonely stage, with nothing left for her.

She rose, slogged into the bathroom, splashed cold water onto her face until she felt on the verge of drowning. And that's when it came to her. She lifted her head, stared at herself in the mirror, and didn't like what she saw. She didn't like it at all.

"Fuck you," she said. And then more forcefully, "Fuck you!"

She was addressing herself, but also all those actors around her who had purported to be her friends. Their masks were down; she heard the lines they uttered for what they were.

"Fuck you!" she shouted, then turned, walked back into her room, pulled on jeans and her favorite sweatshirt, the one with Stewie Griffin from *Family Guy,* holding a scepter, an emperor's crown on his head, above which was emblazoned the motto "Born to Rule." In bare feet, she went out of her room, along the hall, and down the stairs, determined that her days of self-pity were at an end.

She found Hunter in the industrial-size kitchen, a stainless steel rectangle with three refrigerators, four dishwashing machines, two sinks, walk-in pantry, and freezer. Hunter was sitting on a wooden stool at the central much-used butcher-block island. In front of her was an enormous bowl of vanilla ice cream onto which she was squeezing U-Bet from a giant brown plastic bottle.

"Whipped cream's in the fridge on the right," she said.

Camilla noticed not one spoon on the island, but two. Returning from the refrigerator, she set the whipped cream down and pulled up a stool next to Hunter.

"Stewie," Hunter said. "Is that your power shirt?"

"Something like that." Camilla wanted to smile, but didn't. Nevertheless, the feeling of animosity that had been eating away at her insides vanished, and she felt more at ease.

When Hunter reached for the whipped cream, she stopped her.

"No more sex," she said.

"Are you punishing me, or yourself?"

"And no more lies."

Hunter nodded. "Okay."

Camilla took her hand away, and Hunter laid on the whipped cream.

"I saw you with that shitbag Terrier at Jake's World," Camilla said.

Hunter passed the second spoon over. "Dig in."

"That's all you have to say? 'Dig in'?"

Hunter took a huge mound of the sundae on her spoon and crammed it into her mouth. For a moment her eyes closed in ecstasy. Then she made a humming sound, which jolted Camilla almost off her seat. That same vocalization signaled Hunter's orgasm, the first of a chain reaction.

Camilla's temper was up. "Hunter, answer me!"

"What d'you want me to say, 'Guilty as charged'?"

"That would do, yes."

"You're not eating the sundae," Hunter pointed out. "Come on. Enjoy yourself."

"I didn't come down here to have dessert."

"Why *did* you come down here?"

"How did you know I would?" A good interrogator answered a question with another.

"I know you."

"I'll admit you think you do."

Hunter turned to her. "Okay. What am I guilty of, exactly?"

"Of lying to me, for starters."

"Didn't you lie to me?"

"What? When?"

"You said you'd never been with a woman before."

Into Camilla's mind flew Helena and the memory of their college tryst.

"Jesus, how did you — ?"

"Who cares? It doesn't matter. That's the point, isn't it?" Hunter picked up the second spoon, placed it in Camilla's hand. "Now, let's have some fun, and eat together from this enchanted bowl. Nothing better on earth than a chocolate sundae."

CHAPTER
FORTY-ONE

It seemed a long, agonizing trail through the labyrinth of the Afghan cave before Bourne reached Borz and the Chechens. The remnants of the cadre were on the point of moving out.

"What happened?" Borz said as Bourne set Aashir down. "I thought you were lost . . . or dead."

When Bourne told him, he said, "They're dead — all three of them. You're sure?"

Bourne glanced around. "Where's your physician?"

"Also among the dead," Borz intoned. "Along with more than half my men."

Indeed, there seemed more corpses than soldiers standing awaiting the recommencement of orders. None of Faraj's men had made it. Bourne counted five Chechens and Borz, the only survivors of the ambush.

Bourne turned to one of the Chechens. "Fetch the physician's kit, would you?"

The man looked at his leader, and when Borz nodded his assent, he trotted over to where the physician lay, snatched up his pack, and returned to where Bourne knelt beside Aashir.

"How badly is he injured?" Borz asked. He appeared unusually ill at ease.

"He was hit with a stone at close range." Bourne opened the pack, took out antiseptic and sterile cotton pads. He turned Aashir's head gently to one side, exposing the wound, which continued to seep blood. Cleaning the wound gave him a clear idea of how deep it went. No stitches were needed and the bleeding was near to stopping on its own. As he went about bandaging the wound, he spoke to Borz.

"We can't be sure the men in the owl's nest didn't radio for help, though I don't think they did. Still, best to post lookouts on higher ground until we can head out."

Borz barked his orders, then squatted down on the other side of Aashir. "The boy won't die, will he?"

"Not from the wound itself," Bourne said. "The worry is concussion. He's gone in and out of consciousness." He sat Aashir up, spoke to him directly. The eyes fluttered open. "Good," Bourne said. "Aashir, do you know where you are?"

"Yes."

"You remember what happened to you?"

The eyes fluttered closed.

"Aashir! Do you remember — ?"

"What happened to me? Yes. The Taliban hit me with a rock."

"That's right."

The boy's eyes opened, focusing on Bourne. He smiled. "I'm happy to see you, Yusuf."

Bourne turned his head. "He'll be fine," he said under his breath to Borz.

386

"Good." The Chechen slapped his thighs as he rose. "When can we leave this accursed place?"

"Fifteen minutes," Bourne said, "maybe twenty."

"Make it quick as you can, Yusuf. I don't want to run into more of these people if I can help it." He went off to see to what was left of his men.

"How are you, Yusuf?" Aashir said softly.

"Me?" Bourne laughed. "I'm fine. And you will be too, in a day or two."

"I don't know. My head is pounding."

"Try not to move it too much." Bourne pawed through the physician's bag, found a painkiller, and handed Aashir two. "Here. Swallow."

Aashir did, wincing as he was obliged to tip his head back to get them down. He must have become a bit dizzy; he grabbed at Bourne's arm to steady himself. Bourne held him until the blood returned to the boy's face.

"That wasn't so good," he said in a voice pinched by his pain and fear.

"It will get better."

Aashir took several deep breaths. "I screwed up back there."

"You made up for it," Bourne said with a reassuring smile. "You did better than most."

Aashir looked at him for a long time. "Yusuf."

"What is it?"

"I know I can trust you."

"Of course you can."

The boy licked his lips. Now he looked truly frightened. "So now I'll tell you a secret no one else

387

knows." He looked around to make sure no one was near them. He took another deep breath, let it out. "That girl I told you about? The one I wanted to run away with? Well, it wasn't a girl. It was a boy my age." He looked at Bourne, searching his face, it seemed, for either disapproval or validation. A laugh turned into a sob. "Some man I turned out to be."

So this was what Aashir had been wanting to tell Bourne for some time. It had been on his lips at least twice before, but he had lacked the courage or the faith in Yusuf to confide in him. The compressed time that comes with life-and-death situations had cemented his trust in their friendship.

Bourne was still holding him. Though Borz was getting restless, it was not yet time to let him go.

"What happened to your friend?"

"He's dead." Aashir bit his lip. It was clear that was all he was prepared to say about it now, possibly forever.

"Aashir, look at me," Bourne said. "I'm sorry for your loss. I'm sorry you've had to carry this terrible burden."

This produced in the boy a smile, both grateful and rueful. "Strange. It doesn't seem so terrible, now someone else knows."

Then, at last, Aashir allowed himself to cry.

Hunter's midnight-blue '72 Chrysler Imperial barreled down the Virginia highway on its way to Dulles International Airport. The windows were open, the Imperial's speed was redlining, and Hunter seemingly had no worries about being picked up by the highway patrol's radar.

Beside her, Camilla stared straight ahead as her future came rushing toward her at light speed.

"What are you thinking?" Hunter said.

"I'm thinking about Kettle — the dinger."

"And here I was hoping you were thinking about staying here."

"And do what?" Camilla shifted in her seat. "Anselm and Finnerman have their claws too deeply in me."

"Well, at least you have Kettle's real name and photo. Hopefully you'll be able to ID him before —" She broke off, biting her lip.

Camilla shot her a sidelong glance, but Hunter would not meet her eye.

Traffic had thickened, and for a time Hunter concentrated on her driving. There was a lot of weaving going on, as other drivers stared or honked their horns. It wasn't every day you got to see a cherry 1972 Imperial doing ninety-five in rural Virginia.

"Now that I know you're really going, do you have any curiosity what Terrier and I have in mind for you?"

Camilla shook her head.

"What does that mean?"

"That conversation was part of another life."

Hunter turned to her. "You mean you don't want to know what it is?"

"That's exactly what I mean."

Hunter maneuvered the Imperial smartly around a truck. "I don't get you."

"We're not the same people who met for the first time last week, are we? I don't want to be involved in whatever you had planned in Singapore."

"Never say never." Hunter opened her handbag, took out a buff-colored envelope, dropped it on Camilla's lap.

Camilla stared down at it, frowning. "What is this?"

"Read it on the plane. If you decide to. If not, go into the ladies' room at the Singapore airport, burn it, and flush the ashes down the toilet. Will you do that? Yes? Okay." Hunter pressed the accelerator all the way to the floorboard. "You're ready for takeoff."

CHAPTER
FORTY-TWO

"You stink," Islam said, the moment he entered the room. "And whose fault is that?"

Soraya watched Sonya run to him, watched as he gathered her up in his arms, lifting her over his head until she began to giggle.

"How about a shower?" he said to Soraya as he cradled Sonya in the crook of one arm.

"I'd like that," Soraya said. "We'd both like that."

He took them out of the room, down the hall lined with El Ghadan's men, their faces wrapped in headscarves, their dark eyes revealing nothing. These young men with their grim silence, their lack of affect, their oiled assault rifles still chilled her. They were only babies.

Islam ushered them through the second door on their right — a larger space than the toilets, and brighter. It was wider than it was long. Shower stalls lined the rear of the room, tiled and blessedly clean. A stack of thick towels sat folded atop one wooden stool, piles of clean clothes on another.

"I estimated sizes for both of you," Islam said, setting Sonya down.

"Thank you." Soraya turned to him. "May we have some privacy?"

"I'm afraid I have to stay," Islam said. Then, unexpectedly, his eye crinkled, indicating that he was smiling at her. "But I will turn my back so long as you promise not to hit me again."

Soraya surveyed him for a moment. "I promise. Neither Sonya nor I will hit you."

His smile broadened. "There's soap, shampoo, and plenty of hot water." Then he turned away, facing the door.

Warily at first, then more rapidly, Soraya undressed her daughter, then herself. Taking Sonya by the hand, she led her into one of the showers, which was large enough for three adults. The hot water was sheer ecstasy, and for a time she reveled in it, before she got down to work, soaping up Sonya's little body, washing her hair. Then, because Sonya asked to, she squatted down so her daughter could wash her hair.

"You shouldn't be in here with us," Soraya said as she scrubbed herself down.

"I shouldn't be doing a lot of things," Islam said, "but my life does not run along those lines. I have no wife, no children. My job is to wage war. Injustice is all I know."

"Now you sound full of self-pity."

He stiffened. "Not self-pity. Rage."

Soraya placed a soap bubble on the tip of Sonya's nose, making her laugh. "You've been brought up on rage."

392

"Injustice breeds rage. Assaults on our homeland, occupation by infidels, the contamination of Western consumerism, while we are forced into mountain and desert retreats. How would Sonya respond to these violations? How would she react to being oppressed? Don't even respond. You can't know the answer, you can't even imagine it."

Soraya finished her shower in silence, knowing he was right.

Bourne, Ivan Borz, Aashir, and the five Chechen soldiers came down from the mountains without incident. Borz had sent two of his men ahead as advance scouts, but they had seen nothing untoward. There was no sign of Taliban activity. Behind them, the caves looked like cavities in an otherwise healthy mouth. They had the sad look of abandonment, of temporary homes, unloved and unwanted, occupied only by the restless spirits of the forgotten dead.

They spent more than half a day on their trek. Occasionally they would pause for a brief rest. Even the mighty Chechens seemed near the end of their rope. The deaths of so many of their compatriots had worked its black magic on them. They were sullen and dispirited. All except Borz, who seemed as light and buoyant as a birthday balloon. At each rest stop, he opened a map, studying it in relation to the terrain that surrounded them.

"You know where we are," Bourne said at one point.

"Absolutely." Borz made no secret of the map. "Once we were across the border and into the caves we were all right. The Waziri knew where to take us."

"They didn't betray us," Bourne said.

"I know. It's a pity Faraj shot them." By his tone it was clear he didn't think it was a pity at all. Rather, it was a complication Faraj's rage had done away with.

"Where are we headed?" Bourne asked.

"Here." Borz's forefinger stabbed out, indicating a spot on the map. "Not so far now." He looked up at the darkening sky. The sun seemed to have an aversion to this part of Afghanistan. The terrain was cloaked in a perpetual twilight; they seemed to be floating between worlds.

"No point in coming on our destination at night." Borz folded the map and put it away. "We'll make camp here and set out at first light."

They settled in, backs to rocks, the Chechens taking turns standing guard. Bourne noted they used infrared night-vision goggles to pierce the darkness. Borz had certainly been telling the truth when he said he profited by America's wars. Those goggles were American-designed and -manufactured.

They ate their meager rations, too exhausted to know exactly what it was they were chewing. It didn't matter as long as it provided sustenance. At last, they settled down to shallow sleep, but for Bourne the night wore on, the minutes draining away so slowly his thoughts flickered among them like comets streaking in the darkness of space. He didn't want to sleep; he wanted to get on with it. There was no time to waste.

He was all too aware of the hours passing, of the sluggishness of their progress. The beginning of the summit was only a day away now, and here he was embedded in a terrorist cadre whose objective was also the summit. This, at least, had been his working premise ever since he recognized the blueprints on Borz's desk. But Borz was not divulging any information, and Bourne knew better than to push him too hard. That would only cast suspicion his way — the last thing he needed from the Chechen leader.

But time, his implacable enemy from the start of the mission El Ghadan had forced on him, was fast becoming Soraya's and Sonya's executioner. For the first time, he wondered whether he would be able to save them, whether he had taken the right path after all. But the fact was, he could not think of a reasonable alternative — either then or now. There was only faith left to him, faith that the path both he and Borz were on would lead to Singapore quickly now.

"Yusuf," Borz said, as he sat down beside Bourne, "satisfy my curiosity. When did you make your first kill?"

Bourne stared up at the uncountable stars, their brightness banishing all concerns, all negative thoughts; they would only get in his way. "I try not to think about it."

"But surely you remember."

"I remember everything," Bourne lied. "That's why I try not to think about it."

"Death becomes me," Borz said after a small silence. "There is a silence just after someone dies — a special silence I cherish."

Bourne's ears pricked up. "Why?"

"It's only in that silence I feel truly alive."

They made their destination just before midday. The sky was clear, the temperature elevated. The scouts hadn't seen a soul. The blasted landscape they passed through was devoid of all life; they might as well have been treading on the dark side of the moon.

Dust coated them. It had gotten into everything, including their mouths and noses. The taste was like medicine forced on them to stem a sickness. The Chechens had come out of their lethargy into a state of perpetual impatience. This led to irritation, which led to anger. They snapped at each other, their iron discipline crumbling in the face of the hostile environment. It was as if the air they breathed was hour by hour changing them, turning them against themselves. Once, Aashir intervened, breaking up a fight over an alleged slight. Another time, Borz, holding Aashir back, allowed two men to go at it, trusting that their rage would be spent by violence. He was wrong. The bitterness remained, festering like a plague to which all of them had been exposed. Bourne kept an eagle eye on Aashir, but the boy seemed to have shaken off the effects of the concussion. In fact, Aashir did his best to keep the Chechens relatively calm and sane by telling them stories of djinns, living dust devils, and talking serpents. Bourne was impressed not only by his initiative but by how he inveigled the disgruntled men to listen to him. He wasn't even Chechen, but he won the affection of death-hardened men.

The cadre crested a rise, trekked across a plateau so barren they all felt vulnerable to a sudden attack, and

396

so Borz hurried them along. At the far end of the plateau, the terrain dropped into a wide depression, in the center of which was a large item covered with camouflage netting.

"Here we are!" Borz cried, loudly enough for all of his men to hear. They were in need of encouragement.

While two Chechens stood watch, Borz directed the three remaining soldiers to cut away the netting. An Antonov An-140 twin-engine turboprop crouched, awaiting their arrival. The plane had a capacity of fifty-two people and a maximum range of a bit over sixteen hundred nautical miles. Borz must have felt it expendable, Bourne thought. At nine million dollars, it was a relatively inexpensive aircraft as these things went. An Alenia or an ATR went for about twelve to twenty-six million, but the Antonov was sound enough. How Borz had managed to have it flown here was anyone's guess.

At last! Bourne thought. His pulse beat fast in his temples, a rush of blood to his head.

Borz unlocked the door, climbed in, and his men followed. Bourne, the last one to board, felt a strange premonition come over him as he kicked away the chocks, freeing the wheels. He went up the central aisle to the cockpit. Borz was already in the pilot's seat, well into his pre-takeoff checklist. Bourne slid into the seat beside him.

"I don't have a good feeling," he said.

Borz grunted. "You never have a good feeling." His fingers were flipping switches as he watched for any red lights, assuring himself step by step that the plane was ready. He started up the engines and the cabin started to vibrate. "Look, green lights across the board."

Bourne tapped a dial. "The altimeter's off."

"It's an Antonov," Borz said. "Fucking Russians. What d'you expect?"

"I expect everything to be in working order in any plane I fly."

Borz turned to him. "For an Arab, you can be quite amusing, Yusuf, you know that?"

Moments later, they were rolling across the depression. On the far end was a line of trees, dusty, misshapen, brownish green. The Antonov torched the sky, its undercarriage not even close to scraping the treetops.

"Flight time about fifty-five minutes," Borz called over the engines' roar.

Bourne pulled out his rifle, stripped it down, inspected each piece, put it back together. Borz watched him, but said nothing.

Just shy of fifty minutes later, Borz began the Antonov's descent. Bourne, staring out the windscreen, saw them approaching another depression — this one large enough to be termed a valley. In the center, the rocky terrain had been cleared to create a landing field. A long-range jet, fuselage gleaming in the sunlight, stood ready and waiting at one end of the strip. Bourne could make out six armed men. One, scanning the sky with binoculars, raised his assault rifle, pumping it up and down three times.

"All's well," Borz said. He switched the landing lights on and off three times, in response to the signal.

398

They had descended far enough that Bourne could see the airstrip was wider than most, could accommodate both the Antonov and the jet at once. Borz made preparations for the landing. He had entered the critical flight path, was beginning his final approach, when the altimeter suddenly dropped precipitously.

Both men saw it.

"It's nothing, Yusuf."

But Bourne, his premonition returning at full force, knew Borz was wrong.

Without another word, he unstrapped himself, knelt at the rear of the cockpit, unlocked the hatch in the floor, and peered in at the tangle of wires and electronic systems.

"Pull up!" he shouted at once. "Borz, pull up now!"

CHAPTER
FORTY-THREE

Benjamin Landis, code named Kettle, had many attributes that set him apart from his brethren, but possibly the most important was that he looked precisely like the legend given to him by the DOD. He entered Singapore under the name Jack Binder, Inverhalt Fabrications' Far East regional sales manager. Inverhalt had offices in Washington, Paris, and Mumbai, or so it read on his business card. If anyone was curious enough to telephone these offices they would be put through to a dedicated agent at the DOD Foreign Ops section, but no one had ever called, at least not in Kettle's memory.

He was middle-aged, tall, thin, whey-faced, and balding. He also affected the slight stoop of many taller people and the splay-footed gait of someone with fallen arches, which he did not have. Apart from a briefcase filled with Inverhalt information, he traveled without baggage, preferring to buy whatever he needed at his destination.

Finished with immigration, he went immediately to his airline's customer service desk and in response to his query was handed a sealed envelope. He headed to the men's room, where he entered a stall, locking the door behind him.

Slitting open the envelope, he found a set of car keys, a bill of lading, and a slip of paper containing three lines of electronic type. The first was the location of a vehicle, the second was an address, the third was an alphanumeric code. He memorized them all, then set fire to the paper, flushing the ashy remains down the toilet.

The Mitsubishi van was waiting for him in the long-term parking lot. In the glove box was the ticket, plus enough local money to cover the cost of parking and much more. He drove out of the lot and the short distance to the freight terminal. A guard checked his bill of lading, stamped it, and directed him to the proper warehouse, where imports were waiting, having cleared customs. Two men in overalls loaded three long rolls wrapped in brown paper into the rear of the van.

Exiting the airport, he drove to the address he had memorized. He had had several previous briefs in Singapore and so had no need to consult the Google Maps app on his mobile.

The address was a warehouse — one of a row of them — in the southwestern section of the city. To the left of the corrugated galvanized steel door was an electronic pad into which he punched the alphanumeric code he had memorized. The door rose, and he returned to the van and drove it into the interior, which contained only a black BMW sedan.

Opening the van's rear doors, he unwrapped the consignment, which turned out to be rolls of silk from

India. The fabric was wrapped tightly around thick cardboard cores, each one of which contained a piece of the sniper's rifle, scope, and ammo he had had custom made for him.

He checked the pieces, fitted them together, loaded and unloaded the long gun, then broke it down again. Leaving the keys in the van, he got into the BMW, reached under the floor mat, inserted the key in the ignition, and backed out. He pressed a button on the visor and the steel door slid down into place. Then he turned the car and drove into the golden late afternoon sunlight.

"That's the last of the press interviews for today," Howard Anselm said as he handed the Reuters correspondent over to one of Air Force One's uniformed stewards.

Even thirty thousand feet in the air, POTUS's responsibilities never ended. It was the conclusion of a long day, and the president looked particularly haggard, so much so that even Anselm, his mind awhirl with resolving the protocols of four nations, was struck by it. He came into the spacious presidential cabin, closing the door behind him.

"Everyone wants a piece of me." Magnus scrubbed his face with his hands. "I feel like I need a sauna, a rubdown, and a shower, in that order."

"Unfortunately, Bill, those luxuries will have to wait until we're on the ground. Singapore is noted for its practitioners of the healing arts."

"The healing arts are what I need most now." Magnus looked up at his chief of staff. "She knows, Howard. Charlie knows."

"She knows what, Bill?" Anselm tried to sound calm, but his pulse was fluttering.

"About Camilla!" POTUS scrubbed his face again, as if trying to erase the terrifying incident in the Oval Office. "Of all the people to find out! Jesus Christ, what are we going to do?"

Anselm seated himself opposite his boss. "Calm down, Bill."

"Calm down? You should've seen the look on her face."

"I saw the look she gave me."

"And scuttled away like a rat."

"I wanted to give the two of you privacy."

"Oh, don't give me that crap. You knew what was about to happen. You just didn't want to be there when the bomb hit." Unconsciously, POTUS held his hands in prayer. "Anyway, it wasn't anything like what she threw my way." Then he exploded. "Respect, Howard! She's lost all respect for me! My only daughter." His voice cracked, and he lowered it. "She'll never forgive me, Howard. Never. My relationship with her is ruined."

Anselm decided this was not the time to tell his friend that his relationship with his daughter — as well as with his wife — had been ruined years ago. The human creature, he had discovered, possessed an almost unlimited capacity for denial and self-deception.

Instead, he made soothing noises because he knew that was what POTUS needed to hear. "It'll be all right, Bill. We'll work it out."

"How? How? Just tell me that."

"First of all, we will give it time. We'll let Charlie's feathers settle. The air will clear and then we'll go to work on her. She'll come around, you'll see."

"I could get her something," Magnus said. "Something major that'll make an impression. She's been wanting a car, driving lessons. You know. What about a Fiat? They're cute."

Anselm mentally rolled his eyes. "Buy American, Bill. Anyway, let the dust settle before making that decision." Now for the hard part, he thought, taking a deep breath. "In the meantime, you need to keep the presidential mouse in the house."

Magnus's face was mottled, as if he had been weeping. But of course that was impossible. Presidents didn't weep, except at national tragedies of enormous scope. And even then . . . He was commander in chief of the United States Armed Forces, for Christ's sake.

He swung around in his chair, his back to Anselm. "But, see, the thing of it is, I miss her, Howard."

"Who, Bill? Who do you miss? Charlie?"

"Don't be absurd," POTUS snapped. "When we get to Singapore, I have to see Camilla."

Anselm groaned inwardly, thinking, Is there truly no rest for the presidential mouse? "After what we just discussed — ?"

"I know what's coming," POTUS snapped. "I don't want to hear it."

404

"Bill, you must listen to reason. She's been given a brief."

"I don't care. Dammit, I won't be able to function at the summit. That's the bottom line, Howard. I won't be strong. I won't be presidential. You don't want that, do you?"

Anselm wiped sweat out of his eyes. Christ, he thought, it was times like these when no amount of power was worth the angst. "No, sir," he said dutifully, revealing none of this. "No one does."

"Then just do it, Howard." POTUS held his head in his hands, as if battered by a pain beyond imagining. "Just fucking make it happen."

Borz hauled back on the joystick. "What the fuck is happening back there?"

"There's an explosive device attached to the altimeter," Bourne shouted back. "There was a reason the altimeter dial wasn't working correctly. It's been jiggered."

"Meaning?"

"I'm not positive, but it seems most likely that when we touch down the device will detonate."

For the next thirty seconds or so, Borz emitted a stream of the most obscene curses. Then he got down to business. "Can you render the device harmless?"

"I need a needle-nosed pliers and a wire cutter," Bourne said.

"The engineer's emergency toolkit is in the bulkhead just above you," Borz called without turning around.

Bourne twisted open the flush handle, found what he needed, then returned his attention to the explosive device.

"What is it?" Borz asked.

"Semtex," Bourne answered. "Enough to blow us all to kingdom come."

"Christ Jesus!" Borz muttered as he pulled back on the throttle. "Don't take too long, Yusuf," he shouted. "We're running out of fuel."

"How could we be running out of fuel? We've only been flying for an hour."

"The tank wasn't full," Borz said. "It didn't need to be."

All those men, left dead in the Afghan caves; the cadre seriously diminished.

Bourne went for the red wire, but at the last moment, as he settled the jaws of the wire cutter around it, he saw the trap. The bomb maker had set a double blind. Cutting this red wire would not defuse the bomb. In fact, breaking the connection would signal the bomb that it was under attack. It would explode at once.

Carefully, Bourne backed the wire cutter away from the red wire.

"How're you coming? Yusuf, I'll be forced to land in about four minutes. That's all the time we have left."

CHAPTER
FORTY-FOUR

El Ghadan insisted on driving Sara to the Industrial Area in his huge American SUV. He activated a privacy panel that shut them off from the driver and the muscle up front.

"With me, you won't ever have to worry about the police." Sara was still learning the extent of his influence throughout Qatar.

"What is our destination?" she asked.

"Street Fifty-Two and Al Manajer," he replied. "Omega and Gulf Agencies." He turned toward her on the seat. "I'm throwing you into the big pond."

"You really feel the need to test me? After the product I gave you? After I killed Blum for you?"

"This is sink or swim, Ellie. No second chances."

The SUV swung onto the Industrial Area approach road. They were in the southwest quadrant, a section of the city no tourist knew existed, let alone ever saw. No one challenged them, no guard even looked their way. It was uncanny, and, for Sara, another sobering example of El Ghadan's control of this region. They rolled slowly, inexorably toward the far southern edge of the Industrial Area.

The vehicle pulled up to the curb outside a long, low, almost windowless building. Over its steel-jacketed front doors was a sign: OMEGA + GULF AGENCIES. Looking out through the heavily smoked glass windows, Sara saw no vehicles, no pedestrians — just the sunbaked road, hot enough to fry falafel.

"Now what?" she asked.

"Now we wait."

He sat very close to her, his presence like that of a coiled serpent.

"Wait for what? I think I have the right to know what it is you expect of me."

El Ghadan was staring straight at the front doors of Omega + Gulf Agencies. "That is not for me to say."

Sara's brow wrinkled. "Then how will I know — ?"

"It will be for you to make the choice, Ellie."

Choice? What choice? She felt a chill slither through her, even while a bead of sweat rolled down the indentation of her spine.

She tried to take another tack. "What goes on in there? What is the agencies' business?"

"For the moment, you know all you need to know."

His voice had abruptly turned harsh and cutting, and despite her best efforts, she could not help feeling diminished by it.

The doors to Omega + Gulf Agencies opened and a slim young man stepped out into the blinding sunlight. He wore jeans, an immaculate white T-shirt, and Nike sneakers. A pair of wraparound sunglasses shaded his eyes. He oriented himself to the SUV but did not make a move. His mouth was an expressionless slash.

408

"Here is Islam," El Ghadan said with what appeared to be an enigmatic smile. "Go along now. You don't want to keep him waiting."

She slipped slowly, almost dazedly out of the SUV. The sunlight hit her like an anvil.

Because she was on the edge of the unknown, because she was confronting a test the parameters of which were hidden from her, she began to wonder whether El Ghadan suspected she wasn't who she claimed to be — a friend of the fictional diamond merchant, Martine Heur, and a freelance fieldman.

Could he suspect her of being American, or Israeli? Even worse, did he know about her relationship with Jason? She tried to reassure herself. How *could* he know? But then the darkness of the unknown came rushing in. What if he did know? Then what in the world was he playing at here at the corner of Street Fifty-Two and Al Manajer?

All at once, she began to feel the ground soften beneath her feet, until she was sinking into quicksand. Suddenly, she didn't know where she was.

She had lost her bearings.

The nest of colored wires swam before Bourne's eyes as he remembered an early morning in Bosnia when Soraya had been caught by the tripwire that led like a spider's silken strand to an explosive hidden just beneath the icy crust of earth. Sprawled on the snowy ground, she could not move forward or backward. The scents of pine resin and leaf mold filled his nostrils.

"Don't move," he had cautioned her. "Relax. I have you."

Using only his fingertips, he had exposed the explosives — three packs of C4, bound together by black electrician's tape. Unlike other bombs of that type, this one had a timer that started ticking down the moment the tripwire was activated.

There were the four main wires — white, black, yellow, and red. Two were alive, two were dummies. The red was almost always alive, the one to go for. He opened his slender gravity knife, but as he pried apart the black and white wires to get to the red wire, he froze. Four more wires presented themselves below the top four. The digital clock was counting down. Two minutes left, a minute and a half.

"Jason?"

"Right here, Soraya. I almost have it."

But he didn't. Eight wires and very little time to sort through them. Already down to a minute, now less. He examined the wires one by one, working out what each was attached to. But now he had less than thirty seconds until both he and Soraya were blown to smithereens.

It was impossible. There was no way to discover which wire was the correct one to cut — the bomb maker was diabolical.

Fifteen seconds. Ten.

That's when he saw it: At the ten-second mark, deep in the heart of the bomb, a hair trigger moved. He saw at once the wire it was attached to, and at the three-second mark, he cut the white wire in the lower tier.

"Yusuf!" Borz shouted now. "We're running on fumes. I've got to take her down."

Aashir appeared in the doorway. "What's happening, Yusuf?"

"Come here," Bourne said, by way of answer. When Aashir was kneeling beside him, he said, "Lift away those wires. Careful! Slowly!"

And there was the lower tier of wires. Same bomb maker, only this time there was no ticking clock. Instead, the bomb was connected to the altimeter.

"Borz, call off the altitude!" Bourne shouted.

"Two thousand feet," Borz replied. "Fifteen hundred."

Bourne searched for the telltale hair trigger, but he could find no sign of it. And yet it must be there. It was this bomb maker's signature.

"A thousand feet and dropping fast. Yusuf, I'm going to have to land the plane."

Bourne concentrated on each of the four lower wires in turn, but he could see nothing.

"Five hundred!" Borz shouted. "Four hundred, three! Wheels are down!"

At two hundred feet Bourne saw his mistake. The bomber had reversed himself: The upper wires were live, the lower tier dummies. His wire cutter hovered over one of the wires, then another. No hair trigger. Nothing.

"One hundred feet! Yusuf, tell me you've got it!"

He had a one-in-four chance of being right. Not good enough, not by a long shot. But to do nothing meant certain death.

411

"Fifty feet! Wheels will make contact in ten, nine, eight . . ."

Right before Bourne's eyes something shifted. It was minute, but it was the same motion he had discovered in the Bosnian bomb.

"Six, five, four . . ."

He cut the black wire, and then the plane landed, bumping along the ground.

"My God," Borz shouted in triumph, "I'm a fucking puddle of sweat!"

They stood on the Afghan plain, the Antonov crouched at the end of the runway farthest from where they were grouped. A hundred yards away, the Bombardier Challenger 890 CS gleamed in the sunlight. It had been expertly painted with the colors and insignia of Balinese Air Transport, a regional freight line.

If the waiting pilot was surprised by the diminished number of Borz's cadre he gave no sign of it while he and Borz huddled in hurried discussion. Once inside the plane, Borz gave instructions to shave and climb into overalls with the insignia of a Singapore security firm on their chest and right sleeve. Work shoes were awaiting them as well. The men lined up for the toilet, where scissors and razor awaited them to cut and shave off their beards.

Bourne was suitably impressed. Borz seemed to have thought of everything down to the smallest detail. He was a professional through and through.

During his time in the toilet, staring at himself clean-shaven, Bourne took out the piece of the plan he

412

had taken from Borz's office after the drone attack. What he had at first thought was a sewage system was in fact a drainage network, part of what appeared to be a perfect oval. This pointed to a stadium of some kind. The new national stadium was not yet finished. Though there were over a dozen other stadiums in and around the center of Singapore, Bourne knew this one had to be one the president would visit during the week of the peace summit. Then he looked closer at a corner of the plan. There was a section of a watermark: part of a horse's head.

And at that moment he knew the target of Borz's attack.

Part Four

CHAPTER
FORTY-FIVE

Jimmie Ohrent was a man of means. He had no pressing need to be a horse trainer, or to have a job at all. Nevertheless, he was known as the best horse trainer in Southeast Asia. As a boy in Melbourne, he had ridden horses on his uncle Mike's farm. Later, after spending ten hairy but exciting years in the Middle East, he had returned to Melbourne. Finding it both changed and boring, he decided to follow his uncle, crossing the Strait of Malacca to Singapore to make his fortune. Borrowing money from Uncle Mike, he bought a bit of land and started raising Thoroughbreds and Arabians, which he sold at auction. These horses won races at the Singapore Thoroughbred Club, and Ohrent's fortune was made. He sold one Arabian, then another, to key members of the ruling family, both of which went on to win the coveted Raffles Cup. As a result, Ohrent was a frequent dinner guest at the presidential palace. He started gambling runs to Macau with the big boys, and his fortune was lost. He fell into a funk, drank self-destructively like his grandfather, and lost himself.

But he wasn't his grandfather, and he rose from the ashes like a phoenix. In time, he made money again, but not to the same degree. He was not the same man; it didn't matter. Ohrent being Ohrent, he had tired of the limelight. He disliked the cabal of horse owners with whom he had been obliged to mingle, and didn't miss them. He loved horses more than people, but he'd had enough of breeding. He sold his business, because of his neglect at a reduced price. Again, it didn't matter. He became a trainer. He looked after horses and trained jockeys, for a hundredth of what he had been earning. But it was a profession he loved, and for which he had a natural flair.

By the time Camilla arrived in Singapore, Ohrent had been working for the Americans for just over a decade, making nice money that afforded him luxuries now and then. Plus, he was reminded of his days in the Middle East, when green youth made any adventure sing like a diva. His affiliation with them was unofficial, clandestine, and sporadic, which was precisely how he and they liked it. By the time she presented herself to him at the trainers' facilities at the Thoroughbred Club, he had already lined up a horse for her — a beautifully proportioned hot-blooded filly named Jessuetta. Jessuetta was usually jockeyed by a man named Gruen, but Ohrent didn't much like him and had been looking around for a replacement when orders came down from his local American handler.

At first sight, Ohrent had doubts about Camilla. Though she was more or less the right size and weight to jockey, she was untried. But all concerns vanished the moment he saw her ride Jessuetta. He loved her from that moment on — not that he didn't have things to teach her, but she had a jockey's instincts, and she was an instant learner; not once did he have to repeat himself. Best of all, she, like him, possessed a natural rapport with the horses. Jessuetta loved her fully as much as he did. Maybe more.

"The one thing you have to watch out for is not to slap her on the flank," he said. "She'll kick the clacker out of whoever's behind her."

Camilla laughed. "I'm not about to slap Jessuetta anywhere at any time. I can tell she wouldn't respond well to that."

Which comment made him love Camilla all the more, so much so that privately he felt it a pity and a waste to set her up for a fall. By the way she inveigled Jessuetta to reach her full potential far better than Gruen, he was of the opinion that she could jockey Jessuetta to victory if given the chance. But she wouldn't. That was the brief he had been given, and, being both well paid by the Americans and an upright kind of guy, he followed all briefs to the letter, even when he didn't understand or agree with them. Ours not to reason why, and all that, he told himself stoically when he was overcome by a dark hour and the urgent need to ingest a half bottle of whiskey.

But in truth, those moments were few and far between. In the end, there were always his horses, who loved him, never failed him, and would never do anyone dirt. Sometimes Ohrent wished he had been born an animal. Life would have been so much simpler — and cleaner. No skullduggery, no backbiting, no jealousy, greed, or fear. Best of all, he would have lived his life completely ignorant of the inevitable end.

For her part, Camilla was immediately infatuated with the atmosphere of the Thoroughbred Club and Singapore in general. On her first day, as part of her orientation, after she had met and ridden Jessuetta for the first time, Ohrent took her to the National Orchid Garden, where her ecstasy over her fast furlongs-long ride around the racing oval was almost exceeded by the two hours she and her guide spent among hundreds of orchid species, each one more extraordinary than the last.

Afterward, she asked him to take her to a mobile phone store, where she bought a cheap phone with a local SIM card and a half hour of talk time and Internet access.

He took her to lunch at a second-floor restaurant in the Muslim quarter, across the street from a shop that sold alcohol-free perfumes — alcohol being forbidden to Muslims — to local clientele and curious tourists alike. Over seven dishes, each more incendiary than the next, they engaged one another in order to come to terms with their brief. They were both people who found discovering the humanity in their colleagues vital to accomplishing their work.

"You've no family?" she said.

"Oh, family." He took a bite of curried chicken. "Well, it's my experience that families are a nuisance, get me as cross as a frog in a sock, they do. Always earbashing, telling you what to do and how to do it.

420

Now, my horses like everything I do, they like how I do them. No backtalk."

"Still, it must get lonely," Camilla said, thinking as much of herself as of him.

He shrugged. "It's the life I chose." He gave her a canny look. "But you're still a young woman. Why would you choose to be alone?"

"Who says I am?" she said, a bit too quickly.

The well-tanned flesh at the corners of his eyes crinkled when he smiled. "You have the look."

"Really?"

He nodded. "It's unmistakable."

"How dispiriting."

"Well, I'll give you the drum. There's no shame in it. If you want the shadows, why not?"

Why not, indeed? For so many reasons, she thought, not wanting to count the ways. She ate some food instead. Her lips were already numb, but the fire was just starting to kindle in her stomach. How fun!

"But it seems to me," he said, "that the shadow world is not your lucky country."

"My what?"

"Your natural habitat."

"So what?" she said somewhat snappily. "I've adjusted."

"Like to high blood pressure?"

Now it was her turn to smile. She liked this man, with his long, lean body, unbent by either age or disappointment. His informal, straightforward manner relaxed her, as did his slightly off-kilter humor.

"Well, now that *would* be bad for me."

"So can this kind of life. And unlike with high blood pressure there's no little pill you can take to normalize things. Here, where we are, nothing is ever normal, nor can it ever be."

More food, more heat, building into a bonfire. "All the people I know like it."

"Yes, but the question is whether *you* do."

She considered this for a moment, chewing slowly. "I tell myself I do every day."

He put down his fork. "Now that is a troubling sign."

She sat back, all at once overcome with a terrible foreboding.

As if he could divine her thoughts, he said with some urgency, "What's the matter?"

"Nothing." The last thing she wanted was her contact here in the target zone to report her as a risk.

"Hmmm."

This sound, emanating from the back of his throat, made it clear he didn't believe her. But neither did he press her, for which she was grateful. He glanced up as the waiter spoke to him in a language she did not understand.

"There was a time," he said, "when I was as far from here as I was from the place where I was born. I had joined a Bedouin caravan, about to cross the Negev Desert. Three *pops*! like this —" He put a finger in his open mouth and, pursing his lips, flicked it out. "Three pops," he repeated, "and the heads next to me exploded like dropped melons."

422

He stared down at his food for a moment, but Camilla could tell that he was gazing back through time.

"One, two, three. Blood and brains all over the place — on me, the camels, everything." He looked up at her, his expression abruptly bleak. "Palestinians: Hamas, or the Izz ad-Din al-Qassam Brigades. Who knows? And anyway, it doesn't matter. I killed one of them right away, tracked the two others down and shot them at point-blank range. What else was I to do? They were terrible shots. Aiming for me, the bleeding buggers had killed three of my hosts." He wiped his hands, as if they were still covered in blood. "*That's* the world we live in; the world you have talked yourself into."

"Or others have," she said under her breath.

"Finished?" he asked her, only half meaning the meal.

When she made no reply, he spoke softly to the waiter, who cleared the dishes away, piled one atop another, a rickety tower.

Ohrent's gaze settled on her. "Well, now you've rocked up here, and here we be."

Camilla watched him for some time. Then she took out the envelope Hunter had given her. She had not opened it or even tried to imagine what was inside. Sliding it across the table, she kept her hand on it until one of his lifted, landing at its far edge.

"Read it," Camilla said, taking her hand away.

He regarded her with a strange calmness that seemed to reach across the space between them and settle her. She felt perfectly at ease with him opening the envelope, though she could not have said why. Frankly, she didn't care; it felt right.

For what seemed a long time, Ohrent did nothing. Then, slowly, carefully, as if he knew that what she had given him was of great value, he turned the envelope over, slit it open, and read the off-reservation brief that Hunter and Terrier had devised for her.

His expression did not change, but she was aware that he had begun to read it all over again. Only when he was done did he look up.

"Really?"

"It's real." For a moment, she thought she had misread him, that that was not what he had meant.

He dropped the paper onto the table. "Good God, woman, what pressure you must be under!"

She stared at him, and something in her expression must have clued him in, because he said, "You haven't read this, have you? You don't know."

Heart in her mouth, she took up the paper, spun it around. She had only begun to read it when she blanched, feeling as if she were in an elevator whose cable had snapped.

CHAPTER
FORTY-SIX

Sara was ushered into Omega + Gulf Agencies without fanfare or even a word being spoken. She watched the young man El Ghadan had called Islam out of the corner of her eye. He was slim-hipped, hollowed-chested, with the ropy arms of someone born and bred to hardship and backbreaking work. More than anything, he looked like he could use a good meal — several of them, in fact.

Sara had seen countless others like him; sad to say, she had zero sympathy for people whose credo was "I kill to know I'm alive." Still and all, until she could get a grip on the nature of the test El Ghadan had set for her, she knew she needed to keep an open mind on everyone and everything she encountered here.

Islam showed her three large open-plan rooms where busy people were working on . . . what?

"Traffic scheduling, essentially," Islam said without inflection, when she asked. "The company creates the routing and shipping calendars for any number of import-export firms all over the world. Doha is the central hub."

"What kinds of goods?" she asked.

"All kinds," he said, deliberately evasive.

Those three large offices, plus a cluster of smaller ones for management, seemed to make up the extent of Omega + Gulf Agencies' quarters.

"What about the rest of the building's space?"

"Warehousing."

Using a magnetic key card, he led her through a door as thick as a bank vault's. Ahead was a carpeted, well-lighted corridor hung with prints of trains, freighters, and cargo planes, worked in a rigorous engineering hand. It looked more like a hallway in an upscale hotel than an entry to a warehouse.

Partway down, Islam pushed open a right-hand door with his shoulder and they were out of the air-conditioning. The courtyard in which she now found herself was surrounded on all sides by the building's featureless concrete walls, mostly hidden by a fierce riot of climbing bougainvillea. It was dominated by a vast fig tree in its center, gnarled as a fisherman's fist. Beneath the tree was a rough-hewn wooden table and chairs. As they approached, Sara saw that the table was set with a tea service and a number of small hand-hewn plates piled with fresh figs, pistachios, dried dates and apricots, and delicate honey pastries. The spread was more appropriate to a doyen's salon.

Islam ushered her to a chair. He sat at her left elbow, poured mint tea into tall, narrow glasses. The scent of fresh lemons perfumed the air. Somewhere high up in the fig tree a bird sang briefly, then fell silent.

Islam gestured. "Help yourself. Please."

"This is very pleasant," she said, looking around. "Do you work here every day?"

"Are you not hungry? I assure you every bit of food is the freshest possible."

Sara drank some of the tea. Then she put down the glass and smiled at him. "Islam, what am I doing here?"

"You have a man's directness."

"And that's a fault?"

He shook his head. "I merely make an observation. It's unusual."

"Are you uncomfortable sitting here with me?"

"Should I be?"

She watched him for a moment, silent and enigmatic.

"You are El Ghadan's emissary," he said at last.

"And that too is unusual."

"Unprecedented, I would say."

"It's a pity I don't know what being his emissary entails."

"You are his strong right arm," Islam said. "You tell me what to do and I do it."

She stared at him for a long moment. "I feel like I've fallen down the rabbit hole."

He frowned. "I beg your pardon?"

Time to change the perspective. "I see you are unarmed."

"Here?" He spread his arms wide. "We are in the heart of a fortress."

Now we're getting somewhere, she thought. "I am to make a decision, then."

He showed her his teeth. "Precisely." He popped a date into his mouth and seemed very pleased.

"About you? Shall I interview you?"

"Oh, no." He laughed. "However, I imagine I would find it very pleasant to be interviewed by you."

That's what you think, Sara thought. "If not you," she said, "who?"

He reached for a miniature honey cake. "I don't know whether 'interview' is the correct term."

"Then what would be?"

"That depends on your opinion of our guests."

She was a bit taken aback. "Guests? You have guests here?"

"Yes."

"In the warehouse."

He nodded.

"Tell me."

He ate the sweet, licked the honey from his fingers. "Imagine for a moment that you have an enemy. An implacable enemy. Now further suppose you have a mission to carry out. This mission, like all those facing you, is of vital importance. The problem is that neither you yourself nor anyone working for you can complete this mission."

He held a dried apricot that looked like a human ear. Biting it in half, he said, "Desperate times, would you not agree?" He did not wait for an answer. "But there is one person who can accomplish this mission for you. The only problem is he won't ever do that. Why? Because he is that implacable enemy I mentioned. What to do?"

Islam finished off the apricot. "Then an idea springs into your head. What if you were to coerce your enemy into doing what he otherwise would never do? This

428

person does not respond to force or interrogation. He would laugh in your face if you offered him money. But your enemy must have a weak spot, no? Every person does. So you find this weak spot and you exploit it. This forces him to comply."

He raised a forefinger. "Or so it at first seems. The fact is, new information comes to light that your enemy has somehow tricked you. You have given him a mobile phone with a GPS transponder that cannot be disabled. This will let you know where he is at all times. After days of tracking him, your people tell you that the GPS is in fact sending dual signals. One has broken off from the other and is degrading fast, leaving you with the true signal.

"Instead of being in, let's say, Singapore, where he should be, preparing to begin the mission, your enemy is in Afghanistan. Why? You do not know, but it cannot be good for either you or your mission. Your enemy has broken trust with you."

As he recounted this "hypothetical" scenario, his voice increased in tension, and fury came into it, turning it dark and ominous. For her part, Sara knew precisely who he was talking about, and her concern for Bourne increased exponentially.

Careful not to reveal the slightest hint of emotion, she said, "What has all this to do with your guests?"

"They are the coercion, the people who were supposed to force your enemy to comply."

"And who are they?"

"A woman and her two-year-old daughter."

A scream, like an unwanted guest, rose up from Sara's depths. She snapped it off the way a bear will bite off the head of a fish and swallow it whole.

Her voice sounded thick and ungainly as she said, "What kind of decision am I being asked to make?"

Islam lounged in his chair, another square of sticky pastry between his fingertips. "Life for them," he said, contemplating her with a frightening intensity. "Or death."

CHAPTER
FORTY-SEVEN

Knowing the target of Borz's attack and knowing what he planned to do were two separate issues. The Singapore Thorough-bred Club was to be ground zero, and yet El Ghadan had set in motion a dangerous and elaborate scheme forcing Bourne to kill the president. What was to happen at the Singapore Thoroughbred Club and why? Who was Borz's target? Or was it to be the Thoroughbred Club itself, Southeast Asian symbol of consumerist fat cats? Anything was possible. Suddenly, everything was in play.

Bourne, sitting in the airplane just behind Borz, imagined a nightmare scenario where the peace process brokered by President Magnus was sabotaged beyond repair. The stability of the entire Middle East would be in jeopardy. Bourne recalled all too well how the assassination of Yitzhak Rabin had blown apart a nascent accord between the Israelis and the Palestinians that to this day had yet to be advanced. What had followed was bitterness, vengeance, war, and a reemergence of ancient enmity neither side could or would control. As a result, the Israelis had taken more land, the PLO was supplanted, replaced by the militant Hamas and worse. Hard-liners poured out of the woodwork, gaining power with every fresh incursion, every new death.

Borz was in constant discussion with the pilot, a youngish, dark-haired man with a triangular face, bright blue eyes, and a fringe of beard. Borz brusquely introduced him as Musa Kadyrov. For a time, Bourne watched Musa's hands on the controls. When he determined he was an excellent pilot, he rose and went back to where Aashir was reclining across three seats.

"How are you feeling?" Bourne asked.

The young man stared up at him. "I wouldn't be here without you."

"Let's make this about you."

Aashir smiled. "The doctor gave me some pills for my headache. Don't look so alarmed. They took the pain away. Apart from the soreness and the bump I feel fine." He sat up, made a gesture. "Sit here next to me, Yusuf."

"Where did you hear all those stories the Chechens liked so much?"

"My father. He used to tell us stories when we were little. The more fanciful the better I liked them." He gave Bourne a shy smile. "I used to pretend I was far away in those mythical lands. How I would have loved to have been a djinn with a serpent to talk with. An animal, I thought, even a reptile, would understand how I felt, even if no one else could."

"No friends."

"Are you kidding? The day I had my first crush I knew I couldn't allow myself to get close to any other

432

boy, no matter how much I wanted to. My secret had to remain *my* secret."

"Until you met your friend."

"That was years later. Many years. And even then . . ." He looked away. "Even then it turned out to be a mistake." He turned back to Bourne. "It was my fault he was killed."

"You've left that all behind," Bourne said. "It's part of growing up."

Aashir's expression turned thoughtful. "I won't be grown up until I go back home and see my father again."

"I'm sure he wants to see you."

"Desperately, so I hear. But he doesn't know me, does he?"

"I wonder," Bourne said, wanting to draw Aashir out, "how well you know him. What happened to the man who told you stories when you were a child?"

"International Zionism, the rabid dog of the region," Aashir said. "And the American imperium."

Bourne immediately recognized the rhetoric. So Aashir and his father were Iranians. That answered some questions, especially how Aashir stood out among Faraj's Arabs. Iranians were Persian in origin, Muslims, but Shia, a minority, whose members were always, it seemed, on the defensive in their eternal war against the Sunni majority. This imbalance made them desperate, willing at all costs to strike out against their enemies. And their enemies were legion.

"You speak fine Yemeni Arabic for a Persian," Bourne said.

"Adaptability. All part of my cover. I can change to other regional dialects. Which would you like to hear? Tunisian, Iraqi, Saudi, Omani — I can even do that Egyptian thing, where they put the 'shhh' sound at the end of their words."

For a time, then, both men kept up a rapid-fire dialogue, switching dialects every few sentences, following which Aashir, slightly out of breath, laughed softly.

"We are like two grains of sand from the same desert, Yusuf. So alike and at the same time unlike, no two grains of sand being identical."

"When you return home, your father will be proud of your accomplishments."

"As long as I keep from him my secret heart."

"I assume he doesn't know where you are."

"He's been searching for me for a long time." Aashir looked around to make sure no one else was in hearing distance. "No one here knows my real name."

"Not even Borz?"

Aashir let out a breath. "*Especially* not him. He's so venal he'd sell me out to my father in the blink of an eye." He eyed Bourne. "You're not curious?"

Bourne shrugged. "Either you'll tell me or you won't." But he was elated. He had suspected who Aashir was almost from the moment the young man began to confide in him. Now he had no doubt; now he knew the path he had chosen was the right one. The way to saving Soraya and Sonya was like a blinking light finally observed on the far horizon.

434

"If I decide to tell you, Yusuf, I know you'll keep it to yourself. I trust you."

"I appreciate that, Aashir."

The young man leaned toward Bourne, lowering his voice further. "Our family name is Sefavid. We were once a dynasty, the most powerful in Islamic Persia. We brought the Twelver school of Shia Islam to Iran, though our ancient descendants were actually Azerbajiani Sufis. Along with the Ottoman and Mughul, we were one of the so-called gunpowder empires. Our lands stretched from Iran, Iraq, Azerbaijan, of course, Georgia, Afghanistan, all the way to Turkey." He made a helpless gesture. "And now look at what we have been reduced to. That is the well of bitterness from which my father drinks. It is his faith, his rage, his cause. He kills and, possibly, will be killed for it. This is his life."

"But it isn't yours," Bourne said.

"I have no life," Aashir replied. "I am adrift, a leaf allowing the river to take me where it may."

"You can't live your whole life like that."

"But, Yusuf, isn't that what you are doing?"

"Do as I say," Bourne told him, "not as I do."

"But why not? You are a good man. Down to your very core — your soul — you are a good man. You understand things the others do not — cannot. It seems to me I could do worse than to follow your lead."

"Perhaps. But at some point, you must find your own way."

"But, Yusuf, you of all people must know that I don't trust myself to do that."

435

And with that he pierced the final layer of Bourne's armor, and found the place Bourne had so successfully hidden from the world.

Out on the pulsing twilight streets of Singapore, Howard Anselm was at last able to take a deep breath, something he had tried and failed to do during what had seemed to him the interminable flight from D.C. to Singapore. Scheduling POTUS's necessary one-on-one press meetings, hurried meals, calls to the advance party, including Magnus's Secret Service contingent, all the while revising the summit schedules and fielding requests and/or complaints from the press on board, had driven what humanity he still possessed deep underground.

The moment POTUS was settled in his suite at the Golden Palace Hotel, overlooking the river that snaked through the heart of the city, he knew he had to get out from under the crush of arrangements and responsibilities, at least briefly, or risk being buried alive.

He took one of the limousines at the presidential party's disposal to the edge of the Chinese quarter, then, armed with the slip of paper one of the Secret Service agents had at his request palmed him, he took to the street on foot.

Now, as he picked his way through jam-packed Chinatown with its riot of bright colors, odd food smells, and myriad shouted voices, he searched for the large sweets stand at the all-night food market. The

436

business he was looking for was well hidden within the sweetshop, an apt incorporation if ever there was one.

Anselm needed release, both emotional and physical, but the one would not be possible without the other. Which was why he had solicited the address from the Secret Service agent who had been to Singapore. The city-state was the most difficult place in Southeast Asia to find physical relief. It was also the most dangerous. Wickedly strict, the government was notorious for severely punishing even the comparatively minor sins of cursing or spitting in public. Paying for sex was a huge no-no, which didn't stop Anselm in the slightest. He had an itch he was determined to scratch. Fuck Singapore and its dotty laws. In fact, fuck everyone who wasn't American.

It was in this strange mood, an amalgam of lust and aggression, that Anselm came upon the sweetshop. He paused for a moment, stunned at the riotous display of tier upon tier of different types of candies, more than he could ever have imagined. He began to wonder what was waiting for him within.

The paper he was holding informed him that he should ask for Old Numby. The real name of the proprietor of both businesses was Nem-Pang, but no one had called him that since he was a child. Anselm was just about to ask for Old Numby when his mobile buzzed. He would have ignored it, especially in his current mood, but he recognized the vibration pattern he had set up. Finnerman was calling.

"POTUS has a problem," Finnerman said without preamble. "Which means we have a problem."

The familiar hollowness, which rendered all voices flat and toneless, meant that the under secretary of defense for policy was using a scrambled line.

Anselm closed his eyes for a moment, his body swaying slightly from the time change and lack of sleep. He did not want to know about another problem, especially not now.

"What?" he said because he had no other choice.

"The opposition have bum-rushed a major Senate hearing on the viability of POTUS's drone program."

Anselm's eyes snapped open; he was suddenly on the alert. "Overnight? How the fuck did that happen?"

"Families of the kids killed in the drone strike have leaned hard on their senators and congressmen. And of course, they've been joined by the usual lefty suspects. But, Howard, the stink they made went viral — and I mean immediately. Congress had to scramble. And the worst part is there's bipartisan support for dismantling the program."

"Our own party is selling POTUS out?" It was virtually a howl of pain and rage.

"Elements within, yes."

"POTUS will make those fuckers pay."

"We all will, Howard," Finnerman said. "Which is why it's more vital than ever that we ensure the major incident occurs at the summit. POTUS comes home a hero and the drone problem goes away. You're on-site. You have to make certain that no one interferes with the dinger. It's vital Kettle makes his shot."

"He will, Marty. You can count on me." Anselm took a step toward the sweetshop's promised land. "The plan will go down like clockwork tomorrow. Guaranteed."

"It had better," Finnerman said. "Otherwise, POTUS is going to suffer a most humiliating defeat, which means neither of us will get the war we want and need."

Anselm severed the connection, walked into the sweetshop, where he was greeted by a blast of sugar, honey, and whatever the hell else the Chinese used in their candy. Melamine, probably, he thought sourly.

But then he encountered Old Numby and was determined not to let the dire implications of the call reverberate through his fun time. Old Numby was squat, goggle-eyed, and so comically bowlegged that when he walked he rocked back and forth like one of those bobble-heads you saw on car dashboards in Middle America.

There was nothing comical about his demeanor, however. Old Numby was all business. Anselm spoke the code words written on the slip of paper he had been given, and after sizing him up, Old Numby said, "Money. Let me see money."

Anselm showed it to him.

Old Numby nodded, threaded him through gargantuan mountains of candies, into the dim rear of the space.

When they reached a padlocked door, Anselm said, "What kind of selection have you got back there?"

Old Numby grinned, revealing stumps of teeth the color of teastained ivory. "What is it you want?"

Borz came down the aisle to fetch Bourne. "You boys have a nice visit?" Without waiting for a reply, he beckoned to Bourne. "Let's go, Yusuf."

Bourne and Aashir exchanged a brief glance before Bourne rose and followed the Chechen up front, where the two sat together.

"Less than an hour before we land," Borz said. "How are you feeling?"

"Fine."

"No aftereffects from your encounter with the Taliban?"

"None."

"And Aashir? Is he fit? Can I count on him?"

"Absolutely," Bourne said. "He's out to make a name for himself. It's his way of becoming a man."

"A fine way," Borz said approvingly. "His skill level?"

"He's a quick learner."

Apparently satisfied, Borz spent a moment studying the back of the seat in front of him. "You ever been to Singapore?" he said at length.

"A number of times, yes."

Borz nodded. "We're down a lot of men, so I've enlisted Musa. Also, I'm going to need your help more than ever now."

"Whatever I can do," Bourne said, "if the pay is right."

A knowing smirk informed Borz's face. "How does fifty thousand sound?"

"Pounds, euros, Swiss francs, dollars, yen? No Russian or Chinese currency, please."

Borz opened his right hand, and Bourne counted five diamonds.

"Perfect for transportation purposes," Borz said. He let Bourne take one, hold it up to the light. "You know what you're looking at?"

"This one's too flawed." Bourne dropped it back into Borz's palm, took up another. "And this one's a cubic zirconia."

Borz studied him a moment. "You know, Yusuf, I do believe you've missed your calling. A sniper with your range of skills is being wasted."

"I'm just a simple man."

"And I'm just a tourist." Borz laughed. "Will American dollars do you?"

"Dollars will be fine."

Borz opened up a map. "No matter how many times you've been to Singapore, Yusuf, I can guarantee you've never been here."

Bourne looked at the tattered blueprint, but it did not have its corner torn off. It was not a plan of the Thoroughbred Club's drainage system. It was a detailed architectural plan of the club itself.

"What am I looking at?" Bourne said, though he knew quite well what it was.

"The stands of the Singapore Thoroughbred Club." Borz's forefinger stabbed out. "Look here. On the roof of the stands is the lighting array for the night races. It's new, elaborate, state of the art — sodium lights. The best lighting, but also the most delicate. It needs constant tending. That's where we come in. We're going

441

to tweak the lighting array, give it an off-the-grid update." He laughed.

"We're only going to be there about four minutes. That's how long it's going to take us to deal with the security guards stationed there, plant explosives, and make our way out. A press of a key on my mobile will do the rest."

He slapped the seat's armrest. "We're going to blow up the Thoroughbred Club while the president of the United States and the heads of Palestine and Israel are attending the races."

CHAPTER
FORTY-EIGHT

"But first," Islam said. "This."

He must have made some sort of signal Sara didn't catch, because just then the door into the warehouse opened and a jihadist came out. He was as slim as Islam, but shorter. His face was wrapped in his headscarf so only his eyes were visible. He carried a cheap plastic briefcase, which he set down beside Islam's chair, then turned and left without uttering so much as a word.

Islam snapped open the briefcase, removed a laptop, which he fired up, then plugged a small rectangle with a depression on the top into a USB port.

"Give me your right forefinger," he said. When she complied, he pressed it into the depression, then looked at the biometric readout on the screen. "Well," he said, sitting back. "You are something of a mystery, after all. Your prints don't show up on any international database."

No they don't, Sara thought, once again grateful for Mossad's ingenuity. "So this is all about trust."

"We don't know who you are — or even if Ellie Thorson is your real name. You gave us two pieces of product on Mossad, both good. But so what? They might be bait — the solid intel allowing you entrée into the cadre."

Sara said nothing. In view of their rising suspicion, anything she said would now be construed wrongly. Best to sit tight, monitor her breathing, and try like hell to relax. To help her with this, she leaned forward and began to pluck up bits of the food. Eating always helped to calm her down.

He watched her with a curious expression on his face. "We need assurance. Something concrete that cannot be faked."

Time to join in; time to get what she needed out of him. "Something you see with your own eyes."

"Yes."

"I understand completely. I'd do the same if I were you."

"Then we're agreed."

He made to rise, but she stopped him. "Not quite, Islam." She waited until he slouched back into his chair. "I require some assurances, too."

He stiffened. "I don't think you're in a position to —"

"Tell me, Islam. Am I a potential prisoner, or a potential asset? But how could I be the former? I am El Ghadan's emissary, yes?"

He nodded, frowning. "You are."

"Well, then, assurances."

For the first time since she laid eyes on him, he seemed unsure of himself, as if he had suddenly lost control of the situation. Clearly, he did not like that,

444

but just as clearly he didn't appear to know what to do about it.

"Perhaps you want to call El Ghadan?" Her honeyed tone, devoid of all sarcasm, tempered her meaning. The last thing she needed was for him to get pissed off. "But really there's no reason to, right?" Saved him face, shifted their relationship — how much she had yet to discover.

Never taking his eyes off her, he reached into the briefcase, placed a SIG Sauer on the table between them. "Now you will have to make your decision."

Sara deliberately kept her eyes off the handgun, even though it was like a magnet, trying to draw her gaze.

"That is for me?" she said.

"As I told you. The value of our guests has been diminished in a major way."

Sara felt her pulse in her throat. With an effort, she kept all thoughts of Soraya and Sonya out of her mind. "Are the woman and her daughter no longer of any use to El Ghadan?"

"That has yet to be determined."

"By me."

His dark eyes did not flicker even for an instant. "Pick up the gun, Ellie." He rose. "Pick up the gun and we will confront them."

Bourne buckled himself in. "Why are you doing this?"

Borz, clicking his seat belt in preparation for landing, looked at Bourne with a degree of scorn. "Does it matter?"

"I'm a rational man, Borz. I'm not a fanatic or an ideologue. I made that clear from the start. Of course it matters."

"It's theater, Yusuf. All acts of terror are theater."

With a whine, the hydraulic landing gear clicked into place. The wing flaps extended, slanted down.

"That's not enough of an answer."

"Well, Yusuf, it'll have to do."

"I disagree in the strongest possible terms."

Borz stared at him. Then he drew a pistol. "Or I can kill you right here."

"Now you're speaking like a madman," Bourne said. "You may be many things, but crazy isn't one of them. You're a businessman, plain and simple. Whatever you choose to do you do for money."

"Shut up."

They hit the ground, bumped, and began to taxi furiously along the runway, Musa braking hard to decelerate.

"Who's your patron? Who's paying you to kill wholesale?"

"I said shut up!"

Slowed considerably, the jet now rolled calmly toward the freight terminal. A member of the ground personnel in overalls, ears protected, light baton swinging rhythmically, guided Musa through the final phase of taxiing.

Borz turned to Bourne. "Why do you care who's paying the freight, Yusuf? What's it to you?"

"I don't kill people lightly. I need a reason."

"Well, well, a sniper with a conscience. You need a reason to shoot individuals with the long gun?"

"I usually work for myself, so, yes, I need a reason for every kill, so maybe I don't make as much money as you do, but at least I sleep at night."

"I sleep just fine, Yusuf."

"Listen, Borz, you don't want to tell me, that's fine. It's your prerogative, but then count me out. I'll get off here and be on my way."

Borz gripped his wrist. "You're not going anywhere."

"Are we actually going to discuss this? Then put the gun away."

The plane had come to a stop. Chocks had been kicked against its wheels, the engines switched off, mobile stairs had been set in place by ground personnel, and the door had been opened. No one got out of their seats, no one even unbuckled themselves. They sat, waiting for their leader to make the first move. But their leader wasn't going anywhere — not at the moment, anyway. He was locked in a battle of wills with Yusuf.

Borz, having waited long enough to save face, holstered the gun. How he was going to get into Singapore with it was anyone's guess.

"If you want me to stay," Bourne said with a quiet menace, "then you need me. If you need me, then we negotiate."

Borz shrugged, affecting disinterest. "What is there to negotiate?"

"I want a hundred thousand."

"That's not going to happen."

"Or I walk."

"I'll turn you over to the Singapore authorities."

"And risk blowing your cover? I don't think so." Bourne stared out the window. "Look, Borz, it's a beautiful night. Why don't we go out together and enjoy it?"

No sooner had Anselm returned to his room after having his itch scratched in every imaginable way, as well as one or two that had never been on his radar, than there was a pounding on his door. Suffused with a delicious postcoital lassitude, he was just about to order room service, and was disinclined to rise from the edge of the bed where he had plunked himself in a mist of delirium. It was like one of those wet dreams you never want to end, he thought. Only this was real.

The pounding came again, more insistent this time, impelling him to rise and cross the room.

"POTUS," one of the Secret Service agents said when Anselm flung open the door. "Now."

Cursing under his breath, Anselm padded across the corridor in his stocking feet, entering Magnus's immense suite without knocking.

POTUS turned at the sound. "Ah, there you are, Howard." He had been staring out the window at the lights of the city, myriad as the invisible stars in a sky turned every shade of colored neon.

"Where is Camilla?" POTUS said. "I told you I wanted to see her."

Anselm was alarmed to feel a tiny trickle of sweat roll down his side. "Camilla's undercover, Bill. I thought I made that clear to you."

"And I told you I don't care." He waved his arms. "We're on the other side of the world, for Christ's sake, Howard. What could happen?"

"Bill, do I really have to remind you that the president of the United States takes the world with him wherever he goes?"

As it was wont to do when he was forced to face reality in private, POTUS's face fell. He suddenly looked gray and lined, as if he had aged five years in five minutes. Coming away from the window, he collapsed onto a plush chair, scrubbed his face with the heels of his hands.

"Jesus, Howard, what am I to do?" He looked up at his chief of staff. "I need to see her, to touch her, to . . ." He shook his head. "She's all I can think of."

Finally his friend's anguish pierced the pink cloud on which Anselm had floated back to his room. "All right." He sat down on a chair facing POTUS. "I'll tell you what. There is an hour between races tomorrow. You have no more than half that before your entrance into the presidential box. I'll take you to see her." He lifted a warning finger. "But, now listen to me, Bill. She'll be working; you can't interfere with that — we can't afford to have her cover blown."

Magnus blinked. "Thirty minutes won't do it."

"It will have to do. The Singapore president won't tolerate tardiness."

"What the hell's his name, anyway?"

The two of them had a good laugh at that one. Anselm rose, crossed to a sideboard, poured himself two fingers of the special bourbon Magnus liked, and downed it. With the fire streaking down to his belly, he turned.

"Bill —"

"No, no." Magnus waved away his words. "I read the brief. I know precisely what Camilla will be doing there tomorrow." He sighed. "Do your best, Howard." He rose, went to his chief of staff, gripped his shoulder. "But then I have no worries. You always do."

CHAPTER
FORTY-NINE

"Tell me, Islam," Sara said, "how long have you been shuttered here with El Ghadan's guests?"

"Days," the young jihadist said noncommittally.

She cocked her head. "That must be hard for you, being a man of action."

The courtyard was silent. The sun was down and the bird had flown; the leaves of the fig tree were still. The ground, baking in the last of the afternoon heat, seemed to absorb all sound. Only the dust remained, floating in the air in listless patterns.

"Everything is hard for us," Islam said.

"Of course," Sara said. "Otherwise there would be no reason for you to live."

He seemed to glare at her, but it might only have been the way the sunlight struck his face. He tapped the gun lying between them amid the plates of food.

"Decision time," he said.

Sara waited a moment, then took up the SIG. She ejected the magazine, which was empty. So was the chamber.

Islam smiled at her, a hard line in the sand. "But you knew it would not be loaded."

"It would have been foolish to have thought otherwise."

"Still, your decision concerning the disposition of our guests must be made."

She nodded. "Let's do it, then."

They rose and he led her back inside. At the end of the hotel-like corridor stood another steel door with a slot into which he slid his magnetic key card. The door opened with a sigh, as if the area beyond had been hermetically sealed. He ushered her down another, far more utilitarian hallway, past doors clearly marked TOILETS and SHOWERS in both Arabic and English.

At length he stopped in front of a locked door. "In here," he said, turning a key in the lock, but as he made to move forward, she stopped him.

"I go in alone, Islam." She held his gaze, unblinking. "This is the way it's going to be."

He acquiesced far too quickly, confirming her suspicion that he would be spying on her via video or audio, possibly both.

"Just knock when you're finished," he said.

She entered the room and the door closed behind her. Ten minutes later, she pounded on the door, and it swung open.

The moment she stepped out, he said, "Well? What is your decision?"

She was aware of him scrutinizing her face. Her expression betrayed nothing, but seeing Soraya, and especially Sonya, whom she had never before met, was like a dagger twisted into her heart. Brave didn't begin to cover what those two were. In the moment before she raised her fist to pound on the door she despised El Ghadan and Islam more than she ever could have imagined. There was an instant when she lost her professional perspective, when everything became personal, but with a colossal effort she was able to pull herself back from that perilous brink.

"You can ask El Ghadan after I've spoken with him," she said flatly, and strode back down the hall with him trailing helplessly behind.

Camilla looked down at her mobile, saw that Hunter was calling, and didn't pick up. Standing in the stables with Ohrent and the stamping horses, she had no desire to speak to Hunter. Being on the other side of the world had a way of clarifying issues you were too close to at home.

"The horses are restless," she said.

"They're always like this before a race." Ohrent had his hand on Jessuetta's mane. "Eager for the track." His mouth twitched. "It's a good thing. When they're not like this is the time to worry."

He came away from Jessuetta's stall, stood by her side, looking out at the velvet night. Beyond the Thoroughbred Club's environs the sky was lit up as if with the northern lights.

"It's beautiful," she said softly.

"Just another evening in Singapore." Behind them a horse snorted, others answered it. One of them bumped its hindquarters against a stall. "What are you going to do?" His voice was lower than hers had been.

She took out her mobile. "I've decided to trust you," she said.

He did not reply. Instead he waited patiently, in the easy, relaxed manner she had quickly come to admire.

She brought up the extermination brief from Finnerman's office, along with the photo of Kettle, and showed them to Ohrent.

"Huh, a DOD dinger."

"There's more." She played him the MP3 file of Finnerman and Anselm adding her death to Kettle's brief.

He shoved his hands in the back pockets of his jeans. "I think you just answered the question." He shifted from one foot to the other. "In that event, you'd better come along home with me." When she turned to him, he added, "You won't be safe anywhere else."

"I'm not going home with you and I'm not going back to my hotel." She shook her head. "You think I'd be safe with you? Well, I wouldn't. Until this is over I'm radioactive, and I'm not getting you involved in —"

"Camilla, I'm already involved," he said slowly and carefully. "Plus, I'm too old and crotchety to be told by a young filly like you what to do." His eyes crinkled. "You're coming with me."

"I said —"

"Pull ya head in. Not to my place. No, you're right about that. Radioactive isn't too dramatic a word for what you are. But I've got the perfect spot to take you. It's fifty k's south of Woop Woop."

"Meaning?"

"Meaning no-fuckin-one is going to find you there." His smile was so very reassuring. "You'll spend the night without having to look over your shoulder, which is just as well because you look knackered."

She was exhausted. Running on adrenaline could only take you so far before you fell on your face. "Okay." She returned his smile. "I am delivered into your providential hands."

"That's more like it. I'll take you there, then be off."

She frowned. "Off where?"

"Me?" Ohrent began to guide her out the back of the stables. "I'm going to find the dinger and settle his fucking hash."

There was a space in time between the moment Rebeka left Soraya and Sonya and Islam appeared in her place when Soraya could legitimately tell herself that there was a sliver of hope for her and her daughter. She had seen these scenarios all too often in her time at the Company, and especially at Treadstone. She knew the longer they were incarcerated the slimmer their chances of coming out of this alive. She also knew that Jason was doing all he could to free her and Sonya, but though she had been witness to a number of his seeming miraculous feats she was unsure whether this would be one of them.

After all, every winning streak eventually came to an end. There was always someone stronger, better prepared, and, most crucially, smarter. Jason had not yet come up against such an adversary, but the law of averages told her that it was only a matter of time. El

Ghadan was the most powerful jihadist on the planet; he commanded countless men in an array of far-flung places, and he was currently at the top of his game.

These thoughts, piling onto her like a pyramid intent on burying her beneath their weight, seemed instantly mitigated by Rebeka's appearance. Soraya could not have been more shocked if the pope had bustled in with his white robes and gold crucifixes, censers swinging in his wake.

She had met Rebeka several times — Aaron had introduced them. Soraya had intuited Rebeka wasn't her real name, but she didn't care. In fact, she knew that it was far better for everyone involved if she didn't know Rebeka's real identity. However, the woman's essential kindness was unmistakable, and she had liked her on the spot. Now, somehow, some way, she was here and ready to help. Had Jason sent her? Possibly, but the hows and whys mattered less than whether she would be able to free them. Right now, Soraya would settle for Rebeka taking Sonya out of here, far away from these people.

She closed her eyes, knowing she was working herself up into another bout of anxiety. To combat it she began her slow-breathing exercises, and it was when she was sunk deep into *prana* that the door was unlocked from the outside and Islam stepped in. He was carrying the video camera in one hand, a newspaper in the other. She took Sonya onto her lap; she knew the drill.

They were finished almost before she knew it. Her mind was elsewhere while the taping was taking place. She felt humiliated and sickened by the violation.

Then it was over and, tucking the newspaper under one arm, Islam unwound his headscarf, revealing his face. He was a handsome young man, she saw, his face long, bony, eyes sunken on either side of a prominent nose. And yet the sight of him immediately dispelled the effects of her yoga breathing. In fact, it sent her into a full-blown panic.

Islam showing himself to her was a threat, or maybe a harbinger — the surest sign yet that these people had made up their minds that she and Sonya would not survive. Because now she knew what he looked like, now if she were freed she would be able to identify him.

Which meant she and Sonya were not going to be freed. They were going to be killed.

CHAPTER
FIFTY

Bourne spent the night on the outskirts of Singapore, where Borz had arranged for the cadre to stay. Once it had been a warehouse, and possibly still was down on the ground floor, though apart from several wooden crates he saw little sign of it. But a loft space, accessed via spiral steel treads, had been turned into a living space for up to fifty human beings. The cadre consisted of only a fraction of what it had been, of course, and Bourne wondered what Borz had planned to do with so many men. Anything he could think of seemed like overkill. Plus which, in a city like Singapore, with its restrictive laws, small seemed far superior — and less risky — than large. But then the scheme masterminded by El Ghadan, to be carried out by Borz's cadre, had yet to come into focus.

Bourne, once again unable to sleep, padded through the converted rooms. Accessing the mobile El Ghadan had given him, he brought up the proof-of-life videos he had missed while in Waziristan and Afghanistan, and was reassured by their faces that both Soraya and Sonya were alive and being well treated. There were no signs of bruises or swelling on their faces, no sign either that they were being starved, even though Soraya did

458

look thinner, her large eyes sunken in their sockets, surrounded by dark circles of worry and anxiety. For the moment, this was as much as he could hope for.

There was also a brief coded text from Sara, accelerating his pulse. El Ghadan's people had found the false GPS signal Deron had piggy-backed onto the real one. El Ghadan knew he had been betrayed.

"Looking for something?" The pilot, Musa, stepped out of the shadows. A cigarette dangled from between his lips. He never removed it, even when he was speaking.

"A little air," Bourne replied.

"Well, you won't find it here." Smoke dribbled from between his half-opened lips. "I heard you saved the boss's life — twice."

"I was lucky to be in the right place at the right time."

"Still" — Musa sucked in some smoke, held it, let it go — "we all owe you a debt of gratitude, Yusuf."

Bourne nodded in acknowledgment. "You know Singapore well?"

Musa shrugged. He had the beefy shoulders of a mechanic or a wrestler. Though dull, he possessed an air of quiet confidence, as if he could handle any problem, mechanical or electronic, his airplane developed. "Not as well as I know Chechnya. But some. Enough."

"Enough for what?" Bourne asked.

"Enough to get the job done."

And no more, Bourne thought, as he bid Musa good night.

Moments later, he stood out in the humid darkness, just beyond the warehouse's front door. From his vantage point there was not much to see: black buildings beyond which rose the multicolored glow of the Singapore night.

Despite having stolen into the center of the web woven by El Ghadan and Borz, he felt as if he were still in the dark. Because what he had seen and been told didn't add up, he knew he was missing something — something vital, if he knew anything about the two terrorists. No one was telling the truth, him included.

The door opened behind him but he did not turn around, even when he felt Aashir come up beside him.

"You should get your sleep," Bourne said.

"But you don't need it, Yusuf?"

"I need it less than you."

At that moment, the clocks struck midnight and El Ghadan's mobile buzzed. Raising his forefinger, Bourne stepped away. The usual short video of Soraya and Sonya had been sent to him, but a moment later a voice call came in.

"Where are you?" El Ghadan said.

"You know where I am," Bourne said. "It's midnight in Singapore."

"Yes, I know where you are."

There was a pause, ominous in its length, and Bourne's senses went on high alert. He was almost at the finish line. Nothing could happen to Soraya and Sonya now.

"You found your explosives expert?" El Ghadan said, interrupting Bourne's train of thought.

"As a matter of fact I didn't. At least none to my satisfaction."

"In Damascus? That seems odd."

"You don't know what I was looking for."

"So how are you going to fulfill your end of the bargain?"

"I didn't say I gave up. I ventured all the way into Afghanistan for the answer."

"And you found it there."

"I did. This is Singapore, El Ghadan. Lowest profile possible."

"And how — ?"

"Leave the how to me. It will happen at the Thoroughbred Club. He'll be attending the races tomorrow."

"Have you scoped out the site?"

"I plan to do that later this morning. Security will be in the stands hours before the races start, and I'll get a clear idea of the area he'll be sitting in."

"How are you getting in?"

"As part of the light maintenance crew."

"Sounds like you've thought of everything."

Bourne glanced over to where Aashir was waiting for him. "How are Soraya and Sonya?"

"You saw the video."

"Yes, but I want to know —"

But he was talking to dead air. El Ghadan had severed the connection. Pocketing the phone, he returned to Aashir with a certain dread for the safety of Soraya and her daughter. Had El Ghadan bought his story about going so far afield to find the means to assassinate the American president? No way to know, but he had done what needed to be done, in light of Sara's text. It was essential that El Ghadan believe that he was still going to complete his part of the bargain; otherwise, Soraya and Sonya were as good as dead.

"To answer your question," Aashir said as Bourne drifted back to where he stood, "I'm fine."

Bourne eyed him critically. "I don't believe you."

"Listen to me, Yusuf, I don't want to be left behind."

Bourne heard the desperation in his voice, turned to him. "Not likely, considering who your father is."

He seemed guarded now, like an animal that's caught the scent of a predator. "You're not going to contact my father, tell him where I am."

"Why would I do that?" Bourne said softly.

Aashir's eyes were very wide, reminding Bourne of some corpses he'd seen, death coming as an astonishment to them.

"My father has been desperately trying to find me since the day I left. As you may imagine, it hasn't been easy keeping myself hidden from him and his people."

"You did the smart thing," Bourne said. "You decided to hide in plain sight. He would never think to look for you in Ivan Borz's cadre."

Aashir, seeming not to register the compliment, eyed Bourne critically. "He would pay you a fortune if you gave me up."

"I don't need a fortune," Bourne said. "Anyway, some things aren't for sale."

Aashir leaned toward him as if the two of them were magnetized. "Truly?"

462

Bourne nodded. "Truly, Aashir. Too many people have misused you already."

Aashir opened his mouth to say something, but turned away before he could utter a sound, but not before it was clear to Bourne that he had been released from a powerful tension.

The night was very still. The wind seemed to have nowhere pressing to go, It hung thick and hot like a blanket smothering the city. There was no respite from it.

"Tell me about him," Bourne said.

"My father?"

"Yes."

"I hate the name he's taken: Mohamed Sefavid." A tiny smile informed Aashir's lips. "Mohamed is a name he took as a young man. The name his parents gave him is Sameer, but he despised it." He exhaled, relaxing a little as he leaned against the warehouse wall. "My memories of him are partial — or, more accurately, he was home only sporadically. When he was home, he was frighteningly strict. I suppose he might have felt guilty about being away so much."

"What was he doing when he was away from the family?"

"What do you think? Being indoctrinated into jihadism, then weapons and explosives training. He claimed he learned from Al Murad" — Aashir shrugged — "but who really knows? My father seems allergic to the truth. Like Al Murad, he cloaks himself in ever thicker layers of myth and legend, which still inspires awe from my people. 'From awe comes obedience,' my father used to tell me, so often it made me sick to my stomach."

"That's what he tried on you."

Aashir nodded. "When I was very little, he was still around. He told me stories, claimed he was a djinn, that he could spread his arms and fly across the desert wastes. Of course, I begged him to take me with him, what child wouldn't? 'You need to grow up a little,' he told me, and the next morning he was gone.

"When I was older, of course, I learned the truth. Djinns don't kill people, but that's what my father was training to do, honing his skills along with his hate. And death became him. He flourished under its banner. I saw it myself.

"Many times I followed him, instead of attending classes at my school. I watched him change before my eyes. I listened to the indoctrination, the incessant spewing of hate and prejudice: the Jewish demon, fed, clothed, and armed by the American devil. But beneath all the rhetoric and religious rationale, I sensed the fear. Fear for Islam, fear not of the Israelis or the Americans, but of time. Islam has difficulty adjusting to the modern way of life. Everywhere people like my father look the old ways are being supplanted by the new, each of them a knife in Islam's belly. This cannot be tolerated, and for these people, the only answer is death to the infidel. But time cannot be killed. It continues to roll inexorably on."

Aashir shook his head, as if to rid himself of the past. "Anyway, the more people my father killed the greater

464

his reputation became. And then the moment arrived when he killed those standing in his way.

"Then he became El Ghadan."

CHAPTER
FIFTY-ONE

"They're still alive," El Ghadan said. "You didn't kill them."

"I'm not an assassin," Sara said. "I am not a jihadist. Killing people is not my field of expertise. You have soldiers like Islam for that."

El Ghadan's SUV moved like a shark along Doha's Corniche. The scimitar of land lay in dark contrast to the glimmering water. It seemed interesting to her that a desert dweller would prefer to be close to the sea.

El Ghadan plucked his mobile off the seat beside him. "Then I shall call him."

Sara knew everything depended on her staying calm and keeping to her plan. "You sent me in as your emissary, to make a determination."

"A decision," he corrected her sternly.

"A decision is based on absolutes," she said.

He held out his hand, thumb up. "Life." Then flipped it over like a Roman caesar delivering the fate of a gladiator. "Or death."

"In this instance there are no absolutes."

His lips pursed. "Explain, please."

"Soraya Moore is an old confidante of Jason Bourne's. She has stories to tell, secrets to impart."

He grunted. "Bourne's people — the very few that exist — are utterly loyal. They would never betray him."

Sara had been expecting this argument. "You are forgetting Soraya's daughter. She would do anything to save Sonya's life."

El Ghadan's face darkened. "Is that what you promised her?"

"I didn't promise her anything," Sara said. "I merely pointed out a possible exchange."

"You should not have done that, Ellie."

She leaned forward, said to the driver, "Stop the car."

El Ghadan waved away her words. "What do you think you're doing?"

"Getting out. I understand now that you and I can never see eye to eye."

Even though the vehicle was still rolling, she opened the door. Leaning across her, he slammed it shut.

She shook her head. "You don't get it, do you? It doesn't matter how much money you throw at me."

"So it's not a matter of money." He shrugged. "What is it, then? A difference in, what? Philosophy?"

"You devalue life, El Ghadan. Killing someone means nothing to you. And a two-year-old child — it's unconscionable!"

"I've seen too many children shot, beaten, charred in drone strikes. In Syria, they are shooting pregnant women in the belly."

"And you will follow their lead; you're part of those atrocities."

"There are many people who —"

"I don't care about the many people, El Ghadan. I care about the woman and child you hold captive."

"They have outlived their usefulness. I told you."

"And I'm telling you they haven't. I don't care about what Bourne has done or what he hasn't. This is about what this woman can do to save her child."

El Ghadan stared straight ahead. "You are trying to distract me."

Sara knew she had to pitch her voice just right, to remain neutral, leach all emotion from it, evince the dry dispassion of a bureaucrat. "You deal in information as well as in arms, isn't that right?"

"It is." He said it grudgingly, clearly not liking where this conversation was headed.

"Then what could be more useful to you than information about the world's most mysterious human being?"

She waited several beats, not wanting to oversell her thesis. "Consider, almost nothing is known about Jason Bourne. Now you have a direct conduit and the means to coerce her into divulging everything intimate she knows about Bourne." Again she paused, longer this time, to allow him to get used to the idea. "Isn't that worth a stay of execution for them both?"

Bourne heard the tiny catch in Aashir's voice. "But your father is not the nub of it, is he?"

"Well, yes and no."

468

Bourne waited, patient as the desert.

There was a breeze now. It had sprung up from the east, bringing with it a myriad of scents, most from modern-day Singapore, but a few from the town it had been when Sir Stamford Raffles planted the British flag in 1819 and declared it a perfect gateway port between the East and the West. There was still something of Raffles's Singapore if you looked hard enough in the right nooks and crannies, but it was fast disappearing under the steel and glass of office towers and glamorous resorts.

"I had a brother." When he resumed, Aashir's voice was barely above a whisper. "He was born to one of my father's mistresses. He had many, believe me. He needed them, I think — all of them. He doesn't know how to love."

"And your mother?"

"He had to marry someone, didn't he?"

There were a number of threads in Aashir's voice — bitterness, anger, guilt, as well as a longing to be the recipient of his father's pride. Bourne was aware of all these, knew he was successfully leading Aashir toward the heart of the complicated knot at his core.

"I hated her for putting up with it," the young man continued. "She was weak, which I suppose is why he chose her to many. He knew she wouldn't put up a fight. She was wholly traditional. She didn't have one foot in the modern world like a growing number of Iranian women."

"And this child — your half brother."

"*Him*." Aashir's voice turned dark. He might have been referring to the devil. "My father loved him from the moment he was born. He lavished all his attention . . ." He broke off, turned away again, and now a tear appeared at the apex of his cheek. "I don't want to talk about him."

"Is he still alive?" Bourne said, knowing that Aashir needed to talk about his brother.

"He was killed when he was eight." Aashir wiped his cheeks dry as if angry at what he believed was his own weakness. "An American air strike. It killed my brother and his mother, her entire family. My father was devastated. For weeks, he locked himself in his study and would not come out even to eat. My mother was reduced to leaving a tray of food in front of the door three times a day. Sometimes it disappeared, but most often it just lay there until, in a flood of tears, she took it away. I wound up eating most of it so it wouldn't go to waste."

Aashir was breathing hard, as if he had just finished a sprint. Bourne could see he was spent. He put his arm around the young man, turned him, guiding him back into the dimness of the warehouse.

"It's past time for both of us to get some rest," Bourne said.

Sara, waiting for El Ghadan to make his decision, stared out the smoked windows of his SUV, thinking of Soraya and Sonya.

When she had entered the locked room she had heard Soraya telling her daughter a story about

470

Dinazade, had waited to say something until the story was over. Luckily, Soraya still had the discipline not to look or sound surprised at Sara appearing like one of the mythical creatures in her Persian stories.

Sara spoke fluent Farsi, as well as Arabic, French, and Hebrew, among three or four others. Soraya greeted her in French. It was clear from her lead that neither Islam nor any of the other jihadist jailors spoke the language.

"L'histoire de Dinazade m'a tout de suite inspiré." The story of Dinazade immediately inspired me, she had said to Soraya. Her mind suddenly on fire, she spun out her own plan — desperate, far from a sure thing, but so far as she could determine the only chance her friend and her friend's daughter had.

As Soraya was Dinazade, Sara would become her sister, a modern-day Scheherazade; she would spin out tales of Jason that Soraya had supposedly told her. Each day she would bring another mythic bit of information back to El Ghadan. In this way, she hoped to keep Soraya and Sonya alive, giving Jason the time he needed to complete his own plan. Not knowing what it could be was nerve-racking in the extreme, and if she hadn't been an expert in compartmentalizing, she doubted she would be able to keep her fear at a manageable level. But in spinning King Shahryar ever more fantastical tales Scheherazade forestalled her own death until, after a thousand and one nights and a thousand stories, the king fell in love with her, commuting her sentence.

Now it was Sara's turn to spin a yarn for El Ghadan that he would find compelling enough to agree to keep Soraya and her daughter alive. Scheherazade was doubly canny; she made sure she came to a crucial point in her story just as dawn broke, compelling Shahryar to wait for another night to hear the resolution.

It would be up to her to make El Ghadan agree to such a scheme. She had to try to feed him bits of intelligence about Jason that would interest and intrigue him enough to consent to her arrangement. But even if that happened, she had no idea how long she could keep up the stories. She prayed for a quick and dramatic resolution to Jason's current predicament. He was the only one who could save them.

"All right," El Ghadan said, half turned toward her on the SUV's backseat, "begin, and then I will decide."

"No." Sara knew she had to remain firm with him. If he sensed any weakness at all he would put an immediate end to the conversation. "I need assurance from you that if you are satisfied Soraya and Sonya will live."

"For another twenty-four hours." El Ghadan nodded. "Proceed."

"First of all, Jason Bourne isn't his real name."

This news seemed to hit El Ghadan hard. "What is it?"

"Soraya doesn't know. I doubt if anyone does."

"Someone must."

"Possibly, but she hasn't come across them." She regarded him. "Shall I go on?"

He waved a hand at her.

"Jason Bourne was the name of someone in American military intelligence — a traitor who was shot dead for his crime. When the present Bourne was recruited into Treadstone he was given the name of the dead man."

"Why?"

"You remember Carlos?"

"The famed terrorist?" El Ghadan grunted. "Who doesn't?"

"Bourne's first mission was to draw Carlos out of hiding and kill him."

"And did he? I never could quite make out how Carlos died."

"Bourne completed his brief. He was the only one who could have succeeded."

El Ghadan's eyes went out of focus for a moment before his gaze snapped back to her. "I have heard some dreadful things about Treadstone's indoctrination program. Tell me about that."

"It was so far off the books it was illegal. It was shut down."

"I require details, Ellie. I need to know what Bourne is capable of."

"Tomorrow."

For a moment, El Ghadan glowered at her. Then his face broke out into a huge grin. "So this is how it's going to be." He waggled a finger at her. "I know what you're doing. I'm willing to play along, but only so far." His face darkened. "Am I clear?"

"Perfectly."

The SUV stopped. Without another word, she opened the door and stepped out into the Doha night.

After dropping Camilla off at his safe house, Ohrent went straight to the Kampong Glam district, at the outskirts of which was a small, unprepossessing mosque, among the oldest in Singapore. Its front doors were barred. Undeterred, Ohrent went to a small door near the rear of the left side, unnoticed by most. It was as heavily incised as the wall itself.

He knocked four times, waited, then knocked twice. At once the door swung open, and he was admitted by a figure, robed and hooded, hidden also by the lack of clear light. Not that the deep gloom was any deterrent to Ohrent; he knew the way with his eyes closed.

Removing his shoes, he dipped his hands in the earthenware bowl set into a niche. The hooded figure handed him a thin towel with which to dry his hands, then the figure vanished.

Ohrent proceeded down a short hallway that ran along the left side of the central chamber itself. Glancing in, he could make out perhaps a half dozen worshippers, foreheads pressed to their prayer rugs.

Shortly thereafter, he turned right. He was now behind the central chamber. The air was filled with murmured prayers. He entered the second chamber on his left. Two lamps on either side of a narrow bed were blazing. A man on a stool sat at a narrow wooden table.

474

A portable jeweler's lamp, complete with magnifier, lit up a small rectangle within which the man's expert hands were working. He was slim and tall, his shoulders stooped.

At Ohrent's entrance, he turned around.

"Hello, Kettle," Ohrent said. "Settling in well?"

CHAPTER
FIFTY-TWO

If there was one thing Camilla had learned since agreeing to take on the Black Queen brief it was not to trust anyone. She hadn't needed Hunter to tell her that — especially Hunter, for whom her feelings were multiple and confused. And even though she liked Ohrent, recent experience had forced her to question whether she could trust him.

Immediately after he left her, she took out her mobile, sent an email with the two attachments to the phone she had bought earlier in the day, then forwarded the email from the new mobile to POTUS's private mobile number.

A moment later, she slipped out of the safe house, following Ohrent back into the byways of Singapore, shadowing him like a remora sticks to a shark. Along the way, she dropped the new mobile into a trash bin. She had no idea where she was going, or why — she only knew that for her own peace of mind she had to find out whether or not he was telling her the truth.

Surprisingly, the evidence of that answer wasn't long in coming. Ohrent went directly to a mosque, entering through a side door. She heard the pattern he rapped out on the door, but knew she could not follow him without making some adjustments to her attire. She was wearing a pair of her favorite jeans, and she'd had the presence of mind to replace the tank top she had been wearing for a lightweight linen shirt with the cuffs pushed up her forearms.

Now she took out the headscarf she had brought with her from Washington, for she had heard there were a number of beautiful mosques in Singapore she would want to visit. Wrapping it around her head, she approached the door, repeated the pattern Ohrent had used.

The door swung open and she was admitted. However, she had no idea where he had gone, so after removing her shoes and washing her hands, she went down the hallway, past the main prayer room.

Just above the murmured susurrus of the faithful, she heard what sounded like Ohrent's voice in concert with an unfamiliar one. Turning right, she crept along the passageway, silent on her bare feet. Moving closer, she heard the voices more clearly — two men, one of them definitely Ohrent; his accent was unmistakable.

"This brief is cut-and-dried. It will be done, no fuss, no muss."

Then she heard Ohrent reply, "This is Singapore. Nothing here is ever that simple, Kettle."

"Speak plainly, Jimmie. We've known each other too long to beat around the bush."

"I don't give a fig about your primary target, but the girl —"

"What? She's gotten to you already." Kettle snickered. "Christ, Jimmie, you're old enough to be her father — her grandfather, in some cultures."

"She's special, Kettle." It seemed Ohrent was not to be baited. "Back off. Leave her alone."

"You know I can't do that."

"I'm asking you as a friend."

"And as a friend I'm telling you the brief is the brief. There can be no deviation."

"Of course there can. In special situations —"

"Jimmie, the only way you can stop me is to kill me. You're too old and we know each other too well for you to try it. Go home, Jimmie. That's my advice. Go home and forget I'm even here."

A cold fist clenched Camilla's lower belly. She had been right to follow Ohrent. She felt like the protagonist in a Kafka novel. Was there, in truth, no escape for her?

She was inching her way even closer when she became aware that she was under surveillance. Sweating as if she were in a steam room, she swung her head around so quickly her vertebrae crackled.

A small girl of about four or five regarded her from a shadowed corner. For a moment, Camilla was shocked that a small child would be up so late, but then she remembered that imams and their families often made their home in these mosques.

Terrified that the girl would make a sound that would alert Ohrent or Kettle, Camilla put her forefinger across her lips in the universal sign for silence. The girl's lips curled into a smile. She imitated

Camilla's gesture and then her smile widened until it seemed to take up almost all of her face.

Despite her burgeoning anxiety, Camilla felt a smile bubbling up from inside her, and she could not help returning it. Absorbing the child's beautiful face, the large, dark eyes regarding her without an iota of pretense or guile, she was pierced to the quick by the girl's absolute innocence. Here was a creature who had not yet learned to lie or deceive or hate. Here was pure love, and this notion rocked Camilla back on her heels. It was as if a switch was thrown inside her head, as if this child had single-handedly lifted the fog of war that had clouded her mind for the past week, revealing the truth of her own life — what was important to her and what she rejected.

When had her life sunk so deep in deceit, venality, and cynicism? Had it happened overnight while she was asleep or had it crept in so slowly day by day that she, with eyes wide shut, had not noticed until now? Either way, she knew she had to exorcise it immediately, before she succumbed to it or, worse, became part of it. This decision was her survival instinct coming to the fore.

The innocence of this child plopped down in the center of the muddle her life had become was a sign, she was sure of it. Just as she was sure of what she wanted now: a chance to make her own bundle of innocence. To give a child of her own what had been denied her. She never had been so certain of anything in her life.

Still smiling, she put her forefinger across her lips again. Again, the little girl copied her. As she began to giggle, Camilla, breathless with her revelation, turned and, fast as she could, padded back to the side door, where she gathered up her shoes and returned to the blood-warm Singapore night.

President Magnus was up at dawn. In truth, he had never gone to sleep, though he had tried more than a dozen times, while the illuminated clock by his bedside ticked off the minutes as slowly as if they were hours.

Finally, after being able to think of nothing but Camilla straddling him, or Camilla with her lips wrapped around his erection, or Camilla naked, clothed only in the American flag, he had rolled out of bed, slipped on a robe, and entered the living room. Turning on a lamp, he had plopped himself onto the sofa, tried to read a biography of Lyndon Johnson, then the current issue of *Foreign Affairs*, before admitting to himself that he hadn't absorbed anything he had read. And so his mind drifted back to Camilla. Not Charlie. Charlie was Charlie. She was growing up, and years from now, or maybe only months, she would change her opinions, or they would be changed for her. That was the way of the world. But Camilla . . .

Magnus was one of those people who, having made up his mind about an issue or a person, could never be persuaded to change his opinion. Take Camilla, for instance. The moment he met her he had known he wanted her near him, and the job opening was a perfect way to legitimately get what he wanted. And when it

480

was reported to him that she routinely stayed at her job until two or three in the morning, his mind was made up. Even before the fateful lunch that Anselm and Finnerman mistakenly assumed sealed the deal.

It was untrue, Magnus thought, as he stood by the curtained window of his hotel suite, that he had fallen in lust with Camilla at first sight. Dead wrong. That had come later. And it wasn't lust; it was love. Real love, such as he'd never felt for any other woman in his life. He would kill to protect Camilla, he knew that now, as sure as he found sleep a commodity without a price.

And now he knew that he had been a fool to agree to her being the choice for the Black Queen brief. Far too late, he realized what Anselm and Finnerman had been up to in pushing her for the mission. They saw her as a threat. They had plotted to get her away from him, get her out of Washington altogether. But then why send her to the same city he was in? It didn't make sense. He knew he was missing something.

Dawn light rose like a shell cracking open. He ran a trembling hand through his hair, was appalled to find it slicked with sweat. A thought had occurred to him, one so awful, so heinous he could barely get his head around it. And yet it was all too plausible. In fact, it fit the scenario so neatly, so perfectly, that he was forced to admire its audacity before he was shocked all over again.

Coming away from his vigil at the window, he returned to the living room sofa, where he had spent the latter part of the night going over the intelligence reports from the daily Eyes Only pouch delivered to him at midnight because of the distance and the time change. The pouch Anselm usually vetted first, for Anselm had established a habit of keeping a good deal of the daily intelligence chatter from him so that he would not be distracted from the important decisions on his plate.

It was a routine not altogether without merit, but to have kept from him the hints and innuendos that the peace summit was a forgone failure was, to his way of thinking, just plain criminal. Also humiliating. And that was even before he read the latest reports on the revolt in his own party against the drone program. Christ almighty, what else was Anselm keeping from him? he asked himself.

The answer was not long in making itself known. Minutes later, he heard the familiar ding of an email surfacing on his private mobile. Crossing to the sideboard where he had left it, he discovered a message from an unknown sender. He was about to delete it, when a kind of sixth sense made him pause. The account was so restricted and so heavily defended that no spam or phishing emails could get through.

The email itself held no text, but two attachments were waiting for him. The first was a DOD file from Finnerman's office dispatching the wetwork fieldman named Kettle to Singapore to find Jason Bourne and terminate him with extreme prejudice.

Curious, he opened the second attachment, an audio file, and was stunned to hear a conversation between Anselm and Finnerman discussing a verbal extension to

Kettle's unsanctioned brief. When he heard Anselm utter Camilla's name as an additional target, he went ballistic. Then, the first wave of fury having passed, he settled into a surface calm beneath which he was seething. There was much to do and little time to do it in.

In the small hours of the morning he made a series of calls, issued orders. Now, unable to wait a moment longer, and with one hand closed in a fist, he went to the door, opened it.

"Wake the chief of staff in an hour," he said to the Secret Service agent closest to him. "Now bring me my press secretary. And breakfast for three."

CHAPTER
FIFTY-THREE

Returned to the safe house in which Ohrent had stashed her, Camilla punched in a number on her mobile. Hunter answered at once, as if she had been waiting for Camilla's call.

"It's you."

She sounded slightly out of breath, which Camilla knew only happened when her emotions were running high and hot.

"I was worried you wouldn't call me back."

"I need you to listen to me, Hunter. Something's happened I'm sure you didn't count on."

"What do you mean?" Hunter said with a catch in her throat.

"I read the brief you and Terrier drew up."

There was a short silence, during which Camilla imagined many things passing through Hunter's mind, none of them good.

"And?" Hunter said, after a time.

"You need to leave the Dairy."

"Jesus, Cam."

"Leave the Dairy, leave D.C., leave the country."

"You're not going to turn us in. You can't possibly
. . . We are asking you to do nothing, to stand aside, to

let whatever was going to happen happen. Is that so terrible?"

"Do you hear yourself, Hunter? Listen to what I'm saying. I am here to protect the president. I will not violate my brief. I will not kill for you; I will not stand aside, as you put it." Her voice was rising, shrill even. She had wanted to keep everything on an even keel, but now in the middle of the conversation she understood how impossible that was. "Hunter, leave now, this instant."

"And throw Terrier under the bus?"

"He's more than likely going to do that to you the moment he's in custody."

"You can't —"

"You won't get a second chance."

Another pause, this one taut as a bowstring.

"Cam, I can't. I believe what we're doing is the right thing, the only humane thing, to stop —"

"I'm sorry, Hunter. Really, I am."

She disconnected before the conversation could get overemotional, out of hand. She couldn't deal with that now. She had to come to terms with something that had been in her face for some time: Hunter and Terrier were fanatics. And because their plot concerned the president, she called Tony Levinson at the Secret Service, a senior supervisor she had brought in and so could trust absolutely, told him about Hunter and Terrier. She answered his barrage of questions as best she could. "Get on them now," she said, then rang off.

In the aftermath, Camilla felt nothing, less than nothing. It was as if a void had opened up inside her.

Then, without warning, the storm hit, and she wept, sobbing as she had not done since she was a little child in her mother's arms. Even at that tender age, she remembered, her mother had admonished her not to cry, ideally not to show her emotions at all.

"That makes you weak," her mother had said, "and in a man's world you can't afford to appear weak." But a dam long held in place had been shattered, and she wept unashamedly until there was not a single tear left to shed.

She was bone weary. Part of her ached to go to bed, pull the covers over her head, and sleep for a week, but of course she didn't. She couldn't; she was not that kind of person. She poured herself a drink, held it without taking a sip. She was that kind of person, too. Still, she drew comfort from its weight and its aroma, which reminded her of better, less frightening times.

As the sky was beginning to turn gray and pink, she heard a key in the lock and dumped the liquor in the sink. Ohrent, presumably finished with his business with Kettle, stepped in, softly closing the door behind him.

"How did you sleep?" he asked when he came into the kitchen.

"Like a baby," she replied with a smile she had once seen on a crocodile.

"It's London to a brick you'll need some food." Ohrent seemed not to notice the remnants of her tears. "But not too much; don't want your weight on, do we?"

Camilla hesitated. "What about Kettle? Did you find him?"

"You needn't worry about him," Ohrent said. He clapped his hands sharply. "Now come on. We're due at the club in two hours. It's race day."

"Come in, Howard," POTUS said in a jovial voice as Anselm appeared in the doorway. "Good to see you so early in the morning."

Anselm, hair tousled, was still tying the belt around the plush bathrobe with the Golden Palace's sea-blue merlion embroidered on the chest. "It's a big day for us, Bill."

He pulled up short as he saw Marie Engle, the press secretary, smiling at him from the sofa opposite where POTUS sat. A sumptuous food cart stood at POTUS's left elbow.

He greeted Engle, then returned his attention to Magnus. "We have to meet the Palestinian president and the Israeli prime minister at the Thoroughbred Club in a couple of hours."

"Oh, but surely we have time for a bite of breakfast, Howard. Come on now" — he patted the sofa cushion next to him — "take a load off and we'll break bread like friends should."

Anselm sat as directed. In front of him, the coffee table was laden with plates of fruit and eggs and toast, cups, and glasses of fresh orange juice laid out for three.

POTUS reached over, poured him some coffee. Engle already had hers held between her two hands. Anselm noticed no one else in the room — no stewards, no security personnel. Definitely odd.

"Believe it or not, the coffee here is fantastic," POTUS said in the breezy way he handled interviewers. "They say it's from Bali. Who knew the Balinese grew coffee? But I'm telling you it packs a punch. Here."

He handed his chief of staff the cup, and as Anselm brought it to his lips said, "Did you know that I'm a big John Le Carré fan?"

"No, sir, I didn't." Anselm's eyebrows lifted. "Wow, this *is* strong."

He reached for the milk, but POTUS stopped him. "Trust me, its strength is best savored black." POTUS winked. "It'll put hair on your chest."

Anselm obediently took another sip, made a face as if he were drinking slivovitz.

POTUS sat back against the cushions, crossed one leg over the other, as if they were two pals sitting down to breakfast after a particularly active boys' night out. He swallowed some more coffee, said, "Did you know that Le Carré is a nom de plume?"

"I think I heard something about that."

"Yes indeed." POTUS regarded Anselm over the rim of his cup. "Turns out his real name is Cornwell. David Cornwell." Another sip of coffee, his eyes never leaving those of his chief of staff. "It also turns out that Cornwell's father was a con man. That's right. Can you believe it? I imagine that's why the son changed his name. It seems Cornwell père was caught, tried, convicted, and sent to gaol. That's what they call prison in England, isn't it, Howard?"

Anselm, whose pale and waxy complexion attested to his being caught by surprise, said nothing for a moment. "Yes." He cleared his throat. "Yes, I believe it is."

"I thought so!" POTUS cried in the voice of a child coming down the stairs on Christmas morning, but his tone changed on a dime. "When were you going to tell me that the drone program was under attack?"

"I have that under control, Bill. It's taken care of."

"Uh-huh. Just like you took care of this?" Opening the top of the serving cart, he took out a copy he had had made of the Kettle brief, spun it across in a perfect arc so that it landed on Anselm's lap.

Anselm glanced down, then away, as if his boss had thrown him a live cobra.

"Kill it, Howard." POTUS's voice was now as hard and unyielding as a marine's steel sword. "Kill all of it."

"Sir, I —"

"Howard, call Finnerman. Since you two are such asshole buddies, this task falls to you. Tell him to call off his snapper or whatever those idiots at DOD call snipers these days."

"A dinger, sir." Anselm looked stricken, as if he was about to have a heart attack. "A snapper's a prostitute."

"Seems to me snapper's the correct word, then." He bared his teeth. "Get to it, Howard. Or do you want me to make the call for you?"

"Bill —"

"You've lost the right to call me by my Christian name."

"Sir. You're making a huge mistake. If the dinger doesn't take care of Bourne —"

"My security detail is on high alert for Bourne."

"Well, that's good, I suppose. Though, in my opinion, not nearly as good as Kettle."

"Cut the crap, Howard." Magnus raised a forefinger, the stern paterfamilias. "There's something you're not telling me, an addendum you and Finnerman added to the Kettle brief, isn't there?"

Anselm swallowed hard. "I . . . I don't know what you mean, sir."

POTUS pressed a key on his mobile, and to his horror Anselm heard his own voice in brief colloquy with Finnerman.

Anselm seemed to have lost control of his eyes. They were rolling in their sockets like caroming pinballs. "Sir, if you'll only give me a chance to explain. We were trying to protect you from —"

"All explanations have passed their sell-by date," POTUS said silkily, talking right over Anselm. "Now, you will do precisely what I tell you, no more, no less."

Anselm nodded numbly, dug in the capacious pocket of his bathrobe, pulled out his mobile, and punched in a speed dial number.

POTUS watched beneath half-closed lids. "What? No answer, Howard?" He snapped his fingers. "Oh, that's right, Marty Finnerman's mobile has been confiscated, along with his computer at work and his laptop at his home." A slow smile, like the sun rising, spread across POTUS's face. "Your co-conspirator is at this moment in custody — in a solitary holding cell,

490

being interrogated by certain elements of Homeland Security I don't know about." The smile continued to spread like honey across toast. "I mean, just between you and me, I *do* know about them, but, well, you know . . ."

Slapping his hands on his thighs, POTUS rose. "It's your turn now, Howard."

Anselm was almost breathless, as if he were trapped in a room without oxygen. "Look, look, making her a jockey was my idea. Why? So Camilla would be sent for training to the Dairy, where she would be trained by Hunter Worth. Hunter had been on our radar —"

"By 'our radar,' just who do you mean, Howard?"

Anselm took a deep breath to try and steady himself. "Gravenhurst."

POTUS nodded. "The Watchers. But tell me, Howard, who watches the Watchers?"

Preferring not to answer that, Anselm pressed desperately on. "Hunter is a homegrown danger. But she was working with someone. We needed to know whom. So I sent Camilla —"

"It's Terrier."

Anselm gaped. "What?"

"Camilla just phoned it in. Hunter's contact is Vincent Terrier." Magnus nearly exploded. "One of Finnerman's most trusted agents, for Chrissakes!"

Anselm went pale. "I didn't —"

"Shut up, Howard." For the first time in many months, POTUS's face seemed devoid of indecision or anxiety. Without taking his eyes from his chief of staff, he held out a hand. "Marie?"

His press secretary handed over a sheet of paper with the presidential seal. "This is a press release, Howard. It describes in detail how the drone program was the brainchild of Marty Finnerman. I'm pinning the program on him. And he's going to fall on his sword. Why? Because you're going to convince him it's in his best interests. And why will you do that, Howard? Because it's in *your* best interests."

"Camilla did what she was supposed to do . . . I mean, without me —"

"You used her. You put her in harm's way, you shit." Magnus handed over another sheet. "Signing this acknowledgment of your complicity in this affair will keep you out of jail, but nothing more. Am I making myself clear?"

Anselm, unable any longer to get his voice to work, nodded shakily.

"Now get out of here."

Magnus crossed the living room to where a pair of Secret Service agents had been patiently waiting just outside the closed door. "He's all yours, boys. Treat him the way you'd treat the son of a bitch who just screwed your sixteen-year-old daughter."

492

CHAPTER
FIFTY-FOUR

Borz took Aashir by the elbow. "Come with me."

The living area of the warehouse had a narrow catwalk that had once been the province of the supervisor overseeing loading and unloading, but was now rarely used. It was separated from the living area by a thin composite-board wall and a door a rat could waltz through.

When they were out on the catwalk, Borz turned to Aashir. "Yusuf has taught you to shoot the long gun."

Aashir nodded. "He has."

"You're confident in your aim."

"I am."

"In killing people."

"I have done so for you, Borz, have I not?"

The Chechen nodded. "That you have, and very well indeed. You handled the Taliban without fear. Today, you will need all that calmness and courage, Aashir, because once we get inside the Thoroughbred Club you're not staying with the cadre. I have a special assignment for you, one no one else can know about."

His gaze studied the young man's face as if it were a specimen in a killing jar. "I'm trusting you with this assignment, Aashir." He closed the distance between them. "Am I right in trusting you?"

"You know you are," Aashir answered.

For a long moment Borz kept up his scrutiny of the young man's face. Then, as if satisfied, he gave a curt nod. "Bombs are mechanical," he said. "They sometimes don't work, or don't work properly. That's where you come in. We're leaving nothing to chance. Our intel is that all the dignitaries will be sitting in the presidential box for the second race." A cynical smile stole across his face like a sneak thief, and was gone. "The ruling family's horse will be running in it, and if the past is any guide it will win it." He closed the distance again, lowered his voice to just above a whisper. "Because the ruling family will be in attendance, each race will go off at exactly the scheduled time, so everything we do has been planned out in advance, timed to precision. I will show you where to go. You're going to be given the long gun and a roost from which to shoot. You'll be directly across from the presidential box, far enough so the detonation will not reach you. But your role is essential, you understand?"

Aashir nodded. "Why isn't Yusuf being given the long gun? He's the real expert. Don't you trust him?"

Borz sighed. "Of course I trust him; he saved my life in Waziristan. But I don't know him the way I knew Furuque. You have been with me for some time. You're a natural; you're as good a shot as he is."

He leaned in. "No one who enters the presidential box will leave it alive. That will be up to you, Aashir.

Anyone left alive after the bomb goes off — or if it fails to detonate — you shoot him dead. The American president first, then the Palestinian, then the Singaporean."

"And then the Israeli?" Aashir said into the small silence.

"The Israeli?"

"Have you forgotten, Borz? The prime minister of Israel."

"No," Borz said. "I haven't forgotten him. An urgent call will summon him at the precise moment. He won't be in the box when the bomb is detonated."

So that's El Ghadan's plan, Bourne thought. Assassinate the heads of state, scuttle the peace process for all time, and blame it on the Israelis. The resulting worldwide outcry might well spell the end of Israel. An ear to the composite-board wall delivered the conversation on the catwalk as if he were out there with Borz and Aashir. But there was a further aspect to the plan he hadn't told Aashir. Of course he hadn't.

Bourne opened the door, stepped out onto the catwalk.

Borz turned. "Yusuf, what do you want? This is a private conversation."

"Well, it was." Bourne came toward the two men. "Why don't you tell Aashir what his real role in the plan is?"

"You overheard?"

"That wall wouldn't stop a rubber bullet," Bourne said.

Borz's eyes were slitted. He was fairly shaking with rage. "No, no, you deliberately listened in."

"To protect Aashir."

"I've had enough of your interference. Aashir is off-limits," Borz said.

Bourne ignored him. "Aashir, listen to me —"

The Chechen leapt at Bourne, a knife in his left hand. Bourne evaded the first strike, struck at Borz's wrist. The blade, only partially deflected, scored a line down the inside of Bourne's right forearm, where blood immediately welled.

Out of the corner of his eye Bourne saw Aashir step in. He hit Borz on the side of the jaw, a clumsy blow that nevertheless twisted Borz's head and enraged him. Slamming his shoulder into Bourne, Borz grabbed on to the front of Aashir's uniform and jerked him forward, butting him with his bony forehead, them shoving him back against the railing so hard that Aashir bounced off and right into a powerful blow to the gut. As he doubled over, Borz grasped his head. He was about to pound it into the railing when Bourne buried a fist in his kidney.

Borz's face screwed up, his torso jackknifed, and Bourne struck down his grip on Aashir. As the young man collapsed onto the catwalk, Bourne drove his knuckles hard into Borz's ribs. Borz gasped, but still managed to stamp hard on Bourne's instep, then deliver a one-two combination to his midsection.

Out came the bloodied knife again. He slashed inside, going for Bourne's throat, and for a moment the two of them were very close, in a kind of tense stasis.

496

Borz's lips were against Bourne's ear. "You're fucked now, Yusuf," he whispered. He brought his elbow against Bourne's throat, dug it in with a vicious strength. "Lose all hope, you who enter here."

He bent Bourne back over the railing and swept inward with the knife blade. But Bourne had worked his hands to the inside. They were now in the narrow space between his body and Borz's. Grabbing the Chechen's belt, he lifted him off his feet, lifted him up over his own body. Borz's elbow was caught between the two men's chests. He frantically tried to shift it, but Bourne blocked him, and seconds later, the elbow cracked. Bourne heard the joint go with the sound of a rifle shot.

Borz lost control of the knife as he struggled to free himself, but he was too far off the catwalk, his center of balance was too high. He was tipping over. With one last effort, he freed the knife with his good arm, tried to stab Bourne, but it was too late. He had lost his balance, he had no leverage, no power behind the strike.

Then he was upside down, raised by Bourne's powerful arms, delivered into the air. He seemed to hang for a moment at the level of the catwalk's railing. He flung out his arms in a vain attempt to grab on, then plummeted down onto the concrete floor of the warehouse.

His skull hit first, broke open like a ripe melon, blood and brains spilling out. Then his spine fractured as the rest of him struck the floor.

Bourne immediately knelt by Aashir's side, gathered him in his arms. Blood leaked from Aashir's nose and he was going in and out of consciousness until Bourne slapped his cheeks, bringing color to them and blood back into his face.

"Are you all right?" Aashir asked.

Bourne laughed. "I should be asking you that." He grasped Aashir under the arms. "Let's get you up."

Aashir, struggling with his balance, leaned against the railing, holding tight. Then he looked around. "Where's Borz?"

"He went over the side," Bourne said. "He's dead."

"In fact, that's not true."

They turned to see that Musa had appeared on the catwalk. His eyes stared straight at Bourne. "You killed the wrong man, Yusuf. That was Nazyr, one of my lieutenants. He was in charge of the Waziristan cadre."

"One of your lieutenants?" Aashir looked bewildered.

"Musa is the real Borz," Bourne said. "But I'm wondering why you would want Nazyr to impersonate you?"

"Security." Borz smiled. "The Mahsud are no different than any other Waziri tribe. They have given me no good reason to trust them. If my deal with them goes sideways I'm not there to take the fallout."

He shrugged. "Not that any of it matters. Furuque was supposed to be our sniper at the Thoroughbred Club. Then you took over. But the moment you killed Nazyr you betrayed me and this cadre."

498

Aashir threw up his hands. "Wait! What are you saying?"

There was a small, easily concealed .25 caliber pistol in Borz's right hand, and before anyone had a chance to react or even utter another word, he shot Bourne twice in the chest.

Holstering the gun, he glanced at Aashir. "Does that answer your question?"

CHAPTER
FIFTY-FIVE

When Camilla arrived at the Singapore Thoroughbred Club with Ohrent she found it much changed. For one thing masses of flowers were everywhere. For another, a colossal specially made construct of the Singapore merlion, the half-land, half-sea beast, symbol of the city-state, had been erected in the center of the main racing oval. For still another, the club was chockablock with security personnel from the three visiting countries. Not to mention that the complement of Singaporean security personal had been beefed up to three times its usual size.

In other words, the place was alive with new faces and activity, even around the stables, which, predictably, was making the horses nervous.

Opening Jessuetta's stall door, Camilla did her best with voice and hands to calm her to a race-ready state. That was more than could be said for Camilla herself, who had been so unnerved by the events of the previous night, she watched herself as if through someone else's eyes. With mounting horror, she witnessed her hands trembling as she sought to gentle Jessuetta. Who will gentle me? she asked herself. But

500

there was no one; she was entirely on her own in the field, without backup or a local control she could trust.

"I'm going to take her out for a walk around the track," she said when Ohrent appeared at the stall.

"You don't have much time until the weigh-in. When the ruling family is in attendance everything runs like clockwork, not a minute late."

"Once around the stables paddock. She's too het up to stay here."

As she slipped the bit into Jessuetta's mouth and slid the bridle over her face, Ohrent said in a low voice, "Camilla, come out here for a moment."

She looked at him, at the grave expression on his face.

He led her into the deep shadows of a far corner, held out a throwing knife in a slim sheath. "Do you know how to use this?"

She nodded.

Ohrent stepped around behind her, fitted the knife between the skin of the small of her back and the waist of her jeans. He came back around, gave her a thin smile.

She studied him. "What really happened last night?"

"Ask me no questions," Ohrent said, so softly she had to lean in to be sure she heard him.

Camilla was reminded of the parable of the man who always tells the truth and the man who always lies. How do you tell them apart?

Bourne, who had been on his stomach since being shot by Borz, rolled over, pulled himself up to a sitting position, back braced against the catwalk railing. For a moment he stared at the smear of blood on the catwalk where he had bled from the wound Nazyr's knife had scored along his arm. He needn't have bothered, since Borz had ducked inside almost immediately, drawn by a mobile phone call. Aashir, with a look over his shoulder at Bourne, had trailed after him. Within minutes after that, the cadre had cleared out of the warehouse.

Deep pains ricocheted through his chest with every movement he made, so he stopped, spent the next several moments concentrating on deep breathing, to reoxygenate his system. Trauma and shock robbed you of what you needed most.

He looked around for a weapon, but someone — probably Borz — had scooped up Nazyr's fallen knife. Then he pushed two fingers through the bullet holes in his uniform tunic. Unbuttoning it revealed an aramid vest — lightweight body armor he had been wearing since Zizzy had brought him his belongings out of the hotel room in Damascus.

Reaching down, Bourne pulled out the two .25 caliber bullets, flattened now, from the fabric of the body armor. He dropped them on the catwalk, grimaced as he at last stood up. His chest felt as if he had gone fifteen rounds with a heavyweight boxer.

He staggered into the living area. He had to find a spare tunic, one that wasn't torn apart by bullet holes, otherwise he'd never get through security at the Thoroughbred Club.

The morning, clear and blue as a marble, was scorching by the time Borz and his cadre reached the service entrance to the Thoroughbred Club in the vehicle that had been provided for them. He had meant to station members of the cadre across the street from all the entrances to the club, to shoot patrons at random as they fled, but that was only a peripheral part of the theater. Considering the main objective of the plan, that detail would not be missed. It still would be theater on the grandest of scales.

Ivan Borz had assured him as much. He had been in contact with the real Ivan Borz, safe and sound in his headquarters, a heavily fortified medieval castle overlooking the Caspian Sea, from which he directed all his business. Borz never ventured far outside the Makhachkala area, except on his ninety-eight-foot yacht. He was something of a hermit, possibly even an agoraphobe. Musa — for that was the pilot's real name — was another of Borz's trusted lieutenants. He had been with Borz for over a decade, had bloodied his sword — so to speak — in numerous forays for his boss.

Showing their provided ID tags, the cadre passed through security without incident, though the heightened extent of it was perfectly clear. Inside the Thoroughbred Club complex, Musa gave his final instructions to the five members of his cadre and, with a map, sent them on their way.

Then he turned to Aashir, took him in the opposite direction, toward the side of the racetrack opposite the presidential box. The target area was at this moment devoid of anyone save members of the various national security agencies. The rest of the stands were already packed, as the first race was about to begin, and the betting had been fast and furious, as befitting a day when the ruling family was attending.

On the way to the sniper's roost, Musa drew Aashir aside. "Are you certain you're up to this?" he asked.

"Of course I am. Why would you ask that?"

"You became close to Yusuf during his time here, but I tell you the man was not to be trusted. It's far better for everyone that he's dead."

Aashir nodded. He was holding a metal container, which contained the long gun, broken down into three sections.

They had attained the service stairs at the rear of the stands. "When you reach the top of the stairs —"

"I've memorized the blueprint."

"When you reach the top of the stairs," Musa repeated, undeterred, "do you turn left or right?"

"Left," Aashir said. "Until I reach the vertical ladder. Then up that. The roost will be ten feet away on my right."

Musa's dark gaze bored into him. "All right, then." He slapped him on the shoulder. "May Allah grant you success."

He watched Aashir until he was out of sight. Then he turned and went on his own way, which was in fact the only operational section of the plan that mattered.

Outside, on the oval, the horses in the first race were thundering around the track.

504

For Kettle, Singapore was just another stop — one of many his briefs took him to. Like hotel rooms to a traveling salesman, the cities tended to blur one into another. But in some ways even he had to admit that Singapore was different. He knew if he were forced to live here he'd most likely wind up blowing his brains out. The rules and regulations, the strictures on citizenry and visitors alike were draconian, not to mention capricious. Who ever heard of an injunction against chewing gum in public? The importation of gum was banned. No swearing either. Insane. Truth be told, the quicker he finished with this brief the happier he'd be.

He had received the call informing him of an addendum to the brief. A second hit had been ordered. After rising this morning following a deep and dreamless sleep, he had carefully, lovingly taken up the long gun, which in many ways was his closest friend. His only friend. He had other weapons he felt close to, but none had the gravitas of his sniper's rifle. The special case he had made, holding the broken-down sections, looked like nothing more than an old-fashioned physician's bag.

Now he was here, invisible among the swirling, gesticulating throngs, making it child's play for him to find the door marked SECURE AREA — AUTHORIZED PERSONNEL ONLY. It was metal, painted a bright red. It was also locked, but that proved no impediment to Kettle. He had a way with locks, even digital ones.

Fifteen seconds later, he was inside. A minute and a half after that, Camilla, walking Jessuetta, spotted him.

Kettle, in the stables area, was warming to his task. It was always this way, he thought, when the kill was near. Finnerman had texted him that Camilla Stowe was going to jockey a horse in the second race — one of Jimmie's horses.

Jimmie is definitely getting old, he thought. Old and possibly senile. The girl had gotten to him somehow. In a stunning and, ultimately, pathetic example of breaking protocol, he had come to the mosque to beg for her life, but Kettle had been given the brief. It was his now, and he was going to carry it out to the letter as he'd done with all his previous briefs. Jimmie should have known that; clearly the girl had blinded him to good sense. Maybe he'd even lost his operational edge. In any case, he'd have to let Finnerman know; Jimmie needed to be replaced.

He was heading toward the stables themselves when his mobile vibrated. He had only to think of Finnerman and there he was. He took the call. But it wasn't Finnerman on the other end.

"This is Robert Lonan, Department of Justice," the deep voice in his ear said. "You should know that Martin Finnerman is in our custody. Your brief is hereby terminated, as is your position in DOD. You are to turn yourself in to the local authorities, who have been notified of your name and status."

"And if I don't?" Kettle said.

"Then you will immediately become a fugitive from justice. The full power and influence of the United States government will be directed at finding you. Clear? You have one hour to comply with this order."

"Fuck you!" Kettle said in reply, but the line was dead. Robert Lonan, Department of Justice, was no longer in the ether.

Sensing movement to his right, he turned. "Are you Camilla Stowe?" he said to the figure that had emerged from the shadows. A horse stood by her side. The two of them seemed to be watching him.

"Can I help you?" Camilla said.

Kettle smiled, but he was having trouble getting into his legend's skin. "Binder, Jack Binder, but my friends call me Jackie, Inverhalt Fabrications, we make all the racing silks for the jockeys." He said all this far too quickly, speaking one long run-on sentence. What should have been a salesman's breezy spiel came across as overeager, not to say overcaffeinated. The phone call had inflamed an anger he kept safely banked while in the field. The anger made him hurry, and in his haste he lost discipline. Appalled as he was, Kettle pressed on, the only thing to do. "Jimmie told me you're his new jockey. Am I right?" He sidled ever closer. "I'm trying to find him." He waved a hand. "But in all this madness, no matter how many times I come here I always get lost." That was better, wasn't it? he asked himself.

"You're right. I'm jockeying the horse Jimmie trains," Camilla said in a kind of dreamy voice. "I'll take you to him."

"I'd appreciate that."

Before he could edge still closer, Camilla drew Jessuetta around so the animal was between them. Kettle immediately stepped forward, following her, but skittishly. He was clearly uncomfortable around horses, which made it a good bet he knew nothing about them.

Jessuetta stepped sideways, toward a wall she might have mistaken for her stall. It seemed she wanted to get away from Kettle as badly as Camilla did. But her movement put Camilla's back against the wall. Camilla had nowhere to go except past Kettle. One of her hands slid behind her back, her fingers wrapping around the hilt of Ohrent's knife.

Kettle leaned forward. "Listen," he said. "Listen, the truth is . . . the reason I'm here, see, is to take your measurements, get you fitted with your own set of Ingerhalt silks."

"I'm sorry. I don't have time now. Maybe later."

"But, I mean, you can't! Wait, that is." He pushed against Jessuetta's side to get all the closer to her. "You're in borrowed silks now, am I right? Jimmie won't like that. You got to get your own, know what I mean? And ASAP." His voice had now completely slipped the leash of his legend. Instead of overeager, it became manic, something dark and ominous. "Come on now, it won't take but a couple minutes, promise." As he pushed more urgently, Jessuetta stamped her hooves and snorted through widened nostrils.

Camilla hesitated a moment more, then said, "Okay. Sure." She started to come around Jessuetta's rear, but as Kettle all but rushed to meet her, she stepped smartly back.

Unmindful, he came on. He was behind Jessuetta when Camilla slapped the horse hard on her flank, just as Ohrent had warned her not to. The result was instantaneous and decisive. Jessuetta kicked out hard with her hind legs. One of her hooves caught Kettle in the left temple. He went down as if struck by lightning, which, in a way, he had been.

Camilla was so shocked that for a moment she felt paralyzed. Then, gathering herself, she whispered to Jessuetta, apologizing, promising her that she would never strike her again. As the horse settled, Camilla moved toward her rear, always keeping a gentling hand on her to let her know where she was.

Kettle lay where he had fallen. There was a deep indentation on his head where Jessuetta's hoof had struck him with the force of a jack-hammer. Is he, is he . . . ? Good Lord, she thought, he's really dead. She stood in a kind of daze, momentarily incapable of further action, not wanting to think of cause and effect.

People were running toward them, and with a spasmodic movement of self-preservation, she pushed the handle of the knife down past the waistband of her jeans, where it could not be seen.

CHAPTER
FIFTY-SIX

"Kettle's dead," Camilla said, when she had returned to the stables and put Jessuetta in her stall.

"Kettle?" Ohrent's cheeks became mottled with shock and emotion. "Are you all right?"

She made a face. "Of course I'm all right."

He leaned on the stall door, arms crossed. "Well, you don't look all right."

"What are you, my daddy?"

Her irritation masked the horror of how quickly everything had happened. Thoughts and emotions eddied inside her, muddled and unnerving. She had never caused another person's death. Though she had trained for it, tried her best to prepare herself mentally, how could she have really known its effects beforehand? She bore down, concentrating on the fact that he had come after her, would have killed her had she not stopped him. Yet still in the aftermath she had to admit she was feeling slightly queasy.

Apparently, Ohrent decided to take a different tack with her. "What happened?" he said in the crisp, terse tone of a control debriefing his fieldman. "Don't tell me he was the man Jessuetta kicked to death."

When she nodded, Ohrent said, "Well, fuck me dead!" Then, returning to his role as her local control, he said, "Details, please."

So she told him. How he had appeared out of nowhere, taking her by surprise. The people who showed up first had called a doctor, who arrived shortly thereafter. As she suspected, the doctor found no breath, no pulse. Kettle was dead. Moments later, a security team arrived, asked a number of questions, which she answered calmly. No, she didn't know the man. Yes, he had accosted her. Yes, she had tried to get away from him, but she didn't want to leave her horse. When he came around behind the horse, the horse spooked and kicked him. That was all. Witnesses corroborated her story. No one had seen her strike Jessuetta. The security officers checked her passport, asked for her address in Singapore, then thanked her and said she was free to go.

"Afterward, I apologized to Jessuetta," she said in conclusion.

Ohrent stared at her with a grief-stricken look.

"What?" she said. "Do I need to do more? I think she's forgiven me."

All his life he had wondered whether it was possible to laugh and cry at the same time. "Bugger all, I've failed you, Cam."

She handed the knife back to him in a gesture that was almost ceremonial. "You were between a rock and a hard place." Stepping forward, she kissed his cheek. "No worries, Jimmie, you did your best to protect me."

"Trouble was, this time my best wasn't very good." Then a shy smile crept across his face. "And to think you didn't even need protecting."

"I was glad to have it, Jimmie, believe me. It lent me courage when I needed it most."

At that moment, two men entered the stables. It was perfectly clear they did not belong among horses or jockeys. They were not owners, nor owners' representatives. They were as far from tourists as Camilla was from D.C.

For an awful moment Camilla thought she was about to be arrested. Her heart pounded painfully against her rib cage.

"What can I do for you gentlemen?" she said.

"Please come with us," the one on the left said, showing his Secret Service ID. He looked very much like the one on the right. She thought it curious that she did not recognize either man. They must have come on after she had begun her brief.

"Wait a minute." Ohrent interjected himself between them. "What is this?"

"This doesn't concern you," the one on the right said, with absolutely no inflection in his voice.

"The hell it doesn't!" Ohrent took a belligerent step toward them, which put them on alert.

"Jimmie, stop," Camilla said. These were her people, after all. At least they were until she had taken the Black Queen brief.

"Please come with us, Ms. Stowe," the one on the left said. "There's not much time. POTUS requires your presence."

512

Ms. Stowe. She was their boss, but not while undercover. She felt herself relax.

"'He requires her presence,'" Ohrent mimicked with no little derision. "Does POTUS know she's jockeying my horse in the next race?"

The one on the left gave him a jaundiced eye. "Cool your barbie, Matilda," he said.

"Agent," Camilla said, "what's your name?"

"Morris, ma'am."

"Shut it, Morris."

"Yes, ma'am." Morris looked properly abashed. "The thing is, ma'am, we're in the sixty-minute interval between races. The sooner we bring you to POTUS the sooner you can get back here."

"Bugger all!" Ohrent said, throwing up his hands. "Go on, then. What POTUS wants . . ." He let the rest of that sentence hang in the air as Camilla prepared to leave.

"I'll be back in plenty of time, Jimmie," she said as Morris and his partner took up position flanking her.

He glared at Morris. "Bollocks to you, sonny-Jim. You'd bloody well have her back in time or this *Matilda* will have your hide." He turned away, stared at Jessuetta, who looked back at him, bobbed her head and snorted.

"You can say that again!" he muttered as he fingered the knife Camilla had returned to him. "They give me the shits too."

POTUS, nervous as a fox at a hound convention, was waiting for Camilla in a bunkerlike room well below ground. It was the place his Secret Service detail had chosen as the most secure inside the Thoroughbred Club. There was no time to go anywhere outside it.

His heart turned over the moment he saw her; he felt like a teenager with his first real crush, when nothing else in the universe mattered except this girl, filling the room with her intoxicating beauty and sexuality. He was already hard, and forgot to be embarrassed by it.

No one else was in the room besides them. Somewhere close by, they heard the sound of water gurgling through pipes. The place smelled of mineral dust and disinfectant.

"Camilla," he said softly.

He moved to take her in his arms, but she drew back.

"Bill, are you crazy? What part of 'no' don't you understand?"

"None of it. I know when you say no you really mean yes."

She recoiled as if he had slapped her. "Like hell I do!"

He reached out for her. He was still vibrating with the heady power he had exerted in his hotel room. He wanted everything, and he wanted it now. And why not? Was he not the most powerful man in the world?

She turned her head away as he lunged to kiss her. "Bill, you can't —"

"I'm POTUS, Cam." He pulled her, resisting, into his arms. "I can do anything I want."

"Don't I get any say in this?"

"Of course you do." He began to wrestle with her to keep her in his embrace. "But I know you better than

514

you know yourself." He pressed his crotch against her. "You want this, I know you do." He kissed her throat, the side of her neck. "You're just scared is all."

"You're wrong, Bill." She was still trying to twist away from him. "I admit I was scared, back at the White House." It was like struggling with an octopus. "But that's a million miles away. I'm different now."

"Nonsense." He was licking her ear. "People don't change in the matter of a week."

"*You* don't, Bill." She reared her head back, away from him. "You're as immovable as a boulder. But other people — *I* do. I *have*. And I'm telling you I don't want this — not anymore."

"But I love you, Cam. I love you and no one else."

She froze. She felt as if he were about to consume her, swallow her alive. She felt his erection, huge and thick as a cudgel, and she shuddered at the thought of it slamming up inside her.

Then he had his hands on her jeans, unsnapping them, pulling them down over her hips.

"No, Bill," she said, trying to pull them up. "No, no, no!"

CHAPTER
FIFTY-SEVEN

Bourne had passed through security and gained the interior of the Thoroughbred Club by the time a beautiful Thoroughbred was led into the orchid-bedecked winner's circle by his owner. The jockey, clad in purple-and-cream-striped silks, was crouched atop his mount, waving his short crop in triumph.

Excited chatter filled the stands, and long lines had already formed in front of the betting windows for the second race. It looked like Percolate, the ruling family's horse, was the clear favorite.

Bourne made the climb up to the rooftop light array, which at first looked deserted. Then he spotted someone — a Secret Service agent. He froze. Then he saw another and another. It was clear the cadre had not been here, possibly it had never intended to be here.

Borz had played him. Perhaps Nazyr had seen Bourne's interest in the Thoroughbred Club when they had first met, and told Borz. Perhaps Borz had never really trusted him. In either case, at this very moment members of the cadre were planting a deadly bomb in another location — one where it would do the most damage to the dignitaries in the president's box.

Before beginning his descent, Bourne looked across the oval. He spotted Aashir, but only because he knew where to look. Aashir's attention appeared to be focused on the stands across the racetrack.

Climbing down from the aerie, Bourne brought to mind the blueprints of the club. If Borz wasn't planting the bomb on the light array, where would be the best place to put it, the place most likely to kill as many people sitting in the stands as possible? The stands. Of course! The bomb was going to be placed *beneath* the stands.

Following the blueprint from memory, Bourne made his way down through the security and maintenance tunnels. Three times he was obliged to freeze, squeezing back into the shadows as security personnel passed by. But finally he found the correct tunnel that led underneath the stands. Above him roared the cheers and excited shouts of the patrons, and every once in a while the jostling mass caused what felt like a minor earthquake.'

He pushed through a door and came face-to-face with the Chechen with the scar along his chin. The man was so surprised to see Bourne he was paralyzed for an instant. Bourne chopped down with the edge of his hand to render him unconscious, but Scarface shoved him back against the wall, using his assault rifle as a bar across Bourne's chest. At once, Bourne slashed in on the sides of Scarface's neck with both his fists. The Chechen's eyes rolled up in his head as he collapsed. Stepping over his prone form, Bourne crept forward in a half crouch, and almost stumbled over a pair of security guards. He checked them. Both dead. He pressed on.

The passage was lit by a string of spiral fluorescent bulbs protected by steel cages. The concrete undersides of the tiers of seats rose above him, connected by a supporting network of steel beams and girders. Bourne looked up. Through the gloom he could make out a figure hunched over a black oblong the size and shape of an electrician's toolbox. It was shiny, made out of metal or plastic, and as the man settled it into place on one of the lateral beams, it seemed very heavy. A tremor passed along Bourne's spine. It was all too possible the bomb was loaded with high explosives in order to blast through the reinforced concrete underside of the stands.

Bourne knew where the presidential box was located. The spot mandated for the bomb looked to be directly under it. Reaching up, he swung onto one of the lateral beams over his head, then grabbed the next one up and so began his climb to the level where the bomb was sitting. He was moving through patches of shadow and light, but as he rose, the shadows deepened and the light dimmed to a sepia shade.

Above him, the bomber's fingers were long, white, bony, spidery in their movements. Bourne's approach was as silent as an owl's. Nevertheless, the bomber sensed Bourne's presence. In an instant, he had a switchblade out and had thrown it with deadly accuracy.

Bourne spun to the left. The blade shredded the cloth over his right arm, then continued on its way, its

518

downward flight erratic now, slowed considerably. It cartwheeled into the gloom below.

In one leap, Bourne reached the bomber's level. The Chechen rose, but not fully. His knees were bent, his arms cocked as Bourne closed with him. He expected Bourne to strike first and was prepared to counter. Only the span of an arm away, Bourne brought himself up short. The man, caught off balance, made a belated lunge that, had it not been awkward, might well have shattered two of Bourne's ribs if he had not been wearing body armor. As it was, the blow landed heavily, below the ribs and in the armor's seam. Bourne buckled. Sensing an opening, the Chechen lashed out at him. Bourne grasped his forearm and spun, using his own momentum against him, pulling him around and down in an aikido move.

The Chechen landed on his back, already half off the beam, and Bourne struck him twice on the sternum. But the man immediately drew up his knees, got his feet under him, levered himself up, throwing Bourne off and coming at him in a whirlwind of callused knuckles and steel-tipped boots. Bourne was driven back a step, then another. One foot slipped off the beam, hung for a moment in midair. The Chechen pressed his advantage, but Bourne swung so his left side was toward his adversary. The Chechen's strikes missed their target, and Bourne, grasping his wrist, swung him around, using his body as a counterweight to bring himself fully back on the beam.

Now the two men squared off. The Chechen was not big, but his upper body was wide and well muscled, his arms like steel bands. He was wary now, having been suckered by the aikido move. Bourne knew he wouldn't be able to get away with that surprise twice.

Feinting to his right, the Chechen struck at Bourne from the left. A ferocious gust of blows was delivered by both men. Then the struggle seemed to come to a standstill as the two men's physical prowess locked together, like an inexorable force straining against an immovable object.

The Chechen broke free first, and immediately struck out, not realizing that this was what Bourne wanted. He overreached as Bourne slipped sideways, and, off balance, he stumbled. Bourne, bent, grabbed him, but the Chechen twisted over onto his back. His foot hooked behind Bourne's knees, whipped forward, taking Bourne off his feet.

Bourne reached up, but the Chechen slapped his hands away, and Bourne fell. He grabbed the lateral beam just below, hung there, swinging precariously, watching as the Chechen began to climb back up to where he had left the bomb.

Kicking out, Bourne increased his swing until his momentum was such that his feet struck the vertical girder on his left. As they did so, he let go of the lateral beam and flexed his knees. With the power of his legs, he launched himself up to where the Chechen crouched over the bomb. He struck the Chechen, but the sole of one boot knocked the bomb out of the Chechen's hands. The bomber managed to hold on to the beam, if just barely, but the bomb struck an adjacent girder, then arced down through the webwork of steel.

Camilla, deep in POTUS's grip, did the only thing she could think of: She kneed him hard in the groin. With a groan, Magnus let her go as he slipped to his knees. He squatted there, rocking gently back and forth, his hands cupping his genitals.

He looked up at her. "Why are you doing this to me?" Both his face and his voice were stripped of the perfect photo-op expressions and inflections Howard Anselm and the mandarins at Gravenhurst had indoctrinated him in. The imperial mask had slipped off his face and, as at the end of a Greek tragedy, the sorrowful bare bones beneath were revealed. For the first time he was naked to her.

"Cam, I love you," he said like a besotted Montague.

She crouched down in front of him. "Bill, you are the president of the United States. You're married. You have two beautiful children."

"One of whom knows about us," he said miserably.

"What?" Camilla said, like a Capulet. "Who?"

"Who do you think? My genius daughter, Charlie." He looked at her beseechingly. "She knows I'm a bad horse, Cam. She's never going to bet on me again."

Camilla shook her head. "You don't know that, Bill. She's young; you still have time to make things right."

"But it's you I want, Cam. Only you."

"But your wife —"

He waved a hand dismissively. "Maggie and I haven't said three meaningful words to each other in ten months. And as for sex —"

"That's enough, Bill."

This was more than Camilla had bargained for, more than she wanted to hear. For many reasons, she did not want to be embroiled in Magnus's sexual angst. For one thing, she knew it would never end. In a week, a month or two, he'd become infatuated with someone else and cheat on her. For another, Camilla had made her decision to put as much space between her and the Washington Beltway as humanly possible. This was her last brief; she was damned if she was going to allow Bill to rope her into another.

To this end, she rose, twisting away from his outstretched arms and grasping fingers.

"Come on, Cam," he pleaded. "You can't leave me like this."

Involuntarily, she glanced down. The long bulge of the presidential phallus was all too visible. As she stepped past him, Magnus's hand almost grasped her ankle. But he had used that trick on her before, and she was ready for it, high-stepping like a horse at dressage. His fingers closed around air, and he groaned in his misery.

"Cam, where are you going? Don't leave me. I need you. I can't sleep, I can't think. You're all I want."

"Bill, you don't know what you're saying."

"You think not?" His voice had a belligerent edge to it, like a child who realizes he's not getting what he wants. "I'll give you anything you want. Anything. Just name it. I'm the president; I can do anything for you."

With her hand on the doorknob, she turned and looked back over her shoulder. "I know you won't believe this, Bill, but there's nothing you have that I want."

It was the perfect line, preparatory to the perfect exit. The only problem was when she opened the door she smelled a familiar odor. Her mind just had time to register POTUS's three Secret Service agents on the corridor floor before she was struck in the chest.

She reeled back, lost her balance, and fell. Her heart and her mind seemed to beat a vicious tattoo like a war drum. Then she passed into unconsciousness.

CHAPTER
FIFTY-EIGHT

It wasn't the bomber that concerned Bourne now; it was the bomb itself. Thirty feet down, it was caught in the V of a girder and a support strut. By some miracle it hadn't exploded, but if it fell farther, the timing mechanism could be jarred into triggering the explosion. In that event, both Bourne and the Chechen bomber would become irrelevant.

A series of huge roars from the stands above shook the girders like ocean waves, making the footing far more treacherous on the lateral girder. To make matters worse, it was strewn with metal shavings. A slip on any of them could lead to defeat.

Enough blows had been struck for the Chechen to suspect that Bourne was wearing body armor, so he had changed tactics, aiming for Bourne's head and neck. As Bourne had reached for the falling bomb he had gained the advantage, and was now straddling Bourne, a push dagger in his hand, its wicked wide spadelike blade swinging nearer and nearer to Bourne's eyes, like Poe's deadly pendulum. The blade sliced through the bridge of Bourne's nose, and blood ran down either side. One more pass and the blade would reach Bourne's eyes.

Bourne's left hand scraped up some metal shavings from the girder. These he hurled into the bomber's face. Several lodged in his eyes, and the man recoiled. Rubbing at the eyes only embedded the filings more firmly. The bomber's eyes started to bleed, and all thought of Bourne was erased. Bourne rose up and shoved him off the girder.

The bomber fell. Whatever sound he might have made was overwhelmed by the frenzied excitement from the stands. Some or all of the dignitaries had reached the presidential box.

Swinging down the girders, Bourne reached the crook where the bomb had wedged itself. Far below, the body of the bomber lay splayed out, his head at an unnatural angle. Turning his attention to the bomb, Bourne at once saw that it contained twelve wires. It was totally different from the device he had found on the airplane.

He parted the red and black leaders to get a look at the guts of the bomb, only to discover there were no guts. No explosive material at all. The bomb was a dud. No, not a dud: a fake. But why?

Decoy.

Bourne sat back on his haunches for a moment. If El Ghadan's and Borz's plan did not involve blowing up the stands from the light array above or from the understructure below, then what was it? Bourne recalled that El Ghadan seemed fine with him searching for a bomb maker in Damascus, even Afghanistan. Was this all a ploy to keep security off Bourne's back?

Possible.

But that would preclude El Ghadan being a deceitful son of a bitch, who hated Bourne as much as he hated the president of the United States.

Bourne didn't buy it. Recalling the corner of the blueprint he had taken from the building in Waziristan, he pulled it out now. It marked the drainage system for the racetrack, but there were several items specified other than the network of pipes. Maintenance rooms most likely. They were small, without windows, and with only one egress. To Bourne's mind they would make perfect temporary prison cells.

It had to come sooner or later, and frankly, Soraya was surprised at how long it had taken Sonya to have a full-fledged meltdown. Apart from the bathroom and shower breaks, they had been cooped up in the same featureless room for close to a week, maybe more, it was difficult to tell. Soraya had done her best to keep her daughter engaged in the Persian stories, figuring that the fantastic characters would allow Sonya's imagination to become a window onto a larger world. But at last the breaking point had arrived, and no amount of cuddling or storytelling would satisfy her.

And contrary to what Soraya had assumed, Rebeka's appearance had accelerated the breakdown.

"She can leave whenever she wants to," Sonya sobbed. "Why can't we?"

There was, of course, a very good reason, but it wasn't one a two-year-old could absorb, let alone accept.

526

Soraya took her daughter onto her lap, stroked her hair, whispered to her, but Sonya was having none of it. She was far too upset to be mollified. Her sobbing became wails that bounced off the walls, seeming to gain in volume and terror with each echo.

It was at this point that Islam unlocked the door and walked in. Approaching the girl, he knelt on one knee, tried to talk to her, to reason with her. The wrong approach, Soraya thought, trying to reason with an unreasonable child. But she also knew that despite her best efforts, Sonya had slipped behind that wall mothers dread, to the place where chaos ruled. Only the physical could help now.

"I need to take her out of here," she said as she stood up.

Islam, rising, stood his ground between her and the door. "You know that is impossible."

"Then I'm asking for the impossible. Not for me, but for Sonya. You see how she is. The only way to calm her down is for me to take her out of here. Now."

Islam's attention was on Sonya, which was good. The child's hysteria continued to mount.

"If this continues," he said, "I will have to tie her up and gag her."

"Don't even," Soraya said in a voice that cut through her daughter's cries. "You do that and she will never be the same. Is that what you want on your conscience, Islam? To turn a child mad?"

Islam passed a hand across his forehead. He drew a handgun, let it hang by his side. "You see this?"

"Yes."

"You know what it can do."

"Of course."

"Then remember." He gestured with his head. "Come on, then. Ten minutes in the sunshine." The gun swung up, away from his thigh. "But that's it, I promise you."

It was Bourne's nose that guided him. A short time ago, the corridor ahead of him had been flooded with gas. He turned a corner and saw the Secret Service agents lying on the floor. Proceeding cautiously, he picked his way down the corridor at the end of which was one of the small rooms he had seen on his triangle of plan.

He went from body to body. Each one had succumbed to the gas, all right, but they also had had their throats slit, as if whoever was responsible had wanted to inflict the worst land of damage. He had just turned over the third agent when a terrific blow struck the nerve bundle behind his right ear, and the floor came up to smack him in the face. Not that he felt it; he was already unconscious.

CHAPTER
FIFTY-NINE

He awoke in the middle of a stage set: lights, a canvas backdrop. Several feet in front of him was a microphone attached to an expensive video camera. He was one of two actors the camera was aimed at. The other, sitting close beside him, was the president of the United States.

Bourne, wrists bound behind his back with a hard plastic tie, was sitting on a chair. POTUS's wrists were identically bound. The backdrop was artfully painted to resemble a cave. Whoever saw this video would believe it emanated a long way from Singapore — the mountains of Afghanistan, perhaps, or western Pakistan. In one corner, crumpled up, he saw his body armor, which had been stripped off him while he was unconscious.

Three men were in the room: Borz and the two men he was supposed to have left outside the Thoroughbred Club. It was clear now that everything Bourne had been told was a lie, just as it was clear that the dummy bomb was a diversion to keep him from the main event. A more daring and terrible act of terror he could not imagine. While it was true that the terrorist playbook called for large-scale attacks, nothing could vie for people's attention the world over than the public execution of the president of the United States.

Then his attention was drawn to the woman crumpled on the floor to one side. Who was she? What had she been doing here with POTUS? His press secretary, or had she been the one to unwittingly lure him here? Another piece of the puzzle clicked into place.

"How many lives do you have?" Borz, leaning forward on the balls of his feet, peered into Bourne's face. "I think we're about to find out. Your death here in this room — your real death — will serve a higher purpose."

POTUS's chin lolled on his chest. He was still out of it. Bourne knew they couldn't get started until he was both conscious and cognizant of his surroundings. Borz stepped forward, took out a stiff leather case that looked like a cigar carrier. Instead, it held a number of small syringes. He removed one, stuck it in POTUS's arm, and depressed the plunger. Moments later, the president stirred, his head lifted off his chest, and his eyes sprang open.

"What the hell is this?" he said in his most imperial tone of voice.

"What does it look like?" Musa's voice was the opposite of POTUS's, casual in the extreme. He might have been paring dirt from under his fingernails. "We are about to make history, President Magnus. You and your top paid assassin will be beheaded over a live feed. Anyone can plant a bomb, anyone can send a suicide bomber into a crowd, but what is about to happen here is real terrorist theater: the so-called leader of the free world beheaded while billions around the world witness his just humiliation. The United States citizenry will be in paralytic shock for years to come."

"Good God!" POTUS's eyes were all but spinning in his head. "You can't!" He looked as if he was about to succumb to a heart attack. He turned to look at Bourne. "This is a sham! I don't know who the hell this man is," he shouted, "but he sure as hell isn't on the payroll of the United States."

Musa laughed. "Come, come, President Magnus, it is unseemly to die with a lie on your lips."

"But I'm telling the truth." Sweat was pouring down POTUS's face, staining the collar of his white shirt. "You have to believe me."

"Believe an American lie?" Musa laughed again, gestured to the Chechen acting as cameraman. "Time to go live," he said. "The end of American hegemony is at hand."

"It will take a minute or two to link up with the Al Jazeera network," the cameraman said.

In the corner, the young woman stirred.

"Cam," POTUS called, his attention focused on her. "Camilla! Are you all right?" When she did not reply he exhaled a "Jesus," though whether it was a prayer or an expletive was unclear.

"Almost ready," the cameraman said. "But what is the assassin doing?"

Musa looked at Bourne, who was doubled over.

"Get him upright," he ordered his other man. "The camera must record his face as he is beheaded."

The Chechen approached Bourne, grabbed the hair at the top of his head, and pulled. When Bourne's head came up, he mumbled something in Russian. When the Chechen bent closer to hear what Bourne was saying, Bourne smashed his forehead into the Chechen's face. The man reared back, blood pouring from his nose, stumbled as his eyes rolled up in their sockets, and fell beside Camilla.

Musa shouted, headed straight for Bourne, while the cameraman grabbed the heavy .45 at his hip and drew it. He was fully concentrated on Bourne and POTUS. As a consequence, he failed to notice Camilla's hand reach out, draw the fallen Chechen's weapon from its holster. She lay on the floor, used two hands, steadied by her elbows. The narcotic she had been shot with was still in her system. Her vision kept fading in and out, and there was a peculiar buzzing in her ears that at some point she began to recognize as human voices, shouting.

Nevertheless, her training took firm hold, and she sighted, inhaled deeply, let it out, and squeezed the trigger. The bullet slammed into the cameraman's side, the second one took him off his feet in a fountain of blood.

Bourne was ready for Musa as he came toward him. Launching himself to his feet, he leaped backward with all his strength, was rewarded as the chairback struck the concrete wall at an angle and shattered. With his arms free, Bourne drew his knees up, passed his legs between his arms. Now his bound hands were in front of him, and as Musa drew his pistol, he threw a section of the chairback. It struck Musa under the chin. He gagged, was driven back a pace, but did not lose his grip on the pistol.

He fired, but Bourne, already on the move, was outside the trajectory of the bullet. Lifting his arms, he brought his balled fists down on the crown of Musa's head, at the place where, as a baby, the parts of the skull knit together. The blow should have driven Borz to his knees, but miraculously, ominously, he remained on his feet.

The handgun was useless to him now, and he let it drop to the floor, used both his hands in simultaneous kites. Bourne, his hands still bound, was at a distinct disadvantage.

"Let's see how you do without the armor," Musa whispered. The straightened tips of his fingers drove into Bourne's midsection just under the sternum. Almost at the same instant, he slammed the edge of his other hand into Bourne's ear, rocking him backward.

Following up the attack, he closed with Bourne, who met him with a cocked elbow, then a short, sharp swing of his forearm. Unfortunately, he was forced to use two hands, and Musa's fists broke underneath the blow, hammering at the spot over Bourne's heart. It was an old KGB hand-to-hand method that was supposed to interfere with the electrical flow to the organ, inducing a heart attack.

Bourne could feel his pulse pause, as if suspended in time, then flutter, as if having lost its natural rhythm.

His breath was hot in his throat, bitter as if with poisonous gases needing to be expelled.

With an extreme effort of will, he ignored both and, looping his bound wrists behind Musa's neck, twisted them with a vicious torque that spun the Chechen around. Now the plastic tie that bound his wrists dug deeply into Musa's throat.

Hauling with all his might brought the Chechen's head back until he was staring at the ceiling. Bourne slammed his chest into the back of Musa's head and slowly began to squeeze the air out of him, tighter and tighter, until the Chechen's face became empurpled.

Musa's mouth opened, working spastically, trying and failing to inhale. Then a curious smile informed his lips.

"You won't ever know," he whispered in Russian, "until it's too late."

He fell heavily against Bourne, who lifted his arms and stepped away, allowing Musa's corpse to crash to the floor.

CHAPTER
SIXTY

Magnus, bound to his chair, was for once speechless. He worked his mouth like a fish out of water. He was disheveled, a state he had never before experienced, even after sex, which for him was always an exercise of power, dominance, and destruction. He watched the death exploding around him in a state of profound shock; his mind seemed to have fled elsewhere, to a safe place where he was still the president of the United States, still able to command everyone, still in control of even the smallest events.

At that moment, Aashir appeared in the doorway, Musa's bloody corpse between him and Bourne. He seemed transfixed by the carnage. Camilla saw danger where Bourne did not. Still in her prone position on the floor, she swung the .45, centered the barrel on Aashir's heart. She was about to squeeze the trigger when Bourne called out.

"Don't shoot! Don't shoot."

She put the gun up, kept her shooter's position, but the effort she had made was too much for her, and, shaking, she slumped down, her breathing slowed and thickened.

Bourne knelt down, went through Musa's clothes until he found the hard leather case. Extracting a syringe, he pulled off the plastic casing protecting the needle, injected the serum into Camilla's upper arm.

"What are you doing here?" Bourne said as he awaited Camilla's return to consciousness.

Though it was unclear whether he was addressing Aashir or POTUS, it was Aashir who answered.

"Borz ordered me to shoot the dignitaries in the presidential box," he said softly. Producing a knife, he sawed through the plastic tie binding Bourne's wrists. "I couldn't do it."

"You weren't meant to shoot anyone," Bourne said as he helped Camilla to sit up. "Borz was using you as a diversion. He was going to make an anonymous call to the police about your presence in the stands opposite the presidential box. While you were being taken into custody, the real event would be taking place here in this room."

Aashir's shoulders slumped and he leaned back against the wall, as if his legs could no longer hold him upright on their own. "Nothing is ever as it seems," he murmured, possibly to himself.

"Untie the president," Bourne said.

Magnus cringed. "Keep that raghead away from me. What is he, Iranian like El Ghadan?"

"He's Jordanian." Out of Magnus's sight, Bourne looked at Aashir, put a forefinger across his lips.

"Iranian, Jordanian, what's the difference?" Magnus spat.

"For one thing, Jordanians are Arabs, Iranians are Persians."

"A jihadist is a jihadist. They all want to kill us."

"Not all of us," Aashir said.

"And who are you to say, sonny?" Magnus said.

Aashir made no comment. He stepped behind Magnus, slit his bonds in two. The president brought his arms around to his lap with a groan. He rubbed his wrists to get the circulation back.

Aashir, wary of the American president, stepped quickly away from him. "I can't believe what Borz was going to do here."

Bourne gestured with his head. "If that was Borz."

"What do you mean?"

Bourne looked up at him. "Do you seriously believe a man of Borz's stature — the world's largest illegal armaments dealer — would put himself in the field?" Bourne shook his head as he helped Camilla to her feet. "I don't know who that man was, but I'll wager any amount Ivan Borz is safely in Russia or Chechnya or wherever the hell he calls home."

Aashir stared at the corpse for a long moment before picking his way over to the video camera to turn it off. Then he crouched down beside the false Borz, rummaged through his clothing, looking for some means of identification.

"You won't find anything," Bourne said.

But because he was young and in a way still full of hope, Aashir continued to paw through the pockets, patting seams and linings. "There's nothing," he said at last, sitting back on his haunches. "Nothing at all."

POTUS, coming out of his self-imposed paralysis, rose and on shaky legs approached Camilla. "Are you all right?" When she didn't answer him, he switched topics, as politicians sensing trouble learn to do without conscious thought. "Do you know this man?"

She stepped back. "Please, Bill, don't come near me."

He stared at her bleakly. "I've ruined everything."

"We need to evacuate this room," Bourne said. "Now."

"I'm not going anywhere," Magnus said, "until she answers my question."

For a long moment, Camilla said nothing as she regarded Bourne with an expression of curiosity. "No, I don't know him," she said at length, "but I've been shown his photo. I believe this is Jason Bourne."

"Impossible!" Magnus burst out.

But no one was listening to him.

"I was meant to protect POTUS by killing you," Camilla said to Bourne. "I was trained to jockey a horse so I could be on the inside, so I could explore the nooks and crannies where you might be."

"That's as difficult to believe as this man being Ivan Borz." Bourne shook his head again. "Another diversion. This time from the opposite side: from Washington. Your superiors likely sent you into the field to be killed along with me."

"Yes, I know. I was shown the brief," Camilla said to Bourne. "I also heard a recorded conversation between Marty Finnerman and Howard Anselm. They wanted their dinger, Kettle, to kill me as well as you."

"I took care of that," Magnus said.

No, Camilla thought. I did. But on this point she kept her own counsel, wanting Magnus to at least have this victory to himself.

"Both Anselm and Finnerman are in federal custody," POTUS said.

Stepping over the corpse of the false Borz, Bourne went to the door, opened it. "There's another room, several yards down the corridor." As Magnus moved to follow him, he added, "Brace yourself. Your men are dead, Magnus."

Sidestepping the bodies, they moved quickly along the corridor to the room Bourne had identified. Midway, Magnus touched Bourne's arm and they dropped back a few paces.

"I don't want to be in an enclosed space with that towel — that Arab."

"Talk with him, Magnus," Bourne said. "Maybe you'll learn something."

The room, though smaller than the one they had been in, was set up less as a storeroom than a supervisor's office, equipped with a metal desk and several chairs. Three filing cabinets hunkered along one wall. One of the overhead fluorescent lights buzzed when Bourne turned them on.

"Maybe," Magnus said. "Maybe you're right. But the fact is, I can't let anyone or anything impede the peace process. People will be looking for me. In fact, a panic already may be starting. Certainly alarm bells will be sounding from here to D.C. Tensions were already running high between the participants. Now, who knows? If I'm not there to guide them —"

"There are some things I need to tell you," Camilla broke in urgently.

"I'm afraid it will have to wait, Cam."

"But it can't." She told Magnus about the conversation she had overheard between Hunter Worth and Vincent Terrier. "This is what Terrier said, and you know my memory, Bill, I'm quoting verbatim: 'I work in the real America that no civilian sees. Because of that I understand that it runs on a warfare-state bureaucracy that has become so entrenched that no president, no political party can defeat it. It's become permanent. And I also know that the heart of that warfarestate bureaucracy is a place called Gravenhurst.'"

"Oh, for the love of God!" Magnus said.

Bourne knew of Gravenhurst. Both Magnus and his chief of staff, Howard Anselm, were among its illustrious alumni.

"Bill, whatever you think you know about Gravenhurst is a carefully honed facade."

"Come on, Cam. That's got to be a lie!"

Undeterred, Camilla persevered. "Terrier said that Gravenhurst is far more than the conservative think tank manned by like-minded Yale graduates it purports to be. There are no alumni, only members for life, and those members — the most highly placed individuals in the fields of politics, industry, and our infernal war machine — are as addicted to their own ideology as are jihadists like El Ghadan."

540

"This is incredible," Magnus burst out. "Monstrous." But his expression had clouded, an indication that he was beginning to put two and two together.

"It gets worse," Camilla said. "According to Terrier, your peace initiative is doomed to failure. Do you know why? Because the Gravenhurst alumni make too much money on the war machine. Peace is anathema to them."

"I don't believe a word of it," Magnus said stiffly. "People like Terrier are born liars."

"As opposed to your chief of staff and under secretary of defense for policy," Bourne said.

"By Cam's account, this one was crazy enough to plot to have me assassinated."

"And didn't Anselm and Finnerman plot against you?" Camilla said.

POTUS appeared shaken to his core. Still, he felt he had one more swing left in this fight. "Gravenhurst is my alma mater. It's a proud institution, doing invaluable work." He cut the air with the flat of his hand. "Besides, I know all the men working there."

"Perhaps you don't know them well enough," Bourne said. "It sounds as if the entire infrastructure is rotten."

Magnus stared at Bourne. All at once, the air went out of him and he was obliged to sit back down. "Christ, if that's true . . ." He ran trembling fingers through his hair. "What am I supposed to do?"

"Try your best to get the Palestinians and the Israelis to agree on something. A basis for further discussion, if nothing else," Bourne said. "Then when you return to

D.C. find people you can trust and start cleaning house."

Magnus looked up. "Camilla, will you help me?"

She shook her head. "No, Bill. I'm done with this life. You'll have to do this on your own."

His face looked stricken. His near-death experience had frightened him, but his vulnerability had absolutely terrified him. All the dynamism he had felt in his hotel room earlier had been beaten to a pulp by the events of the last hour. And now Camilla looked farther away from him than ever: icy and untouchable.

"Because of what happened before," he said, his voice cracking.

"No, Bill. Believe it or not, my decision has nothing to do with you."

The hard edge to her voice made him wince. "Cam, I've made mistakes. My judgment . . . I've acted poorly. Very poorly."

"You're better served telling that to your wife and children," she said.

Magnus looked ineffably sad. "Are we at the end, Cam, or at the beginning?"

"That's up to you, Bill."

It was up to him, he saw that now. The notion was like spotting a lighthouse in a violent storm. He reached out for it, trying to right himself before he capsized. "Right, then." With a supreme effort, Magnus gathered himself. He was the president after all; he needed to act like one, even if he was still quavering inside. "I have my duties to attend to; I've spent too

542

much time running from major decisions, letting other people make them for me."

"That's what made you the perfect president for your billionaire pals at Gravenhurst," Bourne said.

Magnus regarded Bourne for what seemed a long time. He realized what a fool he had been. "I shudder to think that you and Camilla might be right." He slapped his thighs and stood up. "In any event, it's time for me to leave this underworld, to return to life. After all, I have a peace process to hammer out."

Bourne stood in front of the door. "Magnus, it's vital that you not show yourself for the next few minutes."

"I couldn't disagree more," the president said. After the nasty shock he had received, he seemed to have regained his sense of importance and mastery. "And I resent you calling me by name. I'm the president of the United States."

"You would have been dead if I hadn't saved you," Bourne told him. "In here, you are who I say you are."

Magnus's expression showed he was struggling with the reality of the situation. Clearly, he didn't like it, but what choice did he have?

"You wanted to know what I'm doing here, Magnus. El Ghadan kidnapped a family out of Paris. A Quai d'Orsay agent by the name of Aaron Lipkin-Renais. He married one of your own. Soraya Moore, formerly co-head of Treadstone. The couple have a two-year-old daughter named Sonya. Soraya Moore is an old friend of mine. El Ghadan is keeping her and her daughter hostage because, he told me, he wanted me to kill you. But I was duped. The real plan was to get both of us here so we could be executed on camera in front of the entire world."

A tense and unpleasant silence followed, during which Bourne was aware of Aashir, the alien, the outsider witnessing the worst of Western culture — its greed, venality, and ferocious duplicity. But there was no disgust on his face, none of the fanatic's smirking satisfaction at his screed writ large. He observed, and in observing, absorbed with a grave expression.

Bourne said, "And here we are together in this small room, Magnus. I've saved you, counseled you. I made no move to kill you."

Magnus looked nervously at Camilla, who shrugged at him, as if to say, You can't refute reality.

Magnus's attention returned to Bourne. "You're saying that El Ghadan abducted the child as well?"

"That's precisely what he did. You must help the hostages. If you show yourself at this juncture —"

"Their lives are forfeit," Magnus said. "Yes, I see." He shook his head. "You're not at all like what your file claims you are. You're supposed to be a rogue agent, unpredictable, borderline psychotic."

Bourne laughed. "Files of the clandestine services the world over are like history, meant to be remade by the people in power. I'd take them with several grains of salt if I were you."

"Still, I've been out of sight for too long. I have to make an appearance, and, frankly, the sooner the better."

Camilla turned to him, her expression accusatory. "Then what happens to the hostages, Bill? A mother and her two-year-old girl. Are they to be sacrificed?"

544

"That depends," Bourne said, "on Aashir."

"On the Jordanian?" Magnus shook his head. "I don't understand."

Bourne did not look at the president. "But you do, don't you, Aashir?"

Aashir nodded. "I've been thinking," he said. "I don't belong here; I never did. It's time for me to go home and see my father."

"You're sure," Bourne said.

Aashir nodded. "At long last, I am. Things must change or they must end. That is life's secret, is it not?"

The president's face registered bewilderment. "What's he talking about, Bourne?"

Bourne put a hand on the young man's shoulder. "It's a long story, Magnus."

CHAPTER
SIXTY-ONE

Life for life. The one for the others.

Bourne and Aashir arrived in Doha the next day. They had left Camilla at the Thoroughbred Club. She had been determined to jockey Jessuetta in the race she had been training for. As it happened, she was neck and neck with the president's horse all the way down the stretch, but lost by a nose. It was an exhilarating race nonetheless. And Camilla would not say whether she had reined Jessuetta in at the last moment in order to smooth the ruffled presidential feathers caused by the unprecedented delay. Jimmie Ohrent probably knew, but if so, he chose to keep her secret.

"I had fun," Camilla had said to Ohrent, cheeks flushed, her pulse running fast. "I must say that."

"Then stay around for a while," he had replied.

In Doha the sun was shining, but then the sun always shone in Doha. It was hotter than Hades, even this late in the day, but neither Bourne nor Aashir took notice.

It had been agreed that the exchange would take place at midnight, on the causeway to the Pearl-Qatar. Bourne had set the time; El Ghadan had dictated the place. Begun in 2010, the Pearl-Qatar was a man-made paradise, an island almost a thousand acres in area, that was only possible to construct in the Middle East. Its hotels, marina, malls, and residential towers were still being finished.

The wide, curving causeway, however, was complete. Apart from the two cars, at midnight it was completely deserted. Bourne, with Aashir beside him, sat behind the wheel of a rented silver Opel. On the other side of the apex of the curve crouched a large black SUV.

"Are you sure you want to do this?" Bourne said.

"You've asked me that before," Aashir replied. "Nothing's changed."

"Everything's changed," Bourne said. "An idea has become reality. We're at the crossroads. Now there's no turning back."

"I don't want to turn back," Aashir said. "I have a chance to do something worthwhile. Freeing a woman and her daughter — that's something I can be proud of. It's not enough to make up for what my father has done, but —"

"It's enough," Bourne said. "It's more than enough." He turned to Aashir. "I owe you a great debt."

"On the contrary, I owe you everything," Aashir told him.

Behind the SUV, lights from finished structures pierced the night like comets. Here and there, the vague outlines of enormous yachts rose from the water like leviathans.

Midnight.

Over the curve, one of the doors of the SUV opened and Sara stepped out. It seemed like such a long time since Bourne had seen her. He was struck anew by her beauty, her courage, her presence, which seemed to make the lights over the causeway shimmer, as if they were standing on Bifröst, the rainbow bridge of Norse mythology that connected Earth to Asgard.

"Stay where you are until I call for you," Bourne said to Aashir.

He got out of the Opel, stood staring across the expanse at Sara. Then his gaze shifted to the SUV itself. He began to walk toward it.

"I need to see them," he called to Sara, careful not to use her name nor in any way give El Ghadan a reason to think they knew each other.

"They're in the backseat," she said. "They're fine."

"I need to see that for myself." Bourne's voice echoed eerily across the flat expanse of water, low, black, still, like a sheet of obsidian.

"He wants to see his son."

Bourne turned, made a gesture, and Aashir climbed out of the car.

El Ghadan must have said something to Sara, because she turned, ducked her head, and ushered Soraya out into the night. Soraya cradled her sleeping daughter in her arms. When she saw Bourne tears sprang into her eyes, rolled down her cheeks. She looked thinner than he remembered, and paler, but she certainly did not look older. Wiser, for certain.

"Now have the boy walk up beside you," Sara called.

"He has to show himself," Bourne replied.

She stared at him, did not speak a word, but after a moment the front driver's door opened and El Ghadan appeared. Bourne had insisted that El Ghadan come without driver or bodyguard.

Unlike before, El Ghadan wore a traditional Iranian outfit. His face appeared as pale as Sara's, lined, tense, and all of a sudden Bourne realized that he was almost rigid with anticipation to have his long-lost son returned to him.

"You should be dead, Bourne," he called, his voice flat, like a cast stone skipping across the surface of the water. "I should be angry, but I'm not. You have found my son, you have brought him back to me, and for this I am grateful."

"Okay now," Bourne said softly, and Aashir approached the spot where Bourne stood, facing El Ghadan.

"It's all good," Bourne said when he felt Aashir close beside him. "You'll be with him in a moment. The start of a new life for both of you."

To El Ghadan, Bourne called, "Let them come."

El Ghadan's hand flicked out, and Sara guided Soraya and the child along the causeway, away from the SUV, toward Bourne, who, with his arm lightly across Aashir's shoulders, began their walk toward the apex, the designated spot for the exchange to be made.

The closer they came the more studiously Bourne watched El Ghadan. With his son's life at stake he was fairly certain the father would do nothing untoward, but his training nevertheless required him to remain on guard lest at the last minute he try to shoot Soraya.

When she was near enough, he said, "How are you?"

"Fine, now."

Her voice was strong and steady, which reassured him. Sonya, perhaps hearing their voices in her sleep, stirred, wrapped her arms more securely around her mother's neck, snuggled her cheek against Soraya's breast. "Now that you're here."

"Bourne." El Ghadan's call was sharp, almost harsh, as if his throat was sore. "My son, if you please. It's been such a long time."

Bourne turned to Aashir and they clasped forearms. Aashir kissed Bourne on both cheeks, and they parted without a word. Everything that could have been said between them had been said. It was time to leave, for Aashir to return to his family, to find a way to start a new life. Who knew, Bourne thought as he watched him approach his father, perhaps he would have a positive effect on the fanatic, a taste of the modern world to which Islam, like every religion, had to adapt.

Bourne studiously avoided talking to Sara, or even looking at her, except out of the corner of his eye. El Ghadan would expect him to be focused on the people he knew.

"It's good to see you again, Soraya."

Her eyes were shining, enlarged with tears. "Thank you, Jason. I know no one else could have saved us." Her hand reached out, grasped Sara's arm. "But without Rebeka, I don't know what we would have done."

Bourne looked directly at Sara for the first time, whispered, "You did great work."

Soraya looked from one to the other. "You two know each other?" She laughed softly. "I should have known."

550

It was the laugh — the unalloyed joy in her mother's voice — that must have woken Sonya. Squirming, she turned in her mother's arms, looked Bourne squarely in the face, and, with a huge smile, said, "Mama, the djinn has come at last."

It was then they heard the shot — a single report carrying over the water, ripping apart the night.

Bourne ran without even a conscious thought, over the apex, toward the SUV. Beside it, El Ghadan stood, a pistol in one hand. Just in front of him lay Aashir, facedown, arms spread-eagled. Blood, black as pitch, pooled around his head.

"What have you done?" Bourne cried.

"What had to be done." El Ghadan moved to the open door of the SUV.

By an odd quirk of acoustics the water on either side amplified. their voices, so there was no need for either of them to shout. Bourne kept closing the gap between them, but it didn't seem fast enough.

"He was your son."

"No, Bourne. He was a homosexual. No son of mine can be a homosexual. He brought shame on my family. It is not allowed. The honor of my family must be restored."

"And the reputation of El Ghadan."

As if in a dream, Bourne seemed to gain no ground. He ran harder, full out. But El Ghadan was already behind the wheel of the SUV.

"I leave him to you, Bourne. You loved him. I never did."

He had left the engine running, and now he put the vehicle in gear, made a U-turn, and sped away, leaving Bourne to kneel over Aashir's body, and mourn.

Three Months Later

Abdul Aziz prayed six times a day. Facing Mecca, his forehead pressed to his prayer rug, he felt the complex beauty of Islam, the goodness of Allah, and knew he was blessed.

But today he was not at his enormous office suite, nor at his palatial home, with its Moorish tile fountains, watercourses, and open-air pavilions made of fragrant cedar of Lebanon. Today he was in a hammam deep within the Marrakech medina. It was quiet here, serene, but all around the hammam the clamor and tumult of the teeming market continued in an endless swirl, complex as an Islamic design.

Sitting in the steam room opposite Aziz was El Ghadan. Sara had brokered a deal between the two of them, acting as El Ghadan's intermediary. Every six months or so, El Ghadan changed his shipping companies. He had his own, of course — Omega + Gulf Agencies — but the volume of arms was far too great for any one company to transship without raising unwanted attention from any number of quarters.

This was how El Ghadan had decided on Abdul Aziz. He had heard of Aziz's expertise, and when Sara had come to him with the idea of using the Qatari's services he was intrigued. There began a six-week vetting process, after which El Ghadan was finally satisfied. Aziz had suggested Marrakech as neutral territory, and this very hammam because it was private and discreet.

Unsurprisingly, El Ghadan had arrived with three bodyguards, each of whom looked as if he could take out a UN battalion. Aziz was unfazed. "As long as our business dealings remain between the two of us you can have as much security as you desire."

"And you?" El Ghadan had said when he had arrived. "What about your security, Abdul Aziz?"

"I am a simple businessman," Aziz had answered. "I have no need of security."

Now they were alone in the steam room, sitting on tile platforms built into the walls, their loins wrapped in towels. Lighted candles inside pierced and filigreed Moroccan lamps set in niches threw dancing shadows across their faces.

Two of El Ghadan's guards stalked the hammam like Dobermans hunting rats. The third stood just outside the steam room door, arms hanging loose and ready.

These people were always ready, Aziz thought. Always at the precipice, an inch away from the darkness.

"The arrangement I propose would be for three years," Aziz said easily. "If, at the end of that term, matters are satisfactory to both parties, a longer contract period would be negotiated."

El Ghadan smiled. "My dear Abdul Aziz, I am neither interested in a three-year contract nor a longer-term arrangement. What I propose is that I buy your company lock, stock, and barrel."

The shock on Aziz's face and in his voice was palpable. "But this is impossible! Mine is a family-run business. I inherited it from my father, he from his father. My three sons work in it, and when I retire they will take it over. I have never even contemplated selling it."

"Until today." El Ghadan grinned. "I am prepared to make you a very generous offer." He stated an astronomical figure. "I believe that's overly generous, in fact, beyond the annual profits you now see from it. Forward-looking numbers once I take over will double or possibly triple the current amount within the next three to five years. This is what I want."

"With all due respect," Abdul Aziz said in muted alarm, "it's not what I want."

"I see. Well, I'm prepared to add another quarter of a billion on top."

"You don't understand," Aziz said. "I won't negotiate. If you're not interested in the arrangement I outlined, I consider the matter closed."

As he began to rise, El Ghadan said, "Sit back down," so sharply Aziz could not help flinching.

"I beg your pardon." El Ghadan waved a hand through the billows of steam. "Please be good enough to be seated." He smiled, but it was without an iota of warmth.

"Now" — he rubbed his hands together — "you mentioned your three sons. I assume you would like them to live to a ripe old age, to one day marry — excuse me, Hamad is married, but as yet without issue, yes? — and, Allah willing, give you many healthy male grandchildren to take care of you in your declining years."

Abdul Aziz's voice hardened. "Are you threatening my family?"

"I don't make threats, my friend." His smile, polished to a high gloss, shone like a beacon. "I am just outlining a possible future, one of a number which will either benefit you or take you down a dark road that will cause you grief."

"My path is already determined," Aziz said, "by my own actions and by Allah's grace and beneficence."

El Ghadan seemed to want to keep a neutral expression, but in the end his emotion got the better of him. "You're not afraid of me."

"No."

"Not afraid of dying."

"When that day arrives I will be transferred from the loving arms of my family into the loving arms of Allah."

"And what of your three sons? What if they are no longer around to deliver you into the loving arms of Allah?"

Aziz hated what El Ghadan was saying, hated even more his sardonic tone. But, he supposed, that was how you spoke when you were on top of the world, all enemies defeated.

Time, he thought.

556

"And what of your own son, El Ghadan — or should I call you Sameer Sefavid? Yes, I think that's best. What of Aashir, Sameer? You blew his brains out. Your own son."

El Ghadan was so astonished no coherent word emerged from his open mouth.

"You're not fit for life — let alone taking over my company."

El Ghadan leapt up, calling for the guard outside. Instantly, the door flew open and the man came in. He took one step over the threshold, then fell on his face. The back of his skull was a bloody morass.

Behind him Bourne entered. "No one's left to help you, Sameer," he said. "You're on your own."

El Ghadan looked from Bourne to Aziz and back again. "This was a setup, all along a setup."

"And now it's over," Bourne said.

"Never!" El Ghadan pulled a short dirk from beneath his towel, thrust it forward, but Bourne caught his wrist, twisted it away from him. He slapped his other hand behind El Ghadan's neck, jerked him toward him so they were face-to-face.

"Now everything is over," Bourne said.

El Ghadan winced. "What did you . . . ?" But he keeled over before he could finish his thought.

Bourne glanced at the *mangèr*, the tiny blade, the "serpent" hidden inside the bracelet Khan Abdali had given him to combat, as the malik said, extreme darkness. He had pricked El Ghadan with its point. Its poison had worked almost instantaneously.

Abdul Aziz looked up at Bourne. "I see now this was the only way to get him to emerge from his fortress."

"You had doubts."

"Until we began to speak in earnest." His smile showed many teeth. "The negotiation, such as it was, went precisely as you predicted."

"Some reactions are utterly reliable." Bourne pulled Aziz to his feet. "And now, I think we've both had enough steam."

A Week Later

"It wasn't easy," Sara said, "finding a place for him. After all, he was neither Arab nor Jew."

"He wasn't Iranian either," Bourne said, "at least by their standards. He was without a home. I know what that's like."

They stood in front of Aashir's grave. It was a clear day, clouds running before the hot wind. The dust tasted of antiquity, of the succession of civilizations, and of the blood of the fallen. They were in the ancient Mamilla Cemetery, hard by the western edge of Jerusalem's Old City.

"Added to that," Sara continued, as if he hadn't spoken, "he was a Sefavid. His ancestors declared Shia Islam the state religion of Iran. They also declared the Jews *najis*, unclean, and had them expelled."

"Did you hear what I said?"

Sara bowed her head. "Of course I did."

Above them rose the Temple Mount, and its two sacred monuments dating back to the seventh century. It was where Judaism and Islam intersected: The rock where Abraham bound his son, Isaac, to be sacrificed to God was also the place where Mohammed ascended to heaven.

"This is not a religious issue," Bourne said in a tone of voice that made it clear he was adamant.

"Everything in Jerusalem is a religious issue."

He stared down at the grave, silent.

"Nevertheless," she said, "I understand."

He did not move or blink; he seemed scarcely to breathe, as if he had become rooted to the spot, an old tree, wiser now.

"There was nothing you could have done," she said, her voice pitched lower, as soft as the wind. "You saved Soraya and Sonya. Isn't that enough?"

"It's never enough."

She saw the sadness in his face. "No, I suppose not."

For a long time, the only sound was the wind rustling the treetops. Then, startlingly, a child's voice was raised in song — a nonsense rhyme that so entranced the littlest ones the world over.

"I understand what happened," Bourne said after a time, "and yet I don't."

Sara put her arm around his waist, half turned him toward her. "Being what he was, he never had a chance."

"That's the part I don't understand."

"Then understand that you gave him something precious, something he never could have dreamed would be his. You accepted him, befriended him, helped him to grow up."

"I helped him to his death."

"No, Jason, that was his choice. An adult's choice. Finally, he understood that he needed to put away childish things. He needed to return to his father."

"He tried to fit in," Bourne said, "but he didn't belong anywhere else."

"That's right." She took his hand in hers. "That's all of it." She kissed him hard on the lips. "That's the end."

The child, his voice plaintive against the centuries-old wall, sang on. Soon enough, other voices joined in.